The Queen's Maid of Honour

Book IV

in the French Orphan Series

by Michael Stolle

Table of Contents

Prologue

The gates of hell had opened.

Strands of sulphurous light oozed like poison from wounded clouds so dark that they must be heralding the arrival of the Prince of Darkness. Beyond a shadow of a doubt, the end of the world must be upon them.

Surely any minute now the riders of the apocalypse would appear and give chase, their grinning skulls wrapped in moth-eaten cowls. Hadn't his confessor insisted he should always be ready for the final judgement?

But his home in France and his confessor were far away – why had he ever decided to come to England...

In the end it was not an armada of scythe-wielding phantoms that descended from the sky, but rain, followed by hail, which poured down on them instead and Armand started to wonder if this wasn't worse after all. In vain he tried to shield himself and his precious horse from the sudden onslaught of deadly hailstones, as large as pigeon eggs, and heavy as pebbles. No wonder his horse was shying and rolling its eyes in terror, whinnying in pain and fear.

Thunder had now started, numbing his ears, drowning all other sounds as it rolled through the forest, heralding the apocalypse that must surely be imminent. The sun had ceased to exist; it was dark as deepest night. Only vaguely could Armand discern the silhouettes of the tall trees in the darkness, their branches still bare, for spring was yet to come – if, that is, this godforsaken country would ever see spring or summer again.

How would he find his way in this hellish darkness?

As if someone had been reading his thoughts, bolts of lightning suddenly flashed down, casting blinding flashes in the trees around him. In the dazzling light he saw barren trees with dead branches that reached out to the dark sky, like pitiful skeletons pleading for a last blessing from heaven. Further lightning bolts followed without respite and made the undergrowth spring alive, like crouching phantoms of the underworld, ready to pounce at him.

"By the holy Virgin, I must find some kind of shelter! There must be some kind of shelter in this godforsaken forest," he swore aloud, fighting against a rising feeling of despair. Stuck in his saddle since the early hours of the morning, Armand had been riding through endless pastures and stretches of woods in the hope of reaching Winchester before the thunderstorms were unleashed.

1

Up until noon the shadow of a pale sun had helped to guide him, but soon, far too soon, the sun had disappeared behind the thick curtain of clouds – as was so often the case in this miserable country. Deprived of any guidance from the sun, Armand had lost his way and had no clue where he was or where to direct his horse in a forest that had become a maze. Was he simply riding in circles? He couldn't tell anymore.

Lacking any other guidance, he simply followed a narrow path, riddled with hidden potholes and treacherous roots, hoping and praying that it might lead him in the right direction.

Armand was not only fighting against a mounting feeling of despair; he could barely keep his eyes open, as he was hungry and utterly exhausted. Yet he knew that he couldn't afford to yield to the luxury of taking a rest. He needed to be watchful, not only because stopping and falling asleep in this thunderstorm might be the end of him. Armand knew that a hunt had been set in motion.

This hunt had one aim only: finding and killing the King's men, the Cavaliers, of whom he, Armand de Saint Paul, was one.

The thunder and lightning moved on and Armand's horse calmed as the hail stopped; soon Armand's mount trotted on slowly, tired and placing its hooves with caution. Suddenly Armand had to laugh out loud, but even to his own ears it didn't sound particularly joyful. "What a great team we make: a lame horse and a beaten knight, battling against all odds in this dark hell!"

As if in answer, a black shadow detached itself from one of the trees and automatically Armand's right hand seized his sword, ready to strike. But it was only a black crow that had left its hiding place, disturbed by the approaching horseman.

Eerie stories about the forest came to mind, stories that had been whispered around campfires at night. It had been vastly entertaining to listen to those stories, sitting close to a crackling fire while drinking ale and joking with his comrades. "Witches and sorcerers live down there in the Southern Forest, practising their dark arts since ancient times. Those who had the bad fortune to set eyes on the elves dancing underneath enchanted trees," the story teller had whispered, rolling his eyes ominously, "those poor souls never made it home."

The crow screeched with contempt at the lone intruder who had dared to disturb the peace of the sacred forest before it escaped, flapping upwards in slow circles.

All of a sudden, the sound of thunder stopped completely, but the ensuing silence was almost as disturbing as the previous noise. The heavy rain stopped and turned into a mere drizzle; soon – hopefully – it might stop altogether. If only Armand had more light. And a fire. Horse and rider were drenched and it was freezing cold.

Armand's mind wandered. Cheriton! Would he ever be able to forget such a battle? A battle that had started with all the hallmarks of an easy victory for the King's gentlemen, but had ended up an utter fiasco. Armand closed his eyes. The sound of gunshots and exploding cannon echoed in his mind, he could still hear the desperate cries of the wounded and the dying, the screaming of the horses as they broke their legs and fell to the ground. Armand could still smell and taste the blood – blood that must have been everywhere, horse blood, human blood, a slippery mess on the ground with a penetrating sweet smell, a memory that made his stomach churn.

Angry at his own weakness, Armand wiped a tear away. He had been prepared to die on the battle field, a Saint Paul would never yield. But General Forth had shouted at him, "We're going to lose the battle, Armand, retreat!"

"A Saint Paul never deserts his men and never gives up!" Armand had shouted back, eyes flashing angrily at the general.

"What do you think we're doing here? We're already retreating. Now my task is to save as many of our men as possible. We've lost a battle but now we must make sure not to lose the war. If the Roundheads capture you, they'll skin you alive, they hate the French – and the Catholics. Leave for the coast, go back to France and throw yourself at the feet of this strange prime minster of yours, we need his money and French soldiers or our cause will be lost! Ride to Wintershill Castle first, the Earl of Wiltshire is a loyal man, he'll put you up and will help you find a ship. Avoid the roads though."

"A Saint Paul would never throw himself on his knees, not for anybody, and certainly not for an upstart Italian Cardinal!"

"Swallow your pride, Saint Paul, go and fetch help for us. King Charles needs money, we need fresh troops or our next battle will be lost as well. The Roundheads are no longer a gang of bandits, you've seen them today with your own eyes, they've turned into a genuine army. Leave now, go to Wintershill Castle and then to France!"

Armand had gulped. General Forth had never been so outspoken before. In the meantime the enemy had been advancing fast like the approaching tide, and there was no time left for arguments. Armand had turned his horse, heading south towards Winchester. His mission was clear, he must sail back to France and beseech Cardinal Mazarin to send support. King Charles's position was indeed becoming desperate.

Weary and tired, Armand continued riding through the forest and suddenly his guardian angel must have intervened: like a beacon of hope a ray of light penetrated the clouds.

Armand closed his eyes for a second in relief – but a split second too long – as he failed to see the low-hanging branch that blocked the path in front of him. The obstacle caught him unawares and knocked him right off his horse. It all happened so fast, a first onslaught of pain, a feeling of panic as he fell and crashed down onto something hard, even more pain, and then – nothing.

Maybe this was a blessing, as it meant he didn't hear them coming.

Some Months Ago

The young gentleman waiting in the antechamber of the Louvre palace would have been the envy of any host of distinction. Tall and lean with shoulder-length blonde hair, he was impeccably dressed. His shirt, breeches and waistcoat were tailored from the finest linen and lace imported from Flanders and shining silk from the Orient, and his long boots had been crafted by a true master of his art. The polished leather of his boots shone with a gleam that tended to make his friends downright jealous. Shimmering buttons of mother of pearl and fancy coloured ribbons perfected his appearance, but his muscular body and vivid grey eyes betrayed the fact that François de Toucy would be at home as much on a battlefield as at the royal court of France.

Only a slight tapping of his right hand on the desk close to him betrayed the fact that he might be impatient. The desk was laden with documents, a crucifix, books and a silver stand for quills of various sizes. It was the desk of a man of power – and a man with a frightening amount of work waiting for him.

François sighed. He had been waiting for more than an hour already. His sigh earned a sympathetic smile from the young monk who served as secretary to the Cardinal and who kept arranging the files into neat piles on the desk. "It won't be very long, Monsieur, but His Eminence is having a private audience with Her Majesty and as you may be aware, Her Majesty…"

"…likes to gossip, I know." François finished the sentence for the young monk.

The young monk looked shocked by this candid response but declined to comment, as not even in his wildest dreams would he have taken the liberty of uttering such a casual statement about the Queen Regent of France. But obviously his elegant visitor had no such qualms.

About half an hour later François could discern the noise he had been waiting for in the gallery outside, the tapping of heavy boots of the guard of honour, the shouting of the herald announcing the approach of an important member of the court. The so-far silent wing of the Louvre palace was transformed in no time into a humming bee-hive, only with the difference that it was not the Queen who was expected, but His most honourable Eminence, the Cardinal Mazarin, prime minister of the most Catholic Kingdom of France.

The door was flung open but the Cardinal didn't wait for the ceremonial announcement of his titles – he entered the room with his robes flying, his bright red skullcap sitting lightly askew.

François de Toucy hastened to rise from his chair and dived down to kiss the ring of office of the Cardinal, making him almost collide with the Cardinal, who was still in full flight. His Eminence started to laugh.

4

"I apologize, my son, not only am I late, but I have never learnt to move with the deliberation and decorum I owe to the honour of my office. I imagine it's my Italian heritage, I can never muster enough patience and I have never been able to wait."

François de Toucy marvelled at the difference between Cardinal Mazarin and his predecessor, the Cardinal Richelieu – how often had he heard Richelieu laugh? Had he ever laughed?

The Cardinal sat down behind his huge desk, shoved some piles of the neatly arranged documents to one side, upon which they collapsed and toppled over. This careless movement must have made his secretary wince with mental anguish, as it annihilated in seconds the sorting and careful preparation that had surely taken him hours.

"You may sit down, although I know that this chair is most uncomfortable. I inherited it from my predecessor, the Cardinal Richelieu, may the Lord bless his soul," and he made the sign of the cross. "I would imagine that this chair was his secret revenge for those visitors who'd keep him busy for more than half an hour."

The Cardinal's smile transformed his face. He was by no means a handsome man, but François now understood why his charms were such that he had not only gained the confidence of Queen Anne, the young king's mother, but rumour had it that they were much closer in reality than court etiquette or convention would ever allow.

"I've sat on much more uncomfortable chairs in my time," François de Toucy smiled back, "but if I may permit myself to come straight to the point, why did Your Eminence invite me to come to the Louvre, insisting on such urgency?"

"The French are always so direct…" muttered the Cardinal, and made a sign to his secretary to withdraw. The ensuing discussion would need to be kept absolutely confidential.

"I do apologize for dragging you away from the side of your beautiful young wife, Marquese!" the Cardinal opened the discussion. "If I'm not mistaken, your wife has recently inherited the title of Marchesa de Castelfranco?"

"Your Eminence is never mistaken, but usually I don't use the title in France."

"That's very wise, the French are not always inclined to appreciate foreign dignitaries. I should know."

The Cardinal looked at his desk, strewn with documents and files. He frowned: "Did my servants forget to offer you a glass of wine?"

"I wasn't asked," François smiled back, "but the idea of a glass of wine does hold some appeal. I wouldn't mind."

"*Imbéciles*! Why do I pay servants if they forget the basic rules of hospitality!" Cardinal Mazarin exclaimed and rang the bell, loud enough to wake even the sleepiest of servants.

Minutes later a glass of honey-coloured wine was placed in front of François de Toucy, accompanied by some sweetmeats and candied fruit. François noticed that the colour of the Cardinal's wine was considerably paler, concluding that the Cardinal had given the order to have his wine watered down.

"*Santé*, your health!" His Eminence toasted, raising the precious Venetian crystal glass.

"To the health of Your Eminence and to the health of our royal family!" François replied – he could see that his answer was pleasing to the Cardinal, who quickly added, "Yes, to the health of our Sovereigns, may the good Lord protect them!"

The wine was heavy and thick as honey. *I must be careful*, François thought, *this wine is the perfect way to loosen the tongue of even the most taciturn visitor. What are the Cardinal's intentions?*

Meanwhile His Eminence carefully inspected the candied fruits served on a silver platter while François waited patiently for him to open the discussion.

"Your wife has recently inherited large tracts of land, along with a bunch of titles from her uncle." The Cardinal finally opened the discussion.

"As usual, Your Eminence is well informed. We plan to travel next summer to Venice to sort out the details, our lawyers have warned us there will be mountains of papers to be signed, as at least five different countries and jurisdictions are involved."

"I still maintain some old friendships in Venice," the Cardinal answered, almost absent-mindedly, as he seemed to be concentrating on choosing the most appetizing candied fruit. Finally, he selected a cherry and remarked, "Those were the favourite sweets of the late Cardinal de Richelieu. He always thought that I didn't know where he bought them from, so I left him with that illusion. Richelieu always liked to consider himself master of the game."

His glance went back to François who was starting to wonder about the strange subject of their conversation.

"As it happens, I maintain good contact with my friends in Venice. I also happen to know that two charming but not very loyal cousins of your wife have filed a new law with the council – a law written essentially to disinherit women who have taken the liberty of marrying outside the closed circle of the Venetian nobility, the Golden Book, as they call it."

François kept masterful control of himself, and merely bowed to the Cardinal. "Your channels of information seem to be excellent, as usual, if I may say so. We haven't heard about this new law yet. It's always good to know your enemies."

"You won't have heard, because it has been filed as a secret directive rather than a formal law to be voted on by the full assembly. These cousins are wily, they know exactly what they're doing."

"What does Your Eminence suggest?"

"I can use my influence to keep the decision pending – pending forever, if it pleases me. It will cost a lot of money as I'll need to use my influence not only in Venice but will have to intervene with the Holy See as well. If I wish, one of your wife's cousins will find himself appointed bishop in some very remote part of the Mediterranean. He'll be very pleased at the beginning. He'll carry a lot of fancy titles and he may even govern some islands, just like a true prince. Of course there's a catch – the moment he arrives there, he will open his treasure chests and find them empty. But not many people know about this so far. When he discovers that he's nothing but a poor bishop sitting on a forlorn island that nobody ever wants to visit with the exception of the marauding Turks, it'll be too late."

The Cardinal grinned, full of mischief, enjoying his little intrigue.

"You'll need to pay me back every single *sou* once your wife is sure of her inheritance; I certainly cannot use money entrusted to me by our government for something that must be considered a strictly private matter."

"Certainly we will, but why would Your Eminence do this for me? I guess that – besides my gratitude – Your Eminence might expect some… service in return?"

"Of course I do. I always find it pleasant to discuss matters with someone who possesses a quick mind. If I render you a service, of course I expect something in return, something special."

"May I know then, what I'm expected to do?"

The Cardinal took a sip of his wine and seemed to savour it before he swallowed. "Excellent wine, from the region of Avignon, the winery is still owned by the Holy See, by the way. The Holy Father sends me a couple of casks every year."

François laughed. "I'm starting to become nervous! If Your Eminence is taking this much time to tell me about my part of the deal, I'm afraid that it won't be simple."

"Her Majesty is worried about the state of affairs in England," the Cardinal finally answered. "I assume you're aware of what's going on there?"

"As much as most people are. I'm not aware of all the details though, the situation looks… let's say, complicated. The kingdoms of England and Scotland are ravaged by civil war. I never understood though why things are so bad, it seems that King Charles has fallen out with Parliament – why did he ever let Parliament become so powerful?"

"Money and religion," the Cardinal stated simply. "The usual story. A weak king, if you permit me to say so, with a bunch of useless advisors, not a good combination. And his enemies have a lot of money."

"But why would Her Majesty be worried? France and England have been at odds for centuries, it's good news if an old enemy will be weakened for the years to come. France can only profit from this situation."

The Cardinal looked around him as if to make sure that he didn't want to be overheard. "I'm inclined to agree with your analysis, de Toucy. But the Queen is worried about her sister-in-law, the Queen of England."

"Queen Henrietta Maria, the sister of the late king?"

"Exactly, this means that she's a 'fille de France', a princess of the royal blood of France and Her Majesty is worried that she might fall into the hands of these crazy Puritans, who are lusting after the blood of believers of the True Faith. She has nightmares of what could happen to a member of the French royal family under these circumstances. I do agree with Her Majesty that we must avoid this happening; never should it come to pass that a member of the French Royal family should fall into the hands of the *canaille*, the mob in the street."

The Cardinal made a solemn sign of the cross as if to ward off evil and paused a moment.

"Does Queen Henrietta plan to leave England and to appeal for exile in France or will she join her daughter in Holland?" François asked.

"That's part of the problem. Queen Henrietta Maria insists on staying in England, she thinks that God has chosen her to convert the English and would rather die as a martyr."

François had to digest this information first, and a short silence ensued.

"Your Eminence wishes me to talk to the Queen?" he asked incredulously.

"Yes, someone has to explain to her that – if things become worse – she must leave England. To make things worse, Her Majesty is with child – again," the Cardinal added, and sipped at his wine. "One could argue that King Charles should perhaps have had different priorities at such a difficult time…"

"How does Your Eminence suppose then that I convince a queen to change her mind and leave England if she's expecting a child, unwilling to abandon her country and – most likely – abandon her husband?" François asked in a polite tone, with just a slight raising of his eyebrows betraying his true feelings.

8

"I leave this to you. Don't forget what's at stake for your wife and, by the way, if you succeed, you'll be elevated to the rank of a count in France, Her Majesty has graciously given her consent. At present Queen Henrietta Maria seems to be safe enough, the court has moved to Oxford which is a more secure place compared with London, which is firmly in the grip of Parliament. But my agents tell me that the forces of Parliament are gathering strength every day. In a matter of only a few months the situation could become quite desperate."

The Cardinal selected another cherry and continued. "The government of France has decided not to intervene. We want to save the Queen, not England. In addition, the Prince of Orange doesn't want to meddle, which means that the Dutch have the same attitude; they may pity the king but they're happy to see England weakened. In fact, we know that a considerable amount of money supporting the Puritan cause has come from the Dutch."

He washed down the cherry with a sip of wine and continued. "King Charles may be saved by a divine miracle – but regrettably this happens very rarely in our modern times. If you ask me, he's doomed. As long as I'm serving as prime minister in France, I'll make sure that the parliament in Paris will never gain any power. It's a matter of resources and leadership. In England the Parliamentarians have more money and more men at their disposal than the king. Worse, they seem to have found gifted leaders for their army. Best to get everything ready for a swift departure for England when I call you. It could happen tomorrow – if you accept the mission, Monsieur le Comte."

François de Toucy smiled at the Cardinal, the famous smile that usually made the hearts of the Queen's maids of honour beat faster. "How could I refuse, Your Eminence? Let me know when I'll have the honour of meeting Queen Henrietta Maria in England."

The Cardinal had no such weakness for dashing young men; his weakness was for young, buxom women waiting every night in his bed. Therefore he just smiled back, keeping it strictly business.

"It's all settled then, I knew that I could rely on you, my predecessor recommended you warmly for any such delicate mission." He rang the bell and the young monk entered again. "M. de Toucy will tell you later what he needs, a ship, some gold etc., he has carte blanche, make sure that his requests are fulfilled quickly and give me a weekly report. His mission is highly confidential." He sent a last stern look to François. "No unnecessary expenses though, you know that all expenses will need to be accounted for!"

"Another thing that hasn't changed, the Cardinal Richelieu never accepted unnecessary expenses," said François.

"That's why he made France a great nation! And I shall make it even greater. Trust me."

9

The secretary moved forward and bowed reverently, and François de Toucy found himself dismissed. With the instinct of a bloodhound the Cardinal dragged some documents out of a pile in front of him and, apparently satisfied to have found what he had been looking for, he started reading, forgetting his visitor and the previous topic, as it had now been dealt with to his satisfaction.

**

Accompanied by his faithful footman, Michel, François rode back from the Louvre palace to the new town house he had acquired after his marriage. Although he was vigilant – nobody in their right mind would ride through the dirt-strewn streets of Paris without looking for hidden potholes or thugs roaming the streets – part of his mind was still dwelling on the conversation with Cardinal Mazarin.

As usual, François ignored the intrusive peddlers trying to sell him pastries, fake jewellery or relics straight from the Holy Land, guaranteed to ward off all kinds of afflictions, just as much as he ignored the persistent beggars, some of them mutilated to the point that he could only wonder how they managed to cling on to life. Every Sunday it was customary to hand out alms to the beggars waiting outside after the church service had finished, but today was not Sunday and François was a man of principle – furthermore he had a practical mind, and knew that an army of beggars would follow him immediately if he started to hand out any alms.

Michel had to wield his whip when a filthy and especially bold beggar became too insistent, uttering curses, as obscene as they were imaginative, to ensure that they could ride on without being molested any further.

Therefore, they arrived at François's new home without any major incident. As soon as they reached the entrance, servants sped forward to take care of their master and the horses. Still deep in thought, François de Toucy dismounted and climbed the steps to the drawing room where his wife must surely be waiting for him.

Julia jumped from her chair and rushed into his arms to greet him. François held her tightly and inhaled the scent of her perfume, an extract distilled from rose petals with a secret oriental mixture of ingredients which she had brought over from Venice. Joy filled his heart; he still couldn't believe his luck at having encountered Julia in Venice – had it happened only two years ago?

Julia's waist had expanded somewhat – she was with child. One of the few secrets the Cardinal Mazarin doesn't know yet, François mused as he embraced his wife.

"Tell me, what did the Cardinal want? He didn't invite you just to share a glass of wine?"

"He did offer me a glass of wine, my love," François answered, as he made sure that Julia was sitting comfortably on his lap, "and a very good one, a wine from the Avignon wineries of the Holy Father."

Julia was not very impressed. "The Holy Father should be concerning himself with more important matters than producing wine! Anyhow, the wines from our own estates are much better, I don't know why you French make such a fuss about your wines. The wines from northern Italy are superior to anything I've ever tasted in France. But never mind, I hope you told the Cardinal that you're married and no longer available to render him any services?"

"This is how our conversation started," François answered cautiously.

Julia looked at him critically, sensing immediately that François had no good news to share.

"Do you remember your cousin Giovanni, and that other one, the one who stutters and gets his parlour maids pregnant as soon as he claps eyes on them?" he continued.

"I guess you mean Giacomo, it must be him. He was always scheming with Giovanni, they're the kind of relatives you don't really want to have... What about them? Why on earth would you mention them now? You wouldn't have discussed my relatives with the Cardinal, would you?"

"In fact, we did. The Cardinal told me in confidence that your cousins want to introduce a new law with the intention of getting their sticky fingers on your inheritance – of course they wove it into some general formula that Venetian women who venture to marry outside the venerated circle of the Golden Book should lose their right of inheritance. As I'm not inscribed in the Golden Book you'd be the first one to lose everything, at least the inheritance from your uncle."

"Yes, that would be just like Giovanni and Giacomo!" Julia jumped up, clenching her fists with anger. "What an odious pair. But I'll deal with them, I'll talk with my aunt, I'll have them killed, chopped into pieces and dumped in the Canal Grande!" Julia was fuming.

"Weren't we just talking about wine? There were times when my lovely wife would offer me a glass of wine after I galloped through the dangerous streets of Paris in order to come back to her as fast as possible?" François tried to change the subject.

"If you can tell me how anybody can find a way to gallop through Paris, I might be tempted to believe you, but the streets in this dirty city are so narrow and congested that even the Queen has to move at a snail's pace when she wants to go to church," Julia answered, but took the decanter of precious Murano glass and poured a glass of wine. François thanked her with a long kiss.

"No use trying to deflect my attention, sir," she whispered, but willingly acquiesced when François repeated the procedure.

"The Cardinal offered to bribe the members of the committee and despatch Giacomo, promoted as a bishop with some fancy titles, to some remote island in the

11

Mediterranean. I guess that would be more efficient than having him killed and dumped in the sea."

"I prefer the idea of seeing them dead." Julia was in no mood for conciliation. "But I agree that this could work. But this proposal will cost a lot of money – and the Cardinal Mazarin is no fool, you'll need to pay back every scudo – and more, so what is it that he wants from you?"

"He wants me to render him a special service, in England. But he'll throw in another reward: if I do what he requests, I'll be made a count here in France."

Julia opened her eyes in dismay and swallowed before she replied. "So that's how he got you hooked! I could tell you that I don't care if I get my uncle's inheritance or not, I have more than enough money. But this Mazarin is devious, he knows that you'll do anything to become a count in your own right. My proud husband doesn't like to have to bear the titles of his wife."

"Are you angry with me?" François looked at her with his translucent grey eyes – no living female had ever been known to withstand this look.

"Of course I am, and stop turning your charms on me! I hate you, François de Toucy!"

François took Julia in his arms. Any further protest was silenced by means of a long kiss.

"There seems nothing I can really do, unless go into a tantrum, but that's not going to help," she continued after considerable time, "and doing so would be useless. I'll ask my aunt to travel to Paris and join me. I'll agree to your going to England but only on one condition!"

"What condition?"

"Tell me every detail about your mission, even if the Cardinal has told you that it's top secret."

And so François told her.

***

François changed the subject. "I fancy a nice evening with you in the library this evening. Yesterday I bought a copy of a new play, a comedy, and rumour has it that it's a caricature of some well-known members of the royal court, and I have an idea who it could be. All of Paris will be talking about it."

"I've got bad news for you then, my love, I've promised your mother and sister that we'll accompany them tonight to the hôtel Saint Paul, the Marquis is hosting in great style as his youngest daughter is about to be betrothed. Your mother wants to use the opportunity to present your sister to the Marquise and have her introduce Martine to the court."

François moaned. "This sounds simply awful. Am I expected to look after my sister the whole evening?"

"Stop complaining, I'll be there as well to look after her together with your mother, and don't forget, Armand de Saint Paul and Pierre de Beauvoir will be there – knowing you, you'll disappear to play cards as soon as the Marquise invites us into the salon. As a special treat, a young poet has been invited to read his latest oeuvres."

François's eyes nearly popped out of their sockets. "Poetry!" he groaned. "I hate poetry. It bores me to tears! Daffodils dancing in the wind with nymphs and all that hogwash. Who is it this time?"

"A promising young poet sponsored by the Duchess of Limoges," Julia answered dreamily. "Very interesting. The last time he read a very touching poem about the ethereal beauty of her eyes."

"Oh *mon dieu*!" François retorted. "But let's face the truth, there's nothing else of beauty left in the Duchess, with the notable exception of her castles and her considerable fortune. Doesn't she look terrible with her jowly cheeks? She resembles more and more one of her petulant pet dogs. I won't shock you if I assume that this poet is her newest lover?"

"Oh not at all, it's an open secret," Julia giggled. "But at least he seems to be talented – I mean talented outside her bedroom – more so than her last discovery. I have to say this of Paris, it's vastly more entertaining than Venice. No gentlewoman in Venice would ever dare to appear with her young lover in society."

"That's why our culture is in decline," François answered, resigned to the fact that his comfortable evening at home had turned out to be nothing but a dream.

***

François later had ample time to regret having ever agreed to attend the grand ball. Their coach advanced only at the speed of a tired snail, as too many luxurious carriages and sedan chairs were blocking the entrance of the Palais de St. Paul, home of the Marquis de Saint Paul and his numerous offspring.

Apart from the royal family, it would be difficult to imagine any family of higher rank in France. The Marquis's ancestors had conquered Jerusalem, sacked ancient Byzantium in the name of the Almighty, fought in France for the Valois against the enemy Plantagenet usurpers – or acted as their allies, whichever course of action had seemed more profitable or rewarding at any given moment. Titles, land and gold had been showered on the family over the centuries and the present Marquis was rumoured to be wealthier than the King of France – not to mention the present king's penniless uncle, the King of England.

13

Clenching their teeth, the Saint Pauls had endured the ascent of King Henry IV, the first Bourbon in a long line to come from a shabby and tiny kingdom, forlorn in the remote south, to the sacred throne of France. But the Marquis was not blind to reality. As soon as Cardinal Richelieu had noiselessly but with deadly efficiency removed many influential families from the map of power, the Marquis had astutely made sure that no member of the Saint Paul family would be touched, a silent truce between two powerful men.

"Look, François, isn't this beautiful!" François's sister tugged at his sleeve and pointed at the courtyard as they drew near. Her face was flushed with excitement, for today was her first official ball since she had arrived in Paris.

Gigantic torches placed in wrought-iron holders had been positioned to light the way, bathing the façade of the Palais de Saint Paul in their bright light. The noise of the servants' shouting was deafening, every coach had to be accommodated first, stressing the importance of their noble owners.

Eventually François, his wife, mother and sister descended from the coach and were greeted in due course by the Marquise and her husband. The Marquise de Saint Paul not only held François in high esteem, as he was a close relative of hers, but she was also known to have a soft spot for her handsome nephew.

Until the death of the late Louis XIII (never known to have been a particularly cheerful monarch), the style of dress at court had been sober and plain. The King's sudden death had resulted in a prolonged period of mourning, banning all colours besides subdued grey and raven black. But as soon as it was deemed seemly, a tacit understanding had brought on a wave of new fashion in the most luxurious style. Tonight the hôtel de Saint Paul was glittering with silk dresses in the brightest colours, combined with expensive cloth woven with threads of silver and gold, adorned with sparkling diamonds and precious stones.

As soon as possible, François found an excuse to leave his family in search of his friends Armand de Saint Paul and Pierre de Beauvoir. Eventually, he found them, but not in the gambling room – as he had hoped – but in the great ballroom where Armand was leading the dance with a rather plain faced young lady.

Pierre still looked like a young gentleman aspiring towards knighthood, although he already possessed two titles: on his father's side he was styled Marquis de Beauvoir of France and on his mother's side he had inherited the dukedom of Hertford in England. Pierre and Armand were close friends; it was almost inconceivable to imagine one without the other.

Since Pierre had married last year, Armand was probably one of the hottest remaining prizes on the marriage market in Paris right now. He was handsome, with his curly brown hair, muscular frame and warm brown eyes that were a constant – and very promising – invitation to every beautiful woman.

14

But Armand was known by now to enjoy rather too much the pursuit of pleasure and so far had not had fallen into any of the numerous traps of marriage that had been set for him. Therefore the sour looking matrons in charge of their young daughters had become wary of his attempts at courtship, as he had left too many broken hearts in his wake.

Armand wasn't known to be chasing after a rich heiress, thus there could be only one explanation as to why he was dancing with that girl: his mother must have condemned him to dance with those unlucky wallflowers left without suitable partners tonight, a suspicion that was confirmed by the broad grin on Pierre's face whenever he encountered his friend during one of the complicated dance figures. The music stopped and nothing could have been more charming and courteous than the way Armand took leave of his dancing partner. His duty done, he quickly joined his friends. "Please get me out of this torture chamber. I promised my mother a dance with all the young ladies who couldn't find a partner, but enough is enough! She stepped on my feet twice – can you imagine?"

"Ouch!" commented Pierre. "She does look a bit heavy…"

"She is!" Armand answered, sending a reproachful glance at the stout young lady who now sat at the opposite side of the ball room, whispering and giggling with another girl, probably her sister, as she shared the same plain looks. As soon as the two girls noticed that not only one but three handsome men were watching them they dived behind the shelter of their fans, yet sending inviting glances, in the hope of being asked for another dance.

François changed the subject. "I need to talk with both of you – in private."

"I wish it were something connected with a new adventure," Armand sighed. "Paris has become so boring. I really could do with a bit of excitement."

"So could I," Pierre fell in, blushing. "I mean, I'm a married man – and very happily so – but sometimes…"

François laughed. "I get the point, after I had the pleasure of rescuing both of you during your last adventure in Venice, life here seems a trifle boring. Where and when can we talk in confidence?"

"Later, François, after midnight. After I'm finished here in the ballroom, my mother has ordered me to attend a poetry reading in the blue salon. She wants to show that the Saint Paul family is dedicated to promoting the fine arts," Armand groaned. "By the way, Pierre, my mother demands your presence as well, and I'm to warn you that she won't accept any excuses."

"A room full of middle-aged ladies whimpering for the great poet's attention. I know these kinds of gatherings, they're horrid!" Pierre exclaimed. "You're not seriously proposing to drag me into this!"

15

"I am, and I repeat, no excuse will be accepted. You know Maman... but she'll have to pay me for that," Armand answered darkly. "There's a limit to what even the most faithful son can be expected to do for his mother."

"Let's meet after midnight then, but where?" François asked, secretly relieved that the Marquise had obviously forgotten to find a task for him.

"That's the complicated part, the library has been converted into a gaming room and will be full of noisy guests. I suggest we use my bedroom, if you don't mind. No other place is available tonight to discuss anything confidential."

"That's agreed then, let's meet at the library after midnight and go to your room together. Now I have to dance with my sister." His glance fell on Armand. "Or would you mind dancing with her? She told me that she hates the idea of opening the dance with me. She's convinced that everyone will think that she couldn't find a suitable partner."

Armand's face lit up. "With pleasure, amazing how beautiful your sister has become. I'll make it two if you allow!"

"You dare; one dance will be enough or you'll start tongues wagging. And keep your dancing respectable, nothing else!"

"Trust me!" Armand answered with a wink, his good humour restored.

***

The Marquis de Saint Paul had given carte blanche to his maître de cuisine who hadn't wasted a second in indulging in his most daring dreams and exploiting this rare opportunity. As a result even the most demanding culinary whims were catered for. In the dining room François discovered tables loaded with food, an abundance not even seen at the royal court – in times of war and belt-tightening, who could afford to serve mountains of caviar imported on ice from afar?

A haughty-looking stuffed peacock presided in regal splendour over a mountain of exquisite bites of fowl. He was accompanied by a honey-glazed suckling pig, venison pâté, roast boar – there was no end to the list. All dishes were arranged on polished silver platters, a deliberate understatement as the Marquis could easily have afforded to use his golden ones. But as His Eminence, the Cardinal Mazarin, was expected to pay a short visit tonight, the Marquis had decided not to show off too much of his wealth, and thus risk irritating the prime minister who was known to hoard treasures by the dozen, often using innovative ways to divert anything he fancied into his own capacious pockets.

François was just about to instruct one of the liveried servants what kind of fowl to pile on the plate in front of him when a giant of a man entered the room, exclaiming in a deep voice oozing with satisfaction, "Now, that's the room I've been searching for. I'm positively starving!" His appraising glance went over the food – a strange glance, as the giant had eyes of two different colours.

16

"Charles!" François exclaimed. "I didn't know you were in Paris. You're just the man I need!"

The giant turned and smiled with affection at François. Not only were they close friends, they had shared many adventures in the past.

"You sound just like my wife!" he jested, with his thick English accent.

"But let me take some food first as I'm starving and you certainly don't want me to drop dead of exhaustion before you tell me why you need me. Not difficult to guess though, it's no doubt something extremely troublesome that you want from me."

François started to utter a protest but Charles cut him short. "No use telling me otherwise, I simply know you too well!"

"You misjudge me!" François answered with a wink. "Just a small piece of advice, nothing to trouble you at all. Don't look at me like that!"

Charles laughed, a sound that almost made the room vibrate. "All innocence, as usual, but you can't fool me."

He moved his attention back to the table where he chose with careful deliberation from the best dishes. While they were eating, they exchanged the latest news, though they carefully avoided any controversial subjects in public. François was aware that Charles had been entrusted to carry out a secret diplomatic mission for His Majesty, King Charles, King of England, Scotland and Ireland – but as rumour had it, His Majesty might soon be a king without a kingdom if his luck didn't improve. Given his last interview with the Cardinal Mazarin, François doubted that Charles would be able to change the course of history.

"I'm meeting Pierre and Armand at midnight at the library, would you mind joining us there? We could do with your advice."

"The three of you – this surely means a lot of trouble. I was right – wasn't I?" Charles sighed with satisfaction. "You're lucky, now that I'm no longer hungry, I'm in a conciliatory mood, and might in fact consider joining you. But I must insist, no adventures of any kind, I've had enough of those. I'll never forget that your irksome friends made me gallop day and night through France and Italy to save them from the clutches of Pierre's murderous cousin Henri! Pierre's French relatives are an odd bunch of people."

"No adventures, I promise!" François grinned. "And, by the way, one of the irksome friends you just mentioned is your own cousin. Don't worry, Charles, we just feel the urgent need to drink from the unrivalled fountain of your wisdom."

"You sly little devil, you're mocking me. You'd make an excellent diplomat. See you later!"

17

Looking at the sumptuous buffet, François remembered with a pang of guilt that his wife and his family must be waiting for him, probably starving, and most probably cursing him for his prolonged absence. With more than just a tinge of bad conscience he made his way back to the ballroom in order to look for Julia and his mother, who'd be in charge of chaperoning his sister.

But to his greatest relief François was spared the expected painful lecturing on his negligence. By a stroke of luck, his mother had encountered some of her old friends and he found her in animated conversation while his wife was dancing with Armand, and not at all hiding the fact that she was having an exceedingly good time.

"You don't seem to be missing me very much?" he greeted his wife, through clenched teeth.

"You were absent, sir," Julia answered, opening wide her beautiful eyes. "I must have forgotten, I was having such a pleasant time with a handsome gentleman who took good care of me, he even brought us some wine and sweetmeats, whereas my husband had disappeared..."

"Touché, Julia, how can I ever regain your favours?" François pleaded.

"It will be difficult, my lord, but I might consider it. You could start by asking me if I wanted to dance, for instance, then afterwards a bite of a supper would be lovely."

The evening passed quickly and François almost missed his appointment with his friends. But as it turned out in the end, although late, he was still the first to arrive at the library where he had ample time to finish a glass of wine before Pierre and Armand showed up. The two friends had been playing dice and forgotten all about the time.

"I've invited Charles to join us, has anybody seen him?"

"Oh, Cousin Charles! He's a big shot now, I saw him discussing things with the Cardinal Mazarin and with Armand's father downstairs," Pierre exclaimed. "Better be prepared to wait for some time; Mazarin loves talking – as does Charles."

It certainly took another quarter of an hour before Charles turned up, not at all perturbed at being late. "You're still waiting for me," he sighed. "I had hoped that you'd forget. You're more troublesome than a pack of young dogs."

"How on earth could we forget you, Charles," Armand protested, "your sheer size makes you unforgettable."

"Rascal!" Charles commented good-humouredly. "Now be a good host and organize some wine. If we have to sit in this stuffy bedroom of yours to talk, I don't want to die of thirst."

Armand was the youngest son of the Marquis de Saint Paul. His room was of pleasant proportions but by no means the largest in the house. His eldest brother, heir to the title, had seen to that, he'd need the biggest room – apart from the Marquis and his wife, of course. But the windows of Armand's bedroom opened onto the palatial gardens, which was a nice compensation, as his brother would be disturbed by the sounds of the street.

Until Charles entered the room it had looked more than adequate and comfortable – now the bedroom suddenly appeared small. Charles suspiciously inspected the armchair offered to him before he sat down. Pierre held his breath as the chair squeaked in protest, but it held. Two more chairs were available for Pierre and François, and Armand flung himself on the large canopied bed as there was no chair left, doing so with a sigh of satisfaction, as his feet were hurting.

"Having dances at home are a nightmare… as I'm a gentleman, I'm not going to tell you what I truly think, but I feel as if I have been tortured – body and mind. First I had to dance with the most unattractive girls you can possibly imagine to please my mother, then came this silly poet with his endless 'ode to my nymph bathing in the silvery light of the ascendant moon'. This painted popinjay almost killed me. I've never heard so much nonsense as when our celebrated poet opened his mouth. And you should have seen the ladies, drinking in his words, almost kissing his feet, disgusting!"

"You seemed to have had a good time with Julia though," François threw in, still jealous.

"Oh, Julia! You have to give it to her, she's really special, quite a treasure. I never understood why she married you, one word and she could have had me! One day she'll wake up and understand what kind of terrible mistake she made."

François kicked him, but declined to comment. He knew his true worth.

Charles helped himself to a glass of wine. "Can anybody reveal to me why we need to hide up here like a group of conspirators? I thought I had seen enough of those at home in England."

"I guess it's time that I gave you all an explanation." François shifted his legs to find a comfortable position in his chair; finally he gave up on this fruitless exercise and exclaimed in exasperation, "This chair has come straight from your medieval torture chambers."

"Don't complain about my chair, it has served my family for generations," Armand retorted.

"Maybe it's about time to invest in some new furniture then." But then he went on, "Needless to say, what I'm about to tell you is highly confidential. To cut a long story short, I have the honour of sailing to England, to meet the Queen of England,

and try to open her eyes to the fact that it's about time to return to her family in France – safely. Any suggestions as to how to do this successfully?"

"You're joking?" Charles looked at François as if he had just discerned a new and very unpleasant trait of insanity in his character.

"I'm not, I'm deadly serious. His Eminence gave the order in person. Her sister-in-law, Queen Anne, is worried that events in England might spiral out of control soon and Mazarin shares her view. As a 'fille de France', it would be a nightmare to see Queen Henrietta Maria fall into the hands of the rascals occupying Parliament right now, therefore she absolutely must be convinced to come back home to safety, and the sooner, the better."

"Have you ever heard anything of Queen Henrietta Maria?" Charles asked, while he poured another glass of wine. "I need this now, and I can guarantee you, you'll need this later as well," he added, pointing to the wine.

François frowned. "Yes and no, I mean, the usual things. She was reputed to be a beauty, but we all know that this is probably not true, how can she be beautiful with parents like Henry IV who looked like a peasant with his terrible nose, and her fat Medici mother with her countless chins and a waist like a pig. I also heard that she seems to be running out of money all the time, but most kings and queens do, that's nothing unusual."

Charles took a long sip of wine, scratched his head and replied, "Our noble Queen is a bit special, I admit. She's never been crowned, by the way, as she refuses to attend a church service conducted by a bishop of the Church of England. It may sound surprising, as her father was a stout Protestant, but he changed his faith as soon as he'd change a shirt the minute he was offered to have the French crown put on his balding head. But Queen Henrietta, her husband calls her Marie by the way, was educated by Carmelite nuns and she's as stubborn as a mule, a trait she's inherited from her father. She sees herself as a martyr sent by Providence to the shores of an uncultivated island called England in order to convert the heathens, and she makes a point of saying she would prefer to die rather than leave her husband."

Pierre nodded. "I have received urgent summons from King Charles demanding money and my presence. I hate the idea, but I have no choice, I must make sure that Hertford will not be touched by the war."

Charles replied. "Yes, things are changing by the minute – for the worse. The forces of Parliament gather strength daily. There's a new leader of the army, Cromwell, he's put it into their heads that he's inspired and guided by the Almighty and that the King and the Queen must go."

"Is your Cromwell a sort of English Jeanne d'Arc?" Armand quipped. "She at least had secured her place in history, she rescued us from the English."

Charles ignored this impertinence and went on, "Maybe this Oliver
will find his place in history as well. I can speak openly here, I've nev
much incompetence as in the royal headquarters. Sometimes I think our
are more concerned about their dress, their horses and their rank, rather tha
on a concise plan for how to stem the tide of Puritans that threatens to
kingdom away."

"What about Prince Rupert?" Pierre asked. "He seems to be an excellen
and as I hear, he's also a charismatic leader of the troops – and a stout Prote

"Prince Rupert is a good fighter but his cousin, the King, remains ou
commander. With all due respect to His Majesty, the King is a slow th
worries for a whole day and night before he takes any decisions, if he tak
all..."

"Better a bad decision than no decision, my father used to say," Armand
in.

"That's true, in warfare you need to be swift."

"So, tell me, how should I proceed?" François asked Charles. "I car
London and knock on the door of Windsor Castle: 'Your Majesty, may I sug
take a coach back to France, and, just by coincidence, I have one waiting
already!'"

Charles laughed but then his face changed, his usual sunny demeanour
by a deep frown.

"First of all, you should remember that the court left London long ago,
Windsor Castle was no longer considered to be safe. The King and his cou
Oxford. The city has been fortified and is much easier to defend. The sad fac
London is lost to the Crown, it's firmly in the hands of the Roundheads."

"In Oxford? I didn't even know that there was a royal palace or a castle
Pierre was flabbergasted.

"No, there isn't any castle or palace. The Queen is staying in Merton C
she's opened her court there," Charles replied, "she calls it 'ma court cham
and the King and his staff are close to her but in a different college building.
temporary arrangement only, as he's convinced that he'll be returning to Wh
soon, a point of view I don't share with His Majesty."

François grabbed a glass of wine. "I remember now, Mazarin mentioned O
I do need a glass of wine now, you were right. The Queen will never agree to
her husband in such a situation, it'll look like treason."

"Let me say a word of warning, François, you'll need to be extremely cau
from the moment you step onto English soil," Charles continued. "The Puritan
Roundheads, as we call them, hate the French and they detest anybody w

21

atholic. The moment they realize that you're from France, you'll be arrested as a
aitor, if not killed right on the spot. And as for Pierre, you must be careful as well,
ot everybody will welcome your arrival."

Pierre nodded. "No need to tell me, but I have to go. I already informed Marie
at I need to join the King. She'll stay in Reims until I'll come back."

"I could pass as a French Huguenot fleeing persecution in France," François
iggested.

"Not if you walk and dress like a peacock," Pierre couldn't help interrupting.
Armand and I visited Geneva, the stronghold of the Calvinists, three years ago. I've
:ver seen such a depressing city in my life. If you so much as laugh, they'll shoot
ou. If you want to pass for a Huguenot, first of all you'll need to change your
othes, your hairstyle, and learn to look humble, pious."

"You mean I'll have to cut my hair?" François was shocked.

"Yes – and no velvet breeches or silken shirts, it has to be plain scratchy wool.
ut I bet that Cardinal Mazarin has offered to reward you handsomely, so stop
oaning," Armand smirked.

"When will you need to go?" Charles asked François.

"I don't know yet, the Cardinal is waiting for further news from his spies. King
harles's situation has slightly improved during the past weeks, but the Cardinal
)esn't share his optimism that it'll last. He reckons that by early spring Parliament
ill launch a big counter-attack and he wants me to talk to the queen before then.
ny other advice you can give me?"

Charles frowned. "I agree with Pierre's recommendation, better be careful or
)u'll find yourself straight on a shortcut to paradise, assuming, of course, that this
ill be your final destination." He scratched his head and continued, "I have an idea.
n planning to leave for England in January; what about joining me as my French
iguenot friend? I still have a lot of friends in England – on both sides luckily – and
:ould protect you during your journey to London if you use this disguise. I also
)n't think that it's a good idea to leave at the last minute. If Mazarin is sure that the
uation is going to worsen, better prepare everything in plenty of time."

"Thank you, Charles, I'll gladly accept your invitation. January it will be – what
out you Pierre?"

"I guess I should be leaving around the same time. The King's letter was very
sistent. I still have to take Marie to Reims, but I don't want her to accompany me
England. I'm not sure though what the King expects from me – just my money, or
es he really want me to join his army? I have no experience on a battlefield, I don't
e how I could be helpful in any way."

22

"Compared to most other gentlemen I met at the King's court, you'll be a true gem, don't worry." Charles's sarcasm was barely hidden.

"I'll join you," Armand said. "I won't let you go alone, and besides, you'll need me!"

"Armand, you know that I'm always glad to have you with me – but I'm grown up now, I can cope on my own!"

Armand snorted. "Bullshit, I'm coming with you. That's final."

Charles raised his glass. "A toast to England, to our King and to our friendship. It seems that we'll all be reunited soon in England. May the Lord protect our King – and our venture!"

"If we're lucky, it will be a great adventure! To England!" Armand replied, and raised his glass.

Oxford, the Royal Winter Court of 1643

The last notes of the silvery trumpets echoed through the great hall of Merton College, solemn but triumphant, until they were carried away by the always freezing draughts of winter air. Inside the hall, a stage had been erected, painted wooden white pillars that mimicked the shape of a marble temple located on a fictitious Greek Island, tonight's setting for a masked play.

Light cast by large brass lanterns illuminated the stage and bathed the silver folds of the costumes with their golden glow. Tonight's play was an allegory inspired by Greek mythology, glorifying the wisdom and the prowess of His Majesty, Charles, King of England.

The three ladies finished their play but kept their masks on. As the sound of the trumpets died down, they curtsied low before the King who sat on a canopied golden armchair displaying his proud coat of arms reuniting his three kingdoms. His Majesty was accompanied by his adolescent son, the Prince of Wales, and surrounded by his favourite courtiers and their ladies.

The royal party was dressed in the splendour and the decorum expected when attending a major court event, silks gleaming, jewels sparkling in all the colours of the rainbow. The courtiers' elegant outfits were lined with all kinds of precious furs such as sable and mink – for all its elegance, the great hall was a cold place in winter. Many noses and faces showed a red or bluish tint and this was not entirely the fault of having used too much rouge or drunk too much wine.

Charles, by the Grace of God, was the anointed King of England, Scotland and Ireland. The lilies of his coat of arms still proudly proclaimed the English claim to the French throne, a claim long buried, in truth, as England had lost her last territories on the other side of the Channel. Richelieu had seen to that. But if no miracle came to save them, the three remaining kingdoms might be lost as well – the King's power and his territories were melting away like snow in the sun.

The King smiled graciously, although his mind was in turmoil. *How long will my courtiers remain at my side? I sacrificed Strafford, my faithful minister, but this made the beasts in Parliament lust for even more blood, how will this end? I have to fight, if only for my son,* his thoughts continued. Soon the Prince of Wales would be a man, ready to defend the Stuart heritage. King Charles smiled at his son, and the Prince of Wales smiled back, but not like his courtiers, smiling only with their mouths. The prince's smile and affection were sincere. The Prince of Wales was only thirteen years old and no beauty, and worse, he didn't show any prospect of ever becoming a handsome man. His nose was too long, his face swarthy, on the verge of being ugly, and yet, the young prince radiated a charm that would easily conquer any heart.

I wish I could win my subjects' hearts as easily as my son can. People obey and respect me because I'm the King, but they don't love me... Such thoughts went through the King's mind while he continued to smile; appearances must be kept at all costs.

In fact there was a genuine reason to smile tonight. The King had received encouraging news from France. Pierre de Beauvoir, the young Duke of Hertford, had not only agreed to join his court but to send a large amount of money, enough to maintain the cavalry in Oxford until spring. He couldn't have asked for more. Maybe his luck was turning after all.

The King's smile relaxed and he exchanged a quick glance with Prince Rupert of the Rhine, his nephew and general of the cavalry, a man he could always rely on. Prince Rupert must have been reading his thoughts as he was smiling back, encouraging him. Charles liked his nephew, a dashing young soldier who was ever ready to fight for the Stuart cause, his enthusiasm never dampened by the many setbacks they had encountered during the last months. Rupert was a pillar of strength; if only he were more diplomatic!

The King's attention went back to the stage where two of the ladies curtsied deeply once again, and the third one, much more voluptuous than her two companions, just bobbed her head.

In reply, King Charles clapped his hands and the courtiers joined in, having been waiting for his lead, applauding and cheering the three actresses. This was the sign for the first of the ladies, disguised as Greek goddesses, to remove her mask. Of course everybody had known that the Queen would be among the actors tonight and yet, as was customary, everyone pretended to be astonished to find her on stage. The King stood up, waiting for his wife to join him.

"May I congratulate you, Ma'am, your rendition of the Goddess Athena was truly superb. The goddess of wisdom, what an excellent choice, who else could have portrayed her so well?"

Queen Henrietta Maria blushed under her heavy make-up. She loved the arts, plays and dances – although to the exasperation of her numerous tutors she had never shown the slightest interest for books of any kind.

"You're far too kind, Sire, *je suis heureuse que notre spectacle vous ait pu faire plaisir!*" Henrietta lapsed into French – even after many years spent in England, she still preferred to use her native tongue whenever possible.

"Did you hear that?" the Countess of Portsmouth whispered to her heavily made-up neighbour, a gentlewoman well beyond her prime. "The Queen impersonating Athena, the goddess of wisdom! Pffft, what a joke, she's so stupid. She never reads anything, and worst of all, she doesn't even speak proper English."

Her neighbour just shrugged her shoulders. "She's the Queen of England, all queens are supposed to be intelligent and beautiful, at least that's what we keep telling them," she sniggered, "and that's what we expect to be rewarded for…"

To the extent that the King's supporters were dwindling steadily, Charles had started to rely more and more on the support and advice of his wife. By nature a weak, almost shy person, he found in his wife the unerring strength and reliance he lacked.

The Queen's maids of honour brought a warm fur-lined cape and installed Her Majesty in the second canopied chair next to the King while the festivities continued. A ball was to follow with a sumptuous supper as a highlight. Since the court had moved from London, critics like the portly Earl of Shrewsbury might complain that delicacies imported from the Continent were a rarity nowadays and the dishes served on the golden platters brought from Whitehall were not worthy to be served at a royal court, but an ample supply of venison from the surrounding forests made up for the shortcomings of exotic dishes in most courtiers' eyes. The cook's pantry was well stocked as the Cavaliers and the King would go out hunting whenever they didn't need to follow the routines laid upon the government – there was not a lot of alternative diversion to be found in the small city of Oxford.

The youngest actress accompanied the Queen to her armchair. Standing behind the Queen she removed the mask that had hidden a face of exceptional beauty. While loosening the straps of her mask she must have touched by mistake the strings of her demure silver cap. The cap fell down and released a mass of curly red hair, falling down onto her shoulders like a cascade of molten copper. The maid's hair made a striking contrast with her violet eyes – Lady Elizabeth Huntville never went unnoticed.

Not only did the Prince of Wales goggle at her, as if she were in a fairy tale, but several gentlemen hastened to dive down in order to snatch her cap. Lady Elizabeth thanked the lucky finder, her radiant smile sending the young gentleman into ecstasy. She thanked him with some pretty words, but the young courtier was incapable of reply. Face flaming red, he uttered some incoherent sentences before he withdrew, cursing himself at having missed the chance of a lifetime to invite her for a dance.

"She did that on purpose!" hissed the Countess of Portsmouth to her neighbour, the Marchioness of Halifax, a thin lady with a sharp face. "That harlot, she just wants to show off her red hair, she knows that its makes men mad with desire. I've told my son to stay clear of her! Why are men so naïve? The poor boy thinks that I'm just a jealous mother."

"It doesn't matter if she's a harlot or not, if she expects a substantial dowry. We've seen plenty of harlots in disguise at court. Remember Lucy Hays, Percy's sister? Isn't she still the worst of all? Everybody knows that she's having an affair with that ugly Roundhead – how can one demean oneself like that? But as for Elizabeth Huntville, apart from her lack of composure, she hasn't got a penny, no dowry, nothing. I told James to steer clear of her."

The Countess of Portsmouth made a face. "Your James is rolling in money, not like my son. Why does it matter whether a daughter-in-law can bring in even more?"

"Money always matters, my dear, never forget that!"

"How could I forget? I just hope this war will end soon, we're cut off from our estates in the North, we are totally reliant on the King's pension."

Her neighbour took her arm. "Don't worry, my dear, it should be over soon."

At least for us, she added to herself. *Luckily my husband is clever enough to make sure that we'll be welcomed with open arms in London. Soon this farce here will be over.*

Nothing of these thoughts could be read in her face however, as she continued smoothly, "I love this new gown you're wearing, where did you have it made – not here, I imagine?"

In the meantime Lady Elizabeth had tamed her curls and fastened the strings of her cap. She positioned herself behind the Queen's chair, her violet eyes demurely lowered, pretending not to notice the burning gazes and the whispering of the bystanders.

Lady Elizabeth was content; she had rehearsed the little trick with her cap in front of a mirror until it had looked smooth and entirely accidental. She had hoped that her little scene wouldn't go unnoticed, but now she could see that her little ruse had worked to perfection. All the tongues at court would be wagging tonight but she had learnt the most important rule at court: worse than being subject to gossip was the fate of going unnoticed and being forgotten.

Elizabeth had come to court to be successful and to marry – not to be forgotten. She noticed that the young Earl of Wiltshire was looking in her direction but as soon as she looked back, by coincidence of course, he quickly turned his head away. He was young and handsome, boyish with his fair mop of hair – and yet manly enough to keep her dreaming. But the earl had never displayed any genuine interest – her ancestry probably wasn't good enough for the Wiltshires. The earl was rich, handsome and with a bloodline stemming back to the Norman conquest; he could afford to be picky.

At midnight the Queen decided to withdraw from the ball and the King, unusually, accompanied her to the suite of rooms that had been turned into her private lodgings in Merton College. Long gone were the days when the Queen could have withdrawn to Greenwich, her private palace. The train of the small royal procession moved down the aisle and the courtiers made way, bowing low like reeds in the blowing wind.

Merton College had never been built with the intention of offering the comforts or amenities of a royal residence. But the Queen had brought her complete household, including furniture and paintings, from London and her servants had done a remarkable job of converting the sprawling university college buildings into a miniature palace. Furthermore, the King had allowed her to use the adjacent chapel as a place of Catholic worship. His decision was generally met with a frown but he insisted on respecting the rules laid down in their contract of marriage. If it hadn't been for the stream of bad tidings flowing regularly from all parts of England and Scotland, their stay in Oxford could have been a very comfortable one.

The King and the Queen arrived in her private parlour where the Queen dismissed her ladies in waiting. Her dwarfs were lingering in the corner; they knew that they could usually count on the Queen's indulgence, but tonight was different.

"Leave us alone, I'll ring for you when I need you, and take the dogs and the monkey with you, His Majesty desires peace and quiet."

The ladies curtsied and obliged but it took considerable time until the last snarling dog had been caught and leashed, a reluctant monkey had been plucked from the curtains, and the cage with the screaming parrots had been removed. The dwarfs made a joke of falling over each other, but the Queen barely smiled at them; her mind was elsewhere. The noise became almost unbearable, the parrots and dogs voicing their displeasure as they were removed from the Queen's parlour. Finally the doors closed and King Charles found himself alone with the Queen.

The King breathed deeply; the last few minutes had been very trying.

"Anything in particular you wanted to discuss, Ma'am?" he asked curiously. He knew better than to criticize her penchant for pets.

The Queen was nervous. She plucked at the folds of her silver dress. "I need to talk to you, Charles!"

"That seems obvious, Marie…" he had long ago dropped the name Henrietta, a name she hated.

"I hear that you have received good news today?" The Queen avoided coming straight to the subject.

"I always marvel how fast rumours travel at court, but I have, indeed. The young Duke of Hertford, you may remember him from his stay in London two years ago, will leave France after Christmas and has promised to join my ranks. He's already sent me a bill of exchange drawn on his bankers in London," he laughed, but his laugh had a bitter edge. "The King of England, a pauper in his own land. But at least it means that I can feed my horses during the winter. I just have to find a way to feed my men."

"But Charles, this is excellent news! You'll see, things will improve from now on, I know they will. The Lord is with us, these heathens in London will be destroyed, it's the will of the Almighty, my confessor told me."

The King looked at his wife with a crooked smile. "I wish I had your conviction, my dear. Those heathens have a lot of money and they are raising new troops almost daily. Whereas I, as their anointed King, am a beggar in my own country and losing supporters daily. Hertford is an exception. But let's change the subject, why did you want to talk to me in private, Ma'am?'

"The good Lord has blessed us again, Charles."

"What do you mean, Marie? I don't understand."

"I'm expecting a child, Charles!"

The King swallowed. "Are you sure? I mean…"

"I thought the same, I put the symptoms down to my age, but my physicians are sure now, I am with child."

"When do you expect the birth, my dear?"

"By May or June, I hope we'll be back in London by then." A single tear rolled down her cheek. "Are you angry with me?"

"How could I be angry, I'm just worried – about you, about your safety, about the future of our child, but that's my nature, I'm so happy to have you at my side, *ma chérie*, I thank God every day that He made you my wife."

"Charles, this is the sweetest compliment that you've ever paid me. Our marriage has been truly blessed. I'll pray tonight for our victory!"

"Go and pray, Marie, we could do with some divine help, that's for certain."

He kissed his wife good-night and walked out of the room. As he opened the door, the guards saluted and raised their arms. The King greeted them with the same mechanical smile that he had practised for so many years; he had almost assumed a second personality in public. Nobody should notice that their King had just been compelled to face a new anxiety – with his dynasty assured by his six sons and daughters there was no need for a new mouth to feed. The Queen was way beyond her thirties – would she survive the labours of another birth?

He could only hope that Marie was wrong. He'd pray tonight that the Queen had erred, that she wasn't pregnant after all. She must be wrong, it simply couldn't be true!

***

Lady Elizabeth Huntville had no choice but to follow the example of the royal couple and to retire in the wake of the small procession together with the Queen, no matter how much she would have loved to attend the dances that would continue until the small hours of the morning!

A minuscule room would be waiting for her, a dwelling she was forced to share with a second maid of honour to the Queen. Merton College was almost bursting under the strain of having to house officers, courtiers and servants. Her room-mate, Lady Jane, was about the same age but as bland and colourless as Elizabeth was beautiful. Ever since the ladies had set eyes on each other a cold war had been raging between the two of them. Lady Jane, a daughter of a marquess, judged her position and ancestry far above Elizabeth's, tracing her roots to the first barons who joined William the Conqueror. At any given occasion she voiced her opinion about the pitfalls of fate that had compelled her to share a room with the daughter of some upstart gentry from a remote province of Ireland.

"She's probably great with horses," Elizabeth had heard her saying to another lady. "Well, she certainly smells like one."

She had pretended not to have heard the insult, but Elizabeth had sworn revenge. Jane would regret ever having been born, Elizabeth would see to that. But she could wait, revenge would be sweet.

At least Lady Elizabeth could hope to have the bedroom for herself most of the time for once, as Lady Jane had been released from the Queen's service tonight, seizing the opportunity of a free evening to hunt for a husband downstairs in the Great Hall.

As soon as Elizabeth's duties as a maid of honour had been accomplished and the Queen had granted her leave she shut her ears to the inviting sounds of music wafting through the building and walked through the dark corridors to the attic where her bedroom was located, now freezing cold, as it was winter time.

No sign of any royal luxury was visible in this wing of the building. The long and narrow corridors were lit from time to time by sparse tallow lights placed in wrought-iron holders, their fumes spreading the typically strong, unpleasant odour of the cheap fuel. Elizabeth shivered as she noticed a swift movement across the floor. She knew that rats and mice outnumbered by far the courtiers who occupied the building.

It's not a rat, it's just a shadow, she told herself firmly, *don't let yourself be fooled.*

She clutched her coat, a gift from her aunt. How proud her aunt had been to offer Elizabeth her own moth-eaten mink coat!

"A gift for my lovely Elizabeth, you'll need a fur coat for your stay at court, all the courtiers will be wearing sables, fox and mink, I know this from my own days at court..."

Her aunt's eyes had been moist with emotion. Elizabeth had been tempted to fling the shabby coat in her face, but a warning glance from her mother had commanded her to rein in her temper and she had dutifully thanked her aunt. Later Elizabeth's mother had done her best to hide the shabby spots and with the help of a tailor she had transformed the well-meant gift into a presentable fur-lined coat. As it turned out, this was to become Elizabeth's only fur coat – her departure from Ireland had been swift and much earlier than planned.

Her family might be noble and well connected to court through her mother, but they were as poor as church mice, a fact that never stopped her father from gambling and drinking away the little income that the estate could still produce. If her father wasn't gambling, he was drinking. One night, totally drunk, he had knocked at her door.

"My darling Elizabeth, let your father come in!" he had slurred.

Elizabeth had sat up in bed, confused and frightened. As she didn't dare move, her father had forced the door open and – clad only in a shabby dressing gown – entered her room. He reeked of the self-brewed ale that he consumed every evening and approached her bed, swaying. "You must be kind to your papa, my love. Papa will show you something nice."

Elizabeth had been paralysed, this couldn't be true – this couldn't be her own father who was now clumsily trying to get into her bed. But true enough, he wrapped his arms around her, making her almost vomit as she had no choice but to inhale his breath impregnated with alcohol. He was just about to plant the first kiss on her cheek when rescue arrived in the shape of her furious mother. Resolutely Lady Huntville grasped the jug of cold water standing on Elizabeth's dresser and emptied it over her snorting husband.

"Out of this room, you swine!" she cried, swinging the clay jug like a weapon. Sobered, her father fled out of the room and her mother took her into her arms. Elizabeth had wanted to cry, but she couldn't. Something inside her had broken and she knew that it would never mend.

"I'll leave tomorrow, mother," she finally said.

"I should keep you here, child, but I'm afraid that you're right. Your father will regret it and apologize, but he's a different person when he's drunk. I've learnt to live with it, but it's getting worse every year. It's better that you leave. It may sound harsh, Elizabeth, but let this be a lesson to you. Never marry a poor man for love, my dear, like I did. Make sure that your future will be better than the life I have to live."

Now it was her mother who started to cry and Elizabeth tried to comfort her. But never would she forget this evening, nor the advice her mother had given her, and never would she forgive her father. *Never marry a poor man for love!* Elizabeth had sworn to abide by this advice. The old Elizabeth, the young, romantic and impulsive redhead had died that night. Never would she trust any man in her life. Marriage was a contract and should provide freedom and wealth, nothing else.

Although Elizabeth had hated its shabbiness, she was thankful in the end to have received her aunt's coat for the winter– it would also help to keep her warm in bed tonight. But Elizabeth swore to herself that she would own plenty of fur coats soon.

Mink, sable, fox – she would own them all! She would succeed where her beautiful mother had failed, never would she return to the poverty of a shabby barony in Ireland, although her father had died shortly after she had left. No tears would ever be shed for him.

Her thoughts went back to the masked ball. How this stupid clucking hen, the Countess of Portsmouth, had looked at her. Elizabeth smiled as she remembered the vile glance the countess had sent in her direction. As if I were interested in her son – he might inherit an earldom, but everyone at court knows that he's broke. *I'll marry a rich husband, I've had my share of poverty. I'll never marry for love.*

* * *

Deep in her thoughts Elizabeth walked along the tiled floor. Her soft slippers made no sound, and only her breathing and the rustling of her silver dress were audible in the deserted corridor. The freezing cold seeped through her thin leather soles and made her shiver. How good it would be to lie in her warm bed and snuggle herself into the blankets. Hopefully Jane wouldn't wake her up. Elizabeth was on duty tomorrow morning and would need to get up early to serve the Queen.

There was almost no light at all that could guide her way, but Elizabeth wasn't worried, she had learnt to find her way almost with closed eyes through those cavernous corridors and staircases that all looked identical and were totally confusing for any newcomer. She only prayed that no rat would cross her path – she simply couldn't get used to rats. Especially as the Oxford rats were giants, well fed and devoid of any shyness.

All of a sudden a large shadow detached itself from the darkness, jumping straight at her. She shrieked with surprise as a strong arm pressed her against the cold stones and a gloved hand stifled her cry. "It's Mortimer, my love. Be quiet, I need to talk with you!"

"I'm not your love!" she hissed back. "You almost frightened me to death, do you have any idea how to treat a lady with respect?"

Elizabeth was furious. The general opinion might be that Sir Mortimer Clifford was a handsome man with his broad chest, well-toned body, blue eyes and a mop of reddish hair. But all he could aspire to inherit was a modest estate on the Scottish borders and Elizabeth was convinced that this must be even worse than being buried alive in Ireland.

"I need to talk with you!" he insisted.

"Here, in the freezing corridor? A truly great idea, Sir Mortimer!" Her answer was as glacial as the temperature inside the building.

"Of course not, I've seen to that," he whispered with a mischievous grin. All of a sudden a key appeared in his hand. Quickly he opened an inconspicuous door behind him and before Elizabeth realized what was going on or had time to object, she was drawn into a small bedroom lit by several candles and warmed by a cosy fire. Sir Mortimer had left nothing to chance, he had even gone to the effort of bribing a servant to light expensive beeswax candles, Elizabeth could smell the sweet scent. A bottle of wine and two tin cups were waiting for them. All was set for an intimate rendezvous.

Mortimer closed the door and fell to his knees, kissing the seam of her gleaming gown. Carried away by his emotions he declared, "Elizabeth, you're my goddess, when will you answer my prayers? I'm yours, body and soul, marry me! Don't leave me in despair."

Elizabeth tried hard to fight back a surge of anger. Did he really think he could propose to her in this way? Did he think she would simply fall for a pleasant face, like a kitchen maid?

"Sir Mortimer, stand up immediately! What will people think if they happen to pass?"

Mortimer struggled back to his feet, but seemed determined to go on as he turned the key in the lock. "Don't worry my love, I've got the key."

Elizabeth looked at Mortimer, the very picture of a handsome man, but she had to restrain herself from slapping him. What was he thinking? Was she the sort of woman who could be dragged into a bedchamber, happy to fall into the arms of the first available lover?

Calm down!, she ordered herself. *At least he has proposed marriage to me, not like Viscount Rochester who almost raped me.* Aloud she said: "Sir Mortimer please be reasonable! You know quite well that we can't marry even if you may think today that you are attracted to me. You have no money and I have no dowry. Both of us need to find a better match."

"I'm not simply attracted to you, Elizabeth, I love you! Life will be meaningless if you don't marry me. I've asked Prince Rupert to grant me command of a squadron in the next battle, and either I'll come back a hero and the King will recognize my dedication to his cause, or I'll be dead. I'm ready to die for you!"

He had meant to impress her, but Elizabeth was only angered at his childish outburst. "Mortimer, stop living in the world of dreams! Why would you sacrifice yourself for a king who has nothing to offer? He'll promise you a fancy title, maybe some land, but what land is there still in the hands of the Crown? Cornwall, Ireland, the North? As maid of honour to the Queen, I've many a time been present when the King receives visitors together with the Queen."

She laughed, but it didn't sound kind. "Let me tell you that everybody leaves with a promise, no one will ever be disappointed. Their Majesties promise heaven if need be. But... I've never seen somebody leaving with a deed of land or money. The

Queen is considering selling her last pieces of jewellery to make ends meet – and that's the truth."

Mortimer looked crestfallen, like a boy whose favourite toy had just been broken. Suddenly a wild idea popped up in Elizabeth's mind. Money, it was money that was the key to her future. Detached, she looked at Mortimer who was gazing at her with adoring eyes.

Like a mooncalf, she thought, as all of a sudden a bold plan took form in her mind. *I've nothing to lose,* she thought, and changing her attitude completely she smiled. "Mortimer, I think I could do with a sip of wine, if you don't mind."

Mortimer came back to reality, mortified that he had forgotten the basic duties of a good host. "Of course, Elizabeth, I'm sorry I forgot to offer you some, it's all been prepared."

"I can see that but you have prepared a bit too much – and too early, Mortimer. But let's sit down and talk."

Mortimer sent a wistful glance to the bed but Elizabeth brought him back to reality. "We'll sit here on the chairs and discuss matters like adults."

She raised her cup to him and sipped at the wine. It was strong and sweet, probably imported from Italy or Spain.

"Mortimer, if you really love me, you must prove to me your dedication. How could I ever consider courtship – I only have empty words that you love me."

"Elizabeth, I'm ready to die for you!" and he fell to his knees again – an annoying habit, Elizabeth was finding.

"Mortimer, please keep a cool head. If you ever want to marry me, we'll need money. But both of us are as poor as church mice. The King cannot help, he hasn't got a penny either. His Majesty had a big fall-out with the Queen only last week because she had ordered several new dresses. That's why she is secretly considering selling part of her jewellery collection, and not for the first time."

"Elizabeth, that's treason!" Mortimer was blushing, he was shocked.

"Is telling the truth treason? Let's talk about us then." Elizabeth took a cup and handed it to Mortimer, looking deeply into his eyes. "Your health, Mortimer, may our future be bright!"

Mortimer's eyes were glazing over. Things were developing faster than he had foreseen in his wildest dreams.

"To you, my beautiful love!" he answered and drained his cup. Elizabeth just took a small sip from her cup but filled Mortimer's to the brim.

"You have an uncle in London who's rolling in money, I've heard."

"Uncle Percy!" Mortimer almost spat the words out. "That traitor, may the devil roast his soul."

"Yes, the Earl of Northumberland. A shocking family, I admit, just think of his sister, Lucy Hay. But he has something we don't have – he has connections and money, loads of it... and he would trust you... if you brought him a message from time to time."

Mortimer looked at her in total incomprehension, his handsome face flushed from the warmth of the room, the excitement and the wine. "What do you mean, my sweetheart? You can't seriously propose that I should talk with my uncle, talk with a traitor? He's hand in glove with the Roundheads. The King would have me executed – and rightfully so!"

"Mortimer, the King cannot have you executed for speaking with your uncle. Don't make it sound so dramatic. He won't like it, but Northumberland after all is the head of your family, even the King has to accept this fact."

Mortimer was ablaze with indignation. "I shall never betray my King!"

I need to change my strategy, I need to be careful, Elizabeth thought, as she looked into his burning eyes. *Mortimer is so naïve that it hurts, this will be hard work.* "Don't forget that you're a member of a proud family, Mortimer. The Percy family has more royal blood in their veins than all the Stuarts thrown together. You owe your family as much allegiance as you owe the King."

"Now you sound like my mother, she's always been proud of marrying into the Percy family."

"Your mother is right, you've every reason to be proud of your heritage. My parents will only accept a husband from a noble house and of course what could be nobler than a member of the Percy family..."

Mortimer was still sulking but she could see that slowly he was taking the bait. Elizabeth stood up and walked to a small picture that was hanging on the wall. She needed time to think. Distracted, she wondered why this picture was even hanging here, as it was definitely not attractive. It showed a fat gentleman squatting on his sturdy horse, neither man nor horse particularly handsome.

Being a gentleman, Mortimer stood up as well. His expression was still petulant, he remembered Elizabeth as a pouting child. Elizabeth pretended to be studying the picture in detail in order to gain more time, but much as she tried to find different strategies, there seemed only one way left to change Mortimer's mood. She breathed deeply, she had no choice.

35

Slowly she walked back to him and smiled up at him, her violet eyes radiant. "It's nice and warm in here, how considerate of you to have lit a fire," she said in a husky voice.

Fascinated, Mortimer watched her loosening the strings of her coat and her cap.

"Wouldn't it be the duty of a gentleman to help me?"

Mortimer swallowed hard and hastened to follow her invitation, his strong hands shaking as he dropped her coat onto the chair. As soon as her gleaming hair fell onto her shoulders she could hear him moan, a sound that reminded her of a wounded animal. Elizabeth had taken care to loosen the strings of her bodice at the same time, aware that Mortimer would be able to see the neckline of her perfect breasts.

"Elizabeth, my love," he stammered, his heart beating like a drum. "Make me the happiest man on this earth, marry me, tonight!"

"Mortimer, you possess every quality a woman could dream of in a husband, but we must not get carried away. Don't forget, we have no money to build a home. As I have no dowry to offer, we will be facing the same obstacle to our love again and again. If only you could convince your uncle to help us out with some money, our situation would be so much different..."

Slowly she took the cup and sipped at the wine, careful to leave a drop of the red wine glistening on her moist lips. Then she leaned over the table to fill Mortimer's cup anew, making sure that he could see even more of her breasts.

Mortimer watched her pulsing neckline like a transfixed rabbit, his hands moved up to loosen his collar, he had the impression that he was close to delirium – never had he felt so excited before in his life.

"Let me help you..." Cool hands were softly loosening his collar. "It's terribly hot in here," she added as she opened the strings of his shirt and her soft hand slid down to his chest.

"Elizabeth, I want you, now, don't stop," he moaned.

"Mortimer, I'm not a cheap tavern maid. If you desire me, you must marry me first."

"Of course I want to marry you! Let me find a parson to marry us tomorrow, I have enough money to pay for a special license!"

"Marriages are made in heaven but have to last on earth. Go and talk with your uncle – and our dream will come true."

"What should I say to him?" He laughed but it sounded bitter. "'Hello Uncle Percy, do you remember your nephew Mortimer, one of your fifty nephews, as it happens? I need a piece of land and some money.' I haven't spoken to my uncle Northumberland for at least three years."

He had tried to sound cynical but failed. Mortimer simply sounded thoroughly miserable.

"Of course not, Mortimer, think about some kind of service you could render him, a service that would make you valuable and important in his eyes. Your uncle will only reward you if he gets something in return, everyone at court knows he's a tough old dog..."

Her hand travelled downwards towards his crotch, caressing the soft hair around his navel. She could feel the muscles of his flat belly contracting under her touch. Mortimer could barely keep control.

"Close your eyes!" she commanded softly while she withdrew her hand. Mortimer moaned with frustration but obliged. He felt her silky hair, her lips brushing softly along his lips, caressing his cheek while her hands played with the hair on his chest.

"I love you, Elizabeth, I can't live without you!" he moaned.

Elizabeth slowly withdrew her hands and he heard her whispering while her soft lips teased his ear.

"If you love me, ride to London and meet your uncle. He must be burning with curiosity, wishing to know what's going on at court here in Oxford. I can help you to obtain information. The King often talks with the Queen, she's one of his most important advisors. He trusts her even more than his ministers. Knowledge is money, our money, our future."

"But that's treason!" he stammered, opening his eyes in dismay. "You can't truly mean this, Elizabeth, it's against the law, I mean, it's treason of the shabbiest kind!"

"Are you a Percy or a Stuart? Don't you think that you owe allegiance to the greatness of your own family rather than to some Scottish upstarts? Do you prefer to serve a King who's governed by a foreign wife who never even learnt to speak proper English? If this is the case, then let's say goodbye now, Mortimer. You have just proved to me that your dedication is hollow, just fancy words, you're not devoted enough to the genuine cause of your family, let alone wanting to fight like a true knight for our love. The King is more important to you than I am. Go and find a parlour maid, she may be willing to take my place."

Elizabeth's voice was cold, oozing with contempt as she grabbed her coat, preparing to leave the room.

Crestfallen he looked into her eyes, hurt, suffering like a wounded animal. Elizabeth fastened her cap, and turned in order to leave the room. He could smell the scent of her perfume, the scent of her skin, he still felt the caress of her lips linger on his skin. He imagined how these lips would move on to his chest, to his navel, making him mad with desire.

"Elizabeth, stay, I'll do whatever you ask me to do!" and he fell on his knees, tears in his eyes.

How melodramatic, Elizabeth thought, feeling strangely detached. *I must keep his passion burning, but I don't know if I can endure this comedy for long. He's such a simpleton.*

Nothing of these treacherous thoughts could be read in her welcoming smile when Elizabeth turned back. "Kiss me now, Mortimer – and ask your commander permission to leave for London this week. You can tell your uncle that the Queen is with child again. But remember – we need money. If he wants more information, make him pay. Make him pay handsomely for our future, in silver, not in promises. Fifty pounds, no less."

Mortimer nodded, then kissed her, deeply, hungrily.

***

For the first time ever, Elizabeth answered his kiss, but suddenly she became rigid in his arms and pushed him back.

"What's happening?" he moaned, trying to hold on to her.

Elizabeth's sudden change of mood was explained immediately as the door of the room was suddenly flung open. Wrapped in his cloud of his desire, Mortimer had failed to pick up the noise of the key turning in the lock.

"Elizabeth, what are you doing in here?" echoed the sharp voice of Lady Jane through the room.

Lady Jane was not alone. Elizabeth could see the stout figure of the young Viscount Rochester, the heir of the Marquess of Halifax, standing behind her, groping Jane's thighs. His face was flushed with excitement as much as from an excess of wine. Dark sweaty stains were visible underneath the armpits of his slashed green velvet waistcoat.

Rochester, never a shining example of elegance, stank like a boar tonight. His drunken brain seemed to be unable to comprehend why two persons were already occupying the room he had chosen for his amorous tête-à-tête and, not knowing what to do, he scratched his private parts, unsure what to say and how to react.

As Mortimer only goggled at the intruders in shock, Elizabeth took over. "I could ask you the same, Jane. But in fact, I was just about to leave, the room is yours now. You seem to be in need of it."

Elizabeth's voice was glacial, dripping with contempt.

38

Viscount Rochester smirked. "Stay here, my lovely, but we won't be needing Mortimer. The three of us will be enough for tonight." This statement was underlined by a loud belch that echoed through the room like a fanfare. Jane's face flushed even more, trying hard to hide her embarrassment.

Elizabeth sank into a deep, mock curtsy. "I regret that I must decline your chivalrous invitation. Let me wish both of you a very agreeable night. Lady Jane, my lord Rochester, your servant forever – a small piece of advice though, don't forget to lock the door."

Jane eyed her with contempt, blotches forming on her cheeks. "I will not let your impertinence go unpunished, Elizabeth, you seem to forget who you are and whom you're talking to."

"I never forget whom I'm talking to, how could I?" Elizabeth answered softly and dragged a reluctant Mortimer out of the room behind her. She closed the door not a second too late, as Mortimer was burning to start a brawl with Rochester.

"How could this have happened, I paid for the room! That filthy pig Rochester, he was totally drunk, tomorrow I'll demand that he grant me satisfaction, I shall challenge him." Mortimer was fuming.

"Calm down, Mortimer. Certainly there must be two different servants who have access to the keys of the room. Both of them probably wanted to make extra money by arranging a secret rendezvous." Elizabeth shrugged but then her voice struck a serious note. "Mortimer, if you're a gentleman worthy of your name, I beg you, you must protect my reputation! Forget what you've seen and heard! Rochester was totally drunk, tomorrow he won't remember anything. If you challenge him, my reputation at court will be tarnished forever. You know how things are, the court will be gossiping about both of us and Jane will do her best to keep the tongues wagging. Everyone will say that it's my fault, Lady Jane will see to that."

Reluctantly Mortimer digested the content of her speech, and couldn't but agree to its astuteness.

"I'm afraid you say the truth, my love. I'm ready to relent in order to protect you, but won't Jane do everything to slander your name anyhow? She's got a terrible reputation at court, that's why no man will take her – unless he's totally drunk, like Rochester tonight."

Elizabeth shrugged. "Everybody at court knows that she's got a vile tongue. If there's no duel, rumours will die fast. I agree, no decent man has taken the bait so far, as much as Jane has been fishing for a husband. How degrading for her, actually. Her parents can offer a fat dowry, my Lord, she should be looking at better options than bedding that boar."

Mortimer shook his head like an obstinate child. "Nobody with a sound mind would ever marry a woman like her."

39

He wrapped his arm around Elizabeth's shoulders. "Let me protect you, my love, let's marry immediately!"

"Mortimer, darling, we had this discussion just minutes ago. We need to be concerned for our own future, which means that most importantly we need money. Don't worry about Jane, I'll deal with her. But you must find a way to build our future and talk with Northumberland, fast."

Mortimer looked as if he had just swallowed a toad. "Even if I receive money from my uncle – Rochester is not only rich as Croesus, one day he'll succeed his father as Marquess of Halifax, you can't ask for a better match." He laughed, but it sounded bitter. "Elizabeth, I know that he desires you, I saw his lecherous eyes; he almost stripped you naked with his eyes, the filthy pig."

Elizabeth took his hand. "Rochester promised heaven and earth to me, promised to speak to his father and request his agreement to offer a marriage. But I refused to listen. I find his sheer presence nauseating, I can't stand him. How Jane can endure his continuous bragging and boasting, his horrid smell, I don't understand. Does this answer your question? But whatever you intend to do, please think about our future and make sure to protect my name."

Mortimer sank to his knees. "Forgive me, Elizabeth, I'm a jealous dog, I know. I promise that I'll beseech my commander to grant me permission to leave for London. I love you! Life without you would be meaningless. I vow to throw myself at the feet of my uncle to obtain his blessing on our marriage – and to give us the money we need."

***

Half an hour later, Elizabeth sank into her ice-cold bed. She spread her coat on top of the heavy bedspread and heaved a big sigh. Tonight had been hard work. Despite the cold biting into her bones, she felt strangely content. Not only had she convinced Mortimer to leave for London and speak with his uncle, the fact that Jane was staying with Rochester spared her Jane's usual catty remarks at bedtime. Mortimer would certainly come back from London with money, she was sure of that now. And she would make sure that money would keep flowing every month; being close to the Queen, Elizabeth knew all kinds of details that must be valuable for the Earl of Northumberland and his allies in Parliament. Maybe she'd simply make up stories – as long as Northumberland was prepared to pay for it, she didn't care.

How wonderful it would be to possess money! Fifty pounds was a lot of money, more than she had ever possessed in her entire life. She'd buy a new coat, several elegant evening gowns and there'd still be enough money left to hire a maid. Soon, very soon she would have her own maid!

Elizabeth huddled into her straw mattress and drew her coat over her head to protect her face from the cold draughts that were sweeping down from the attic. Even

40

the mice must have sought shelter tonight as she could hear no noise, no night-time sounds of scurrying little feet on wooden floorboards. All was quiet.

Slowly, very slowly, Elizabeth found a bit of warmth in the bedclothes, and despite the biting cold she found sleep faster than she could have hoped for.

***

It was still early morning and no sign of daylight was trickling through the small leaded window panes when a young maid scratched at her door in order to wake Elizabeth up and bring her warm water from the kitchen. Elizabeth groaned and was very much tempted to ignore the unwelcome interruption, turn over in her bed and go back to sleep. But the scratching at the door became more insistent. It was a custom the Queen had introduced, inspired by French royal court etiquette where knocking at doors was considered to be highly unfashionable, a relic of less civilized times.

She knew that there could be no excuse for staying in her warm bed, as Elizabeth remembered only too well that she was on duty today. Queen Henrietta Maria was not known to be lenient with those maids of honour who dared to show up late.

Elizabeth therefore worked up all of her courage and left her warm bed, shivering in the cold but still numb from sleep until she splashed a handful of water in her face. The water woke her up quickly – as usual, it was almost cold. She hadn't expected otherwise, as the route from the kitchen to her room was far too long to keep the water hot during winter.

She chose a soft coloured woollen dress, a gift from the Queen. Luckily Queen Henrietta Maria handed down gowns from time to time which she considered to be out of fashion or which she had simply started to dislike to those maids of honour she found worthy of special favour. The warm yellow colour was a perfect match for Elizabeth's hair – although the rules of conduct and propriety demanded that her luxurious copper locks must be tamed and hidden under a demure cap.

On her way to the Queen's apartments she passed through the kitchen where she snatched a bowl of steaming porridge and warm milk from the protective clutches of the sour looking cook, a female dragon who was the undisputed queen of this realm. But as soon as the cook's attention was diverted by a boiling stew that needed urgent attention, one of the cook's young apprentices quickly dropped a large spoonful of honey and cream into her porridge bowl. Elizabeth thanked him with a radiant smile. The young lad turned bright red and made her a sign to sit down at the table and remove the precious bowl from the sight of the stingy cook.

Breakfast finished, she felt warm and comfortable for the first time since she had left her bed. Now it was high time to leave the warm kitchen and steer towards the Queen's wing in Merton College. On her way, Elizabeth had to pass through paved courtyards where an icy wind was blowing. Apart from some random guards, all was silent, as it was still early morning, but the frozen dew made the cobble stones slippery and she had to be careful not to fall.

41

Tired ivy climbed up the walls of the college building, as if flinching from the biting cold. But Elizabeth could still feel the comforting warmth of the sweet porridge in her stomach and reached the Queen's apartment in high spirits, cheeks glowing.

The Queen's antechamber was almost empty. Her Majesty was still in her bedroom.

"Her Majesty is in a good mood today though she told her chambermaid that she feels terribly exhausted after the endeavour of yesterday's masked play and the ensuing ball." The young liveried page who proffered the information, lowered his voice. "As the Queen was generally praised for her performance and the play, Her Majesty is inclined to be very gracious today," he whispered with a wink and added, "She shouldn't be too trying today."

The pageboy worshipped Elizabeth, and so she tolerated him, as he was one of her most faithful and reliable sources of information.

He made a sign to invite Elizabeth to sit down next to him on a comfortable armchair normally reserved for visitors of rank. He might be young – but not too young to try a bit of flirtation. Elizabeth rewarded him with a smile to encourage him to go on gossiping, but she would take care not to encourage him too much, as she had no intention of squandering her time with a boy from the minor gentry whose voice had only just started to break.

In any case, as she was on duty, she had no option but to stay and wait for the Queen to arrive. Trying to kill time, her glance wandered across the room in the hope of detecting something new that might awaken her interest.

The dean's quarters of Merton College had been transformed into a suite fit for a queen, but the small rooms were almost bursting with all the furniture, paintings, tableware, not to mention all those useless decorative items that the Queen had insisted on bringing from her palace in London.

At least the usual cacophony of barking dogs, shrieking parrots and joking dwarfs was banned from her rooms during the morning. Elizabeth knew that the moment Queen Henrietta Maria would appear, this wonderful spell of silence would be gone, as the Queen expected to be entertained and to be close to her little darlings, as she used to call them.

Savouring this rare moment of peace and quiet, Elizabeth settled into an armchair and picked up her embroidery, the Queen's favourite past-time, as Her Majesty found reading a very demanding task and tired quickly of it. Dutifully Elizabeth tackled her work, and stifling a yawn she started to add stitch after stitch. She was a neat worker and from time to time the Queen condescended to praise her work, though taking most of the credit for Elizabeth's efforts whenever visitors marvelled at the intricate patterns.

Another one of these silly, useless altar cloths, Elizabeth thought as she measured the red yarn. But no hint of this treacherous thought was visible on her face as she continued her work. Having a task to complete helped her to kill the time. *What colour should I use now?* she mused. Threads of gold would be perfect but supply was rare nowadays. Saffron yellow would have to do.

Noon was not far off and Elizabeth was growing hungry when she picked up the first noises behind the door – footsteps and the sound of a single dog barking excitedly, as only the Queen's favourite pet dog was permitted to stay with her at night. The doors were flung open by the liveried servants and the pages and footmen sprang to attention.

Elizabeth rose quickly from her seat in order to sink into a deep curtsy to greet the Queen. Behind Her Majesty she could see the arrogant face of the Queen's chambermaid and – dressed in a sober dark dress like a raven – her nemesis, Lady Jane.

Elizabeth was surprised. Jane wasn't supposed to be on duty this morning. And yet it wasn't difficult to guess why Jane had left the arms of Rochester at dawn in order to seek a private audience with the Queen. Her glance said it all: she was glowing with triumph.

The Queen granted Elizabeth only a short nod. The message was clear, Elizabeth was out of favour. Dramatically the Queen raised her hands, rubbing her temples. "We are still feeling indisposed, our headache is getting worse, in fact, we're afraid it will develop into a migraine. Mary, hurry and ask the apothecary to prepare us a potion, *allez vite!*"

The chamber maid curtsied deeply, "Yes, Ma'am," and rushed out of the room to fulfil the errand as the Queen's tantrums whenever her commands were not followed immediately were legendary.

The Queen looked at the remaining servants including Jane, her face set in a mask of dismay. "Please leave us alone, we wish to talk with Lady Elizabeth in private. Peter may stay."

Peter, the black and white spaniel, wagged his tail as he recognized his name. A maid led the spaniel to a silken cushion, fittingly embroidered with the lilies of France and the lions of England. He graciously consented to lie on his cushion, bribed with a juicy bone while Jane sank into a deep curtsy, trying hard to hide her satisfaction before she swept out of the room.

She looks like a black spider, Elizabeth thought, *a spider of the most poisonous sort.*

The room was quiet again. Elizabeth was alone now with the Queen. Her Majesty was visibly upset; she didn't sit down but stood erect. She tapped on the floor that was covered by several layers of carpets that had been brought over from London. A

43

single clock was ticking on the mantelpiece, and even the dog had stopped gnawing on his bone. All was silent.

Elizabeth sank once again in a deep curtsy. "Have I done anything to upset you, Ma'am?"

The Queen frowned. "*Je suis scandalisée!*" she hissed.

Elizabeth had learnt to speak French fluently during the time she had spent in the Queen's service but she hoped fervently that she would be spared a whole lecture in the language. Luckily the Queen changed to English although she would never master the language without mistakes. "You have indeed, Elizabeth. Lady Jane brought an incident to our attention which displeases us greatly. We do expect that our maids of honour are exactly what the title says, ladies who respect the *honneur* of the *maison royale* of Stuart and who stay away from…" She was searching for a word before she uttered with full contempt, "… amorous adventures of the lowest kind imaginable."

"May I understand that Lady Jane has informed Your Majesty of such an incident… probably with the greatest maidenly reluctance…"

"Don't be insolent, Elizabeth! Yes, she did tell me as she found it her duty to do so. Lady Jane has been raised very strictly. *Une véritable comtesse venant d'une bonne famille!* Don't forget that she's a member of one the most prominent families of our realm, it was quite a shock for her to find you… *c'était l'horreur!*"

The Queen was lost for words although she relapsed into French from time to time while she kept wringing her jewel-studded hands, forgetting to use the majestic 'we'. Red blotches had formed on her cheeks, a stark and not very becoming contrast to the leaden white of her make-up.

"I do apologize, Ma'am. I did not mean at all to upset Your Majesty. I'm deeply sorry for this and can only beg for your kind forgiveness. I do admit that Lady Jane encountered me yesterday evening, just at the very moment when" – she blushed and pretended to search for words – "the moment Sir Mortimer Clifford… proposed to me."

"He proposed to you?" the Queen cried, opening her hands. "But how wonderful, Elizabeth, he's such a handsome man, a loyal subject, Lady Jane must have completely misunderstood the situation. You should have told us!"

Elizabeth tilted her head slowly and smiled sadly. "Lady Jane is absolutely right to criticize Sir Mortimer's bold behaviour. I did not encourage him and had no option but to reject his proposal."

"But why, Elizabeth? Sir Mortimer is all a lady of rank could ask for, broad shoulders, a dashing smile, he comes from a very good family, why would you reject his proposal? Let us be outspoken, you have no dowry to offer and the days are gone when the King and I could offer you some help. We can confide in you as you know how things are. All of our money is being swallowed by this terrible war."

"Your Majesty is very kind, I don't deserve such kindness, Ma'am, and never would I expect anything from the royal treasury, it's an honour for me to serve you, Ma'am."

She sank down on her knees and kissed the Queen's gown to show her devotion. The Queen's eyes became moist with emotion. "I know, Elizabeth, that you're one of our most loyal subjects!"

Elizabeth continued, encouraged to see that her strategy was working. "I may not have the same background as Lady Jane, but my mother has always been very strict and very clear to me regarding my duties as a gentlewoman. She insists that I should never accept a proposal that has been brought forward without the consent of my own family and the family of my future husband. I therefore had to ask Sir Mortimer to wait with his proposal until he obtains blessings from the heads of both our families."

The Queen wrung her hands. "How romantic, Sir Mortimer is such a handsome man. But we must congratulate you Elizabeth, for being so steadfast, we realize now that we were carried away by our emotions, it may be excused by our French heritage. Of course Sir Mortimer has to ask for the blessings of the family first, that's the rule. Who's the head of his family, we know that Sir Mortimer is related somehow or other to half of our leading noble families?"

"The Earl of Northumberland, Ma'am."

The Queen quickly crossed herself. "That horrible traitor in London? But that's a disaster!"

"I know, Ma'am." Quickly she wiped her eyes as if holding back her tears.

"Don't cry, my little lamb." The Queen took her hands into hers. "There must be a solution."

"Would Your Majesty put in a good word with the King in case Sir Mortimer asks leave to meet his uncle in London? "

"Of course we will. Charles is always worried that people are going to betray him, but this is an entirely different story. We will tell him." She looked as impish as a young girl now. "You should have noticed that I still hold some sway with His Majesty."

Elizabeth sank into a deep curtsy. "I'm ever so grateful, Ma'am, I don't deserve such a great favour! May I add one more remark, Ma'am?"

"Of course, Elizabeth!"

"When Lady Jane surprised me with Sir Mortimer, she wasn't alone..."

"What do you mean?" the Queen exclaimed sharply.

"My lord Rochester came into the room together with Lady Jane, and this has been worrying me greatly."

The Queen sank into an armchair and nodded. "It's impossible to live at a relatively small court like ours here in Oxford and not to hear... some rumours."

Elizabeth sent her a knowing glance. "My lord Rochester has built up a reputation, I'm reluctant to go into details. I myself had to make it very clear to his lordship that I'm not disposed to becoming an object of, let's call it... his attentions. I'm worried that Lady Jane is far too inexperienced and that she possesses a mind that's far too pure to understand that my lord Rochester might not have matrimony in mind when he approaches her..."

"Elizabeth, you're absolutely right. Jane is such an innocent girl!" The Queen was quite distressed.

So innocent that she's dragged half of the court into her bed already, Elizabeth couldn't help thinking, *but nobody goes so far as to offer her a wedding ring...*

"How could we help Jane? We can speak with her, of course!" The Queen spoke almost to herself, deep in thought.

"This is a very delicate matter and I don't want Lady Jane to think that I'm slandering her name when she's not present. I do remember though that Your Majesty is considering sending a delegation to France shortly?"

"Yes, we'll be sending a mission to my dearest sister-in-law, the queen of France, a plea from sister to sister to help us in our distress. Queen Anne is such a good person, she'll help us! Soon our troubles will come to an end."

"Wouldn't it be a good idea to appoint Lady Jane to accompany this mission? She comes from a very good family and will add lustre to Your Majesty's delegation. This would be an elegant way to remove her from the undesirable attentions of my lord Rochester."

"What a brilliant idea, Elizabeth! Of course, we'd probably have come to the same conclusion, but maybe not today. We shall do this, she can hand over the altar cloth we're about to finish. This will add a very nice, personal touch. Queen Anne is so charming, her court is so refined, how much we long to go there ourselves."

"Since I've had the privilege of serving you, Ma'am, I have always been impressed at Your Majesty's dedication to fulfil your duty. This is not only my personal opinion, but the whole court admires your example and your elegance."

"Elizabeth, don't flatter us, please." Henrietta Maria was, however, visibly delighted at the compliment, and suddenly she dropped her regal pose. "You may call the servants now, Elizabeth, I miss my dogs and my dwarfs. I feel much better, my headache is gone, although this lazy maid hasn't even come back with the potion yet."

Minutes later an avalanche of dogs, dwarfs and servants carrying cages with colourful parrots poured into the room which was almost bursting under this sudden onslaught. Elizabeth could only wonder how the Queen could endure this cacophony of noise, joking, laughter, shrieking parrots and barking dogs. The dogs chased each other around the room, as silver bells attached to their collars kept ringing frantically as the dogs circled around the laughing queen who dispensed some delicacies to them. The Queen glowed with satisfaction, as she hated to be alone. She hated silence and the boredom of contemplation.

As soon as possible, Elizabeth withdrew to the antechamber pretending that her embroidery needed further attention. She longed to be on her own in order to savour today's victory. Not only had she cleared the way for Mortimer to visit the Earl of Northumberland, she had elegantly removed Lady Jane from court, making sure that her foe would be absent for months to come – if ever she came back at all. Ships were known to sink, maybe she'd be on one of them.

Tonight Mortimer will receive his first chaste kisses, I need to keep him motivated, she thought dispassionately, looking like a cat that had just finished a large bowl of cream. Then she smiled. *I will teach Mortimer, the more money he brings, the greater will be his reward. I'll wager he'll learn quickly.*

Sailing to England

The twelve days of Christmas festivities were drawing to an end. François de Toucy could only congratulate himself that he had insisted on leaving the big house in Paris and shepherding his family (under the howling protest of his sisters) back to his family estate in Picardy, in northern France. Here they had spent a peaceful Christmas far away from the hustle of the royal court and its eternal and never ending festivities and intrigues. If only he could stay here forever!

The latest news from England was encouraging. The King of England had not only been able to strengthen his position in Oxford but had succeeded in negotiating a surprise deal with the ever so rebellious Irish, permitting him to withdraw troops from this misty island to secure his remaining stronghold in the North of England.

"Excellent news, Julia!" he cried out, reading the last letter that Charles had sent from Paris. "There's a chance that King Charles will hold on and I won't have to go to England after all."

"That's really excellent news!" Julia smiled at him. François's heart was beating faster as he looked at his wife. Julia's pregnancy made her seem even more radiant, if this was even possible.

In the north of France the weather in January tends to be cold and unpleasant and this year was no exception – it was freezing cold. Here in Picardy, with its endless rolling fields and its low skies, the cold was not like in the mountains, dry and crisp, but wet and humid. Not even the thickest woollen felt coats could withstand the humidity for long. In the early morning, ice and frosted dew would cover the fields and roads with a hard sugary coating, cutting into the cloven feet of the sheep that were grazed on the pastures outside.

As often as possible, family and servants would huddle close to the fireplace where heavy logs of wood and glowing coal were kept burning day and night. Stories and fairy tales – handed down from generation to generation – would be told while heavy earthen bottles of cider or eau de vie would be passed around. From time to time the cook would throw in some chestnuts from her pantry, to be roasted in an iron pan with a long handle on the open fire, their delicious scent filling the house and making mouths water.

Night fell early here in the north and lasted many hours during wintertime. Not surprisingly, everybody was craving the first rays of sunlight after weeks of darkness – but the sky was always covered by a thick blanket of clouds. No matter if it snowed or rained, a leaden coloured sky hovered above them, brooding and menacing. Julia missed the light and gaiety of her native Italy, but she wouldn't complain; as long as François was there, his love kept her warm.

It was mid-February when a new messenger arrived from the capital, his cap glistening with melting snow. He carried two letters from Paris, but this time, the

48

news was sobering. The royal forces of England had suffered a crushing defeat at Nantwich as a sudden surge of the local river had divided the royal army and had made them easy prey for the newly formed troops of Parliament. A sure and easy victory had turned into defeat. The Roundheads were proclaiming that the Almighty had intervened in their just cause, and the people of England – always eager to witness a divine miracle – were only too willing to listen, and believe.

As an immediate consequence, King Charles was forced to hand over large territories in the North of England to the enemy. There could be no embellishing of this situation, the King's position had become precarious.

"You look worried," Julia stated. "I don't need witchcraft to see that you have received bad news. It's about England, *chéri*?"

"Yes, my sweetheart, Cardinal Mazarin is worried about the safety of Queen Henrietta Maria. He thinks that I should leave as soon as possible for England as King Charles has lost an important battle. Pierre and Armand will be leaving in a fortnight. It might be a good idea to join them. Cousin Charles can give me a lot of help there as he keeps good relations with both camps. Don't ask how he manages to do this, but behind the façade of a jovial gentleman, there's a very clever diplomat."

"Sounds like he's Italian, not English," Julia commented with a quick smile. "I hate to let you go, my love, but I promised to be a good wife and I'll try very hard to keep my promise."

François embraced her hard; he didn't dare talk, as he was afraid that his voice might betray him. And yet, as he had given his word to the Cardinal, he had no other option but to leave. It was a question of honour.

The days passed quickly now. Although François was vain, he had understood that only the disguise of a French Huguenot might save him a hanging from the nearest English gallows if ever he got caught by the Puritans. Choosing clothes was the easiest task – even if it amounted to an act of denial and utter self-sacrifice.

"I look dreadful," he sighed as he looked at his image in the polished mirror. "Why do the Huguenots like to wear those strange hats, they look like a cooking pot – they don't even come with a nice feather to adorn them. And don't even mention the terrible clothes, I never wore such itchy breeches before in my life."

Julia looked critically at her husband, but not even the simple cut and the rough wool of his dark clothes could hide his broad shoulders and his handsome looks.

"Stop complaining, you don't look like a Huguenot at all!"

"How do I look?"

"Like a peacock in disguise," François's mother cut in. She had entered the room and had overheard the conversation.

"I'll cut your hair now – and no complaints please. Please also learn to look humble, if you even know what this word means…"

"With a mother like this, who needs enemies?" François sighed, but refrained from further moaning as the scissors cut mercilessly at his blonde locks.

"Now go and shave and I'm certain that nobody will recognize you ever again," his mother stated with satisfaction in her voice.

"I won't either," François grumbled as he left upstairs like a dutiful son in order to ask his valet to remove his proud moustache.

***

François de Toucy left his home a week later, accompanied only by his faithful groom Michel. Never a great talker, Michel preferred to remain silent after they had crossed the borders of their estate. A short glance in the direction of his aloof master told him that François's face was set in a mask. Small wonder – leaving his young, pregnant wife and his home hadn't been an easy decision to take.

Their journey was a smooth one though, and no snowstorm or heavy rain blocked the roads to the capital. Only three days later a familiar silhouette with its spires and turrets appeared on the horizon. As soon as they had passed through the city gates and into Paris, François steered his horse immediately towards his town house, only to find himself refused entrance by his own guard.

"You'd better open your eyes, you simpleton, and let our master enter his own house!" Michel intervened roughly.

The guard's face turned crimson red as soon as he recognized Michel and hastened to open the gates, uttering as many apologies as he could possibly think of.

François only laughed. "My disguise seems to be convincing. Don't worry, now, let's see how Cousin Charles and our friends react when they set eyes on me."

This question was to be answered almost immediately. As soon as François de Toucy was greeted by his major-domo, he was informed that a message from the Marquis de Beauvoir was already waiting for him. François could only marvel at the remarkable self-control of his major-domo. Not a twitch of his face showed the slightest surprise at finding his master in a disguise that was as unbecoming as it was unfitting for a gentleman known to be one of the icons of elegance at the court of the Louvre.

"How do you like my new outfit, don't I look fashionable?" François challenged his major-domo.

Only a light raising of his eyebrows betrayed his servant's true feelings. "I think my lord has looked, on occasion, more elegant… but I'm sure that my lord has excellent reasons for wearing the clothes of a… ahem… Huguenot."

"You have a point there. It was a sacrifice, but *hélàs*, I have a new mission to accomplish." François smirked at his reflection in the Venetian mirror, which had been brought over at great expense by his wife.

"Will your lordship be changing his attire for this evening's invitation at the hôtel Beauvoir?"

"Of course not, that would spoil the fun. I'll just freshen up, get the dust out of my breeches and change into a fresh shirt, and don't even think about adding a fancy lace collar tonight! And yes, I'll keep this odious hat, I seem to have grown attached to it."

A moment of pain was visible in his dutiful servant's face – but it was gone in a flash. The major-domo bowed reverently and replied with all the dignity that he could muster, "Your lordship's wish is my command, as usual. May I suggest changing your lordship's boots though?"

François looked critically at his mud-covered boots. "You may indeed, they're a disgrace. By the way, I may look like a Huguenot but this doesn't mean that I can abide a life of frugality, what about some wine and a decent lunch?"

"Lunch will be ready in ten minutes, sir, you'll find everything exactly as you desire! The servants are already setting the table in the dining room."

"I knew that I could count on you!" François flashed him a thankful smile and disappeared upstairs in order to change into a fresh shirt.

***

François made sure to be the last guest to arrive for dinner at the hôtel Beauvoir, the palatial Parisian townhouse of the Marquis de Beauvoir. Knowing from experience that Armand would always be late (Charles on the other hand would certainly arrive early, as he was always hungry), François arrived almost an hour late, an unusual occurrence, as he was known to be punctual.

As François de Toucy finally crossed the threshold and entered the vast dining room Pierre de Beauvoir jumped up, crying out, "You unfaithful dog! We already thought you must have forgotten about our dinner app– " then suddenly stopped as he took measure of François's new appearance and just uttered, "Oh my God!" before he sank down again on his chair, speechless.

"I greet my Brethren in Christ!" François answered in measured tones and walked into the middle of the room, shoulders demure, hands folded in prayer.

"May the Lord bless you all and may He be praised!"

"Amen," Charles answered with a broad grin, rising from his chair. "François, let me congratulate you, this disguise is perfect. I've been wracking my brains for how to smuggle you into London, but your idea is a stroke of genius, the Roundheads will welcome you as one of their own."

Armand jumped up. "You really shocked me, François, don't do such a thing ever again! For a second I thought I was back in Reims, in the monastery school. You have no idea what kind of terrible memories you're stirring up!"

Pierre grinned. "Stop your moaning! I remember very well that you spent a lot of nights outside school and would catch up with your sleep during class, therefore the memories can't all be that bad..."

"Can we start with dinner now, I'm starving!" Charles pleaded.

"No surprise there," Pierre replied, and rang the bell. "Let's start, my friends, unless my Huguenot visitor prefers a more frugal diet of bread and water."

"I spent a week in La Rochelle some years ago and found that the food there was excellent. No frugality there. What upset me greatly though were the sheer endless sessions of prayers before we were allowed to start. That's sort of annoying when you're hungry." François grasped a glass of wine. "Let's drink to our new adventure in England!"

The meal started with a delicate venison consommé, followed by freshly baked bread, a rich duck pâté and pickled vegetables. The food was accompanied by a light wine from the Loire, produced in Pierre's own winery from his castle Montrésor.

"How do we travel to England?" François asked, after he had savoured the first bites. "I guess you've got everything planned? Did you find a vessel that will cross the Channel and that won't go down when the first winter storm hits us?"

"The *Beatrice* is waiting in Calais for us," Pierre replied.

"The *Beatrice*?"

"Don't forget that our little Pierre is a grand personage, an English Duke, and therefore his Grace is using the comfort of his own private ship. Luckily his Grace has condescended to offer us a small space on his boat – but I recommend not to test his Grace's temper tonight. I only pray that I'm not supposed to pay for the voyage. I guess it's an open secret that I'm totally broke – again," Armand quipped.

His confession evidently didn't impair his appetite, as he tackled a juicy piece of roasted suckling pig while he was speaking.

Pierre kicked his friend. "His Grace is tempted to leave you behind in Paris. I wonder how you manage to be always broke, no matter how much money you have at your disposal. Your mistress must be the most expensive Paris has ever heard about."

"I like quality – regardless of price," Armand replied simply.

"Do you remember our last journey on the *Beatrice*?" Pierre changed the subject.

"Of course I do, Richelieu almost had us gunned to pieces. That was quite an adventure!" Armand revelled in the memory. "And our Pierre dressed as a girl, a pity that this image hasn't been preserved for posterity. It would have made quite an alluring change in that depressing gallery of ancestral portraits that you keep in Hertfordshire. "

"It would!" Pierre laughed. "I agree, it could only improve the average look of them, what a bunch of miserable looking ancestors I have."

"You're not the only one," Armand added. "Never visit the Saint Paul gallery at twilight, you won't be able to sleep afterwards."

"We were talking about England, I think…" François gently reminded his friends.

"Charles is in charge of planning everything, one couldn't think of anybody more English than Charles, could one?" said Pierre.

Charles stopped his fork mid-motion, looking at it with suspicion. "I can't decide if these French forks are a good invention or not, in England we're used to eating with a dagger and our hands – you can really touch your food, somehow it feels more authentic."

"It's handy, see the fat dripping on the plate? It's really practical to use a fork… but we were talking about England, what are your plans?" said Armand, encouragingly.

Charles sighed. He hated to be interrupted while he was enjoying his food. "After our arrival in Dover I propose that we split. If we remain together, we'll be spotted in no time. I'm expected in London and therefore I propose that I travel together with François to London first. Pierre and Armand will have to ride to Oxford on their own. The challenge will be to do so without falling into the hands of the Roundheads. Later we'll join you in Oxford. François can talk with the Queen and try to convince her to leave England. But on no account must his plan be known beforehand! Otherwise François will be a dead man and the Queen will be lost, there're plenty of Parliamentarians who want to see her captured and sentenced to death. She's hated by the English, you couldn't imagine how much."

Exhausted by his long speech he snatched a leg of guinea fowl and gnawed at it, smacking his lips. "Delicious, I think your cook must have smoked it beforehand, it must be quite sinful!"

François tasted the juicy bite offered generously by Charles and agreed. "Yes, it's truly delicious. Our plans seem to be settled then, looks like a smooth journey and a lot of joyful meetings ahead of us."

"Nothing is smooth in England, these days, you mark my words," Charles replied and snatched a second helping of the guinea fowl. "You'll discover the truth soon enough."

"I was joking. I can only hope that the Queen is willing to listen to reason." François frowned.

"Well, boy, I'm willing to take any wager that she won't, I've never met such an obstinate woman as her before," Charles answered and grabbed his glass of wine. "No use being negative though, cheers to Her Majesty!"

* * *

"Let's play cards!" Pierre suggested. "There doesn't seem to be much else that we can do."

The *Beatrice* was rolling on the stormy winter sea, her wooden planks creaking and moaning under the onslaught of the wind and the furious hammering of the waves. She was a solid ship and Pierre wasn't too concerned that they might be shipwrecked. But it was difficult to stay good humoured in a small stuffy cabin that was poorly lit. Four lanterns cast their gloomy light, flickering in the rhythm of the rolling waves.

As soon as they had left the port of Calais, a nasty winter storm had gripped their ship and since then they had been riding on vicious waves. Charles and Armand had escaped early from the cabin to seek relief from their sea-sickness at the relentless rolling, and only François was left as a companion.

"Yes, let's play cards, it'll help to pass the time. I guess it'll take a few more hours to reach Dover, the captain told me that the crossing will be fast despite the storm. The strong wind is helping us, actually."

"What are your plans for Dover?"

"Charles told me that he has arranged for horses and four armed grooms to be waiting for us in the port. The Governor of Dover is a distant cousin of his, there won't be any problem. But as the port has chosen to support the forces of Parliament, I must remain in disguise as a Huguenot merchant, one of Charles's many friends, accompanying him to London."

"What about us? I'm worried about Armand. His French accent will give him away too easily. And he'd rather die than pass for a Huguenot," Pierre replied.

"Keeping Armand silent will be a true challenge," François grinned. "Our friend loves to talk and talk... By the way, I have started to learn English – what a terrible language! I seem to have knots in my tongue after each sentence."

Pierre laughed. "Yes, it's a strange language. But you'll get used to it. So what about us? How are we to reach Oxford?"

"Charles wants you to stay on the boat, he made sure that the master of the port would be bribed to keep his mouth shut. Before nightfall he'll have horses and two guides ready. Armand and you will ride straight to Oxford, two young gentlemen on their way to meet some relatives. If you meet any Cavaliers, you are on the way to relatives loyal to the King, if you meet Protestants, you'll need to change the story: you'll be on the way to Hertfordshire as you intend to join the forces of Parliament with your own men."

Pierre made a face, but suddenly Charles entered the cabin, meaning he filled it almost entirely. "Why such sour faces? I was the one being sea sick, while both of you had a good time. I should be looking sour, not you!"

"I'm giving Pierre instructions about the story he's got to tell if he meets anybody on his way to Oxford." François repeated the last piece of conversation.

Charles was distracted as he looked suspiciously at the low bench. "This bench doesn't look very solid, you should be able to afford better furniture."

"You should eat less," came the merciless reply from Pierre. "But don't worry, it's made from mahogany imported from the colonies, it'll hold."

Charles sat down, albeit with a suspicious look, but the bench held. He heaved a sigh of relief and continued. "Needless to say, Pierre, you'd better avoid meeting anybody. Your story is quite thin and you're bound to encounter a lot of trouble. I've hired two men, acting as grooms who'll guide you through the countryside. They've received instructions from me to avoid all towns and the major toll roads. It will be wise not to meet or speak with anybody until you reach those parts of England that are still in the hands of the Crown. One of them is quite clever actually, he lived in a monastery before he decided, ahem, to change career."

François grinned. "I bet that your 'grooms' are experts in several fields, did you by chance hire experienced smugglers...? How much I wish that Michel could come with us. A shame that he needs to go back to France!"

Charles grinned. "Yes, Michel is a gem. But we can't risk taking him, it's too dangerous! Now back to the grooms I chose, they're a bit shady, I admit. Of course I'd never support any illegal trafficking, but it did cross my mind that a detailed knowledge of the English landscape might come in handy in our case..."

He eyed the cards. "What about playing dice, I'm still not feeling fit enough for cards?"

They got the hint and changed to dice and although they were playing for modest sums only, a solid heap of silver coins next to François showed clearly who the winner was today. A smug looking François pocketed the coins as soon as the cries outside heralded the sight of the white cliffs of Dover.

"Huguenots are not allowed to gamble, you'll end up in hell," Pierre grumbled, as he saw his money disappear into François's pockets.

"They are, as long as they take the money away from the heretics," François answered, unabashed.

Now as the *Beatrice* entered port, all of them went on deck to reunite with Armand in order to check on the skills of the captain and his crew, but not even the harshest critic could have discovered any flaw in the way she was manoeuvred into harbour.

Once they had moored the boat, armed guards came forward to welcome Charles at the embankment, and it was time to say goodbye.

"Take care, don't do anything stupid," Charles admonished Pierre and Armand.

"Of course not, how could you ever associate the word 'stupid' with us?" Armand protested.

"I can remember some occurrences in the past..."

"Pah! That's a long time ago and we were mere children!" Armand objected.

"I don't see any major change!" followed the immediate dampener.

In a Strange Country

As Charles had bribed the master of the port in a most generous way, the search of the *Beatrice* by the port officials was finished before it had even started. Four soldiers, their pockets filled with silver coins, turned a blind eye to the contents of the ship and concentrated solely on the task of accompanying Charles and his Huguenot friend to Dover Castle. Charles had been invited by the governor, therefore no questions about his Huguenot friend were posed, a man who seemed by no means remarkable, with the exception that he was strangely taciturn for a Frenchman.

Later during the afternoon two grooms approached the *Beatrice* accompanied by two spare horses.

"I guess those gallowbirds there are our guides," Armand stated.

"Yes, they look just like the kind of guides you can trust wholeheartedly. I'm relieved that I wrote my last will and testament before I left my native shores."

"I didn't," came the cheerful reply. "But you know that I tend to be more optimistic. Well, we were after an adventure, and this looks very much as if we're back to having some fun. Cousin Charles did mention that they might look a bit shady."

"A bit too shady for my taste, and they don't look all *that* much fun to me." Pierre was less enthusiastic.

The grooms bowed reverently and greeted their new masters, dutifully removing their worn felt caps from a nest of thinning, greasy hair. Their mumbled greeting ended in a grunted sound that could be interpreted as 'm'lord'. But it was difficult to understand them, as not only were they speaking with a heavy dialect, the fact that several front teeth were missing didn't really improve their ability to enunciate.

A closer look disclosed that they must be younger than they looked at first sight. But there could be no doubt, life had taken its toll as their faces were wrinkled and weather-beaten. One of them looked rather simple, but the man who introduced himself as John looked alert, obviously making it clear that he was the leader.

It took some time for Pierre to be able to catch the meaning of John's words and he translated to Armand. "He proposes that we ride to an inn located outside the city, in the direction of a hamlet called Barham if I understood correctly. We'll sleep there and then ride on the next morning. The inn is owned by his cousin, we'll be safe there."

"At least they have a plan, but I can only hope that the inn is a bit cleaner than our gallowbirds. I wonder why Cousin Charles couldn't have found someone more presentable to guide us."

Pierre grimaced. "You have a point here, but we don't really have any other option. We can't stay on the *Beatrice*, and Oxford is waiting for us."

The hamlet of Barham was located only a few miles from the port of Dover. The two guides might not be icons of elegance but they certainly knew their way round and – as Charles had promised – they knew how to avoid the controls by Parliamentarian soldiers who were roaming the region. As Dover was an important port and a stronghold of Parliament, it was heavily guarded.

Luckily their guides knew the region like the back of their hand and they left Dover unnoticed. Pierre kept a rather tedious conversation going with John as soon as Dover Castle was out of sight and their guides started to relax. He was informed by John that they were making a large detour to avoid the major roads that would be heavily guarded but Pierre shouldn't worry, they'd arrive before nightfall in Barham.

"We'll be having some good roast meat and fine claret there, m'lord," the guide announced cheerfully.

"Excellent!" replied Pierre. "This will be most welcome, much better probably than the food you had in your monastery when you were young. *Ave Maria, regina coeli.*"

His remark was met by a blank look. John cleared his throat. "Sorry, I don't speak French, m'lord."

The second guide mumbled something to John and his attention was immediately distracted. It appeared that they must turn west now, facing the setting sun. Pierre looked thoughtful but followed their lead.

Half an hour later the inn came into sight. It was located far away from any town or village, a low thatched building not able to hide its worn state and respectable age. Pierre could only wonder what kind of guests it thrived on. A closer inspection proved that Armand's hopes of finding the inn cleaner and neater than their guides would not be fulfilled. The taproom looked filthy and run down, although dirty dishes heaped on a table were at least a silent witness that they had not been the only guests to choose this establishment.

The landlord appeared, shuffling his feet and bowing deeply. He introduced himself as a cousin of John's. "I'm ever so happy to serve guests of distinction, my lords. You will find everything to your lordships' liking!"

As if to underline his dedication to service, he grabbed his apron, stiff from an impressive variety of stains and grease, and wiped the table, inviting the two friends and their two guides with a grand gesture to sit down.

"I'm preparing special roasts for tonight, wild boar, mutton and there will be a side-dish of a duck pastry." He beamed. "And the best wine will be waiting for you, my lords. Nobody should ever say that Adam Thomason is thrifty or doesn't know how to cater for noble guests."

"May I see our room first?" Pierre interrupted the landlord's loquaciousness.

"Of course, my lord! We've reserved our best room for you."

They all climbed a steep staircase leading to the first floor. The attic rooms upstairs were small and their appointed room was probably the biggest, but it was stuffy and smelled of an unpleasant combination of dust, stale kitchen odours and mould.

"*Mais c'est dégoutant!*" Armand hissed.

"Yes, it is disgusting," Pierre whispered back. "I don't like this. I don't like this at all."

He turned to the landlord. "You may bring us some soap and water, we need to freshen up before we sit down for our evening meal. You may leave us now, we'll meet at dinner."

Their guides looked at them with surprise. Their idea of using water and soap was probably limited to special occasions such as a marriage, Christmas and Easter. But as Pierre insisted, the two guides left together with the landlord in order to go down to the kitchen and fetch a piece of soap and a bowl of warm water.

"What a terrible room!" Armand grumbled as soon as the three men had left. "I may sound spoilt, but this room looks like a prison to me."

"That's exactly what it's going to be if we're not careful," Pierre replied calmly.

Armand turned around as if stung by a wasp. "What do you mean?"

"Those guides are not the ones Charles chose for us."

"How would you know? I admit that they do look strange, but why are you so sure? They knew our names and know the surroundings perfectly well, just as Charles had told us."

"Do you remember that Charles told us that one of the guides had been educated in a monastery? But neither of them understands even the most basic words of Latin. I cited, 'We greet you, Maria, Queen of heaven' and they didn't understand a word. They've never seen a monastery from the inside. I'm also convinced that Charles would never have chosen such shabby guides for us, I'm sure. The whole story smells very bad!"

"Your mean, we've walked into a trap?"

"Exactly, my friend, you were craving an adventure, and now here we are!"

"Why don't we just walk out then?" Armand asked.

"Our assiduous landlord will have posted guards, I'm sure."

Armand looked at the small window realizing for the first time that it was barred.

"We're trapped," he stated.

"Yes, my friend, we're trapped. Like greenhorns."

"But what can we do, they'll skin us alive?"

"Armand, your fantasy is running wild, alive we're worth a fortune, dead not a lot. They'll want a ransom. A duke is worth at least 50,000 pounds and you... maybe 10,000."

"I'm worth more than that! The Saint Pauls are one of the oldest families of France, we were counts when your family was still toiling to earn a simple barony!" Armand was dismayed.

"Great, why not tell them that, they'll increase the stake immediately. Go on!"

"Maybe we should find a way out?" Armand proposed, forgetting matters of rank.

"Maybe we should!"

A Journey Through a Strange Country

François lay in his bed, relieved that his first day in England was over. He had accompanied Charles to Dover Castle but once they had been greeted by the governor's men, they had to separate. Charles had been treated with all the reverence reserved for a guest of honour but François, having been introduced as a simple Huguenot merchant without title, found himself relegated to the draughty part of the castle, reserved for random guests without rank. He had been forced to swallow all of this pride when a mere footman had admonished him harshly. "Move your arse man, the governor will be arriving any minute and he won't be pleased to find a scarecrow like you hanging around. The merchants' quarters are down there, close to the kitchens."

Ignoring the kind of speech that would normally have led him to draw his sword, François left the great entrance hall and followed the footman down to the quarters never meant to be seen by members of the gentry. Here, he had to share his room with a jovial man of undefined age, travelling to Canterbury, a stout Protestant as well, as he insisted.

Luckily they didn't need to share a bed, but having a companion in his room meant that he was forced to uphold his role of a diligent Huguenot, including half an hour of evening prayers until he could sink into his bed. At least his nightshirt made from coarse linen was a welcome change from the itchy woollen breeches. François swore that Cardinal Mazarin would have to pay dearly for all of those inconveniences!

The next morning – morning prayers dutifully accomplished – he met a grinning Charles who greeted him with the correct degree of condescension that would have been expected of a high ranking member of the British aristocracy who had been kind enough to let a simple Huguenot merchant travel with him.

Charles declined the well-meant proposal by the governor to have them escorted by his soldiers, which meant that they could talk freely as soon as they had passed the gates of the castle.

"How was your night?" Charles asked.

"I was tempted to strangle the fellow they had placed in my room, he snored like a pig! How do those Huguenots ever get anything done if they waste endless hours just saying their prayers?"

"No idea, I keep mine as short as possible. I had an excellent night, the governor and I are not only relatives by some obscure aunt, but we're old friends. He changed sides not too long ago, but in his heart he's still a Royalist. But he's clever enough to understand that King Charles is a sinking ship, as he calls it."

They rode on in silence, which was unusual for Charles.

"What's bugging you?" François finally asked.

"The governor made a remark that I find quite disturbing, not to say alarming."

François made a sign to go on.

"Until now, I was under the impression that somehow King Charles might be defeated sooner or later but that we'd settle with Parliament, like a new Magna Carta, appoint his son as his successor and that the kingdom would be run by the usual bunch of noble families. I believed that the Earl of Essex or the Earl of Northumberland would aspire to act as a sort of regent for the young prince Charles. But the governor told me between these four walls that we must be prepared for radical change. The majority in Parliament has shifted and is no longer in the hands of families like us. I'm not sure that I like it. I think that Essex, Northumberland and their cronies have created a monster that very soon they won't be able to control any longer. I'm no longer sure that it was good idea to let Pierre and Armand go to England. I encouraged Pierre as I was concerned about the honour of the house of Neuville – but what if England becomes a republic?"

"A republic!" François was shocked. "But that goes against the divine order!"

"Venice has been a republic for several hundred years now, I never had the impression that the Almighty had any particular problems with this," Charles answered drily.

François had to digest this first. What if Charles was right, what if the Almighty didn't really care if there was a king in England... or in France? Hadn't his own mother remarked some years ago that times were changing? François liked things to be well organized and orderly, he wasn't sure that he was ready to welcome this new world of liberty and disorder.

"What are your plans for London?" he finally asked, changing the subject.

"We'll stay in Hertford House, you can remain there as well during our time in London, it's a perfect hiding place for you. I haven't been in London for ages and I promised Pierre to have a look into the administration of his estates as well. It's never healthy when the lord of the manor is absent. During this time, I'll have confidential meetings with my friends in order to find out what's really going on. And... I want to meet this man Oliver Cromwell, they say that he'll be one of the new leaders soon."

"That doesn't sound very loyal towards King Charles!" François exclaimed, dismayed by an attitude which he could only qualify as treacherous.

"I admit it, it isn't. But I've been trying to get some reason into the head of our anointed sovereign for years but His Majesty won't listen, he prefers to listen to his wife. Loyalty is a great virtue, but I'm of the opinion that I owe my true loyalty to the house of Neuville and must make sure that our family, and especially Pierre as the head of our house, doesn't get into trouble. It's not the first time that England has headed into chaos. Our family survived the Black Death, the War of the Roses, we'll also survive King Charles's follies."

He laughed. "Come on, François, don't look so shocked. You served under Cardinal Richelieu, you should know how politics really work!"

"Yes, Cardinal Richelieu was the undisputed master of intrigue – and it's true that it was he who created the new France, not Louis XIII!" François continued, and sighed. "You're right Charles, maybe it's about time to face realities! I can only hope that I can convince the Queen to leave England."

"That sounds better! After spending some time in London I suggest that we leave together for Oxford, it's not very far. If the Queen won't listen to you, I suggest soliciting an audience with the King. He'll listen as he's very concerned about her safety and worries constantly about her well-being."

Their journey to London was not a very long one, but as it was winter time, they could only ride the few hours during daylight as night fell quickly. Therefore they had to interrupt their journey and stop at an inn along the road to London.

"I know the innkeeper, his food is excellent and the rooms are clean. I could do with a good dinner." Charles almost licked his lips, he was always hungry.

"Almost anything will be better than the room I occupied in Dover Castle."

"For a humble Huguenot traveller you sound quite spoilt."

"Less spoilt than people hungry for dinner, even though they had a big luncheon before they left Dover…"

They rode on at a leisurely speed, knowing that they'd easily reach the inn before nightfall. On their way they crossed villages, small towns, pastures and open fields. Charles grew more and more quiet; he was shocked to see to what extent the war had ravaged Sussex, a county by now wounded and impoverished by the civil war.

Fresh traces of violence were showing their ugly face, barren fields were in urgent need of being tended, burnt-out houses pockmarked the former pleasant landscape, vast pastures lay idle. Anxiety covered the South of England like mildew, suffocating the countryside. All signs of joy and merriment had disappeared. Now the dull colours of the Puritan apparel were abundant and most men were proudly wearing the strange-looking haircut of the Roundheads, witnessing that the people had – at least officially – embraced the cause of Parliament.

"If this is the future of England, may the Lord protect us!" Charles said grimly as they sighted a row of gallows where crows were feasting on the remains of the poor souls that must have had the misfortune to be caught fighting for the wrong cause. He couldn't hear François's answer as the crows were making a deafening noise, their number was such that they darkened the sky. Charles, not easily given to feelings of foreboding, shuddered. This was a glimpse into the apocalypse.

Finally they reached their destination for the night. Luckily the inn had been spared the ravages of war and sat there in the evening sun, nestled neat and plump next to the road like a clucking hen. Charles was immediately recognized and welcomed, and minutes later the portly landlord arrived to greet his distinguished guest in person.

"Oh, dear Lord, what has happened to you, James?" Charles asked, aghast, as he eyed the landlord.

"It's no longer James, my lord, I have assumed the name of Jeremiah to show my dedication to the true faith."

"May I assume from your new haircut and name that you have joined the ranks of the Puritans, James?"

"It's Jeremiah, my lord. Yes, I had the privilege of hearing our new leader, Oliver Cromwell, and I was enlightened. I understand now that it's time for change. Our King is under the influence of a French harlot, therefore we have to set an example and fight against the Catholics. The heretics are abusing the name of the King and the law, enslaving this country and they are a disgrace to our Lord in Heaven."

"Stop talking and wasting precious time!" came a sharp voice from behind. Seconds later his wife appeared. Although she didn't even reach her husband's shoulder, it soon became clear who was in charge at the inn.

"I must apologize, my lord, my poor husband has been gripped by religious fervour. Like so many of our men, I may add. I may only be a weak woman, but I understand enough to know that religion doesn't fill bellies and doesn't look after horses. Let me look after your lordship and you'll find all will be to your liking, my lord." She spotted François. "Is this guest travelling with you, my lord?"

Charles, happy to have escaped the loquacity of the landlady, seized the opportunity to introduce François. "Yes, let me introduce a friend, a visitor from France. He's a Huguenot merchant and has suffered much during recent years, he hopes to settle in England and to be free to practise his religion here."

"You're welcome, Sir, the guests of my lord Charles are always welcome! Later, we can pray together!" The landlord was delighted that Charles had brought along a brother in faith.

"Pray, pray, pray…" came the sharp reply from his wife. "Heaven can wait, now it's time for work. Hurry, husband, the private salon must be prepared, please ask my lord what he desires for dinner and have an eye on the gentlemen's horses in the stables. I'll take care of their rooms in the meantime."

She hurried away, still shaking her head and mumbling, "Pray, pray, what nonsense, when there's such a lot of work to be done! Men can be such nitwits!"

The landlord withdrew after having taken orders for a sumptuous dinner. To Charles's great relief the religious fervour that had taken possession of his landlord's spirit hadn't affected or diminished the culinary standards of the establishment.

But as soon as the door of the private salon had closed, Charles sighed. "If these zealots govern England in the future, I'm afraid that we're heading for calamity!"

"How can these *canaille* deem themselves worthy to judge their king?" François was scandalized. "How could you ever let it happen that people are allowed to call their sacred queen a 'harlot', this man should be hung, drawn and quartered."

"England is different, François, our people possess great spirit of independence. It's not as easy as in France where the word of a man like Mazarin can bend the rules. But I agree, this goes too far and this story will end in misery, if not disaster. I really need to meet with Cromwell; just imagine, I might end up becoming 'enlightened' as well."

"That's no joke, you'd do better to run your sword through him."

"I'm afraid things are a bit more complicated, François, there are hundreds of Cromwells in the making in England and Scotland right now. But whatever the future will bring for us, a good dinner will help us to deal with it. They have excellent chicken here, cooked in a sauce of cider and some secret ingredient, James will never tell me what it is, although I offered him twenty pounds to tell me his secret. Maybe it's tarragon, come to think of it…"

"How can you talk about dinner when your kingdom is falling to pieces!" François was dismayed.

"If we go to bed hungry, what will that change? The only difference will be that we'll be feeling even more miserable tomorrow morning. If you think that you'd rather feel miserable, just go ahead, skip dinner, I won't force you to eat!"

Suddenly François saw the funny side of things and he had to laugh. "You've beaten me, Charles, let's have dinner together. You're right, if we eat or if we starve tonight, it won't make any difference to King Charles… or Cromwell."

"Finally, finally!" Charles exclaimed. "And I had almost given up hope that a Frenchman could have at least a little bit of common sense in his head!"

***

"How do I look?" the Queen glanced nervously in her polished silver mirror. The truth was that Her Majesty didn't look her best. Red blotches marked her bloated pale face, and she looked tired. Her pregnancy was turning out to be a difficult one – and it showed.

Since Lady Jane had left for the shores of France, it was Elizabeth who had become her confidante and first Maid of Honour. The Queen had not only got used to relying on Elizabeth, she had long dropped her regal pose when they were alone.

"Elizabeth, don't tell me that I look wonderful, you know that I'm suffering. I must look dreadful."

"Ma'am, let me be honest, you do look a little tired, indeed. May I suggest a cup of coffee? The Italian ambassador told me that it's like a miracle cure, it should restore Your Majesty's spirits and beauty in no time."

"Are you sure, Elizabeth? I do remember that it tastes like medicine, very bitter." The Queen's voice was petulant but as Elizabeth gently insisted, she agreed to try the coffee. The King's adjutant had announced a visit by His Majesty later this afternoon – unusual for this time of day – and she wanted to look her best.

It took some time before the coffee arrived from the kitchen, but finally the precious brew arrived. Elizabeth poured the liquid into a tiny cup of Chinese porcelain and added a spoonful of the scarce cane sugar, a delicacy reserved exclusively for Her Majesty and her favourite guests. Sceptically the Queen tasted the thick black liquid and made a face. "The taste is disgusting, Elizabeth, how can people drink coffee when they could have a wonderful cup of hot chocolate?"

"Your Majesty will feel the effect after you have finished your cup. May I suggest that you recline on the sofa and close your eyes for some minutes as soon as Your Majesty has finished her drink?"

The Queen sipped the remaining coffee, closed her eyes obediently and let Elizabeth heave her swollen feet onto a low stool. Resolutely Elizabeth chased a maid, three dogs and a pair of dwarfs out of the room and a soothing silence ensued.

About fifteen minutes the Queen opened her eyes. She looked refreshed and exclaimed, "The taste of this coffee is horrible but you were right, I do feel much better. I should appoint you as my physician and not this useless charlatan we found here in Oxford. I wish I had my doctor from London back, but the King told me the good man is afraid to travel in these troubled times."

She studied her face in the mirror. "I do look better – but not at all like a queen should. Fetch the maid, my make-up needs to be restored."

She made Elizabeth run after some blue silk ribbons for her hair that she suddenly fancied which must be lying in a chest in her bedroom, then chased another maid to fetch the matching sapphire jewellery until she was happy with her attire, and only just in time, as they could already hear the footsteps of the approaching guards.

The Queen's lackeys sprang to attention as the doors opened and King Charles entered the room. He looked haggard; the disastrous defeat in Nantwich had aged him by at least ten years. Never an optimist by nature, he looked brooding and worried.

"Your Majesty!" Elizabeth sank into a deep curtsy.

The King greeted her with a short nod but walked straight to his wife and took her hands. "Let me tell you, you look absolutely flourishing, my dearest Marie, an adornment to our court."

"Charles, you flatter me! How wonderful to have you here at this time of day, shall I order some wine and sweetmeats?"

"Some wine would be nice. I have news, but I'd rather speak to you alone."

The Queen made a sign for the lackeys to withdraw but as Elizabeth prepared to leave the room, she told her to stay. "You may stay and serve the King a glass of wine and for me a fresh cup of this fortifying coffee, Elizabeth."

She turned her head towards the King. "You may talk freely in front of Elizabeth, she knows all my little secrets and I can vouchsafe for her, she never gossips."

The King bowed. "I trust your judgement, Ma'am."

Elizabeth curtsied once again deeply and went out to give orders to have wine and coffee brought to the Queen's apartments.

When she returned the King was already in conversation with the Queen.

"... he's coming incognito and will bring his friend Saint Paul along, you may remember, we made him Earl of Worthing some years ago upon the request of Hertford. Hertford paid me handsomely at the time to ascend to his grandfather's dukedom."

"Oh, of course, I do remember them! What a handsome pair they were when they came to London some years ago. Both are French actually, I used to dance with Armand's father, the Marquis de Saint Paul, who was *very* handsome as well. Ah, those times, when I was still a princess living at the royal court in France... Those balls, I shall never forget the refinement. We danced until morning."

The King looked slightly taken aback. He did not appreciate the Queen's nostalgic retrospection and cleared his throat. "Ahem, very well. Their arrival in Oxford will be seen as a positive signal by the court, but it will create lots of difficulties and complications. Hertford is not the highest ranking duke of our kingdom but of course he'll precede the Marquess of Halifax – and I'm afraid that the Marquess may not appreciate this. Halifax's lands in the North are still loyal to the Crown. If I show any preference for Hertford, Halifax will be annoyed."

The King started to stride up and down like a tiger in a cage.

"Then there is the problem of apartments. The duke will request a suite of rooms – which means that somebody else has to move out – and the person that has to move will be dismayed…"

"Charles, my dear, that's a problem to be solved by the major-domo, not us. Stop worrying!"

The King smiled affectionately at his wife, but it was a sad smile. "Whatever the major-domo does, someone will be offended and I'll have to deal with the consequences."

He took a sip of the wine that Elizabeth offered to him but continued pacing the room. "The biggest problem will be the army. Of course Prince Rupert is the uncontested leader but Hertford would precede the Earl of Northampton in rank – knowing that Hertford has never seen a battle horse in his life, how could he aspire to lead my troops? It would be certain disaster. And yet, how could I not offer him to lead a regiment at least, by rank and honour of his family, he must be expecting an important assignment?"

The Queen made a soothing noise, she knew that she wasn't really expected to answer those brooding questions. Elizabeth tried to blend into the background but her heart was jubilant. This information was worth a fortune, she must meet Mortimer in the gardens later today, there would be a lot to discuss.

"I think I made a big mistake by demanding the duke's presence in person, his money would serve me better now," the King continued, more or less to himself.

"Charles, darling, stop brooding. What's been done, has been done. You'll find a way to deal with the duke's presence, I'm sure." The King was standing close to the Queen now and she patted his hand to comfort him. "Your enemies will see the arrival of Hertford as a strong sign that our cause is just and our power is still undisputed – it will certainly make some people at our court think twice before changing sides. It's a very positive development," the Queen continued.

King Charles's face lit up. "You're absolutely right, Marie, it's a strong signal and after all, the duke will bring fresh money, rather a lot, actually. I'm afraid I do tend towards the pessimistic from time to time."

The King stayed for about thirty minutes but then he had to leave, as the Dutch ambassador was waiting for him.

"Does he have news about our dearest daughter Mary? I receive her letters of course, but it would be nice to hear in person from the ambassador if she is comfortable in this strange country," the Queen exclaimed.

"Mary seems to be thriving in the Netherlands. I think we made an excellent match!"

"If it weren't that she's married to a heretic!" the Queen sighed.

68

"You're also married to a heretic, my dear," the King pointed out, with a wry smile.

"That's why I pray for your soul every day!" the Queen replied, crossing herself quickly.

"If it helps, do the same for our daughter then, Ma'am!"

***

The King left and the Queen took up her embroidery with the best intentions of finishing her work. But – as usual – after a few stitches Her Majesty complained that her eyes were starting to hurt. Elizabeth knew this excuse and dutifully replied, "Your health is very fragile, Ma'am. I don't think Your Majesty should force herself to go on with this tedious task, I'll finish it later for you. Should I call the dwarfs, they may have some new gossip and jokes from the servant's quarters?"

The Queen's face lit up immediately, she loved to listen to gossip.

"That's an excellent idea, Elizabeth, you really do look after me so well. I'm being selfish now, but it's a good thing that Mortimer hasn't yet received an answer from this monster Northumberland, at least I won't be losing you too soon."

Suddenly the Queen cleared her throat. She seemed a little upset. "There's one issue I would like to tell you of."

"Yes, Ma'am?"

"The Prince of Wales will ask you for a dance tonight."

"That's a great honour, Ma'am, he may be still very young but his Royal Highness is a very graceful dancer."

The Queen's face lit up. "He is, indeed. Rarely has a mother been blessed with such a charming son. But that's part of the problem, please Elizabeth, I insist that you grant him a single dance only, even if he pleads for another, it would be… "

"Quite inappropriate, Ma'am, I fully agree. The Prince of Wales may be still very young but he's old enough to set tongues wagging at court. Please be assured that I'll make sure not to feed any rumours. There's no need for Your Majesty to worry."

"You're a gem, Elizabeth, you may call the dwarfs now. I need some diversion."

***

They had found a small abandoned shed close to the gardens and the stables. A dirty wheelbarrow, wooden spades and an array of other discarded gardening tools were waiting for spring to see daylight again, but during winter the shed lay

69

forgotten. It was not in excellent repair but would protect them from the cold winds and – most importantly – hide them from the view of others.

Mortimer had already been waiting for Elizabeth and greeted her with a deep and hungry kiss. The time when she could keep him content with chaste kisses was long gone; since he had started reporting to his uncle and bringing her the money she had asked for, Mortimer was demanding more in return.

"You make me mad, Elizabeth. One day I'll lose my mind because of you," he moaned.

She stroked his curly hair and murmured some reply, as her hands made their way down to his navel and further down into his breeches. His heavy breathing intensified, echoing through the shed as his moaning climaxed.

How long can I keep him at bay, it's getting more difficult every time we meet, she reflected, strangely detached.

She kissed him again and let him fasten his breeches as they settled on a blanket that Mortimer had laid down in the shed for their comfort.

"I have important news." She opened the discussion, repeating the major points of the King's monologue.

Mortimer whistled. "That's what I call important news. Hertford will have to pass through territories controlled by Parliament if he wants to join us here. If I tell my uncle that he's on his way, I'm not sure if he'll even arrive. Maybe that would be better for us anyhow. Halifax will be raging when he hears about that, and what is Prince Rupert going to do with two pompous lads who have never even seen a battlefield?"

"You sound like the King, he didn't seem very pleased to have them coming."

"The King's not stupid, he knows that their arrival may cause more trouble than it's worth. I'll make sure that my uncle gets the information fast, it may be better if Hertford and his friend never arrive in Oxford. What sum should I demand from him?"

"One thousand pounds," Elizabeth said calmly.

He jumped up, shocked by the enormous amount. "Are you crazy? That's the price of a barony."

"If they catch Hertford and Saint Paul, they can ransom him for a fortune. Fifty thousand will be nothing. Our information is worth one thousand – and your uncle has enough money. Ever since he changed sides, he's become even wealthier than he was before."

70

"I'm baffled, Elizabeth. I don't know if I should despise you or if I should admire you – sometimes you even scare me. I'll ask for a thousand pounds. We shall have enough money then to marry and I'll be able to buy a barony close to London as soon as this war is finished."

Elizabeth kissed him instead of giving an answer.

I have to see how to get rid of him afterwards, she thought. *I can't keep this up forever. But when I have the money, things will be different. I'll be free to do what I want.*

The Journey Continues

The delicious smell of roasted meat wafted through the inn, seeping into the room where Pierre and Armand were waiting, covering the stale scent that had been assailing their nostrils thus far.

"Hmm, finally a nice smell." Armand sniffed the air like a dog. "I do feel hungry!"

"I'm not sure if we'll be able to sample any dinner at all. Now let's draw lots, it's you or me."

Armand held two wooden sticks in his hand. Pierre closed his eyes and drew one of the sticks. As he opened his eyes, Armand grinned and waved the second stick under his nose. Pierre had drawn the shorter piece.

"Why do I always lose? You must be cheating!" Pierre groaned.

"No cheating, I swear, but it's a fact, some have it, some don't," answered his friend smugly.

Pierre sighed. "Go on then, but don't cut too deep! And make sure your blade is clean, remember what brother Infirmarius told us in Reims."

"I'm an artist, not a butcher!" Armand was dismayed. "And I do remember what he told us: clean knives make good healings."

He grabbed Pierre's arm and cut without hesitation into it.

"You bastard, you're bleeding me like a pig!" Pierre hissed, not amused.

"That was the intention, stop moaning like a sissy!" came the unfeeling reply from his friend. "Make sure that you spread plenty of blood on the pillow and onto the blanket."

Pierre obliged and soon the bed was covered with large stains of brightest red.

"That looks brilliant." Armand looked at the effect with the satisfaction of an artist seeing his oeuvre accomplished. "But enough is enough. Let's close the wound."

He bound a scarf around his friend's arm to stop the bleeding.

"Now hide your dagger and huddle in the bed, don't forget to moan and sound delirious when I come back!"

"You seem to be relishing every minute of this." Pierre was still miffed.

"Why not, it's an adventure. I'm truly looking forward to seeing their faces!"

"While I have to spend my time in a stinking bed, looking at a dirty wall," mumbled Pierre.

Armand ignored his friend's bad humour. He bumped against the door making a lot of noise, then he opened the door and rushed into the narrow corridor. As expected, one of their grooms had been placed as sentinel, hovering on a chair next to a smoking tallow light. It was Matt, the dumb groom, and he looked at Armand as if he'd seen a ghost.

Armand cried in despair. "It's urgent, help me, call the others, I need help, fast! It's a question of life or death!"

Clearly this scenario had not been foreseen, and Matt didn't know how to react. He stared at Armand with wide eyes, trying to understand – and to come to a decision.

Slowly the urgency sank in and he scratched his head before replying in a gruff voice, "The guv'nor is downstairs." But he didn't move.

"Come on, you simpleton, move your arse. My friend will die if we don't act fast!"

Matt scratched his head once again but Armand's plea sounded genuine enough and he got up. "Come on then."

Together they descended the squeaking staircase, Armand pushing him, urging Matt to move faster.

The taproom was empty, no other customers could be seen. But the noise of their hasty descent had not gone unnoticed. The door of the kitchen was flung open and John appeared, followed by the innkeeper. Now that the door of the kitchen was standing open, the smell of the roasted meat was simply overpowering, making Armand's mouth water. As he hadn't eaten anything since the early morning, it took all his self-control to concentrate on the task in hand.

"My friend, Pierre…" he stammered.

"What about your friend?" asked the innkeeper.

"I don't know, please have a look. I mean, I do know probably, but it can't be, may the Virgin protect us!" he crossed himself.

"What do you mean?"

"Have a look! It's terrible, terrifying, oh my God, save me!"

73

Armand turned back to the staircase and all of them rushed upstairs towards the small bedroom. He opened the door and they discovered Pierre, moaning and writhing in pain, his bed covered with fresh blood stains, glistening ominously in the light of the candle.

"It can't be true," Armand whimpered. "I mean, there was a man on our boat with the same symptoms, but how on earth could Pierre have caught it so quickly? See, he's coughing blood – he's suffering, please help him! Dear Lord, have mercy, help my friend."

Armand noticed with satisfaction the gleam of panic in the eyes of the three men. They looked at each other in fear, but were unsure what to do. Unable to resist adding even a bit more drama, Armand sank to his knees. "Oh my God, save me, my heart is starting to race," and he stopped, interrupted by a nasty cough. When he uncovered his mouth, his scarf was blood stained.

"God help me, I'm bleeding! Pray for my soul, I'm lost. Call a priest!"

Arms wide open he jumped up and staggered towards the three men.

The innkeeper screamed, "Don't come close, you idiot. It's the wasting sickness. May the dear Lord save us!"

His face had turned pale, and sweat was glistening on his balding head.

This was the final straw for John and Matt, who with panic in their eyes raced down the stairs. The door of the inn flew open and minutes later Armand could hear the noise of their horses' hooves on the gravel of the courtyard.

The innkeeper was still standing in their room, paralysed with fear, wringing his hands. He was in total shock. His instincts told him to run – but how could he abandon his inn, leave it in the hands of mortally sick strangers?

Once Armand had ascertained that their false guides had made their escape, he dropped the blood-stained cloth and his behaviour changed completely.

"Now to you, my friend! Our little comedy is finished."

To his shock and amazement, the fat innkeeper saw the fatally sick Pierre rise like a ghost from his blood-stained bed as Armand leapt forward and seized the innkeeper's arm. Pierre placed his dagger underneath his fat double chin. "Let's go downstairs together, but you utter one sound of warning and you're a dead man."

The innkeeper nodded, quivering with fright. "Spare me, my lord, I have a wife and children," he whimpered.

"You should have thought about your wife and children before," Pierre answered, not amused.

"Where's our money, where are our weapons?"

"I don't know, my lord! Surely John and Matt must have taken all of it." He whimpered again.

Finding him not worthy of a reply, Pierre increased the pressure of his dagger until the first drops of blood started to trickle onto his stained apron.

Seeing his own blood spreading like ink on the apron, the innkeeper started to scream like a pig. "Have mercy, my lord, I have everything downstairs, nothing is missing, I swear. I'll give you your weapons, take all of my money, take all I have, but don't kill me!"

"We're gentlemen, not thugs," Armand replied.

They descended to the tap room, keeping their captive firmly between them, dagger pointing at the fat innkeeper, ready to forestall any attempt to escape or raise the alarm. They crossed the tap room and entered a small room that housed a large chest and a bed. Inside the chest, they discovered their swords.

"Where's the rest?" Armand asked gruffly.

Instead of giving an answer, the innkeeper fell down on his knees and dragged a smaller chest out from under his bed. It was a chest made by a master craftsman, secured by a large wrought-iron lock and must have cost him a small fortune. Nervously, the innkeeper reached inside his shirt and produced the keys.

As soon as it was unlocked, Armand could only marvel at their find. The chest was filled to bursting. They discovered jewellery, rings, necklaces and chains made of silver and gold, miniature pictures painted on precious ivory – and a surprising amount of Spanish, English and French coins.

"We're not going to steal his money!" Pierre protested, as he saw his friend grabbing the coins with both hands.

"I wouldn't if I was sure that this was really his money. But this man is nothing but a common thief, I don't have any qualms taking any of this. It will serve us handsomely during the coming weeks," Armand answered unruffled and stuffed the coins into his pockets.

"Who else is staying here?" Armand asked the innkeeper.

"Only my kitchen help, John and Matt didn't want anybody else to stay here tonight." The innkeeper wailed, watching Armand with dismay and growing anger as the latter continued to deplete his treasure chest.

"Let's go and search for him then," Pierre proposed.

"Yes, but let's make sure first of all that our new friend can't do anything silly," Armand replied.

Before the innkeeper realized what was happening to him, he found himself gagged and bound, then bundled into the darkest corner of his taproom.

"You look much better like this," Armand assured the innkeeper who had started to sob. "Alternatively we could have dumped you in the dung heap, would you prefer that?"

The innkeeper shook his head violently and became quiet.

"We're in agreement then," Armand answered cheerfully.

"Let's go to the kitchen and find this help he's been talking about. And then…"

"And then what?" repeated Pierre.

"And then I want a big slice of that roast, I'm starving, the smell is tormenting me."

Swords drawn, they entered the kitchen, Armand first, ready to strike. But to their disappointment the kitchen was empty, there was nobody inside. They continued their search in the larder – but again, nobody was hiding here.

"At least I found this!" Armand grabbed a piece of fresh bread and munched on it happily. "Try it Pierre, not as good as our bread in France, of course, but quite edible."

"I'll go for this!" Pierre had discovered jugs filled with ale and he took a long swig.

"I needed that!" he sighed with satisfaction as he wiped his mouth. "Don't forget that you almost killed me with your dagger, you stuck me like a slaughtered pig!"

"Weakling!" grinned Armand. "It was about time you left your comfortable home, you've turned into a spoilt brat."

They were about to leave the kitchen and to continue their search in the stables outside when Pierre spotted a large oaken chest. It looked strangely odd for a simple kitchen chest.

"Let's see what's inside this chest. Our innkeeper seems to have been running quite a large business of buying and selling stolen goods."

Pierre opened the lid – but to his surprise the chest was totally empty.

"Look, Armand, isn't this strange?"

"Why should it be strange to have a chest inside a kitchen?"

76

"It's strange because it's large but totally empty. Why should he keep an empty chest inside his kitchen? Can you hold the candle please?"

Armand obliged and held the candle while Pierre got down on his knees and examined the chest in detail. Suddenly he exclaimed, "That's it, clever, but not clever enough!"

Grinning triumphantly at Armand, he pulled at an iron ring that was attached to the bottom. The bottom plank creaked and yielded to give access to a narrow staircase that led into the darkness of the cellars.

Armand whistled. "Sometimes you're a clever boy. I just wonder why it doesn't occur more often."

Pierre ignored his friend's insolence and shouted into the darkness, "I know that you're down there, come out or we'll set the house on fire and roast you alive."

He repeated his threat once again until a faint voice from the bottom of the staircase could be heard: "Have mercy, I've done nothing wrong!"

"Nothing will happen to you if you surrender, show yourself!" Armand assured him.

Seconds later two raised arms appeared, followed by a face. "I'm not armed, have mercy!" he repeated, seeing Armand's drawn sword.

As the man climbed out of the chest they could assess him fully. He was a man, still fairly young with the kind of short reddish hair that was so typical of this part of the country. His frame was lean and he had the weather-beaten face of someone who was used to spending more time outside than inside. He was not at all the kind of stout servant that one would have expected to find inside a kitchen. Pierre liked his face, he didn't look at all like a villain. But hadn't he learnt the hard way never to trust appearances?

"Are you the only one here in this inn?" Armand asked.

"Yes, sir."

"I'll kill you if you lie!"

"I'm speaking the truth, sir. My innkeeper's business was such that he didn't like to have too many servants around."

"What were you doing here?"

"Hiding, sir – and helping out."

"Who are you hiding from?" Pierre wanted to know.

The man didn't answer immediately. His eyes assessed the two friends, trying to judge how best to answer. "I'm in your hands anyhow. Let me be straightforward with you. I was doing errands for a group of Cavaliers in Sussex, but a man I considered to be a 'friend' gave me away to the Roundheads. I escaped but killed a Roundhead during my escape – and they're searching for me now. Since that day, I've been living like an outlaw. Adam agreed to hide me but I had to give him all of my remaining money and had to help with any kind of work – free of charge. I also had to look after the stables and… his other business. His cook left us a fortnight ago, that's why I was also doing the cooking."

"You seem to have an amazing number of talents. Adam is the name of the innkeeper?"

"Yes, sir, and the worst cut-throat I've ever met. He'd sell his grandmother to the devil. All he desires is cash and ever more cash."

"What's your name?"

"James, sir."

"Why is half of England either called John or James? It's very confusing," Pierre lamented.

"Pierre isn't that original either," Armand objected.

"You can call me Jim, sir, most people do, actually."

"It's Jim then," Armand decided. "Jim, if you're an enemy of the Roundheads, you're our man." He fished deep in his pockets and threw a nice heap of coins on the table. "I guess some of those are yours then, help yourself."

Jim's face lit up. "Thank you, sir, I'll never forget this."

He carefully counted the coins, shoved some of them back and remarked as he pocketed the others, "Thanks, I've taken back exactly what Adam stole from me plus some shillings as I have been working for free since I arrived. I hope you think that's fair?"

"That's fine with us, Jim, but there's no hurry, I'm hungry. Can you serve us some of this roast and I saw some fresh bread in the larder. Let's sit down and talk while we have supper."

They sat around the kitchen table and Jim served the roasted lamb, fresh bread and ale from the larder to be followed by a cake glazed with honey and nuts.

"I feel born again!" Armand sighed, giving a grunt of satisfaction as he dug his teeth into the fresh bread, to be followed by a muffled, "What a crazy day."

Jim still looked wary. It was obvious that he was still wondering what kind of strange foreigners who had come from nowhere were dining together with him. But he ate heartily – apparently Adam had not been a very generous employer.

"May I take the liberty of asking you, gentlemen, what you are doing here? Maybe I can be of help to you?" he said cautiously, opening the discussion.

"The two gallow-birds and this greedy innkeeper of yours tried to abduct us. We met them in Dover where they were pretending to be the guides we were waiting for. Pierre –" he pointed to his friend, "soon became suspicious and we found out that they wanted to keep us here, hoping probably to ransom us. It was quite fun to get rid of them, but now we have to find our way to Oxford."

"You want to join our King?"

"Yes, Jim, that's the plan. We'll have to find our way North. It's not too far, I guess two days' travelling should do it. But we don't know the countryside and we could do with a guide."

Jim looked at them and cleared his throat. "May I speak openly?"

"Please do!"

"If you two gentlemen travel north, dressed like foreigners and speaking with a French accent, you'll be skinned alive in the next village you enter. All the land between Oxford and Dover is in the hands of the Roundheads. The Roundheads hate the French and the Catholics, you won't stand a chance!"

Pierre and Armand looked at each other, then they looked back at Jim.

"Are you sure that it's as bad as that?" Pierre finally asked.

"I'm sure, sir. The Roundheads are spreading stories about French agents. They tell the people that our Queen wants to bring back the old times, like bloody Queen Mary. Everyone here is scared to death. A fine bounty has been set on the head of any French agent, dead or alive. But may I ask how you escaped?"

Pierre quickly explained their little comedy of faking a mortal sickness and a quick smile flashed over Jim's face.

But Armand was still dismayed. "Are you sure that they'd kill us? Just because we're French? Barbarians!"

"That's the truth, sir. Money is scarce nowadays and a prize will be paid in silver for the head of any French agent."

"What do you suggest we do, Jim?"

Pierre was starting to like their new acquaintance. He reminded him a bit of his faithful valet Jean who had been compelled to stay behind in France to ensure the safety and well-being of Pierre's wife.

"First of all, I propose leaving at dawn. I don't think that Matt and John will come back, and listening to your story, I'm sure that they'll be far too scared. But the innkeeper's family and some of Adam's cronies will be back tomorrow and they'll move heaven and hell if they find you here with the innkeeper bound and gagged. I propose that we ride to my sister's farm. I'll ask her to sort you out with new clothes – with all due respect, you cannot parade around in this part of England dressed in silk and velvet of the most vivid colours when all other gentlemen are following the new fashion for dark and sober clothing. It must be simple clothes and dark colours – and the new hats, I'm willing to bet that you're wearing French-style musketeer hats, adorned with a big feather?"

"Yes, of course I brought my nicest hat. Are you telling us that we need to wear those ugly, shapeless hats that look like black buckets and that I saw everywhere in Dover? How depressing!" Armand sighed. "But I admit, you have a point here, our hats may attract unwanted attention…"

"I agree, we can't parade around like parrots if everybody else looks like a sparrow," Pierre concluded.

"All right, we agree, we need to change our outfits before we travel onwards. But then comes the next question: How do we get to Oxford?"

"If you will trust me, gentlemen, I propose that I become your guide and servant. It would be an honour for me to serve gentlemen who support our King. I know the way to Oxford well enough. But we'll take more than a week, as I suggest avoiding all major roads and anywhere near London. For security reasons I suggest travelling mostly during the evening and night – at least whenever the light of the moon and the weather will permit."

"That sounds reasonable enough. Let's ride together, Jim. My name is Pierre and this is Armand."

"Sir Pierre, may I make a last suggestion?"

"Certainly, Jim, what is it?"

"If we do happen to meet people, may I humbly suggest that you pretend to be two gentlemen going home to Wales? This would explain your accent. But frankly speaking, it would be better if Sir Armand did not speak at all, it's rather too obvious that he comes from France."

Pierre grinned. "I see your point, what should we call ourselves, what would be true Welsh names?"

"I suggest that you should become Sir Pedr and your friend should be your cousin, Sir Aderyn. Sir Peter and Sir Edwin in English."

"How come you know about Welsh names?"

"I have family in Wales. If someone should enquire about your family name, say something long that nobody will understand but drop a hint that your family is related to the Tudors. The Tudors are held in high esteem, especially by the Roundheads. You should be safe enough then."

Armand started to yawn. "I'm hellishly tired. Where can I sleep? I'm certainly not willing to put a foot in our filthy room again."

"You're unbelievable!" Pierre protested. "I had the pleasure of lying in that filthy bed and playing the sick man and now you tell me that you won't even set foot in the room because it doesn't please your lordship!"

"But now it's even worse," Armand argued. "You messed it all up with your blood, don't forget."

"May I propose you use the private rooms of the innkeeper, they're not luxurious but at least they're clean and more comfortable than the guest rooms upstairs," Jim quickly interjected.

A quick inspection confirmed that the innkeeper's bed was far more inviting and as soon as Jim had brought fresh sheets and blankets, Armand went to bed, leaving Pierre and Jim to remain on guard. They'd change watch after midnight.

"Let's play dice," Jim suggested.

"Good idea, it'll help to pass the time."

Thus they passed their time chatting about life in England and playing dice while they emptied a second jug of ale. Pierre was asking many questions; he had the impression that in a matter of three years, England had become an alien country.

Jim obliged and it soon became obvious that Jim had led a colourful life. "I never wanted to spend my life on our family farm, even as a boy I dreamed of seeing foreign countries, and especially the sea. My father wanted me to take over our farm but I wanted a life of adventure, to see the world. Father was very cross with me, but luckily my sister married a farmer and she looks after our farm now. I never regretted my decision. I sailed to Virginia, I've been to Spain and France. If those damned Puritans take over the country, I'll leave England once for all. I'm tempted to go to India. The East India Company is recruiting sailors in the major ports, they'd sign me up immediately. I heard that the women of India are the most beautiful in the world."

Pierre laughed. "We usually say this about the women in France, but Armand swears that he's never seen more beautiful ladies than in Venice. I guess there'll never be a way to tell which country has the most beautiful women."

"Let's drink then…" Jim raised his cup. "To beautiful women everywhere!"

***

The next morning started with a large bowl of steaming porridge prepared by Jim, who had plundered the innkeeper's sacred reserves of honey and clotted cream. Fortified by a hearty breakfast and ready to take on the world they made their way to the stables.

"*Merde alors! C'est quoi ça? Des chameaux?*" Armand exclaimed as soon as they set eyes on the horses.

"Not camels, I'm afraid, those creatures are supposed to be horses. Although, I do admit, they don't really look it."

Pierre examined the sorry looking animals that had been left behind in the stables. Their false guides had taken flight on the beautiful thoroughbreds they had brought over from France.

"We'll never be able to ride to London on these bony creatures. They'll collapse after two miles at best."

"We'll change horses later today, let me organize it," Jim replied with a smile.

"What's your plan?" Pierre was curious.

"Elham Manor is fairly close, maybe one, maximum two hours' riding, even with these creatures. The Roundheads have ousted the loyal lord of Elham Manor, accusing him of supporting the King. In truth, these bastards only wanted to lay hands on the manor's stud farm, it's famed throughout the country."

"Excellent, this means we can nick their horses and will dispense justice at the same time!" Armand concluded with a wide grin.

"Yes, exactly, sir. Even the bible commands us to give the Emperor what is due to the Emperor."

"Let's trot to Elham then, we won't even call it 'riding'." Pierre started to saddle the first sad-looking mare. He fastened the last straps and looked critically at the skinny horse.

"I hope she survives until we reach Elham, I do have my doubts."

"I think she's quite tough, luckily you're not too heavy, sir," Jim consoled him.

By divine miracle, or maybe not, they reached Elham before noon without any major incident. Here Jim suggested a break in a small forest so they could watch from their hiding place the long thatched building that housed the stables and the barns.

"Let me check if there are any guards on duty. I'll simply pretend to be wanting to know when the next batch of yearlings will be for sale. Stay here please until I come back."

Jim didn't wait for a reply and directed his horse towards the manor. A silence ensued, and Armand and Pierre looked at each other.

"Do you like this?" Armand finally asked.

"Not really. What if…"

"…what if he betrays us instead of checking up on the horses?" Armand finished the sentence.

"Better hide, let's see if he comes back alone or not."

"Even that won't tell us much, we can only pray."

***

It was a long wait. Pierre and Armand didn't speak much, but a palpable tension hung in the air. They kept hidden in the undergrowth, expecting the worst.

"What if he comes with a group of armed grooms?" Pierre whispered.

"Say your prayers then, there's no way we can escape on these wonderful horses. You were always the good scholar in the monastery school, at least you'll remember plenty of prayers."

"I do, but I'm rather sceptical that they'll help us now," Pierre replied.

Finally, after an endless period of waiting, Jim came back from the stables. But he did not ride in their direction, instead turning his horse and disappearing down the road to Dover.

"You said that you liked him!" Armand hissed at Pierre. "I always found him a bit suspicious."

"I only said that he reminded me a bit of my valet Jean. I never said that I trusted him! I'm not that naïve!" Pierre was annoyed.

"What do we do now? Jim has left us and any minute we may expect a battalion of armed grooms or soldiers to spill out of the stables and pursue us." Armand was nervous.

"Better leave then, back through the wood, it's better that way, nobody can see us!"

They took the reins and started to guide their horses back along the small path they had taken before.

Only minutes later they found their path blocked.

"Did you truly think it a good idea to sneak out of the woods?" asked the voice.

Armand and Pierre drew their swords – what other kind of answer could they give?

London

Charles and François were not disappointed. The quality of the lodgings and the food in Jeremiah's inn were excellent, beyond any possible reproach. The newly converted landlord Jeremiah, alias James, had fully embraced the Puritan spirit and therefore might be inclined to consider the luxury of soft pillows and duvets as frivolous. But luckily his wife had different views on such matters. Her beneficial and comfortable influence could be felt everywhere.

Dinner had been excellent, exactly as Charles had remembered it, and well worth the detour. The next morning a lavish breakfast with cold meat, bread and an ample supply of home brewed ale was already awaiting the travellers in a private salon.

"Today we should arrive in London," said Charles, opening the discussion. "By the way, you should keep your Huguenot name and remain M. de Tavaillon even in London. I propose that you stay close to me, ah yes, I almost forgot, please let me handle the discussion with the guards at the gate. Just play the humble merchant and don't look them in the eye if you can avoid it. A shilling slipped into the right hands will work miracles in stopping any enthusiastic questions."

"Charles, I'm not a baby, I know what to do!" François protested.

Charles's apology came in the form of a quick grin but his mind was already dwelling on the pleasures of breakfast, as he was helping himself to a large slice of cold beef. François shuddered. He found the idea of having a breakfast composed of tepid ale and cold, almost raw beef simply disgusting. He longed for a hot chocolate and some nice sweet pastries.

Glancing across the well-stocked table he discovered some freshly baked bread and homemade butter and found them edible, in fact, rather good. The moment he detected the homemade jam and a pot of honey, he started to feel better.

"As soon as we arrive at Hertford House," Charles continued, "I'd rather keep you hidden from society until I know how the wind is blowing nowadays in London. I have an idea, of course, but I'll need to meet some of my good friends before I can tell you who's calling the tune in Parliament nowadays. Is it still Northumberland? I still have problems believing that a nobody like Cromwell is daring to challenge our rightful King. But Oliver Cromwell's name is popping up more and more often in the letters that I receive from my old friends. Maybe I'm old fashioned, but it appears strange to me that a man from the lower gentry should be a challenge to our rightful King."

"Yes, the world is going mad. And yet Mazarin told me as well that this Cromwell is to be reckoned with – and he's rarely wrong."

"Yes, your Mazarin is clever, I wish our King had a prime minister like him. But I'm convinced that the Dutch are also playing a false game. They should be supporting our King as his daughter, Princess Mary, is the spouse of their future sovereign. But it's an open secret that they are pumping a lot of money into the pockets of the rebellious Puritans."

François scratched his chin. "Because they're brothers in faith?"

Charles laughed. "Brothers in worshipping the god of mammon? Not only that, the Dutch are hard-boiled merchants. They calculate that England will be weakened for many years, probably for a whole generation, if the King loses this struggle. A tempting scenario for the Dutch, as this would grant them ample time and opportunity to enlarge their overseas territories – and that's what they want, that's where the wealth can be found nowadays."

Several hours later they reached the outposts of the famous London Bridge. Arriving from the south bank, François saw the silhouette of London lurking behind the River Thames for the first time, but he was far from impressed. Instead he found it disappointing. London might be the fastest growing city in England, attracting hundreds, even thousands of new townspeople every year, but its sprawling and chaotic mass of low built wooden houses crouching under wintery clouds of acrid smoke lacked the grandeur and the notable highlights of a civilized city like Paris.

Not even the towers of the venerable Westminster Abbey that Charles pointed out to him could rival the famous, soaring spires of Notre Dame Cathedral. Only the Tower of London came close to François's ideas of regal splendour. The river Thames might be larger than the Seine in Paris but whereas in Paris several bridges allowed easy passage from one bank to the other, all traffic arriving from the South of England had to pass through the bottleneck of the only bridge that had ever been constructed, London Bridge. The Londoners must be a pack of rebellious and thrifty peasants, François concluded secretly.

As they passed the gates of the bridge on the left bank, François noted that Charles seemed to be well known and was warmly welcomed by the officers. Several coins minted from dazzling silver passed discreetly from his large hands into the eager hands of the commander on duty. Such generosity ensured that not only were they spared any awkward searches or questions, but the commander saw to it that they were escorted by a good dozen soldiers on their way into the city.

Those guards were indeed of great help, as the famous London Bridge was not only the sole access to the capital from the south. A steady inflow of traffic from the south collided with curious visitors, pedlars and passers-by, as the bridge was lined with shops and stalls of all sorts. As a result, the bridge was utterly overcrowded. Curses of the worst sort were exchanged between people and brawls erupted as soon as people, horses, coaches or carts collided or blocked the way.

Luckily their guards were used to the daily chaos. Stoically they used the wooden shafts of their halberds without hesitation to make way, and just as the sea had parted in front of Moses to make space for the escape of the chosen tribes of Israel from Egypt, people made way as soon as they understood that the soldiers would not hesitate to use the sharp ends of their weapons as well. Although the crowd on the bridge cleared their path, curses and obscenities continued showering down on the guards and the visitors. François stated with surprise that the people of London were a confident lot, to the point of being cocksure, even in front of the authorities. This country was truly different from France.

Once they entered the city, a new disappointment was waiting for François. Compared to Paris with its newly constructed large avenues and modern buildings with their large windows and façades of light creamy sandstone springing up on every corner of the city, London looked like a dark city still in medieval times. Low wooden houses were crouched tightly like scared sheep against each other whilst narrow streets meandered through the overcrowded city without any obvious pattern.

London shared one common trait though with Paris – dirt and filth was everywhere. Stinking rubbish piled up in the streets, spilling onto the old and worn cobbled streets.

But the worst thing for François was the London air. He had always been convinced that no big city could stink as much as Paris, but he found London to be even worse, with its thousands of blackened chimneys huddling under a blanket of dark smoke and thick fog, a mixture that made his breathing difficult, as it seemed to stick like glue to his lungs. And yet Charles didn't seem to take any notice of the dirt and the bad air. He breathed deeply and cried out, "Wonderful to be back in London, no city like it, is there?"

François made a face but declined to comment.

Thanks to Charles's generosity, nobody had bothered to ask any stupid questions about this strange French Huguenot visitor who accompanied Lord Charles Neuville. From time to time Charles would address a remark to him, to which M. de Tavaillon gave only a short reply. Apparently the Frenchman was no great talker.

Their final destination, Hertford House, was located on the banks of the Thames, not far away from Whitehall Palace. But as the London streets were blocked and they were only advancing at a snail's pace, Charles's patience was wearing thin and so he decided to hire a barge. François later was to discover that using the River was the preferred method of avoiding the daily traffic in London for the privileged. He marvelled at the oarsmen who plunged their long wooden oars into the water with all the precision of German clockwork. The barge picked up considerable speed and quickly they passed along the royal compound, heading towards Hertford House and its private jetty.

On their way they passed along Whitehall Palace, which was reputed to be the biggest palatial building in Europe, but to François it looked rather like a vast assembly of brick buildings, adorned with some random towers and a grand façade, rather than an imposing royal palace in the style of the Louvre.

Therefore it came as no surprise to François that Hertford House was no ducal palace either but rather a large stately house hovering on the banks of the Thames. As soon as their arrival had been made known they were met in the great entrance hall by the major-domo and his staff, offering the newly arrived guests tankards filled with steaming mulled wine.

"That's just what I needed! Is it always so cold in London?" François asked after he had emptied almost half of his tankard.

"I guess it must be the damp coming up from the river. It tends to feel a bit cold, but you'll get used to it," Charles replied unperturbed. "Let's meet in about an hour for dinner, it's going to be dark soon."

François, being received as a friend but also a commoner, was not accommodated in the rooms reserved for visitors of high rank but found himself tucked into a neat guest room close to the servants' quarters. But his room had a large bed and even the luxury of a chest and a chair, therefore he couldn't really complain. It did feel very cold though. François wasn't sure if he'd get used to it. Why had he ever agreed to leave his comfortable home and his beautiful wife just to satisfy the whim of Cardinal Mazarin and to travel to a country devoid of any comfort and decent civilization?

François was still rubbing his ice-cold hands when a young footman knocked at the door carrying a basket with coal and logs of firewood. In no time the brushwood inside the fireplace caught alight, the flames flared up and licked hungrily at the dry wood and the coal. Soon the warmth of the fire spread into the room and François started to feel more comfortable. But the long ride had taken its toll: *I'll just close my eyes for five minutes*, he thought and looked at the bed. François sank down and found it surprisingly soft and comfortable; there was even a luxurious feather bedspread. Warmed by the fire he gave in to temptation and fell asleep.

A good hour later he was woken up by the young footman who had returned with the order to search for the guest and guide him to the remote wing of Hertford House where the private dining room was located. This dining room was used for more intimate family gatherings, as the official dining room was the size of a chapel and as cold as the grave in winter. Not surprisingly, it was rarely used. François – for once – was happy to be disguised as a simple Huguenot merchant, as this spared him the effort of changing into elaborate evening attire. He quickly changed his shirt, combed his short hair, splashed water on his face and was ready to join Charles.

Hertford House had been built and enlarged over generations and it took them almost fifteen minutes to reach the dining room.

"Where have you been?" Charles greeted him. "I'm dying of hunger."

François almost replied, *You're always dying of hunger, nothing new there*, but remembering that he was only a merchant guest in the eyes of the servants, he quickly reined in his tongue and replied instead, "I was following your footman through this maze of corridors and rooms! What an amazing building."

"It tends to be a bit confusing when you come for the first time," Charles admitted, barely able to hide his pride.

"I think the oldest part of the building dates back to the reign of the Plantagenets. At this time King Henry I elevated one of our forefathers, the baron Neuville, to the rank of first earl of Hertford."

Charles suddenly chuckled. "He was later nicknamed 'the skewer baron'."

François rose an eyebrow. "Why so?"

"Baron William, later earl William, was a choleric character and liked to run his sword right through those unlucky opponents who had the misfortune to arouse his ire," Charles laughed.

"But one day he did it with the wrong person, a friend of the King, and ended his life on the block – unrepentant though, as the legend goes. Since those days the headless skewer baron is known to haunt Hertford House. Not surprising as such – presumably the pleasures of a heavenly paradise were denied a sinner like him."

Undisturbed by the ghost of the infamous Neuville ancestor they tackled the sumptuous dinner that was waiting for them. François was not astonished to find it quite excellent. He knew that Charles was prepared to accept many compromises, but never when it came to dining.

After they had sampled a choice of different main courses they attacked a board of cheeses accompanied by a bottle of claret.

"This cheese is very tasty," François conceded. "It could even rival our French cheeses."

"It's called Cheddar," Charles replied, helping himself to a large slice. "It's better than anything you have in France. Although the cheese they call brie that I had in Normandy was not bad at all!"

Before François could seize the opportunity to defend French honour and insist on the superiority of French cheese, the door opened and a very excited butler entered the dining room, bowing deeply several times.

"I do apologize, my lord, for the intrusion," he stuttered, deeply agitated.

"In the hall downstairs, my lord, there is an individual, the kind of man whom I'd have rebuked immediately under normal circumstances, my lord, but he insists strongly that he must speak to your lordship immediately! He says it's a matter of life or death."

The butler's voice had taken on a slightly dramatic tone. He was evidently revelling in the notion of having landed in the midst of a drama.

Assuming the airs of the polite host towards François, Charles bowed slightly in his direction. "I do apologize, M. de Tavaillon, but it seems that I must attend to this urgent matter first. May I ask you to be so kind as to wait for me?"

"Of course, my lord, always your servant!" François answered politely, although he was burning with curiosity to know who this unknown visitor might be and suppressed the urgent desire to accompany Charles downstairs.

Charles left the room and François was left on his own. Trying to kill time, he fetched a bowl of nuts and a nutcracker, and having nothing better to do, he spent his time cracking nut after nut. He had already piled up quite a number on his plate when the doors opened and Charles entered, accompanied by a lean man with a large, reddish nose. From his bearing, François was certain that the man must have been a soldier in his previous life. He positioned himself next to the table and immediately stood to attention.

François could see at once that he was extremely ill at ease and the explanation was easy. Charles's expression heralded a storm – the news must have been bad indeed.

"Can you repeat once again, what you have just told me," Charles thundered.

The man seemed to shrink but he followed the command instinctively. "My name is Able, sir," he began.

"I think your parents committed a fatal error when they chose that name." Charles's voice was pure sarcasm.

Able swallowed deeply and continued, stuttering now and then. "We were supposed to meet Sir Pierre and Sir Armand in Dover, my lord, as per your lordship's instructions. Waiting for the vessel *Beatrice* to arrive, we spent the night in 'The Lions of England', it's an inn inside the port area. We decided to order dinner…" He paused, unsure how to go on. Then he mustered all of his courage and continued, "and my friend Tom befriended a lady. She invited him to follow her upstairs into her room."

The man's face had turned scarlet and François couldn't help commenting, "She was a lady of great virtue, most probably."

"Very much so, I assume," answered Charles. "Go on, tell us, what happened next?"

"I waited in the taproom but as my friend didn't come back after a good while, I started to become worried. I got up, wanting to have a look myself and told the innkeeper to show me to her room. But then someone must have hit me from behind.

The next thing I can remember is that I woke up in the same room as my friend Tom, both of us bound and gagged. We had been fooled like young greenhorns."

Able breathed hard and continued. "I don't know what to say, I apologize most sincerely."

"Nobody can apologize for being stupid and negligent." Charles was furious.

"How did you free yourself?" François asked, not sure if he should believe the story or not.

"Tom was able to loosen my bonds and the rest was easy enough. The innkeeper pretended not to have noticed anything. But of course our horses had been stolen as well. Luckily I have good friends in Dover and I was able to borrow fresh horses. We rode immediately to the port where we found the *Beatrice*, still at anchor. There we learnt that Sir Pierre and Sir Armand had been met by two men who must have pretended to be us. Immediately we started to search and found out that the false guides had left with the two gentlemen in the direction of Canterbury. But after Dover we lost all trace of them."

Able stood at the table, kneading his hat into a shapeless mess, a picture of misery. "I'm sorry, my lord, we have failed miserably."

"I wonder, how would the other men have known that you were intending to meet my friends?" Charles asked.

Able's face turned an even deeper shade of scarlet, if this was at all possible. "I'm afraid, my lord, that my friend and I shared a tankard of ale and discussed some details of our mission."

"That only confirms my previous assessment. You're an idiot, both of you are, your friend even more so." Charles was fuming.

"Leave us for now, but stay around in case I have further need of you. I have to think. The only reason why I haven't had you whipped is that at least you had the decency to come and confess immediately," Charles grumbled.

"Maybe you should allow the messenger to have a bowl of soup and some ale, it would be a gesture of Christian charity," François proposed, playing to perfection the role of the humble Huguenot.

François was met by a thankful glance from the guide. He must have rushed up to London without a break or having dared to take the time to eat. Charles didn't reply, he only snorted. But as he didn't object, the butler took it for a yes and led the visitor downstairs to the servant's kitchen.

"What can we do from London to save our boys? They have walked right into a trap. I could kick myself that I chose those guides. I'll never forgive myself!" Charles exclaimed after the door had been closed and they were alone again.

"Nothing we can do from here really," followed the instant reply from François. "Maybe pray. But it's not your fault, stop dramatizing. The boys were stupid, such things happen."

"Maybe, but one thing is sure, I don't think that any kind of prayers will help them," Charles replied. "I think I had better ride down to Dover and search myself."

"And tell the whole world that two fat pigeons are on their way to the King's court – in the middle of enemy territory. Charles, just think about it, that would be sheer madness!"

Charles hesitated and threw himself into a chair. Ignoring the chair's remorseful squeaking he continued, "You're right. We must be careful. But what can I do? I wonder that you can stay so calm."

"Maybe I'm wrong. But those two are prone to getting into trouble, therefore you won't find me really surprised. Since I met Pierre for the first time about four years ago, it's always been like this, they lurch from calamity to calamity. But they seem to have excellent guardian angels, and I'm also comforted by the fact that Armand is accompanying Pierre, as Armand is an excellent fighter. Let me make a suggestion: if we have no news by tomorrow, give me one of your best men and I'll comb the region. I can be pretending to be looking for a good wool supply, nobody would find it strange for me to be roaming the countryside."

Charles's face lit up. "That's an excellent suggestion. I'll ask Benjamin to accompany you. He's almost six feet tall, a bright lad and a stout Protestant, so there will be no stupid questions as long as he's at your side."

"That's settled then. Hopefully we'll have news by tomorrow – or I'll go and search for the boys."

Charles smiled affectionately. "Thank you, François. You know, I care very much for my little French cousin. If you're out searching for them, at least I know they have the best chance of being found. You'll find them. I know it."

***

The next day passed. While François waited impatiently for a messenger to arrive from Dover, Charles left Hertford House in order to visit old friends in the capital who were well connected in the circles of the rebellious Parliament that had de facto taken control of most of the counties of England.

By noon there was still no sign from the two friends and there was no doubt in François's mind that his departure was imminent. Therefore he set him himself the task of trying to extract as many details from the unlucky Able as possible. As it turned out, Able knew the south of England like the back of his hand – including those sleazy inns that would never be on the map for any gentleman worthy of the name. But both men were in agreement that those were the places where they'd need to start their search.

During the day François had arranged everything for his departure. Horses had been chosen, he had selected a pair of handy pistols from the Hertford House armoury that he stowed into his leather bag and he had acquired a thick felt coat as the threat of heavy rain was looming once again in the sky. Rain in February would be a miserably cold affair and for a moment François had been tempted to buy a fur coat. But it would be highly unusual for a Huguenot merchant to travel clad in an expensive fur coat without raising eyebrows – and provoking unwanted attention.

At dinnertime Charles was waiting for François once again in the dining room. As soon as dinner had been served, Charles made a sign for the footmen to withdraw.

"Now we can speak openly."

"Did you hear anything interesting in the city?" François interrogated him.

"A lot, the city is humming with rumours and stories of all kinds; very difficult sometimes to make out what's real and what's just fantasy. First of all, and I guess that's at the moment the most important information for both of us, there is no news or rumours about Pierre and Armand. This means that their arrival in England is still a secret."

"As they disappeared only yesterday, that's probably to be expected," François commented. "News does travel fast, but not that fast. What does London say about the King?"

"They're now saying openly that the King has to go," Charles answered bluntly. "Some months ago a delegation of members of Parliament approached the King with the intention of mediating and coming up with a new agreement. They had a sort of new Magna Carta in mind, granting more powers to Parliament and reducing the sovereign's prerogatives – especially raising ever higher taxes and charges. Rumour has it that the King was open to discussing a compromise but that the Queen intervened and advised him to fight and not to give up any rights she judges as being granted by the Grace of God and which should never be relinquished."

"Very French attitude," François commented. "But maybe not the best advice she should have given him in this difficult situation."

"Exactly. Now the doors of communication between Parliament and the Royalists are shut and the Puritans are gathering strength every day. Those of my friends who are always the first to scent any political change have already changed their position, praising the virtues of a new government to be led by the Puritans. "

"Is Oliver Cromwell taking a leading role in all of this?" François asked.

"Not at all. That's the strange thing. In London most people still think that he's just one of the many members of the new Parliament, a toy that the noble families will throw away when they choose the next king. But those of my friends who're clever, they see that this Cromwell is gathering more and more influence as he's pulling the strings in the army, calling it a 'new model army'. My friends are willing to bet that we're creating a monster that will swallow us all."

"That doesn't sound good at all. Is Cromwell such a brilliant leader?"

"In a strange way, yes, he's convinced that the Holy Spirit has touched him, that he has been enlightened. He instils such strong faith in his men that they're ready to follow him to the gates of hell if need be. I guess that's the kind of quality that makes a great leader, making people believe that they're invincible."

"It is. Richelieu had this gift as well. When Richelieu wanted something, it was impossible to resist."

"There's another rumour circulating. One of my friends told me in confidence that a year ago a charismatic fortune teller arrived from the South of Europe. Since his arrival in London, many members of high society have become his regular customers. My friend told me, in confidence or course, that he knows that even Cromwell is seeking his advice."

"Very strange indeed, wouldn't this be totally against Puritan teachings?"

"Absolutely, it's not what you'd expect from a man who cites the bible at any given moment. And yet, according to my friend, Cromwell's attitude changed completely after he met this strange person. From that day on, he's been convinced that he's been chosen by Providence to cleanse the country of the sinful reign of the Stuarts."

Both men exchanged knowing glances. They had been long enough acquainted with the highest circles in politics to know that Providence rarely intervenes in human matters, but that very often human greed is skilfully disguised as divine intervention.

"As soon as Pierre appears in Oxford, I'll have to meet and talk with him. We'll need to find a good reason to remove him from England as fast as possible and safely weather the brewing storm back in France."

"And I'll have to convince the Queen to leave for France, don't forget, that's why I've come to England after all," François sighed.

"From all I've heard about Queen Henrietta Maria, it won't be easy…"

"It isn't easy at all, especially as the Queen is pregnant again, I'm not even sure if she's capable of travelling. I've heard that she's not well," Charles answered.

François grabbed his glass of wine and took a mouthful of claret, then he cleared his throat. "I know that she says she's pregnant. The Cardinal Mazarin told me about her pregnancy, his spies know everything. But are they sure about that? The Queen must be in her mid-thirties by now, I've heard that sometimes women of her age develop symptoms that can be confusing… "

"Sure, that could be an explanation. But I met the Earl of Northumberland and I never saw him so gleeful. He thinks that he'll be the next king, stupid idiot. The earl has several spies at court in Oxford, the King and the Queen can't even breathe without him knowing all the details. Northumberland not only confirmed that Her Majesty is pregnant, he told me that her pregnancy is complicated this time."

"Looks that my mission is an easy one then... a missing cousin and his missing friend, a pregnant queen who can't and won't travel, what else could I ask for?"

"Oh, there's no limit, is there? Better avoid being arrested by the Puritans as a French spy yourself. The mood in this country has become strange, people are being dragged to the gallows faster than they can ever imagine."

"*A votre santé*, my lord, thanks for cheering me up!" François toasted him.

"Cheers, my friend, welcome to the new England, the land of peace, brotherhood and unity!"

A Kingdom for a Horse

Armand looked at Jim, who was blocking his way and hissed, "Come on then, you coward, if you dare to fight."

"Is your lordship convinced that this would be a good idea?" Jim pointed towards the undergrowth behind him. "What if my men are hiding there?"

"Oh really? So where are they?"

"Men, show you're there!" Jim cried. The holly bushes started to move. Armand didn't answer but he clenched his fist.

"Name your conditions, Jim," Pierre intervened. "What do you want?"

"I desire that you put away your swords, my lords, and…"

"And?"

"… and that you should be more careful if we are to travel together! If I really had any evil intentions, you'd be dead men by now. May I suggest that you are a little more careful in future?"

Pierre put his sword back into its scabbard and grimaced. "You've got a strange kind of humour, Jim. You scared us. But point taken, I admit, we were a bit careless. Tell us now, who's hiding in there?"

"It's only Jack. Jack, come forward and greet the gentlemen!"

Jack moved forward, leaving the shelter of the thick holly bushes. "Your servant, m'lords," he mumbled.

"Jack's my youngest sister's husband, he happens to work as first groom at Elham Manor. Jack's agreed to help me to get hold of three decent horses when we need them."

Jack grinned back, revealing a gap in his front teeth and nodded.

"Thank you, Jack, but why would you do this for us?" Pierre couldn't help asking.

"Jim's family." He scratched his head. "And them new masters of Elham are thieves. I only serve me true lords."

This long speech had cost Jack considerable effort and he became silent. Jim smiled at his brother-in-law affectionately. "He's a right one, is Jack."

96

Armand had recovered from those first awkward moments but Pierre knew that his friend's pride must have suffered badly. Armand would never forgive himself for walking into a potential trap like a blind idiot.

"How will we ever manage to steal some horses?" he asked incredulously, "I'm sure that there will be plenty of guards. I saw them with my own eyes while we were hiding in the forest."

"We don't steal horses." Jim was all indignation. "We just *exchange* our horses against theirs. That's not stealing!"

"Point taken, but how do we execute the 'exchange'?"

"Jack will lead five good horses to a meadow together with a second groom, he'll make sure to pick his best friend to accompany him. We'll stage a struggle, bind them to a tree. Then we'll pick three horses and make sure that we make a lot of noise."

"But the guards will arrive on the scene straight away."

"Sure, but Jack and his friend will lead them in the wrong direction."

"Clever, I like that!" Pierre smiled.

Jim shook his hand. "It's a pleasure to serve you. You helped me to escape from the inn and it's my honour to pay back the debt."

"But where will we stay tonight?" Armand asked, still feeling somewhat resentful towards Jim. "Soon it's going to be dark and it'll be freezing cold."

"If you agree, my lords, I propose we sleep on my farm. We'll be safe and warm there and my sister will help us to organize new clothes. We'll get the fresh horses tomorrow and then ride on to Oxford."

Jack said goodbye and they left the wood following a narrow path. From there they rode a good mile until they entered a smallish forest. The imposing oak trees had kept their brown withered leaves as if they wanted to hold on to the memory of their summer glory. From here they followed a meandering narrow road. Deep tracks filled with muddy rain made their path difficult but Jim knew his way and avoided the most dangerous potholes.

"See the tracks?" Armand whispered to Pierre.

"Smugglers' carts?" Pierre answered.

"What else? Who would transport something heavy across country to a forlorn farm at the end of winter? If it were in autumn, maybe, but in winter, it seems pretty obvious…"

Armand, always inclined towards optimism, replied. "Let's look on the bright side, probably his sister can serve us an excellent French or Spanish wine if the smugglers use her farm. I could do with a good glass of wine, how these people here can drink tepid ale day and night is beyond my understanding."

It was almost dark when they reached a small farmhouse, which looked as if it had been in use for many generations. Doors and windows showed their age, the tiled floor of the kitchen was pockmarked and rough, as were the walls of uneven cut sandstone darkened by age and decades, if not centuries, of kitchen fumes. Jim led them inside and Pierre noticed with satisfaction that the pots on the stove were giving off a delicious smell. He was as hungry as a wolf.

Their hostess, Maggie, sank into a deep curtsy, overwhelmed by the splendour of the two gentlemen that her brother had brought along as surprise guests. Flustered, she tried to arrange the hair beneath her bonnet while she uttered a mild reproach towards her brother. "Gentlemen, welcome to our humble house! But Jim, you're impossible! You should have told me earlier if you planned to come with gentlemen guests, nothing is prepared, the kitchen looks like a stable and the children will come in at any minute from helping Pa in the pig shed. I can't even offer a decent dinner suitable for your noble guests."

We must look like peacocks that have landed in a nest of sparrows, Pierre thought, while he smiled reassuringly at their hostess. But his smile had the opposite effect of confusing her even more.

Jim laughed. "Believe me, our visit wasn't planned at all, Maggie. I'm sorry if we've bothered you. The gentlemen helped me out of a big mess and I owe them a service. Can we all sleep here tonight and could you help us to find some clothes for these gentlemen that will attract less attention? Everybody can see now that they're Cavaliers. We must ride on to London tomorrow and if people see them dressed in velvet and silks, you can imagine what's going to happen!"

Maggie wrung her hands. "Of course, you can sleep here! It's your farm after all! I'll prepare our bedchamber immediately, we have nothing better to offer. I hope our noble guests will find it comfortable enough. But for sure, my lords, you must change your dress, you look like gentlemen who support our rightful king and those idiot Londoners will immediately arrest you, if not worse. We've heard terrible rumours down here, those Roundheads must be a dreadful lot. I heard that they even forbid dancing, playing cards and singing in the streets! What's life going to be like without a few small pleasures? But I'm talking too much. Let me prepare you dinner first and then I'll see what I can do to find you suitable clothes."

Resolutely she silenced all protest from Armand and Pierre who assured her that they'd be happy to sleep in the stables. "Certainly not, my lords. I may not be a noblewoman, but I know what a good hostess is. You'll sleep in our bed!"

Like a whirlwind she sped around the kitchen adding water and some ingredients from the larder to the soup was that boiling on the hearth. Meanwhile Pierre, Armand

and Jim settled at the large kitchen table and helped themselves to the bread and ale that Maggie had already brought from the larder.

"No wine?" winked Pierre.

"No wine," sighed Armand.

"Let's drink to the health of our King!" Jim proposed, and raised his tankard.

"To His Majesty!" Pierre and Armand replied. But the ale was surprisingly good and they complimented Maggie on it.

"My husband brews it himself," Maggie answered proudly. "Out here we have to make everything ourselves, we only go to the market in town once or twice a year. We're lucky to have enough land, we can even afford to sell a good part of our harvest."

Her last words were drowned by the noise of four children who bounced into the room like an avalanche followed by their mud-covered father.

"Mum, the fox tried to get into the chicken shed again. Papa will hunt him down and said I may join him!" cried a freckled boy of seven years. His words died in his mouth as he noticed the two strangers sitting at the kitchen table. He stood there, transfixed, as never before in his short life had he seen such fine clothes, or such fine hats made from leather and the finest felt adorned with an ostrich feather.

The children and Maggie's husband goggled at the foreigners sitting at the table by the light of tallow candles and Jim quickly introduced his guests. But despite his efforts, he couldn't really break the ice, and only the smallest child was brave enough to climb up on Uncle Jim's knee and examine the strangers, his mouth wide open, from the safety of his embrace.

Therefore Pierre and Armand were happy to be able to withdraw into the tiny bedroom that Maggie had vacated for them, sinking into the large conjugal bed that normally would also serve as the bed for two of the youngest children.

"I feel like a giraffe," Armand muttered. "They kept looking at me as if they'd never seen a Frenchman before."

"Usually you like it when people admire you," Pierre quipped.

"Very funny, *Monsieur le Marquis*, very funny indeed."

Although Pierre was convinced he would never be able to close an eye next to his snoring friend, he soon fell deeply asleep and the pair were snoring in unison. The day had been eventful and tiring.

The next morning Maggie was waiting for them with a steaming bowl of porridge. Her husband and the three older children had left early to collect brushwood but

Pierre reckoned that they been sent from the house under firm orders from Maggie. As soon as the guests had finished their porridge and a glass of milk, Maggie pointed to the clothes she had prepared for them. "Those are the old Sunday clothes of my husband and my father, Lord bless his soul. I'm afraid we have nothing better to offer you, my lords," she apologized.

"That's very kind of you!" protested Pierre. "Let's try them on immediately."

They vanished into the bedroom and put on the woollen stockings, breeches and the stiff shirts made from coarse linen.

"I hate it!" Armand complained. "Not only are the clothes ugly, they stink, and do you feel how itchy these stockings are, are they made from nettles?"

"You big sissy! Let's parade around in silk and velvet straight to the gallows, shall we? But look at these breeches, they're far too big for me. Maggie's father must have been quite stout."

Armand looked critically at his friend, deriving some consolation from the fact that Pierre must look even worse than he did in his new clothes.

"My dear friend, you look terrible, there's no other way to describe it. Why not simply put on an old jute sack, you couldn't look any worse!"

"I just love your compliments, my friend."

Jim tapped at the door. "Are you finished, my lords?"

"Almost, Jim, but no more 'my lords', from now on, you'll see."

Pierre opened the door and let Jim in; he couldn't hide his broad grin as soon as he set eyes on the two friends.

"You look very different... quite convincing. Nobody will ever think that you're the King's men."

"That was the intention. But I'll need a belt or I'll lose my breeches," Pierre laughed. "Your father must have been a stout man. And by the way, no more 'my lord' – please just call us 'sir', we must now assume our new identity and will be simply gentlemen travelling back to our home in Wales."

Jim grinned. "Yes, sir, my father liked a good roast and his ale to wash it down – and it showed. I'll get you a belt but I'll ask Maggie to take the breeches in, with all due respect, you do look like a sack, sir."

"Just what I said," Armand stated complacently. "But Pierre wouldn't listen."

"What about the shoes?" Jim asked.

"Absolutely not!" Pierre and Armand cried almost at once.

"I tried them, they're far too tight and too short." Pierre shook his head. "And we'll need the long boots for riding."

"Your boots are far too elegant, they look as if they cost a fortune. Only Cavaliers would wear those."

"What can we do, I can't ride in my stockings?"

"In that case I'm afraid I have no option but to ruin them, that is, if you'll allow me, sir. I'll have to rub a lot of mud onto them and rough them up, they must look old and used."

Armand looked at his gleaming boots and sighed. "There's no end to sacrifices today, I can feel it. Go ahead, Jim, torture me, ruin them!"

Jim looked ill at ease and he cleared his throat.

Armand looked suspiciously at him. "Spit it out Jim, you're about to tell me something else that's going to be very disagreeable, I can feel it."

"It's your hair, sir."

"No!" Armand shouted.

"We must cut it, at least, just a little," Jim pleaded. "No Puritan would ever wear such long hair."

"He's right," Pierre conceded. "Cut it Jim, better you cut our hair than those bastards cut our throats."

"When you put it like that, it has a certain poetry to it," Armand sighed. "It's a comforting thought, at least, that there's not a lot of chance of meeting anybody from France on our journey, they'd make a laughing stock of me at court."

One hour later they left the farm house. Maggie had quickly stitched up the baggy breeches and Jim had done his best to ruin their boots, which now looked muddy and worn. As they were about to leave, a light rain set in and dutifully Maggie asked them to stay on and wait for a dry spell.

"If we wait for good weather in England, we risk staying for another two months at least. Thank you very much, Maggie, you've been most kind. Take this as a thank you." Pierre placed several silver shillings on the table but Maggie refused to take them.

Pierre insisted. "We have to pay for the clothes, at least!"

Jim nodded. "That's alright, Maggie, take the money. Thank you, sister, and see you again, whenever this will be!"

He embraced his sister and they were gone.

***

"Now let the fun begin, gentlemen. Let's ride back to Elham Manor where Jack is already waiting for us." Jim laughed. "I'd love to see the faces of the new owners once they set eyes on those old nags we're leaving behind. They'll have a fit."

"How come Jack's waiting already for us?" Armand asked.

"I asked Maggie's husband to ride over to Elham this morning and tell Jack that everything must be set up and ready by noon. I want to be in Maidstone before nightfall, I have a friend there. It's close to Bossingham."

"I've never heard of Bossingham or Maidstone in my life. You could be leading us anywhere, how should we know? All I want is to get rid of this creature as soon as possible, I'm not even sure she's a real horse. A living insult to my riding skills," Armand muttered.

They traversed the same small stretch of forest they had passed through yesterday and soon the three were heading towards the meadow where Jack was supposed to be waiting for them.

All went smoothly, exactly as Jim had planned it beforehand. Jack had led five beautiful horses to the meadow Jim had chosen. They could be heard whinnying from afar. Obviously the horses were nervous, they must have sensed that something unusual was going to happen.

As planned, Jack was accompanied by a second groom, his best friend.

"Now let's cover our faces, you never know what's going to happen, better make it look authentic."

The friends followed Jim's advice and tied their scarves around their faces, leaving only their eyes free and stormed forward.

"I feel like travelling back in time," Armand grinned. "I rather like it, this reminds me of the time when I was a kid pretending to be fighting against the royal musketeers. We'd always win, of course."

They caught their willing victims and bound Jack and his best friend to a tree. Both men pretended to fight against the masked villains and were howling in protest. Pierre had to stop himself laughing at the whole farce.

Once this was done they set to the task of choosing their horses – not an easy task, as all the horses were of exceptional beauty, and saddled them. Now as they were about to leave Jim fired two shots into the air in order to make sure that their assault should appear as authentic as possible and should alert the guards of the manor to come and free Jack and his friend.

They had just turned their horses, ready to escape in the direction of Bossingham, when they froze in their saddles, as they suddenly heard answering shots from only a short distance away. Seconds later a group of armed soldiers appeared on the horizon.

"God's blood!" Jim cursed. "Those must be the new lords of Elham Manor, coming back early from Canterbury. Let's go, fast!"

Jim turned and galloped at full speed across the meadow seeking the shelter of the forest bordering the pastures, followed by Armand and Pierre. A hot pursuit ensued but luckily the three horse thieves had fresh horses which took advantage of their freedom and set off at a fast gallop.

As they entered the forest, they could hear a salvo of new shots.

"*Merde alors!* They're not joking," cried Armand. "Quick, let's ride on, they're falling behind, their horses must be tired."

Pierre kicked his horse when he felt something burn his arm. But there was no time to stop, he knew that he must follow the others. He couldn't afford to fall behind.

"Left!" Jim commanded. "I know the way, we'll cross a brook over there and then we'll be safe."

Pierre felt the pain explode in his arm – it felt like fire was eating through his arm while he was still alive.

"Keep going!" he told himself. "Must keep going! I mustn't faint or it'll be the end of me."

But why were the trees looking so blurred all of a sudden?

The Sorcerer of London

Colonel Oliver Cromwell left the Houses of Parliament together with a friend. It had been a long day of futile discussions – yet again. Discussions that yielded no result, as usual, and time was slipping away as the news had leaked out that the King was recruiting new troops in Ireland and Scotland. But what did these weaklings in Parliament do? Nothing!

As had become customary, some delegates from the North had sung the praises of the leadership of the Earl of Northumberland, but it was all far too obvious, everybody here knew that they must be on the secret payroll of the powerful earl.

"Does my lord Northumberland truly think that we want to get rid of our King just to put the crown on his head? All of our efforts would be for nothing! Our glorious revolution, our brethren who died for their faith; should we sacrifice all of this for the vanity of this man?"

His friend made soothing noises, he knew that Cromwell could go on for hours once he was convinced that the revolution, *his* revolution as he saw it, was in danger of being overtaken by what he used to call the forces of darkness and evil.

"We need Northumberland, of course, he secures large territories for us. But we cannot continue to rely on the armed forces of the old nobility and the untrained militia of the gentry. We have to build a new army and I have my ideas as to how this army should look."

His friend listened with awe to the plans Cromwell sketched out.

"But Oliver, this means that the head of the new army will become the most powerful man in the kingdom!" he exclaimed.

Cromwell turned around, his eyes burning with the light of the fanatic. "Exactly. One man, enlightened by the Almighty, this man will have only one noble task: to purify this country. Believe me, this is the only path to redemption! If we fail, this country will fall back into the dark ages, into the clutches of the Catholics, with only superstition to guide us instead of pure faith. Imagine: people dressed in cloth of gold praying to dusty bones instead of worshipping the Almighty! But the Lord will guide us, the good Lord has enlightened me and my brethren: we shall win! The forces of evil will be banished!"

As they parted his friend drew him into an embrace. "Oliver, I'm your man! Let the Almighty guide us! See you tomorrow again in Parliament."

Cromwell bade goodbye to his friend. Still feeling elated by his own speech, he made sure he saw his friend disappear among the London crowds before he hired a coach, as his next visit had to stay absolutely secret; it was an extremely delicate appointment.

The coach driver stopped in front of an inconspicuous timber building in a shabby part of the city, far away from the elegant quarters where the noble families resided. Cromwell was content to have his pistols and his sword close by, for this part of London had an infamous reputation.

"Wait for me!" he ordered the driver.

The driver, having recognized the military bearing and the fine quality of the fabric that Cromwell was wearing, was hopeful of a generous tip and accepted gladly.

"Aye, Sir, I'll be waiting here!"

Oliver Cromwell looked carefully to his left and right. It would be disastrous for his reputation if he were recognized in front of this house. It might look run down and insignificant, but everybody in London society knew this address, for it was the home of London's most powerful and fashionable fortune teller.

The fortune teller himself was an enigma, a man who had arrived in London about a year ago, from nowhere. His accent had a southern twang, but did he originate from the Ottoman Empire, from the depths of Russia or the sunburnt shores of Spain or Italy? Nobody knew. To make things even more secretive, the man had never revealed his true name. Nobody had ever seen his face, as he wore a black leather mask whenever he received his customers. The fortune teller was a riddle nobody had been able to solve so far.

Not only were his services rumoured to be outrageously expensive, but he had in fact created an uproar when he had informed his customers that he'd only accept payment in golden coins, in French louis d'Or, adding in a haughty voice that they could keep their cheap English silver coins for themselves and should better stay away if they couldn't afford to pay him.

Regrettably the fortune teller had a point, as it was generally known that every single English king or queen occupying the throne during the past hundred years had tampered with the quality of the coinage in order to stretch out the contents of the always emptying royal coffers. Now, in times of civil war, who with a sane mind would still trust the English shilling? No matter if the coins were minted in the name of the King or Parliament, only gold could be trusted.

Some influential people had tried to scorn the fortune teller, had accused him of being a charlatan not worth his money. But those voices were silenced fast as soon as several spectacular events he had forecast were known to have become reality. Since that day there was no end of people flocking like devoted pilgrims to his door – who cared about rumours of dark arts and sorcery as long as he could foretell the future?

It was in fact the Marchioness of Edgehill who had been one of his first prominent customers. Burning with curiosity she had visited the fortune teller. Only two weeks later she lost her husband in a riding accident – exactly as had been foretold to her.

Her husband being twenty years older, her tears for the defunct Marquis were quickly dried, as consolation in the form of a dashing viscount was already waiting for her. The now dowager Marchioness spread news of the secret fortune teller's success among her friends in the highest circles in society – in the greatest confidence of course – and in this age of war and uncertainty, everybody was eager to listen and to knock at the fortune teller's door, wanting to know their own future.

But this fortune teller was a difficult man. He only accepted select customers, choosing them carefully but without any apparent reason. Many gentlemen or gentlewomen found themselves rejected, knocking in frustration at doors that firmly remained shut – regardless of the amounts they offered just for the honour of being received.

To his surprise, Oliver Cromwell had been among those who had been received. The fortune teller had not only received him, but he had forecast his success and fast ascent through the military ranks. This came as a complete surprise to Cromwell, as he had never received formal military training and in his mind had seen his future in Parliament. But the fortune teller had been right – in the military his career had advanced fast, and the army had become his new home.

Today Cromwell felt exhausted and tired. Not only had discussions in Parliament been long, tedious and boring (as usual), but to make things worse, he hadn't slept well last night. Didn't the holy scripture forbid fortune-telling? Had he been lured into the sin of curiosity by the forces of evil? Late at night, Cromwell had been sitting in his chair, the holy scripture in his hand, tormented by his conscience. But finally – it must have been early morning by then – the Lord had shown mercy and enlightened him.

He, Oliver Cromwell, was not going to see the fortune teller for his personal profit. He was going to seek him out for guidance, as the tribes of Israel had sought and received divine guidance from the prophets of the Old Testament. Comforted by this logic, Oliver Cromwell had extinguished his candle and had found the peace of mind and the sleep he had been longing for, but it was to be a short sleep only, as he was expected to appear in parliament early in the morning.

Still ill at ease, Oliver Cromwell let the iron knocker bang against the solid oak door. Almost immediately the door was flung open and a young man in dark livery greeted him with a punctilious bow. The young servant was exceptionally handsome but it would have been impossible to guess his origins. His black hair and olive-coloured skin were witness to Spanish, maybe even oriental blood, but he had piercing Nordic eyes, a most unusual combination. His livery was of the darkest grey, almost black, and no coat of arms adorned the simple cut of the waistcoat, but once again, first appearances were deceiving.

The livery and the servant's breeches were made from the finest lambswool that only the weavers of Flanders could produce, the shirt with a deceivingly simple cut collar was made from soft silk – his dress revealed only at a second glance that it must have cost a fortune. It was most unusual to squander that kind of money on the

106

clothes of a mere servant, a frivolous display of luxury in times of war and economies.

The young servant greeted the visitor. "Welcome, Colonel, please follow me to the waiting room."

Oliver Cromwell followed him through a dark and narrow corridor into a surprisingly large room. He was still ill at ease as he sat down on the comfortable armchair that was offered to him. A remainder of doubt still lingered in his mind – how could he be sure that the forces of evil were not guiding him?

Cromwell's Puritan soul abhorred the display of wealth that greeted him inside the room. The heavy silver chandeliers were lit with genuine beeswax candles. The candles spread their agreeable scent, mingling with the subtle smell of perfumed spices brought from the Ottoman Empire. The walls were hung with paintings and woven tapestries showing mythological scenes and landscapes in ancient Greece. The floor was covered by thick silk carpets, so soft and shiny as he had never seen before, not even in the royal palace of Whitehall. As the carpets absorbed all noise, the room was silent as a graveyard.

"The Master will receive you as soon as he's ready. He's still saying his prayers," the servant informed him and placed a bowl of nuts and glass of straw-coloured wine on a low table next to him. Oliver Cromwell scowled. He hated to be kept waiting.

The servant closed the door behind and Cromwell was left alone. Having nothing better to do, he inspected the bowl, as he had never seen such kind of nuts before. They looked almost like beans, light brown, with cream-coloured shells that opened shamelessly to display their tempting green kernels inside. He decided to try one of them and found it surprisingly tasty. The wine was excellent too, sweet and mellow such as he had never tasted before.

The young servant entered the room where his master received the guests. "Our guest is here, my lord."

"What does he want, Antonio?"

"The same as everybody, my lord, to drink from the fountain of your lordship's wisdom," Antonio grinned.

"Don't be insolent. What does he really want?"

"My friends tell me that Cromwell is hatching plans, together with several of his men, to create a new army."

The fortune teller whistled. "Planning to take over power in this country?"

Antonio nodded. "A professional army with a new leadership, no longer under the command of the old lords. If they succeed, Parliament will no longer have anything to say in this country."

107

"Right, Antonio, but if he succeeds, not only will Parliament lose its power, but the King and all the leading noble families will go down. At best they'll become puppets, and he'll be pulling the strings." *It was a wise decision to invest some money and bribe clerks in the Houses of Parliament,* he thought. *Interesting to hear from the clerks those things that will never be put down in writing. Everybody thinks of them as part of the furniture, but they have eyes and ears and understand very well what's going on, maybe better than most members of parliament.* Aloud he continued, "What's the general idea, will Cromwell succeed?"

Antonio scratched his head. "The Dutch have promised a lot of money if he and his allies go forward. Not directly of course, it will arrive through the usual channels, the Earl of Warwick and of course Lord Holland are in on the game and will be supporting him."

The fortune teller frowned. "From what we know, Cromwell holds a lot of sway with his fellow army men, and if he receives enough money and has some powerful families behind him, it will be difficult to stop him. What about Northumberland and Essex? Can they stop him?"

Antonio took some time to reply. "Essex certainly not, he's too stupid. Northumberland doesn't seem to understand what's going on under his nose, he's too conceited and still thinks that the Stuarts are his only enemies."

The fortune teller nodded. "Exactly my understanding as well, Northumberland is too arrogant, he can't even imagine that an upstart like Cromwell could ever become a danger for him. Let our visitor wait a bit and help me to prepare the room, we want it to look fearsome and rather macabre today, I have a reputation to uphold."

Antonio grinned and lighted the candles in the skull that was placed to the left of the fortune teller. Then he removed the polished crystal ball from its hiding place, placed it on a scarlet velvet cushion close to the skull and extinguished the remaining candles in the room. The room now looked dark and foreboding, the only light cast onto the fortune teller coming from the lighted skull and its eerie reflection in the crystal ball.

"Which mask today?" Antonio asked.

"The red one for a change."

"You'll frighten the poor colonel, master."

"Hold your tongue, remember where I found you," came the sharp reply.

Antonio fell to his knees and kissed the fortune teller's hand. "I'll never forget, my lord."

The fortune teller watched Antonio leaving the room. One night – almost a year ago – the fortune teller had been looking for some entertainment in a sleazy brothel close to the docks on the River Thames. It was there that he had found Antonio, a youngster without a name and without a history but with a beautiful face and body – and those brilliant, piercing eyes.

The fortune teller had invited the boy to come and stay with him and, as the young man had no name he was attached to, they had agreed to call him Antonio from then on. No one knew how old Antonio was, anything between late sixteen and early twenties was possible. A product of a more or less passionate embrace between a cheap port whore and an unknown father, Antonio had spent his life in the port of London, selling unsavoury gin, Spanish fly or his own body to any customer who'd offer enough money to help him survive to the next day. There had been enough vice in his short life to vouchsafe being sent to hell for all eternity on the final day of judgement. But Antonio was clever. In the taverns of the port he had picked up several languages – and now had made a considerable effort to polish his English.

Very soon the fortune teller had discovered that Antonio was a valuable asset for his business and trained him to become his spy and factotum. Never had he come to regret his choice. Antonio had become his door to the world, his eyes and ears, allowing him to enter the highest circles of society and astound his customers.

It was Antonio who had developed the idea of bribing the groom of the unlucky Marquess of Edgehill and making him saddle a young and shy horse, unused to the noise and traffic of London, and it was Antonio who had scared the young horse to make sure that it would rear up and unhorse the Marquess. Their prophecy of a deadly accident had been fulfilled and from that day on their reputation was secured.

***

"The Master is ready now, his hour of prayer and contemplation is finished," the young servant announced to Cromwell.

Cromwell rose and accompanied Antonio into the room where the fortune teller received his guests. The door was opened by the servant, slowly, as if his entrance were part of a religious ceremony. Cromwell stopped on the threshold, holding his breath.

An eerie sight greeted him: the fortune teller was sitting behind a carved desk, wearing a mask glistening in the candle light, the bright colour of fresh blood. The only source of light came from a collection of candles, bright flames burning inside a skull. The skull had been cut open at the rear, shedding its light like a halo onto the fortune teller while its gaping mouth grinned at the visitor with its remaining teeth – was it mocking him?

Oliver Cromwell was not a man endowed with a vivid sense of fantasy, but this sight left him speechless.

"Sit down, Colonel," said the voice behind the mask. "I gather you have been promoted since we last met?"

Oliver Cromwell cleared his throat. "Yes, sir, indeed."

109

"What kind of service can I render you this time?" asked the dispassionate voice behind the mask. Maybe it was the effect of the mask, but the voice sounded detached from this world, almost ethereal.

Cromwell had rehearsed his speech several times, but those cold glittering eyes and this unnatural voice behind the mask were unnerving him. Finally he pulled himself together and answered, "I want to know … if my… plans will succeed," he stuttered.

"That's what most people want to know when they pay me the honour of a visit," the voice answered politely.

"… and if my plans … shall receive the blessing of the Almighty," Cromwell added with an effort, his face flushed, ashamed of behaving as awkwardly as a young boy, rather than the future leader of the new army.

"You don't tell me which plans you're talking about, Colonel, but then of course you could object that it's my role to know what you're talking about."

Cromwell prided himself on having a sound mind and being a good judge of other people, but this faceless voice escaped any judgement. The voice continued, even and devoid of emotion. "Your plan is very ambitious, Colonel, very ambitious indeed. If you succeed, you'll change the course of history. You know this, of course, therefore you judge it wise to try to find out if your bold plan will be blessed by the Almighty. But in your mind you've decided to go forward anyhow, you're ready to make the ultimate sacrifice for your faith and for England – even if it won't be called a kingdom anymore."

Cromwell jumped up, shocked. "You know about my plans? Who else knows?"

He could hear the mocking smile in the voice now as the fortune teller replied, "Of course I know, I'm not one of those charlatans who tell silly young girls that they'll meet the husband of their dreams if they pay me in gold. I have the gift. I can see the future, this is why you've come and this is why you'll pay me handsomely. I know a lot of things about many people, but their secrets are safe with me. You're not the only one in London who's thinking about the future of this kingdom. Don't worry, I never betray the confidence of a customer."

Cromwell wiped his forehead and sat down again. "Will I succeed?" he finally asked again. "Will my people follow me?"

"Yes, they'll follow you," the voice said. "But stay away from London, first you must win the hearts of your soldiers. You'll never succeed if you stay in London."

Cromwell nodded. "I see this now, you're right."

"Of course I'm right," confirmed the voice.

Cromwell sat on his chair, brooding. "Will the Almighty give me his blessing?"

110

"Why don't you ask one of the preachers of your church?" the voice replied coldly. "Why would you ask me? You don't even know my faith."

Cromwell hesitated, finally answering in a low voice, "Because I need to know the truth … I absolutely need to know the truth, and my brethren in faith may be biased and blind in their eagerness to fight against evil. Will the Lord truly bless my venture?"

"I can't tell you… today. Come back in fourteen days, but I warn you, I'll charge you again. If the Lord will speak to me, I shall be able to tell you the truth. If not, I'll tell you that I don't know. But be warned, the Lord giveth and the Lord taketh away. Think about Abraham and the price he was willing to pay. You'll need to pay such a price as well, that much I can tell you already."

The voice snickered and pointed at the crystal ball. "I didn't see this in this ludicrous ball. I had a true vision. Are you prepared to pay the price?"

For a minute, Oliver Cromwell was taken aback. He had the impression that a cold hand had touched his heart. Finally he whispered, "I'm prepared. And I'll come back, I need to know!"

Minutes later Cromwell was back in the cab. Somehow it felt comforting to get back to reality, to normal life. The London clouds were still black and brooding but a light rain had washed away the acrid smoke and made breathing easier.

"The Lord giveth and the Lord taketh away," the cold voice had told him. If the Lord demanded a sacrifice, he was ready to make it. He would change the course of history, he was sure about that now. In truth he was ready to sacrifice everything, even his own soul. He must save this country from a rotten aristocracy and a king who was a papist at heart. He had a mission to accomplish.

He had only one true love, one obsession: England.

***

Antonio returned after he had made sure that Oliver Cromwell had climbed into his cab.

"You left our good colonel quite rattled, my lord."

The fortune teller laughed. He had an attractive face, although a large scar disfigured part of his right forehead.

"He'll come back, charge him four louis d'or next time."

Antonio whistled. "That's a lot, will he cough up that much money?"

"He will, he's hooked. Now help me out of the chair, I'm going to lie down."

Antonio helped his master out of the chair and with Antonio's help he limped upstairs to the bedroom.

"This London weather is poison for my body," the fortune teller stated.

"Soon we'll have enough money to travel south, my lord. You promised to show me Italy!"

"Did I?" replied the fortune teller, but for the first time his voice held a note of affection.

Antonio kissed his hand. "You did, my lord, and in the depths of your heart you know that you need me."

"I didn't know that I had a heart. Let's hope that you're right."

Heading for Oxford

"Follow me!" cried Jim and directed his horse straight through the forest. Low-hanging branches blocked their way, a constant menace for the two other horsemen who were speeding behind Jim. They bent low, crouching low over their horses' necks in order not to be swept to the ground – or worse, to be impaled on the sharp end of a branch.

Their luck held. Jim's strategy was working and the sound of the pursuing soldiers was growing more and more distant. Soon the forest thinned out, and the trees were no longer a solid obstacle, but had changed into smaller clumps of trees, until they reached the bank of the brook Jim had mentioned earlier, but in winter it had swollen to the size of a small river. Well nourished by heavy winter rains, the normally tame waters had spread and inundated large parts of the river banks, a formidable flood that swept along at full speed, carrying all manner of dead trees and debris. It was here that Jim stopped his horse.

"Now let's cross the river, but beware, it's quite deep after the rain of the last few weeks. The good thing is that soldiers from Elham won't be able to follow us, their horses are too tired and they're too heavy with their iron cuirasses and arms. Once we've crossed the river, we'll be safe," Jim panted.

"Let's go! I'm not scared of a bit of water!" Armand cried. He was relishing this new adventure and drove his horse straight into the muddy river.

Pierre was the last to follow. His sight was blurred, and it was pure instinct that made him follow the others. What had happened to his eyesight? His grip on the reins slackened but luckily his horse followed the lead of the others and went straight into the river.

The water was ice-cold, which was a blessing as the sudden cold woke Pierre up and numbed the pain in his arm. By a whisker he avoided falling into the swollen waters as his horse swam through the river, following the trail of the two horsemen in front of him.

Ages later – or so it seemed to him – they reached the other side of the river, half dead, frozen and stiff.

"Let's go on now, my lords, my friend's farm is not far away, we can hide the horses in his stable and sleep there over night!" Jim cried, his face flushed.

"Yes, let's go! What a pity I won't see their faces when they set eyes on the old nags we left behind for them!" Armand cried, in high spirits.

Hearing no reply from his friend behind him, he turned around. "What about you, Pierre? Are you ready?"

113

"Is that you, Marie? I can't hear you?" Pierre answered.

Amazed, Armand saw his friend slowly slide from his saddle towards the ground.

"*Merde!*" Armand cursed. "Jim, quick, come before the horse panics, Pierre must have been hit by a stray bullet!" He pointed to thick undergrowth bristling with holly bushes still adorned with their red winter berries. "Let's hide in here."

They tethered the horses to a tree and Jim helped Armand to drag Pierre into the shelter of the bushes.

"How can Pierre be so heavy when he looks as thin and pale as an asparagus stalk," Armand complained, trying to mask his rising concern with a joke. Closer examination showed a gaping hole in the left arm of Pierre's soaked jacket, where the river had washed the wound in his arm clean. But now, as Pierre leaned against a tree, blood started to seep out of the wound again.

"He's been hit by a bullet from those bastards, it's a miracle that he didn't faint before and fall from his horse." Jim was furious. "Those pigs almost killed him."

"Pierre's tough as shoe leather, even if he doesn't look it." Armand tried to sound confident but he was worried. Jim continued to examine the wound, which must have caused Pierre considerable pain, but Pierre barely reacted.

Jim frowned but didn't reply. Luckily he was not given to bouts of panic, and was already tearing a spare shirt into strips. "We have to stop the bleeding and he'll be fine, the cold water has helped and I don't think that the bullet is still inside his body. As far as I can see, it's just a flesh wound."

They were distracted as the noisy pack of the pursuing soldiers had reached the other side of the river. Armand tore his mind away from his suffering friend and hastened to silence their own horses. Hearing the whinnying of the horses and the shouting of the soldiers on the other side of the river, they were starting to grow nervous.

The Elham guards were shouting at each other, apparently disagreeing as to what to do next. Some were pointing to the opposite river bank, indicating that they were willing to cross the river, but the majority were apparently refusing to follow. After nerve-wracking minutes and further long disputes, the Elham soldiers turned around and disappeared back into the forest, firing their weapons into the air to vent their frustration.

Jim's ruse had worked.

"We'd better wait a bit, you never know..." Jim whispered.

"I agree, it could be a ruse and they might come back again," Armand replied.

They waited half an hour until they dared to leave their hiding place. In the meantime all Armand could do for Pierre was to wrap his friend in his coat, trying his best to keep him warm in his arms.

"I'd better put Pierre on my horse," Armand suggested.

"We don't seem to have any other option, your friend can barely hold his head up, he can't possibly ride a horse. Let me take care of the other horse, luckily it's not too far now." Jim tried hard to appear optimistic.

"What do you call 'not too far'?" Armand asked suspiciously.

"About three to four miles, sir."

"Hmm, I wish you'd said 'only a mile'. Let's ride on, the faster my friend can be got into a bed, the better."

After what seemed like hours, the hazy silhouette of a forlorn farm in the midst of vast fields appeared on the horizon and Armand uttered a long sigh of relief as they approached the weather-beaten limestone building that huddled behind thorny hedges planted many generations ago.

"That's my friend's farm. Don't be surprised, Bill hardly ever talks, but he's a close friend of mine and will take good care of us." Jim grinned. "I bribe him with a good bottle of smuggled wine from time to time, that's our deal."

Jim was proved right. Bill hardly raised an eyebrow when Jim and his strange guest carried an almost unconscious Pierre straight into his tiny bedroom. Realizing that Pierre was severely wounded, he helped undress Pierre and tucked him with surprisingly tender movements into a warm bed, which he covered with an additional fur blanket on top as soon as he realized that Pierre was shivering with cold.

Armand was relieved. Not only was his friend in good hands now, but he also noticed that the bleeding had stopped. A sip of homemade, strong liquor brought a bit of colour back into Pierre's cheeks. Only minutes later Pierre lay sleeping peacefully in Bill's bed.

"Thanks, Bill, the poor gentleman needed rest badly. But now it's about time to restore our own strength. Anything we could steal from your larder?" Jim asked full of hope.

"Yes, I'm as hungry as hell! Dinner sounds like music to my ears," Armand proclaimed and added after a short pause, "By the way, thanks a lot to Bill and you, Jim, you were a tremendous help!"

"Nothing to thank us for, sir," Jim answered gruffly but Armand could see that his compliment had pleased him greatly. "But now it's time we got rid of our wet clothes or we'll definitely catch a cold."

Both men stripped out of their wet breeches and stockings and huddled in front of a bright fire, wrapped in blankets while their clothes and boots were drying close to the fire.

"That feels so much better!" Armand sighed.

"Bill, do you still have a bottle of the wine I brought last year?"

"Of course, Jim, it was far too precious to finish it all by myself."

"Then let's open a bottle or two – the gentleman will pay you, don't worry."

"You're my guests, no need to pay. But I need to feed my pigs first," Bill answered and made for the stables. Minutes later they could hear the noise of excited pigs battling for the last morsels of their evening food.

"First time in my life that a pig was granted priority over me," Armand reflected. "A sobering thought –my father will be in fits of laughter when I tell him."

Jim grinned. "Bill's a farmer, his animals will always come first."

As soon as he came back into the kitchen, Bill banged a large cast iron pan on the stove, and minutes later bacon and eggs were sizzling in fat, emanating a smell that made Armand's mouth water in anticipation. A visit to the larder produced a loaf of bread, cheese, a bowl with nuts, apples and pears preserved from last autumn's harvest. Next to the pan, a solid black iron pot was steaming on the hearth.

"Chicken broth, nourishing, but nothing fancy for the gentlemen," Bill apologized. "But hot soup is best for your wounded friend."

"I'm famished. Thank you so much!" Armand raised his cup. "To Pierre's health!"

Armand and Jim ate in silence, savouring the food. The heavy wine spread like an agreeable fire throughout Armand's body.

"The wine is delicious, where is it from?"

"Somewhere in Spain, the wine happened to be part of my booty when I crossed the Channel for a … let's call it an excursion," Jim grinned.

"Truly exceptional! Next time think about me when you cross the Channel!" Armand laughed.

They wolfed down the food that Bill had prepared for them, praising their host who told them they should stop talking nonsense, eat up and shut up.

Armand was fighting sleep but the effect of the heavy red wine combined with the heat radiating from the fireplace was overpowering. He wanted to thank Jim and

Bill, say something witty, but suddenly his eyelids dropped and Armand fell asleep, right in his chair.

"Them nobles," Jim looked at Armand with a smile. "A bit of riding and they're dead tired."

"Aye, them nobles," Bill replied. After a long pause he added, "Where're you riding to?"

"Better you don't know," answered Jim.

"Aye, I may look like a hermit, but I know a cavalier when I see one," Bill replied unmoved.

"Still, better you don't know."

Bill grinned, took up his cup. "To the King, may he have a long life!"

"To the King!" Jim replied and emptied his cup.

"I'd better look after the wounded gentleman, he must have some soup before the night is over. He lost a lot of blood."

"Thought I'd lose him on the way. Didn't want to tell his friend, but it was tight."

"I'll better give him some more soup then," Bill concluded and set to the task of feeding a sleepy and very reluctant Pierre.

***

Antonio opened the door of their house and entered the hallway. The cook was preparing lunch and the tempting smell of a venison stew was wafting through the house. Antonio inhaled the delicious smell; it still seemed like a miracle to him that he could have a meal every day. How often had he gone to sleep tormented by an empty stomach!

His master was already waiting for him as Antonio was the only one allowed to serve him at table. As he entered the dining room the fortune teller was already seated at the table, reading a book in some foreign language. At least Antonio was convinced that it must be a foreign language. He had never learnt to write or read therefore all books looked secretive to him and utterly fascinating. One day he'd learn to read, he had sworn that to himself, he'd make the master show him.

"Before you start serving the meal, Antonio, tell me if there is any news."

"There's always something going on, my lord. Parliament is bracing for a new battle with the King, or should I say with Prince Rupert. Lady Hay, the sister of the Earl of Northumberland has a new lover."

117

"Nothing new there, she likes to change. Has she dropped my Lord Pym?"

"Not completely, my lord, nobody ever knows for sure what Lady Hay wants and whom she fancies. She might come back to my Lord Pym's bed sooner or later."

"So I gather, she doesn't know herself, typical woman. Now as we've covered war and love, is there any other news?"

"Yes, but it's back to war actually. Colonel Cromwell has been discussing – secretly, or so he thinks – with my Lord Pym the financing of his project, he calls it the new model army. His lordship was greatly impressed and has promised his support to come up with a scheme for how to fund it."

"That's important. We will therefore tell the brave colonel that I have had a vision and he has heaven's blessing. Pym has a lot of influence – and he has the skill to find the money. Bad tidings for King Charles indeed, I hope he's already drawn up his last will and testament..."

"There's something else, my lord, an event that might improve the situation of the King." Antonio looked up, studying the face of the fortune teller.

The fortune teller frowned. "That's important then. What on earth could happen to save the King?"

"There're rumours that the young Duke of Hertford has landed in England and that he's on his way to Oxford. Rumour also has it that he has promised a lot of money and a whole battalion of Italian mercenaries to the king."

"The Duke of Hertford!" The fortune teller almost spat the words out, his face went scarlet, and only his scar pulsed an angry purple as if it had taken on a life of its own. It was a frightening sight.

"Are you sure?" he exclaimed.

"Yes, my lord, I'm sure. The Marquess of Halifax is furious, he had to move to smaller lodgings in Oxford because the duke outranks him. He sent a message to Lord Pym, he's considering changing camp now and joining Parliament in London. The news is fresh, not a lot of people will know about it. The duke hasn't arrived in Oxford so far, nobody knows where he is and where he'll land, but he's supposed to be arriving any minute from France."

The fortune teller had calmed down. "If he comes from France, he'll have to pass through Parliament territory unless he chooses to land in Cornwall – but that seems unlikely. Things can happen, must happen, on his way... Antonio! I congratulate you, you're worth every penny."

"But you never pay me, my lord."

The fortune teller allowed himself the shadow of a smile. "I tend to forget that, but didn't you tell me that you'd be my slave forever? An expensive slave all the same, look at your livery."

Antonio grinned, unabashed. "Don't they say that good and devoted servants are priceless?"

"You may shut your mouth and serve lunch now," the fortune teller commanded, ignoring the last statement.

"Yes, as it please you, my lord," came the meek reply.

The fortune teller preferred to eat in silence and Antonio knew better than to irritate his master further with a flow of conversation he knew his master wouldn't appreciate. His master's bouts of temper were legendary. Cook had told him, swearing Antonio to confidence with big eyes, that the previous valet had simply disappeared, overnight! She had rolled her eyes: "He's a sorcerer, never forget that, and beware, Antonio!"

But Antonio had only laughed. "If the master ever casts a spell on me, I hope that he'll turn me into a horse or a dog, I'd hate to become be a frog, or worse, a snail."

Cook had made a face and shrugged her shoulders in despair. This lad was far too careless and cocksure!

But Antonio didn't care. He had seen with his own eyes that the sorcerer's tricks were nothing but trumpery. How could he believe Cook? She was nothing but an old superstitious woman. And yet, an inner voice told him to be careful with the master as life had taught him to assess men quickly. He sensed that his master was not only a man of great charisma, but ruthless, a dangerous man. But didn't this also make him fascinating?

Lunch was finished and for Antonio this was the sign that he was allowed to converse again. "May I tell cook that you appreciated her lunch today, my lord?"

"You may, not that it will make any difference," came the bored reply.

"Did I understand correctly that your lordship would like me to ascertain the Duke of Hertford's whereabouts? And do I also understand correctly that your lordship wouldn't be too chagrined... if some kind of accident, even a fatal one, might befall his Grace?"

The fortune teller's ice-blue eyes suddenly blazed. "You did understand correctly. As I'm... indisposed..." pointing to his lame leg, "I am counting on you, Antonio. I want something to happen to him, the duke must die."

"Is the duke your enemy, my lord?"

"Worse, Antonio."

The fortune teller smiled, but it was not a pleasant smile. "He's my cousin."

On the Way

It soon became obvious that Pierre had escaped by a whisker, and it was only sheer luck that the bullet had only penetrated his arm. Armand didn't beat around the bush. "Dear Lord, you bled like a stuck pig! You must stay in bed at least another day."

No protest would help, Pierre was compelled to stay another night tucked firmly into Bill's bed before he felt strong enough to get up and try to mount his horse.

"I feel as weak as a kitten," Pierre moaned as he finally succeeded in mounting his horse.

"You're mewing like a kitten," his unfeeling friend replied. "Just be happy that it's not your funeral today."

"What a wonderful friend you are," Pierre muttered.

Armand looked critically at his friend. "You can't ride like this, you look like a ghost. We'll stay on for one more day."

Thus they spent another day emptying Bill's hidden reserves of wine and his larder before the party of three could finally leave for Oxford.

It soon transpired that Jim was an excellent guide, who knew the countryside like the back of his hand. Keeping an eye on Pierre they chose a moderate speed while they zigzagged across fields and unknown forests, avoiding the busiest roads and made large detours around those towns that were known to be in sympathy with the detested Roundheads.

But their mood, buoyant at the outset because they had mastered so many challenges, soon became more sober. As they were riding through the countryside they discovered the ugly face of a country in agony and torn apart by civil war: untended fields, the grim skeletons of burnt houses, horrifying gallows with swaying corpses – all grim reminders that there were winners and losers in this strife and that the winners wouldn't be lenient with those who simply had the bad luck to be on the wrong side.

Armand was used to the ugly face of war, he had seen it often enough in France. But he couldn't help noticing that not only had the country changed, more importantly, so had the people. Laughter, fun, colour had disappeared, replaced by a new severity and an air of sobriety that covered the country like a sickening mildew, suffocating the joy out of life.

"What are the Roundheads doing to this country? It's becoming a prison," Armand stated with a shudder, not really expecting an answer from his friend.

"Bringing the tidings of joy and eternal life down here on earth?" Pierre proposed.

"If paradise is in any way comparable to this country as it looks now, then send me to hell, please!"

"That's where you'll end up anyhow, I'm sure a nice, warm place in the fires of hell has been reserved for you already," Pierre joked.

"You know what's good about that?" Armand asked giving it some thought.

"Not really?"

"All the interesting people will be there as well – and most probably all of the exciting women will go to hell as well."

"You have a point there," Pierre admitted. "It does sound most probable. Giving it a bit of consideration, the promises of heaven do sound a bit boring."

Jim only grinned. "Let's meet down there then! By the way, we've almost arrived at our destination."

"Hell?"

Jim laughed. "No, Oxford! A sort of hell maybe, after all I've heard. Early this afternoon we'll be there. The next town is already part of the King's territory. But now we face a new challenge."

"What kind of challenge?" Pierre asked.

"We have to explain why we look like Puritans," Jim answered. "They won't like it."

"You've got a point. What a pity that I had to leave my beautiful hat at your farm! It cost me a fortune. I'll never get such a nice feather in Oxford," Armand lamented.

Jim and Pierre exchanged a knowing smile. It had not gone unnoticed by Jim that Armand was extremely vain when it came to his appearance.

***

In the end they managed to avoid unpleasant encounters and any kind of awkward questioning by the loyal subjects of His Majesty. It didn't take long before the spires of Oxford came into view. As they approached the town, they could see that Oxford had been transformed into a city at war. Large fortifications had been erected around the city, fitted with cannon and surrounded by moats, ready to defend the city against the enemy.

As they reached the outer fortifications they were immediately stopped by the guards.

"Hey, three blind mice walking right into the trap, are we?" a portly soldier with a large moustache smirked. "Tell us what kind of mischief you're up to. We can always help with a pair of thumbscrews if your memory should fail you. Did you really think that we'd let any of you stinking Roundheads walk freely into this town! Start saying your prayers, you'll be greeting the Lord in Heaven in no time."

"The Lord in Heaven will have to wait," Jim replied. "These gentlemen are Cavaliers in disguise and are expected by the King."

The second soldier laughed. "Nice try, mate. My friend is the pope in disguise. I don't see any gentlemen, I just see stupid, green Puritan youngsters destined for the gallows."

"You'd better open your eyes then," Pierre replied, "or you'll be sent to Ireland – I imagine that's probably worse than hell. Let me speak immediately with your commander, you may show him this ring as my identification."

Pierre took the heavy seal that he had inherited from his grandfather from his finger, showing the proud coat of arms of the dukes of Hertford and their fighting stags.

"You may tell your commander that Pierre de Beauvoir, Duke of Hertford, has arrived. Maybe he still remembers me, I stayed several months at Whitehall Palace, I know most of His Majesty's officers."

The soldier digested this speech delivered with the natural arrogance of a titled gentleman. He looked at the ducal ring complete with its coronet and strawberry leaves and it dawned upon him that he might have made a mistake, the kind of blunder that could get him in a lot of trouble. He still looked suspicious but his attitude had changed. "I'm just doing my duty, sir, ahem, my lord. I'll go and fetch the commanding officer now, please wait for two minutes."

It still seemed rather improbable that this youngster, dressed in the drab clothes of a Puritan and wearing a rather abominable haircut, should be a true peer of the realm, but Pierre's self-assured pose had impressed him greatly. Furthermore he had heard rumours that the Duke of Hertford was expected to join the ranks of the King – this was an open secret in the army, as everybody was speculating what reinforcements he would offer the King while the officers were worrying which battalion the young and inexperienced duke would be leading into the next battle – and into probable extinction.

It therefore seemed wise to report to his commander and leave all further decisions to him. Life had taught him never to meddle with the likes of the aristocracy.

The commander appeared quickly, ready to have the imposters arrested and sentenced. It seemed utterly impossible that the Duke of Hertford would arrive without his retinue of guards and in the disguise of the arch-enemy. Never had he heard such a crazy story before!

"I may look a bit strange to you, Sir William, I hope you remember me. We played tennis together at Whitehall." Pierre greeted the officer with a crooked smile.

Sir William was flattered that the Duke of Hertford remembered the occasion and his name. His face flushed scarlet with delight. "That's very kind of Your Grace! I must admit that your disguise has almost completely deceived me. Let me apologize for the rough reception, but in times of war... "

"We had to ride through the territory of the enemy and decided that it would be better to avoid any undue curiosity."

"Very wise, Your Grace, we're living in strange times indeed. Let me be your guide, it's my pleasure to be Your Grace's servant."

"Your friend is a duke?" Jim was flabbergasted. "He never said a word, he's so young, how can he be a duke?"

Armand grinned. "Not only that, he's a French Marquis as well. But why should we have told you, you brought us safely to Oxford, that's all we needed."

"I've travelled and dined with a genuine duke," Jim said to himself. "Bill and my sister will never believe me!"

Sir William called four soldiers to improvise a guard of honour and slowly they rode through the cramped and narrow streets of Oxford to the venerated college buildings that had been converted (under strong protest from the university dean and the Oxford townsfolk) into the new military headquarters and provisional royal court of His Majesty, King Charles. For a brief moment in history Oxford had become the capital of the Royalist Great Britain – and its inhabitants deeply resented the disturbance caused to their peaceful life and the new role that had been imposed on them.

They passed through a city that resembled an army camp in a state of siege. The city, known as the cradle of learning and boasting the oldest university in England, had lost its peaceful sleepiness. Soldiers dressed in proud colours strolled around while their loud voices, the whinnying of their horses and the grinding noise of cart wheels echoed through the cobbled streets. All kinds of military equipment and debris occupied the little space that had been left inside the fortifications and the first rows of thatched houses.

"It's a bit cramped," Sir William commented good-humouredly. "Oxford was only chosen because it's damned easy to defend and we're close to London. His Majesty is confident of being back in London by the end of the year at the latest."

"We all hope to see His Majesty back in Whitehall as fast as possible," Pierre replied politely, but as they rode towards New College with its imposing bell tower his doubts increased that this city was indeed hosting an army destined for glory.

"What do you think?" Pierre whispered to his friend as they dismounted from their horses, having arrived at the sprawling college building that served as the temporary headquarters of King Charles.

"*Un désastre*," Armand answered in French, in order not to be overheard. "*C'est le chaos*. Look at the soldiers, either they're standing around idle or they're strutting around like peacocks, there's no discipline, no proper training going on, they don't even realize that it's a bloody war. I've heard that Prince Rupert is an excellent leader, but how could he ever succeed with an army that's in such bad shape?"

"I've no experience at all in these matters," Pierre admitted, "but it does look strange to me."

I have to find a way to get our heads out of this noose before it's too late, Armand decided secretly. But as Armand was ever ready to be optimistic he added aloud, "Soon we'll meet Cousin Charles, it can't be very long before he arrives here from London. I bet he'll give us some good advice."

Sir William handed them over to a pompous royal servant dressed in livery embroidered with the King's coat of arms. The servant introduced himself as the person in charge of overseeing the lodgings, but – he insisted – only for those high ranking aristocrats who were considered to be guests of His Majesty.

He led them to a suite of two small rooms, complete with a salon and a pleasant view onto the courtyard. The servant stressed several times that this apartment was nearly as big as the Queen's own suite and should be considered a sign of royal grace and appreciation. On the same floor there was a bigger room, equipped with several beds. This room had been reserved to accommodate the duke's entourage.

Pierre pointed to Jim. "This is all the entourage we have for now, not that impressive, I admit," he smiled. "But I'm sure that soon enough more servants will be brought over from Hertford."

Jim didn't mind having a big room all to himself, especially as he had been promoted on the spot to the position of duke's valet.

Assuming his new importance, Jim took control of their small household and was soon exhibiting all the hallmarks of the arrogance expected from a duke's valet towards those he considered to be mere minions, especially to the young page boy who had quickly been recruited. Jim regarded him as his personal slave and had no qualms sending his new servant relentlessly on different errands around the college grounds.

But however hard he tried, Jim's abilities as a perfect manservant proved to be limited.

"If only Jean were here," sighed Pierre.

Jim had done his very best to find suitable breeches, clean stockings, shirts, lace collars and fur-lined silk waistcoats for the two gentlemen, generously bribing other valets to open the chests of their owners as no tailor in Oxford could be trusted to deliver clothes suitable for an appearance at court in a matter of hours. Jim had also done his best to polish up their boots – but as they had been ruined before by him, no shoe polish known to man could ever restore them to their former splendour.

"I wish as well that Jean were here. I look simply dreadful. These breeches are too loose and this waistcoat is a joke, I look like a stuffed sausage! How can I ever face the King in these clothes?" Armand lamented.

Pierre snorted. "Don't worry, the King will primarily be interested in knowing how much money we can offer. His Majesty won't be bothered too much about our clothes. I'm afraid that there's not a lot of splendour or sophistication left at this court, we're not in Paris."

"But I still have my standards when it comes to dressing. And this," he sent a vile look at his image in the mirror, "is most definitely not up to standard."

"Me neither," Pierre replied. "But we're expected to support the royal cause, by tradition, it's our duty. So we'd better not complain, it's pointless."

"Well that's what we're going to tell everybody, at least: that we're staunch supporters of His Majesty, staunch pillars of support he'll be able to count on. But now, let me tell you what my father would advise us to do: best be done with this comedy as fast as possible and leave England, but of course taking care not to damage our reputation. My old man is a fox, he can smell trouble miles ahead."

"Abandon the King, like the famous rats leaving the sinking ship?" Pierre's voice was bitter.

"You could say that... intelligent animals, by the way, my father always says. Man has never been able to beat them. Maybe it's about time that we learned from them?"

Pierre made a face but he had to admit that Armand had a point. If the Saint Paul family had survived and had become one of the most powerful families in France over the course of the past centuries, this was certainly not due to a blind fervour in following their anointed kings or queens. Kings came and disappeared, but the Saint Paul family stayed on, always keeping their own interest firmly at heart.

"I found a tailor, my lords!" Jim burst into the room, interrupting Pierre's thoughts triumphantly.

"Jim, your manners need urgent improvement, a valet is supposed to knock or scratch at the door first!" Armand was not amused.

"Forgive me, my lord, but I thought you'd want to know immediately – I'm sure that you'll be delighted."

Indeed Jim was soon forgiven as he dragged a scrawny man behind him into the room, bent with age and totally awed by the fact that he should be working for a peer of the realm.

Armand looked at him with suspicion. "Are you really a tailor? Not that any more harm could be done to these clothes, they look like rags already, but how can we trust you to make us look presentable?"

The small man was flustered but catching the accusing tone of Armand's question he pulled himself up to full height, which wasn't much, and full of indignation exclaimed, "Of course I'm a tailor, my lord, I even worked for one of the Queen's maids of honour recently!"

"Hmm, let's hope she had more taste than honour, but let's give it a try. We have no time to lose. Can you put some kind of shape to this waistcoat and make my breeches fit? This lace collar looks like a bride's veil, it's impossible!"

"Of course, my lord, it will be done immediately."

The tailor hummed around the two friends like a busy bumble bee, taking their measurements and placing pins in the most awkward places. He left them with a promise to be ready in the evening, just in time to attend the dinner invitation that had been delivered by a royal page boy earlier.

"I wonder what Charles and François are doing right now? And I must send a message to Marie saying we have arrived safely in Oxford. She'll be worrying about me day and night."

"Knowing Cousin Charles, he's probably eating. Whenever I meet him, he's always telling me that he's hungry."

Pierre had to laugh. "That's him, he's always hungry. I hope that François isn't bored to death sitting in London, how good it will be to see them again. I do miss both of them!"

**

"Nothing, sir, nobody has seen or heard anything about two strangers."

François de Toucy sighed. He had come to expect such an answer. They had combed through even the smallest villages and towns close to Dover, had knocked on the door of every inn in the vicinity – but to no avail.

Had there really been nothing? Now, as he tried to remember all the different encounters with more than a dozen inn-keepers (fat, bald, sympathetic, arrogant, lean, tall – a surprising variety, in fact), there had been one, who in hindsight had appeared fishy, far too smooth when it had come to answering his questions.

Where had it been? Close to Elham or Whitfield? Or maybe in Barham? François didn't remember. He'd need to ask his groom Benjamin, these villages with their thatched houses, endless pastures and the square towered, weather-beaten churches all looked the same to him. But in retrospect this man had been an elusive character, a smooth talker, almost too friendly – and hadn't his assurances not to have seen any strangers been a bit too smooth? An inn located only a few miles from Dover was bound to see strangers – at least from time to time.

It was a difficult game he was playing. As a French Huguenot wool merchant, François was supposed to appear humble and grateful for any information that was proffered to him – it was difficult enough bringing up the subject of two French cousins who might be travelling together through the English countryside without raising any eyebrows or encountering open hostility.

François crept into his bed and blew the candle out. The bed was uncomfortable, damp from the winter rains and he tried hard to ignore the stench of mould that emanated from his straw mattress. But his mind was still on the inn close to Dover. He had made his decision, tomorrow he'd take action. If François had experience of one thing in life, it was that his intuition almost never failed him.

Soon sleep overwhelmed him. Being stuck on the back of his horse the whole day had taken its toll. Searching the countryside for the two friends had never promised to be an easy task, but as nothing concrete, no trace worth following, had appeared until tonight, it had been an endless nightmare. Pierre and Armand had vanished from English soil as if they had never existed.

The next morning François gave orders to Benjamin to ride back to the coast. After a short discussion with his groom it had become clear to him that they must ride back to Barham. This meant more hours on horseback but it left François enough time to develop a strategy to get the truth out of the inn keeper. His face was grim; his strategy wasn't going to be a very subtle one.

A soon as they reached the inn, François gave orders to Benjamin to enter the tap room and send the innkeeper out to the stables under the pretext that his master had a problem with his horse and needed urgently to speak to the landlord. Waiting for Benjamin to come back, François took cover close to the entrance of the gloomy stable.

The stable was filled with acrid smells wafting over from the pig sty. François wondered if it had ever been cleaned at all. The only other inhabitant of the stable was a pitiful mare that had been chained to its empty stall, too old and too tired to care about the stranger.

Minutes later he could hear the puffing noise of the innkeeper arriving.

"What's the matter with your master's horse? Why couldn't he wait or come himself, does he think he's the King? I have plenty of things to do, many important guests are expected tonight, I'm not a rich man, I have to work and have no time to be idle."

He continued complaining as he waddled into the stable. François waited until he had passed the entrance door. Then he jumped forward, like a vengeful devil from the very depths of Hades.

The innkeeper screamed like a stuck pig as a monster closed its iron hand around his jowly neck.

"If you want to live, tell me where the two Frenchmen are right now, you know, those men who stayed at your inn about a week ago!" breathed the voice next to his ear while those terrible hands of iron seemed to be wringing the last remaining air out of his lungs.

"I'll tell everything," he gasped, "but let me breathe…"

"I'll let you live, but only if you tell me where they are."

"I don't know, sir, but let me live, I'll tell you everything I know!"

François loosened his grip. The fat innkeeper choked and greedily inhaled the stinking stable air. But as soon as he recovered his breath, he tried to bargain with his captor. "What will you pay me for the information?"

François didn't answer but the merciless hands started squeezing the innkeeper again until he started to stutter, "Let me live, I'll talk!" he moaned.

"Two gentlemen speaking French were brought to my inn by two acquaintances of mine. They stayed one night here and then they left – they pretended to be ill. But it was all a sham! They shackled me and left me helpless – without paying their bill! For me those two can go to hell, both of them!"

François heard enough genuine indignation in the voice of the inn keeper to find his words credible, only he didn't believe that mere 'acquaintances' had brought Armand and Pierre to this sleazy place.

"I'm ready to believe that they left, but tell me who brought them to you and why, if you want to leave this filthy stable alive."

The inn keeper was writhing like a snake in his hands, but he was no match for François. Knowing he was beaten, he croaked, "I'll tell you all. But let me breathe!"

"Go on then. Tell me!"

"It was two of my friends from Dover who brought them. They had overheard that two French bigwigs were expected to arrive in the port. By chance they overheard a conversation between two men, who should have served as their guides. The rest was easy, they followed them, lured away one of the guides with the help of a whore and the second one was put out of action easily with the help of two drinks and quick blow to the head. The plan was to keep the French gentlemen here as guests in my inn, everything had been prepared for their comfort."

"I can believe that," said François, his voice pure sarcasm. "Every comfort indeed. And in the meantime you'd have auctioned them to the highest bidder, either in London, Oxford or in France. You're a bag of scum, a just fit for this stinking stable of yours."

The inn keeper cringed at these unflattering words.

"Bind him. I don't want him to raise the alarm when we're gone."

In no time the inn keeper was bundled and placed roughly like a sack of grain on one of the horses.

"What are we going to do with him?" asked Benjamin, who had thoroughly enjoyed the whole scene.

"Lose him somewhere in the woods. Maybe dump him in the nearest river," François answered, ignoring the vivid protestations of the inn keeper. "I couldn't care less. Then we must ride back to London, let's go!"

François didn't know what to make of the story. It seemed obvious enough that his friends had escaped the trap that had been skilfully set for them – but the idea that they must be riding right now through enemy territory made his blood run cold – how could they possibly reach Oxford safely?

Suddenly the sun broke through. "Let me take this as a sign from heaven. They must have a guardian angel – or be in league with the devil, those idiots. They'll probably reach Oxford before I do."

***

"What's the matter with Jean?" Pierre's wife, Marie, asked Céline. "He's so distracted, I have the impression that it's getting worse every day."

"I wouldn't worry too much, Jean tends to be a bit moody. Maybe he'll be back to his normal self tomorrow, you know, he's always worried when your husband is absent."

Céline put down on a low table the play that she had been reading; despite having a lurid title it had not lived up to her expectations. She noticed that Marie was still frowning at her. "Calm down, Jean's always been a mother hen when it comes to looking after Pierre."

They were sitting in the large, sunny drawing room of the chateau that Charles Neuville had acquired for his wife Céline after their son had been born in Reims. Life would have been perfect if only their husbands hadn't left on a madcap journey to a war-torn England.

"It's our duty, a question of honour!" the men had explained in one voice. Céline didn't share either of those opinions. Yet, she knew that the opinion of a mere female didn't count for much in such matters. Women were supposed to agree with their husbands and keep quiet. Therefore she had deemed it much wiser to keep her mouth shut and her rebellious thoughts to herself. Secretly she was of the firm opinion that women were a good match for, if not superior to, any man when it came to matters of intellect and to risk one's life for matters of honour seemed to verge on stupidity to her. Men might outshine the female sex when it came to hunting or any kind of physical exercise, but as for the rest…

"I'll be looking after little Pierre in the nursery," Marie finally decided. "I feel like I haven't seen him for ages. "

"You're right, it must be two hours at least," Céline replied with a wink. "But I'll come as well. I'll have a look in the stables in the meantime, one of the new stallions apparently created a lot of commotion this morning. I'm curious to see if he's settled down. The horse is one of Charles's expensive follies – I hope he hasn't made a costly mistake. My father was just the same when it came to buying a promising horse, he was prepared to spend a fortune."

"The difference, however, being that Charles has the money and your father didn't," Marie replied.

"That's true, you can't imagine how comfortable it is to wake up in the morning and not have to worry about how to pay the servants. It was so embarrassing."

They parted on the best of terms. Céline put on a woollen coat as winter in the Champagne region was wet and cold. An icy wind was blowing from the east as she crossed the courtyard and she was content to be entering the shelter of the warm stables. Inside the stable building she almost bumped into Jean who was standing in front of a horse box, staring into the darkness.

"What's the matter, Jean? This box is empty, what are you doing here?" Céline chided him gently. "You've been really absent-minded recently, don't pretend that it isn't true. I know you too well. Are you worried, is it something related to the Marquis?"

Jean blushed, although it would have been difficult to see in the half light of the stables, as he had inherited the soft bronze-coloured skin of his Caribbean mother.

"It's nothing, my lady, please don't worry yourself. I apologize if I have not been attentive enough. I will take more care in the future," he answered stiffly.

131

"Jean, that's not fair, you're not telling me the truth. I swear I won't say anything to Marie, but you must tell me what's really going on, you look dreadful!"

Jean opened his mouth, with the intention of denying it, but suddenly he broke down. "I can't sleep at night, my lady, it's those dreams again."

"Dreams? Related to your master?"

"Yes, Ma'am. Not dreams exactly, it's more like nightmares. My master is in danger and I… I can't do anything to protect him while I'm here."

Céline looked at Jean with alarm. She knew that he had inherited a sixth sense from his mother, and had learnt to take Jean's visions very seriously.

"In danger? We all knew that going to England in such unsettled times would be risky, but would you be able to tell me more?"

"In my dreams, there's a man, a man of evil intentions, but I don't know who he is. He's hiding his face behind a mask and has a laughing skull in his hands. It's dreadful."

Céline suddenly felt a chill, although the stables were warm and comfortable. "That sounds terrifying, indeed. Jean, you have to leave for England and warn Pierre and Armand. This sounds very alarming."

"But I had to swear to my master that I'd look after Marie and their child. How can I break my word?"

"Jean, don't come to me with another silly story of honour and duty. I've had enough of this brainless stuff. I'm perfectly capable of looking after Marie and the child, I have a son as well and he's thriving, although always hungry like Charles. It's your duty to warn Pierre now and let me take care of the rest. Tomorrow you may leave for England, let me think up some story that we'll tell Marie."

Tears welled up in Jean's eyes although he tried hard to keep a straight face. "Thank you, Ma'am. You may have saved me from becoming insane. I'll leave for London as soon as possible. I know that my master needs me. I must go, you're absolutely right."

***

Dinner had been an informal affair, although the table had been covered as usual with plenty of mouth-watering dishes.

"Cook simply can't get used to the fact that Charles is absent, she always prepares way too much," Céline complained while contemplating the table, trying to decide if she should opt for cheese or the apple pie. The pie won.

"The servants will be happy to finish the leftovers." Marie shrugged. "I always tell you that you spoil them too much."

"I can't forget the time when I was poor and my old servants looked after me, nurse even took on some tailoring work to pay for our daily bread and cheese," Céline explained with a forgiving smile. "Old habits die hard. But let's change the subject. I have a very difficult request to make and I hope that you won't be terribly upset with me."

"Of course not, whatever I can do, I will do. You're not only my cousin, you're my best friend as well."

"Thanks, Marie, that's very kind. Do you remember the letter Charles sent some days ago?"

"Of course I do, you read it to me. I hope that Pierre will send me a letter soon as well, he really should do." She frowned.

Céline steered Marie's thoughts firmly back to Charles's letter, not wanting to discuss the fact that Pierre hadn't sent any message to Marie since he had arrived in England.

"Charles said that they had all safely arrived in Dover. But I overlooked a line that he had scribbled underneath, you know Charles, he's a bit forgetful from time to time."

Céline could only hope that these words would never reach the ears of her husband. Encouraged by Marie's smile she continued. "He forgot one of his seal rings, a ring he'll need to finish some legal transactions in England. I've been thinking of sending a messenger but I think that I'd only trust Jean to take it, the ring is very valuable and must not end up in the wrong hands."

"I wouldn't mind, Céline, really. The fact is that Jean will be delighted to join Pierre, but don't you think that Pierre will be very upset? He's such a darling, he has almost chained Jean to my side to guarantee our comfort and security here."

"I'll take that responsibility. But I'll be greatly reassured knowing that the ring will be delivered safely. Pierre will certainly understand this. Do I have your blessing to ask Jean if he'd be happy to render me this service?"

"Of course, don't be a goose, I'm convinced it would be much better for Jean to go to London. He's sitting here with a face that could turn milk sour, he's dying to see Pierre. It'll be a relief for all of us when he's gone. I'll write a letter for Pierre tonight. Jean can deliver it."

Oxford

Armand looked at his reflection in the polished silver mirror that Jim was holding in front of him. He frowned. "Move the mirror to the left." His frown deepened. "Now turn it to the right." Armand sighed.

Jim held his breath, finally plucking up the courage to ask, "Are you not satisfied with the tailor's work, my lord?"

"How could I be satisfied? I look like a provincial country squire, you can smell the stables when you look at me. Elegance is a notion that seems to be unknown in this country. Look: simple silver buttons, not even mother of pearl. At court in Paris I'm used to wearing diamond buttons…"

Armand shook his head, unable to believe that the image in the mirror could be him. He looked again at Jim. "But you may tell the tailor that – taking into account the shortage of time and lack of decent cloth – I won't criticize him too much and he may work for me again. I need riding attire worthy of a gentleman. Tell him to be ready tomorrow. I can't possibly mount a horse in my old clothes, I hope you burned them."

Jim looked relieved and turned to Pierre. He'd worry later about how to satisfy the whims of my lord Armand who was acting with all the nonchalance of someone who had never in his life needed to bother about practical details of household life or dealing with tailors and shoe makers. His eyes turned to Pierre. "And you, Your Grace, are you content with the tailor's work?"

Pierre smiled. "I won't surpass anybody tonight when it comes to matters of fashion, but maybe that's just as well, we've created enough turmoil with our arrival, or so I've heard. It's better if I don't outshine anybody. But I'll also need some more clothes such as some decent riding attire, can you take care of that?"

Jim nodded in agreement. In truth he couldn't find any fault with either of the gentlemen. He had never seen such elegance before, he simply couldn't imagine that anybody could look more fashionable or more handsome than his masters. Pierre's blonde hair might be too short for the prevailing fashion of the Cavaliers, as was Armand's short curly brown hair. But both were exceedingly handsome and dressed in gleaming silks and velvet. Jim was sure that they'd create an uproar among the female members of the court and a lot of envy among the gentlemen as soon as they set foot in the great hall where a stately dinner was to be served tonight in their honour.

A royal lackey had been sent to guide them to St Alban's hall, which was located among the other college buildings, a hall with gothic style triangular arches that towered over the other college buildings in the vicinity. It looked impressive, more like a church nave than a college building, providing the majestic setting for tonight's stately dinner.

For many centuries it had been customary for English royalty to travel with their court through the countryside, an old tradition dating back to medieval times. Setting up a temporary court in Oxford therefore had been almost a routine task for the royal household and all amenities deemed necessary for the royal couple had been moved to Oxford.

Preceded by a royal lackey who walked at a dignified pace, Pierre and Armand entered the hall where their entrance was announced by a royal herald who rattled through their long list of titles with the ease of long practice. Armand stayed behind, as Pierre was a duke and a peer of the realm, and so took undisputed precedence; anything else would have been unfitting and a severe breach of royal protocol.

"We greet our beloved cousin, the most noble Duke of Hertford." The King rose from his golden armchair to embrace his visitor, a rare and telling gesture of appreciation.

Both men exchanged formal greetings as dictated by court protocol, in a language and style that must be centuries old. Exchanging formal kisses, Pierre looked closely into the King's face. He had met King Charles three years ago, but tonight the King looked at least ten years older. Pierre discovered a man worn out by a never ending succession of daily disasters, almost waiting for the final blow to come.

The King's eyes were blood-shot from lack of sleep, and he looked exhausted. His Majesty's valet had done his best to rejuvenate the King's sagging cheeks with the help of make-up, but Pierre thought it simply made things worse, and the King just looked like a painted parody of the powerful sovereign he had once been.

After this ceremony had been finished, Pierre stepped forward to greet Queen Henrietta Maria and pay her the formal compliments that were due to a queen. She was eager to greet him, lapsing immediately into the comfort of her native French. Having never really felt at home in this strange country called England she craved news of her home country and the last rumours circulating at the court in Paris.

The Queen's pregnancy had taken its toll on her health, but she was vivacious as ever, wanting to know plenty of details about her family in France: was her nephew, the little King Louis, thriving, and how was his mother, Queen Anne? But behind this façade of benign talk, there lurked something. Pierre could almost smell it – the Queen was scared.

Suddenly Pierre felt a pang of compassion for his sovereigns, two people who had been catapulted by the whim of history into a position that was becoming more and more precarious day by day. Whom could they trust? Who would really defend them and their cause? When would the next disaster befall them?

"Hertford, may I present to you my son Charles, the Prince of Wales?" the King intervened and made a sign to his eldest son to step forward.

Pierre held his breath. He had seen the prince as an infant boy from time to time at court, but now as he approached manhood, his swarthy complexion had worsened. The prince's face was now dominated by a prominent, hook-shaped nose. Whatever the court scribblers might write down, trying hard to embellish the truth, the prince could only be qualified as being exceptionally ugly. But as soon as the Prince of Wales smiled at him with his brilliant and wistful eyes, Pierre forgot his first impression and he smiled back warmly before executing a bow of greeting. Immediately it struck him that this prince had a rare quality. He might be no beauty, but the Prince of Wales could engage people, make them want to follow and serve him. If ever his father lost the struggle for his throne, Pierre thought, this young prince might be able to win it back.

Armand stood several yards behind, waiting for his turn to be called forward and greet the royal couple. Having nothing else to do, his glance roamed around the hall, assessing the various members of the court in the hope of finding a lady his own age. A stately dinner had been announced and all the courtiers had dressed in their best finery, with precious furs and expensive jewels. The country might be suffering, but so far, its nobles were not.

It was obvious though that the ranks of the nobility present at court had shrunk considerably compared to numbers he had seen three years ago. Armand recognized many faces from his last stay in Whitehall, but he also discovered some fresh faces. Young aspiring knights who had just started their career at court, eager to win their spurs. Those young gentlemen were probably content to be born in this era of war and upheaval where promotions and titles seemed so easily gained.

All of a sudden, as he had almost given up hope, Armand discovered a new face. The world stopped turning, his heart was pounding like a hammer. Right behind the Queen, there stood a young maid of honour, a lady of such outstanding beauty that he didn't dare to trust his own eyes.

He pinched himself – was she real? He marvelled at her wonderful copper locks, barely tamed by a dainty cap that matched the brilliance of her golden gown, when her eyes suddenly met his, eyes of the intense blue of cornflowers, promising the heat and the pleasures of summer.

Armand was spellbound. He knew that his behaviour was grossly impolite but he couldn't tear his gaze away from her. Did he see the shadow of a smile on her face? He must meet her, talk to her!

The herald's staff banged on the floor once again, impatiently. "The Right Honourable Armand de Saint Paul, Earl of Worthing." The herald's voice echoed through the hall.

Armand suddenly awoke from his trance, addled and almost blinded, and stumbled forward, as it was his turn now to greet the royal family. He felt awkward, like one of those mechanical dolls he had once seen at the court of Louis XIII in

France, dolls without a human brain but who would move and even eat by the means of some miraculous hidden mechanism inside.

But the court routine of many years helped, and he greeted the King and his son who now stood next to him, finally proceeding to greet the Queen who was still sitting on her golden armchair. He had to force himself to kiss the Queen's hand as he was immediately distracted by the presence of the beautiful lady in waiting who stood behind the Queen's chair. She was so close now that he imagined inhaling the sweet scent of her perfume.

He couldn't help but stare at her once again, but the lady looked straight through him: beautiful, stunning, unapproachable, aloof, a goddess.

I must speak to her, he thought, while he answered automatically some polite questions that Her Majesty had the graciousness to address to him. *I must.*

Armand's mind was made up. He'd move heaven and earth to conquer this lady.

***

Later a sumptuous dinner was served in the Great Hall. Whereas Pierre was seated at the table of honour among the royal family, Armand found himself seated further away. While his thoughts were still revolving around the mysterious maid of honour he was seated next to a neighbour who had certainly passed his sixtieth birthday, an Irish earl, as he found out. From time to time his lordship mumbled something into his grey beard in a language and with an accent that Armand was incapable of understanding.

"Don't even try to understand what father is saying, we gave up ages ago," sounded the cheerful voice next to him.

Armand grinned. He took an immediate liking to the young man, who introduced himself as Martin. The young gentleman had a boyish face framed by a short fair beard, a short Roman nose and laughing grey eyes with a tint of blue that gave him an aura of innocence, belied by the mischief that lurked behind his gaze and promised a sharp sense of humour. Martin assessed Armand and they decided they would become friends.

"We're from Cork, Ireland, if you have any idea where that is!"

Armand smiled apologetically. "Not a clue, thanks for giving me the hint about Ireland – should I know anything about Cork?"

Martin sighed. "The truth is, almost nobody does. We might as well come from the moon. But we breed the best horses in Ireland, that's why we're here. It's no secret that the King needs fresh horses, plenty of well-trained battle horses, actually."

"Let me introduce myself then," Armand answered, ready to go into details.

"No need, Armand, the whole court has been gossiping about both of you for weeks, I think we know more about you than you'll ever know about yourself."

"Court gossip," Armand nodded knowingly. "I'm not that surprised."

"Exactly. In fact, the court has become, well, shall we say, a bit more secluded than in the past. We know each other far too well, cooped up in such a small city. This has been going on for months now and it's become a bit boring, not to say tedious, to see the same faces every day. No surprise that everybody is happy when new blood arrives. We like juicy scandals too, but who doesn't?"

"I understand, we were the talk of the town. What do people say about us, if I may ask?"

"Some dislike you, as they think you'll ingratiate yourself with the King, which would mean in due course less influence for others. Some hope that the duke will donate enough money to allow the King to muster new troops and," he grinned, "we hope that he'll be able to buy more horses with your money. Rumour has it that the duke will even buy a battalion of Italian mercenaries." Martin lowered his voice. "This would be immensely costly. Is this so?"

Armand lowered his voice. "Martin, I'm sure you've been at court long enough to know that I wouldn't answer you – even if I knew."

Martin grinned. "I gave it a try. Now it's your turn, you may ask me an impertinent question."

Armand hesitated but then he asked, "How do you judge the King's chances of winning this war?"

Martin whistled. "That's a very dangerous question…"

He looked at his father who suddenly started mumbling something into his beard. Martin translated. "My father says that we all wish that His Majesty will win, but he needs more money, troops and ships. I tend to agree with him. Between you and me, even a battalion of Italians won't make a big difference. We've heard rumours here that Parliament is recruiting a huge new army…"

"I wouldn't like to be in the King's boots," Armand whispered back.

Martin nodded. "Nobody here would, believe me."

They paused for a moment, as a servant was filling their glasses anew with wine. Suddenly Martin turned his eyes again at Armand and he noticed little devils of mischief dancing in Martin's eyes. "Everybody here could see that the lady Elizabeth has impressed you greatly."

"I have an inkling that I know whom you're talking about... Elizabeth is her name? Was it that obvious? I'll need to throw myself at her feet and apologize to her."

"It was, Armand, the royal herald repeated your name three times before you woke up, it was hilarious, you made our day. The court will be talking about nothing else for the next few days."

Armand ruffled his hair in comic despair. "My reputation!"

His eyes were suddenly pleading. "Tell me more about her, Martin. Don't let me stew here. I guess she's not married yet, as she's a maid of honour? Could I meet her? Can you introduce me to her?"

"Elizabeth is the hottest prize here on the market. All men are mad about her. I'm an exception, of course, as I married recently..." Again his eyes were dancing. "Be careful though, Armand. Sir Mortimer claims that he's betrothed to her and has made it clear that he'll skin any man alive who dares to approach his bride to be. So far it has worked and even the most notorious philanderers are keeping their distance."

"Who's this Sir Mortimer, is he here?"

"See the man on the left, two tables behind us?"

Armand turned his head and saw a young gentleman, has face flushed with anger. His eyes were glaring furiously at Armand.

"I'm afraid Mortimer isn't likely to become my soul mate," Armand commented drily.

"I can only marvel at your quick perception, my lord," Martin replied. "I'm afraid you'll be challenged if you continue showing interest in the lady. Mortimer is like a tinder box, ever ready to explode. I guess it's linked to his being a fiery redhead."

"What would life be without a bit of challenge or suspense..." Armand looked back at the table where Elizabeth was conversing with the Queen.

"She'd be worth a bit of trouble, wouldn't she?"

"You'll be risking your life." After a short pause he added with a wink, "But I do agree, she'd be worth it. How sad that I'm a married man now and even worse – my wife holds the purse strings. No more adventures for me."

***

"You made such a fool of yourself," Pierre stated as soon as he and Armand were back to the tranquillity of their rooms.

"I'm afraid I did, but isn't she gorgeous?" Armand had closed his eyes, raving about her. "Elizabeth is her name. A name like music to my ears. She's a goddess! Did you see her hair, like spun copper? I've never seen such a beautiful girl in my whole life. Pierre, believe me, I'm ready to die for her! I must meet her."

Pierre pulled a face. He had heard it all before. "That's the same story you tell me whenever you meet a woman who sets your heart on fire. Please try to remember that your object of worship is a maid of honour of the royal household and the Queen will not appreciate it if you pursue Lady Elizabeth like a stallion in rut."

"Pah, who cares about the Queen?" Armand waved his arms as if he were swatting a fly.

"You should. I have the feeling that we don't have a lot of friends here at court. Most of the men who're close to the King have treated me with the minimum respect they could possibly get away with. It was fairly obvious that they wish me back in France as fast as possible. If you make trouble, it won't help."

Armand came back to reality for a second. "I had exactly the same feeling. We all know that with the exception of the Vatican maybe there's no place more putrid and hypocritical on earth than a royal court, but Oxford is worse: everybody here is constantly on alert."

"On alert, yes – to make sure not to be the last rat that leaves the sinking ship," Pierre added. "There's no doubt about that. And the worst thing is that the King knows exactly what they're thinking."

***

"The King was *quite* taken in by the young Duke of Hertford, how endearing."

The Marchioness of Halifax had invited her husband to join her in her bedroom after both of them had attended the dinner given in honour of the duke, followed by a ball.

"Wait outside, Ellen!" She dismissed her maid as she wanted to be alone with her husband. Frowning at her own image in the mirror she took off her diamond bracelets followed by a diamond necklace adorned with a remarkable centre piece, a ruby the size of a pigeon's egg.

"These beastly eardrops are so heavy, I wonder why I wear them at all?" she mused, not really expecting an answer.

"Because your diamonds are the largest at court, my dear, and you love it when even the Queen is sending you that jealous, almost vitriolic look. She'd give an arm and a leg to own them."

"That's possible, now that you mention it, I do rather enjoy that." She smiled with her thin lips. "How well you know me, my dearest husband."

140

The Marquess of Halifax performed a mock bow. "You're always a source of never ending inspiration to me, Margaret. I understand from your remark that the duke needs to be removed?"

"I adore your powers of perception, dear husband. Yes – and fast. He's young, charming and rich, the King and the Prince of Wales will soon want to count him among their inner circle of friends. And we don't want dear King Charles to be straying from our path and drop you and our son Rochester, before we decide that it's time to leave the court."

"Not as long as King Charles can grant us more titles or land. As long as he needs me, he'll have to come up with a new incentive every month." He paused a moment. "What about an accident?" the Marquis proposed. "Accidents do happen…"

"How crude!" The Marchioness was not amused. "In this small town everybody is watching everybody else, there's always a danger that the truth might be known. Be a bit more subtle and creative, my dear…"

They stared at each other. The Marquess finally jumped up and started thinking aloud whilst pacing up and down. "Send him on a mission to fight the Scots or the Irish with a battalion of untrained losers? He has no experience of leading soldiers, if he never returns, nobody would be astonished."

"He might be more astute than you think. He probably he won't go if his friend, Armand de Saint Paul, doesn't join him. It took me only a minute to understand that this Armand is the clever one, he won't walk into such a trap."

The Marquess replied, "Armand, you may have noticed, is just about to make a total fool of himself over Lady Elizabeth."

The Marchioness smirked. "Most of the men at court do, I'm not blind. We'll need to separate Armand and Pierre. That's essential. Think about some other way."

The Marquess continued walking up and down, then suddenly he exclaimed, "I think I have an idea, Margaret."

"Stop making me nervous with your pacing up and down, sit down and tell me, husband."

"Armand has military experience, he has served in the French army and rumour has it that he's quite astute. I'll have him appointed as adjutant to General Forth. He won't be able to refuse this appointment if the King commands it, he might even be flattered actually, it's quite a high position. We'll pretend to be searching for an even higher position for the duke, as naturally he can't assume the position of an adjutant, being a duke. Some days later I'll have Hertford appointed to lead a secret mission to London."

"A mission to London?" the Marchioness was impressed. "That's even better than an accident, he'll never come back. They hate anybody who's French and will eat him alive. But how to justify sending him into disaster? No blame may ever fall on us. The duke's cousin Charles will kill you if he ever finds out."

"The story will go like this: a secret truce between the moderate forces of Parliament and the King must be negotiated. You remember that a delegation from London contacted us some months ago with the same intention, to set up a secret agreement between the King and Parliament, similar to creating a new Magna Carta. At that time the Queen convinced the King not to enter into any negotiation, blabbering about the forces of evil. But since then the King has lost control of even more parts of his kingdom. I'm sure that he must be open to reason now and ready to put a toe in the water. I'll arrange for the Lord High Treasurer to cover us. The Duke of Hertford will be presented as the perfect mediator, I'll sell him to the King as someone being almost neutral but loyal to the Crown, the ideal man for delicate negotiations."

The Marchioness smiled but her smile was not a pleasant one. "I gather the duke will carry a letter granting him free passage… but I suppose a secret letter will reach London before he does?"

"You can be sure of that, my dear. The King's enemies will be informed on time and make sure that the duke will never reach the negotiating table."

The Marchioness sighed. "Life can be so cruel. Pierre de Beauvoir should have stayed in France. It's much safer there, or so I've heard."

A Royal Mission

His Majesty was not amused. Why had the Lord High Treasurer insisted on arranging this urgent audience, early in the morning, together with the Marquess of Halifax? King Charles had the suspicion that both men – once again – wanted to pressure him into quick action or into taking some kind of fast decision he'd regret.

Of course they'd pretend, as always, to be motivated by the pure and noble spirit of serving the kingdom. They were good at that, they would be smooth, well-spoken, persuasive. This was why he hated them; he preferred the advice of the Queen, never diplomatic, always to the point. The Queen's world was simple, there was good and evil, never was there any doubt. What a pity that his own mind was never that clear, how often was he confused as to whom to trust and what to believe – and what to do?

A servant announced the arrival of both men. They were dressed in sober colours, faces serious, two men ready to tackle the task of a difficult and important mission. The King's heart sank, it must be a grave matter indeed that they were about to broach.

The Marquess and the Lord High Treasurer bowed deeply.

"Your Majesty's servant, forever." The Lord High Treasurer started the greetings. "May I compliment Your Majesty on your speech yesterday, it was an example and encouragement for all of Your Majesty's subjects." He bowed deeply.

The Marquess followed with similar platitudes, and then the King answered in kind – when would the two men come to the point?

"Thank you my lords, I know that the Queen and I have no better and more loyal servants in our kingdom! What is that you wish to discuss with us? The matter must be pressing?"

The Lord High Treasurer made a sign to the Marquess to start.

Halifax cleared his throat. "Your Majesty, we have fresh intelligence that the rebellious forces are gathering a new army."

"That's hardly what I'd call *fresh* intelligence, my lords. The Roundheads have been doing nothing else for the past two years."

"Your Majesty is well informed – as always. But new commanders are being appointed and a whole new army is about to be created and trained. As Your Majesty is aware, we have bribed a clerk in Parliament – there's no doubt that the war will soon enter into a new and potentially dangerous phase."

"And what kind of wise advice do you have to offer to us? How are we supposed to counter their actions, have you found the money we'll need to strike back?" The King's voice was bitter.

The Lord High Treasurer found it about time to intervene. "We've launched negotiations with Your Majesty's son-in-law in The Hague to raise fresh troops and ships and we're very confident of receiving help from Your Majesty's sister-in-law in France. But time is pressing and we should be looking into new avenues until those reinforcements have arrived…"

"Such as?" the King asked, eyebrows raised. He knew as well as his ministers that no reinforcements were on the way.

"Such as entering into negotiations with Parliament, Sire."

"Absolutely not!" shouted the King and leapt to his feet. "Don't you dare!" And then his voice faltered. "I'm a Stuart, by the Grace of God, King of England, Scotland and Ireland, and I shall never surrender to this rebellious mob!"

The Marquess of Halifax took over. "It would be a ruse, Your Majesty, a cunning ruse. We'd engage our enemies in lengthy and useless talks with the sole intention of buying time. Time is all we need to make sure that Your Majesty will crush our enemies, we all know of course that the royal army will be victorious in the end."

The King sat down again. A silence ensued; the King had always been a slow thinker.

"Who would be ready to go into the lion's den and start the negotiations? Whom could we trust? And – are you sure it's nothing but a ruse?"

"Your Majesty has immediately perceived the most difficult obstacle. To be credible, the person must be of sufficiently high rank to be perceived as a true mediator – and yet he may not be important enough to be indispensable for the continuation of our military campaign. We may not risk weakening our ranks in the army – it's merely a ruse after all. The messenger must be seen to be in Your Majesty's trust and favour – but must not be aware of all our secrets, so as to avoid a major slip of the tongue or risk betrayal."

"This is well thought out indeed, Halifax, but where to find such a person? It seems like what my wife would call a *mouton à cinque pattes* – the impossible animal."

"The Duke of Hertford, Your Majesty, is heaven sent, the ideal person for this mission. His grace has just arrived, he doesn't know any details of our military secrets or campaigns. Besides, being one of the highest peers of the realm, Hertford is a member of the Church of England, therefore the duke would be received even by the staunchest supporters of the Roundheads, even if only for reasons of curiosity."

"You suggest sending the young and inexperienced duke to London – why not feed him immediately to the lions? Are you serious?" The King was not pleased.

"Your Majesty, we don't have many options. There would be another advantage to the duke accepting this mission. It would be a strong sign of Your Majesty's support for moderate forces in Parliament and a heavy set-back for the rebellious faction. The war won't stop, but we'd win valuable time to strengthen our battalions. If Your Majesty harbours any doubts, may I suggest that we ask Prince Rupert for his valuable advice? There can be no doubt about the prince's integrity and sound reasoning."

The King's face had taken on an unhealthy pallor during the discussion, as if all blood had suddenly been drained out of it. But the mention of Prince Rupert brought him back to life. "That's an excellent suggestion. I'll ask the prince, he'll advise us. Your proposal still sounds strange to me, but maybe the prince has a different opinion."

I paid the prince's most pressing debts yesterday, the Lord High Treasurer thought. *I'd be truly astonished if the prince should dare to object to anything that I suggest...* "As Your Majesty wishes, I understand that Prince Rupert is expected to lunch with Your Majesty today, that would be the perfect opportunity to discuss this matter in all confidentiality within four walls."

The Marquess of Halifax quickly changed the subject. "Sire, I took the liberty yesterday of speaking with General Forth about Armand de Saint Paul, the Earl of Worthing. We need to find a position that matches his rank. The general would in fact be keen to have him serve under his command. Saint Paul apparently enjoys an excellent reputation in military circles in France and would be a welcome reinforcement to our troops. Would Your Majesty favour such an appointment?"

"Of course, my lords, of course. Any capable man is welcome. I must confess that sending the duke on a mission to London might solve a potential dilemma as well, we have not yet been able to find a position in our army that would reflect his rank, as sadly the young duke has no military experience at all."

"Your Majesty's powers of perception are impressive. The Marquess and I are honoured that Your Majesty has graciously listened to our suggestions, it is our greatest pleasure to be the most humble servants of Your Majesty."

The two men bowed like twin brothers and left the room.

"Why do I have such an uneasy feeling?" the King mused. "Every single word that they said made perfect sense – and yet I'm sure that they want the duke removed from court. I'll ask Rupert, he must decide. Maybe I'm starting to see phantoms where there are none."

***

"I don't know why I ever bought these jewels!" the Queen said to Lady Elizabeth in a petulant voice. "Look at them, don't they look .... *un peu vulgair?*"

Elizabeth took the garnet necklace in her hand and frowned. Suddenly she smiled. "I remember now: Your Majesty wore a dark velvet dress and you were looking for a necklace that would be more subdued than the rubies your late brother sent you as a gift. But I admit that without this special dress the necklace looks a bit bland. But nothing would ever look vulgar if it were worn by you, Ma'am."

The Queen smiled affectionately at Elizabeth, her good spirits restored. "You're right, Elizabeth, I do remember now. Do you want to have them? I think I gave the dress to you."

For a second, Elizabeth was tempted to accept but then she remembered that court gossip was already at the point of becoming dangerous, she had to be extremely careful. The fact that this Armand de Saint Paul had made a fool out of himself in front of the assembled court because of her wouldn't help. Mortimer had been incandescent with rage.

"That's very kind of you, Your Majesty!" Elizabeth sank to her knees. "I don't deserve to serve such a kind mistress. But I cannot accept such a valuable gift."

"Don't make such a fuss, Elizabeth. It's only garnets, nothing special."

Elizabeth looked at the necklace again. "I think it's the setting, Your Majesty. May I suggest having it reset in a new setting, the King will be delighted to see that Your Majesty is willing to be frugal and wear the garnets once more."

The Queen's face lit up even more. "That's a wonderful idea, I'll have them combined with something a little more sober... let's think. Sapphires will do brilliantly! And just a few diamonds to lighten it all up, not too large of course. The King will be so proud to have a wife who knows how to be economical in difficult times. Call the jeweller as soon as possible, I'll request him to make a pair of fitting eardrops and a bracelet as well."

Elizabeth kept her expression under masterful control while she promised the Queen to follow up her requests. The Queen would never understand what the notion of saving money really meant.

Elizabeth took the necklace. "Would Your Majesty grant me leave to see the jeweller?"

"Of course, Elizabeth, tell him to be ready next week, I want to surprise His Majesty."

Elizabeth curtsied but went straight to her room. She needed to think, in peace and quiet.

Since yesterday her life had changed, and her mind was in continuous turmoil. Never had Elizabeth thought that something like this could happen to her. The idea of falling in love had always seemed utterly ridiculous, after all that had happened to her – here at court and back in Ireland. Since she had left home, life had been nothing but an eternal battle: for money, for safety, for power. Love simply didn't happen, it was a concept from a different planet, a planet she must have left ages ago.

But since yesterday evening, wherever she went, whenever the Queen allowed her one minute of calm and reflection, she saw those brown eyes and that short curly hair in front of her, the dashing smile, lips that challenged her, sending shivers through her body. Whenever Mortimer had touched her body all she had wanted to do was to scream and to tell Mortimer to stop – since yesterday she could think of nothing more desirable, more exciting than to be held in the strong arms of this French stranger, to melt into his embrace. *You're behaving like a silly goose, like a young maid*, she chided herself.

In vain she tried to chase those dangerous thoughts away that kept haunting her, and remain cool and composed. But to no avail. In her lucid moments Elizabeth was aware that she must have completely lost her mind. And yet, she wanted Armand, and not only as a lover, she wanted to be his forever.

If this meant leaving her present life and position at court, and journeying to a forlorn corner of France with Armand, she wouldn't mind, so be it. One instant in life had changed everything and she was possessed by only one wish, one obsession: to be close to him and forget the world around her.

There were voices saying that the young Duke of Hertford was even more handsome, but was he really? Elizabeth hadn't noticed, but she knew for sure that her treacherous heart started beating at a dangerous speed as soon as her thoughts turned to the image of Armand de Saint Paul – and this happened far too often for the comfort of her soul. *You're behaving like a fool!* she told her reflection in the small mirror that stood on her desk. There was no doubt, the image in the mirror nodded in agreement. *What a great fool you are, Elizabeth!*

***

Another dinner and ensuing ball had been arranged for tonight, as the routine of court life and a pretence of normality must be upheld at any cost. As usual, Elizabeth would be serving as maid of honour but the Queen had let it be known that she wouldn't mind if Elizabeth danced from time to time. Mortimer would be present and Elizabeth knew that she'd be obliged to dance with him if she didn't want him to create a scene. But nobody could object – besides Mortimer – if she danced with Armand as well. It would be one dance only though, no more, as the courtiers would be out there, watching her. Dangerous beasts they were, scrutinizing and commenting on every move, every smile, every gesture, desperate for a scandal to feed their dirty minds.

I must make sure to leave Armand enthralled, wanting more – but I must remain aloof, send him the message that I'm not chasing after a man. It will be a challenge for me, but that's the only way to keep a man like Armand interested. She sat on her bed, thinking about the best strategy for tonight. She must impress him: the low cut dress with the flesh-coloured bodice that looked almost transparent from afar would be the perfect answer. She knew from experience that this dress drove men wild – and yet it was giving nothing away that would be improper. She'd tame her copper hair with a golden net – bowing to the rules of virginal propriety – which highlighted the glorious shimmer of her hair.

Elizabeth smiled. Yes, she'd look gorgeous, she'd make him mad with desire. In the beginning she'd ignore Armand, then grant him the favour of a single dance. Let him simmer and suffer – just as she was suffering right now.

***

"Your Majesty looks wonderful!"

"Elizabeth, don't flatter me. It's a nice gown, but you know that I'm in a delicate state… I've looked better than this many a time."

"We're all looking forward for a new prince or princess to be born, it will be a good omen in difficult times, Ma'am."

"Maybe, Elizabeth, but it's a fact that I do not look my best. And I know it. Ask the maid to apply some more of the French rouge and the white powder Queen Anne was kind enough to send me as a gift."

Elizabeth thought secretly that the Queen had applied too much already. She looked more like a painted tavern maid than the Queen of England. But she knew her mistress well enough, any objection would be useless, and therefore she instructed the chamber maid to come forward and follow the instructions of her royal mistress. The girl made a questioning face but obliged; she obviously shared Elizabeth's opinion.

"By the way, Elizabeth, Sir Mortimer asked me yesterday to grant you permission for a dance. Knowing that you're almost betrothed, I knew that I shouldn't refuse, you have my blessing."

Elizabeth curtsied, trying very hard to look grateful. "You're too kind, Ma'am." Cautiously she continued, "It might be that the French gentlemen will also ask for a dance, Ma'am. It seems that this is quite common at the court in Paris, for the queen's ladies to engage in dancing after dinner?"

"It is indeed, Elizabeth, now that you mention it. I do remember that our ladies in waiting used to dance after dinner most of the time. I had almost forgotten," she sighed, "but this court will never reach the level of refinement and elegance I was used to in Paris."

She sighed again, travelling back in time. Finally she came back to reality. "Of course you may accept a dance with our guests of honour, the King has insisted that they should be made welcome at court." She lowered her voice. "I'm not betraying any state secrets when I tell you we are hoping that the duke will pay for a battalion of Italian mercenaries, it seems that Hertford is considering His Majesty's request very favourably…"

Elizabeth congratulated herself. Not only had the Queen almost commanded her to dance with Armand, she also had fresh news for the Earl of Northumberland, news that would be worth a lot of money. Suddenly she stopped in her thoughts. *I can't continue this game! I must stop feeding news to Mortimer and betraying the queen, it's time to start a new life. Northumberland is the enemy now.* Her dream of making ever more money had become irrelevant. The new Elizabeth would stop spying on the queen – hopefully it wasn't too late.

***

The next task was a daunting one: she had to keep Mortimer at bay. For today this looked easy enough. Elizabeth sent a page boy with a message letting him know that she'd been assigned to the Queen for the whole day. As she knew that Mortimer was also on duty with the King's guards, her excuse was credible, although normally she'd have tried to sneak away for a quarter of an hour to meet him. Mortimer sent an answer, telling her how much he loved her and that he was looking forward to the coming ball to hold her in his arms.

When the evening came, Elizabeth took special care on her appearance, making her new maid work hard until her copper locks were shimmering in the light of the candles as if a fire had been lit. The envious glances of the footmen guarding the Queen's chambers confirmed that her appearance had achieved the desired effect; they obviously couldn't take their eyes off her.

"You look lovely, Elizabeth, Sir Mortimer will probably never want to leave your side tonight." The Queen was in a good mood today, ready to dispense compliments.

"Your Majesty is too kind, I thought that we needed to show our French guests that the royal court of England can be as elegant as the court in Paris, thanks to the inspiration of Your Majesty."

"Between you and me, that's so true, Elizabeth, I'm doing my best to bring a bit of culture to this country. Not that many people here appreciate this. Do you think we should organize a masked play for the gentlemen? I do hope that they'll stay here in Oxford for some time, the court has become a bit boring lately, don't you think, Elizabeth?"

"I fully agree, Ma'am, the presence of the duke and his friend is an agreeable change, let's hope that it's a change for good."

Later Elizabeth thought that her words must have been prophetic.

***

"Why have you been avoiding me?" Mortimer hissed, his eyes flashing bolts of lightning. Elizabeth looked down and tried to concentrate on the complicated figures of their dance. She needed time to reply. Finally she answered, "I haven't been avoiding you, Mortimer! The Queen has been very demanding, she expects me to attend her even more than usual. Her condition is making her very moody."

She smiled radiantly at him, only too aware that half the court would be watching this little exchange, hoping for a scandal. But Mortimer didn't care about them, his face looked as dark as thunder.

"Why didn't you come to our usual meeting point after lunch, I can't believe that you were on permanent duty – twenty-four hours a day?"

The dance separated them but soon, far too soon for Elizabeth's taste, they met again.

"You've fallen for this ridiculous Frenchman, but I'm not going to take this! I'll challenge him and blow a bullet through his stupid skull," Mortimer hissed.

Elizabeth's smile remained firmly pasted onto her face. "Don't be ridiculous, Mortimer. The Queen has been instructed by His Majesty that we must please the newly arrived guests. If the Duke of Hertford asks me for a dance, Her Majesty has given orders that I am to accept. If you challenge the duke, you might as well sign your last will and testament, the King will never forgive you. The same goes for the other Frenchman, I forget his name, something with Paul, the one with the dull brown eyes."

Mortimer hadn't expected this kind of answer. Maybe he was seeing ghosts? As Elizabeth had apparently forgotten the stranger's name, he must be overreacting. But the mere thought that Elizabeth could be touched by another man or the mere idea that he could lose Elizabeth drove him to madness. Better dead than a life without Elizabeth.

Deep in his heart Mortimer knew that his infatuation was insane, but he was helpless. As soon as Mortimer woke in the morning, he saw Elizabeth's face, imagined touching her lithe body and this obsession wouldn't leave him until he settled down to sleep again. He was almost looking forward to leaving Oxford with General Forth in a week. A fortnight away from Elizabeth might restore his balance of mind. If only those damned frogs hadn't turned up.

After the dance Elizabeth returned dutifully to the Queen's canopied chair. The Queen immediately let her know that she wanted to speak to her. "The Duke of Hertford has asked me if I would grant permission for you to dance with him." The Queen beamed. "Isn't he handsome? And this wonderful, pure French, ah, if only I were young again…"

Elizabeth held her breath, waiting for the Queen to continue and mention Armand, but the Queen changed the topic. Elizabeth's smile remained frozen on her lips while she nodded and automatically uttered some remarks but her thoughts were elsewhere. *Where is Armand? Who cares about the Duke of Hertford?*

She walked to the dance floor led by Pierre, aware that the eyes of the entire court would be following her. The fact that the young duke was married wouldn't matter, the hungry beast of the court was ever ready for a juicy scandal, she must be very careful.

The music started and Elizabeth discovered that the young duke was a pleasant partner. He engaged her in light conversation, danced well and after a short time Elizabeth started to relax and enjoy the dance.

Respecting the strictest formalities, Pierre accompanied Elizabeth back to the Queen's company as soon as their dance was finished. Standing close to the Queen they exchanged more small talk but Hertford's behaviour was above any criticism. Not even Mortimer would be able to utter any reproach.

In the meantime Elizabeth had caught a glimpse of Armand, but that had been all. She was boiling with frustration and anger – how could he dare to neglect her completely? Knowing that hundreds of eyes were watching her, her frozen smile didn't leave her face. But she would find a way to teach this impertinent Frenchman a lesson! If he wanted to play games, she could play as well. Her anger felt good, as it helped to soothe the feeling of disappointment and emptiness that was gnawing at her.

If love felt like this, life would be better without it.

"Are we bored, mademoiselle?" A familiar voice with a French accent suddenly spoke behind her.

The voice continued, smooth and persuasive. "I am, or at least I was, until I found a chance to speak to the most beautiful lady at court."

Why was her heart suddenly beating in a crazy rhythm she had never experienced before, her blood throbbing in her veins as if they were about to burst?

Elizabeth turned her head, forcing herself to look composed. "I am never bored when I'm on duty with my Queen, my lord." Her voice sounded cold and detached – on no account did she want Armand to know that she had missed him.

Armand chuckled. "That's rather difficult to believe. But I marvel at your dedication. What a morose crowd tonight, look at the lady over there with a nose like a beak. I'm sure she's hiding a rotten tooth or two behind her thin lips."

Elizabeth couldn't help smiling, despite her firm intentions of staying aloof. "That's the Marchioness of Halifax – you are very perceptive, my lord, the Marchioness is known to inspire fear..."

"Especially in her husband, I'd imagine." Armand finished the sentence.

"And her son. That's true. They tremble in their shoes when she speaks to them."

"Let's change the subject and talk about something pleasant. Would you grant me the honour of a dance, Lady Elizabeth?"

"You'll have to ask the Queen, my lord, it's not my decision," she replied with a cool voice, although her treacherous heart was jubilating.

"I happened to ask the Queen earlier, didn't she tell you? *Sa majesté* gave her gracious permission and I'm most grateful. But now I need yours…"

Armand looked at her with wide pleading eyes. He suddenly looked so vulnerable – and yet his eyes retained a promising and very challenging look at the same time. How could he do this? Never had Elizabeth met a man like him before. How could he convey the message that he'd be mortally wounded by a refusal – and yet promise earthly paradise at the same time?

"I might consider it, but for one dance only."

"I'll take this for a yes, Lady Elizabeth, one dance only and I promise you as a gentleman that I'll return to this bunch of country bores afterwards, and pretend to be having a wonderful time with them."

Armand led her to the crowded dance floor in the middle of the great hall. The musicians started to play a courante and, not entirely to her surprise, Elizabeth discovered that Armand was an accomplished dancer. But unlike most men he didn't need to concentrate on the succession of the steps and moves, they came naturally to him. He therefore could allow himself to focus his attention on Elizabeth, who felt his eyes caressing her body while she moved to the rhythm of the music.

How often had she performed these moves and turns since she had arrived at court, young, ambitious and so naïve! But until this moment dancing had been a meaningless exercise to her, a mere ritual of court life. Only tonight, all of a sudden, she understood that every move was meant to be seductive, a subtle provocation for the opposite sex, a thinly veiled invitation to her dancing partner.

Elizabeth looked up and met Armand's eyes. His message was bold and explicit: *You will be mine.*

His eyes challenged her. Gone was the pleading, he was now provoking her openly. The dance continued, they met again and the next figures demanded him to take her arm. As soon as Armand touched Elizabeth, molten fire passed from his hands straight into her body. She wanted to withdraw her arm but he held her firmly and whispered, "You're adorable. *Je t'adore.*"

Bewildered and stunned, Elizabeth looked away and it came as a shock to her to discover Mortimer standing only a yard away from her. Mortimer's face was murderous, his lips were pressed tightly together, and his blue eyes had turned to icy daggers.

For a precious moment only, Elizabeth had felt removed from reality and time, but now she came back to earth. Quickly and firmly she withdrew her arm and made sure to touch Armand only lightly during the following moves. Knowing that

Mortimer was still watching her, she remained very elusive as soon as the dance was finished and Armand accompanied her back to the Queen.

"I think I've made an enemy tonight," Armand said lightly as he guided Elizabeth back to the Queen's chair. "Is this murderous looking gentleman your fiancé?"

"Sir Mortimer has given me the honour of a proposal, indeed," Elizabeth answered, hoping to detect a trace of disappointment in Armand's face.

"What man wouldn't?" Armand smiled at her. "Don't tell me that you've accepted this bore's proposal?"

"He's not a bore, he's an honoured member of the King's court, Sir Mortimer has been assigned to serve as adjutant under Prince Rupert shortly. This is a great distinction," she answered hotly.

"He's a bore, he looks it and you know he's a bore. You didn't answer my question, Lady Elizabeth, did you accept his proposal?"

"That's none of your business, my lord," she snapped back.

"You didn't then. Well, better follow my advice and don't. A gentlewoman like you should have better options in life than spending the rest of her life tucked away in a small barony in the middle of nowhere under the thumb of a jealous husband – sadly, I must repeat that this Mortimer has all the hallmarks of a jealous bore."

Elizabeth realized that it would be useless to continue arguing and was now very much aware that hundreds of eyes must be following their conversation. She concluded, "All of this is none of your business, my lord. You will have to excuse me now, the Queen is waiting for me."

Armand grinned, but if she had hoped to snub him, her words had clearly failed to have the desired effect. He bowed punctiliously and left to join Pierre who was standing close to the King, surrounded by a group of older nobles in animated discussion.

Armand was satisfied with his work today. The lady Elizabeth had been like a citadel, all defences in place, but he was sure he had skilfully managed to break through those walls that guarded a stunning beauty. The lady might want to appear like an iceberg but he was sure he had lit a fire underneath. She would be his, he was sure of it now.

Playing Games

"We've been invited to play tennis today," Pierre sighed. "I vaguely remember that you need to chase a small leather ball – or was it a ball made from feathers? I played it once in Paris with François – he beat me of course."

"Of course, I remember!" Armand smirked. "François chased you around like a headless chicken."

Pierre pulled a face. Taking pity on his friend, Armand conceded, "I agree, it's quite tricky to hit the ball with the racket. Especially when the ball bounces against the walls and you need to drive it over the net to gain points. I used to play tennis from time to time at the Louvre with my fellow officers from the royal guards. But King Louis didn't like the game, he preferred to hunt. The secret is to be quick, and run fast, and King Louis was always a slow runner."

Pierre shook his head. "The English are besotted with this game, unless of course they can ride out and hunt, that's their second obsession. Yesterday we talked more about hunting and tennis than about the war, can you imagine, Armand?"

"Who wants to talk about the war if things are looking as dire as they do at present? Everybody knows the next battle will happen soon. And after this battle, another one is bound to come. The King's enemies are like the hydra, you cut off one head and more new ones grow."

Pierre frowned. "Mazarin will not move a finger to help England, we both know this; that's why he's sending François to get the Queen out of the country before it's too late. By the way, did you hear anything about Cousin Charles, did anybody mention him?"

"I did, actually, the Marquess of Halifax mentioned that Charles would be expected here in Oxford next week at the latest. He let everybody know that he found it *extremely* strange that Charles hadn't come immediately to join us in Oxford, insinuating of course that your cousin is not loyal to the royal cause."

Pierre laughed bitterly. "It only took me a short time to understand that the marquess is a bag full of slime. The kind of rogue who plays a careful game, probably accepting money from both sides. That this cockroach should dare to point to Charles as being a traitor, is an insult!"

Armand shrugged. "There were others who defended Cousin Charles immediately by saying that he was using his excellent connections in London in the King's favour. But rumours will never stop, today it's Cousin Charles, tomorrow it'll be somebody else. Better let's try to get hold of a tennis racket and get ready, as half of the court ladies will be watching. I don't want to be seen playing like a loser."

"That's what it's all about, you're hoping that Lady Elizabeth will be present and my friend wants to impress the lady."

"Of course I want to impress her. She's a rare diamond and a bit of flirting with Lady Elizabeth will be a nice distraction until we've worked out how best to leave Oxford. Have I already said that? I hate this boring town, I hate this travesty of a court. I truly hope that Cousin Charles will help us to leave this country as fast as possible. My only ray of hope is Lady Elizabeth."

Pierre looked at his friend. "Halifax was suddenly very friendly to me, I'm not sure if I like this…"

Armand frowned. "That's dangerous, clearly he hated both of us from the start. If he's nice, it means that he's up to something. Probably this sour looking wife of his is behind it, people say that she's clever enough for the two of them."

"Nothing we can do now, in any case. Let's call Jim, we need rackets and he has to find a place where we can train for a bit."

Pierre's mind was back on practical issues, even if he didn't wish to impress Lady Elizabeth as his friend did. He had no desire to ridicule himself in front of the other gentlemen and ladies of the royal court.

***

"It's done!" The Marquess of Halifax was purring like a fat cat that had caught a mouse.

"Hertford will be despatched to London?" his wife enquired.

"Yes. And his friend will be assigned as adjutant to General Forth who's going south soon, both will be removed from court by next week."

The Marchioness allowed herself the indulgence of a rare smile.

"Now, my lord, we need to find a way to get rid of this curious cousin, Charles Neuville, as soon as he sets foot in this town. I've known Charles since he was a most annoying toddler, he's got a bright head on those lazy shoulders of his. He'll understand immediately what's going on and will rush back to London to protect the young duke. I never understood why, by the way. If Pierre dies, Charles could easily become his successor – as if this wouldn't provide plenty of motivation to get rid of him. But some people are blind when it comes to taking care of their own interests, very emotional."

Not that you'll ever be accused of being emotional, her husband thought as he looked at his wife's sharp face.

"Why are you looking at me all doe-eyed?" the Marchioness asked in her high-pitched voice.

"Nothing, my dear, nothing," the Marquess hastily replied. "I was simply distracted for a second. I agree that we have to find a solution regarding Charles Neuville. Let me think about it, another mission, I would think. That's the advantage of the war, there's always some kind of mission to be sent on. Wales would be good, he owns some estates over there, we can always say that he's the ideal man to go to Wales."

"Wales is as good as sending him to the moon, I agree. Very clever." The Marchioness patted her husband's hand as she would have patted an obedient dog and they started to discuss the latest rumours from London.

"I don't like the talk about recruiting a new army." The Marchioness frowned. "In the end our allies in Parliament may lose their grip, aren't they afraid of creating a monster they can't control?"

"Northumberland doesn't seem to be worried. As long as this happens outside London he can control the city and Parliament. He says that the military needs improvement but as they've appointed two men of the lower gentry, in truth it's the noble families who will keep control."

"Northumberland has always been a fool. Only his sister is clever, but she's a slut. He'll regret this decision one day, mark my words."

***

Pierre was led by a footman into the king's audience chamber, wondering why a royal herald had requested his urgent attendance. He would have loved to drag Armand along but his friend had been absent, as usual. Lately Armand was using any excuse to stroll over to the buildings reserved for the Queen and her retinue. Pierre was starting to worry about Armand's infatuation; it would be a terrible scandal if his friend seduced a Queen's maid of honour – and the maid's bridegroom-to-be, Sir Mortimer, had murder in his eyes whenever they met.

Pierre had explained this again and again to Armand, but his friend dismissed any such arguments as simply irrelevant or downright faint-hearted.

"His Grace, the Duke of Hertford, Marquis de Beauvoir." The footman announced his arrival. Pierre entered the small room that would serve for the audience today.

The King was not alone; the Lord High Treasurer was waiting with him. While the King sat on a brocade-covered armchair, the Lord High Treasurer was standing, and bowed slightly as Pierre entered.

"Your Majesty's servant. My lord." Pierre greeted the King and his minister and waited for the King to open the discussion. But it was the Lord High Treasurer instead who started talking. "We would like to thank Your Grace for being so kind as to having come immediately."

Pierre raised his eyebrows. "You made it a very pressing request, indeed, my lord!"

The Lord High Treasurer cleared his throat. "Indeed, Your Grace, we have a serious matter to discuss, a matter of such delicacy that it will demand Your Grace's utmost discretion." He paused to underline the serious nature of his speech before he continued. "In fact this is a state secret that will be divulged to Your Grace, information that may never be mentioned to anybody outside this room."

Pierre started to feel uncomfortable but kept a straight face. He had seen the Lord High Treasurer conversing on different occasions very intimately with the Marquess of Halifax, a man with the reputation of being involved in every court intrigue.

Pierre only nodded and replied curtly. "It goes without saying that you may fully trust me, my lord. I'm afraid this may not be the case for all those at court, if I may say so."

The King blushed and the Lord High Treasurer was taken aback, they were not used to such blunt speech at court.

"Regrettably Your Grace's answer holds an uncomfortable element of the truth." He cleared his throat. "It's an open secret that the situation of the kingdom is precarious, Your Grace. Although we all know that justice will prevail and the rebellious forces will be crushed in the end, we cannot close our eyes any more to the fact that His Majesty needs more time and more funds to organize the final victorious assault on London."

Are they going to ask me for even more money? Pierre mused. *I've already offered ten thousand pounds, I'd be interested to know how much Halifax has contributed, if anything at all.*

Maybe the Lord High Treasurer had read those thoughts in Pierre's eyes as he replied quickly, "His Majesty is aware that Your Grace has been most generous with your contribution, it's not about asking for more funds from Your Grace. We're expecting help from France and the Netherlands to be forthcoming soon as discussions are progressing well. Queen Henrietta Maria has sent a sisterly plea to Queen Anne of France and we expect a positive reply shortly."

Suddenly the King intervened. "In essence, we are talking about winning time, not just money. Irish troops will arrive shortly and reinforce ours. We would need a person in our trust and of the highest rank to travel to London and start discussions with the moderate forces of Parliament to elicit whether a peaceful solution can be found. Once these forces see that our position has been strengthened they might be ready to recognize the prerogatives of their rightful King."

Pierre swallowed hard. "I'm flattered that Your Majesty should even consider me but I have no experience in such matters. I hardly know anybody in London, such a mission would risk ending in great failure! Certainly the Marquess of Halifax would be in a much better position to negotiate on your behalf, Sire?"

The Lord High Treasurer smiled indulgently. "Hertford, the fact that Your Grace is not involved in British politics at all thus far is Your Grace's biggest asset. Everybody else here at court is known for his political leanings. The Marquess of Halifax is ill-liked in London for being the Roundheads' arch-enemy, to express it plainly. Your Grace may have the opportunity to break this mould and open new avenues for discussions. If Your Grace should fail, we will be no worse off than today – on the contrary, we'll have won precious time."

"I understand, my lord, I'm supposed to go to London, chiefly to bargain for more time. But I'm not sure if I can really accept this mission. I'm not at all convinced that I'm the right person. Surely you should be able to find someone better."

The King raised his hand. "Hertford, view it as my royal wish – or command. I have talked with Prince Rupert and my royal cousin agrees that Your Grace will be the perfect person for this important assignment. I'm confident that Your Grace will bring the desired results. Your grandfather would be proud of you and I'm confident that I shall never regret the day that I elevated you to the status of a duke of the realm – against the wishes of some of your relatives, as Your Grace may remember."

Pierre understood that he had no option but to accept. As soon as he saw the fleeting smile on the lips of the Lord High Treasurer he was sure that he had been lured into trap. But why? What was the background? If only Cousin Charles were here.

"When am I expected to leave for London, Your Majesty?"

"As soon as possible, the Lord High Treasurer says that we have no time to lose. And I tend to agree," the King replied.

And so – conventions barely respected – Pierre found himself dismissed. The King had plenty of pressing appointments this morning, as his minister pointed out with a faint smile on his lips.

***

In the meantime, Armand had been lingering around the buildings that housed the Queen's small court. Finally, after plenty of false alerts that made his heart beat faster, he saw a slender figure that he had been longing to see step out of the doorway. His luck seemed to be holding, Elizabeth didn't appear to be in a hurry.

"What a coincidence, meeting you here, Lady Elizabeth!" Armand greeted her, his eyes almost devouring her. The weather had turned mild today, a first timid harbinger of spring. Therefore Elizabeth had discarded her coat and was only wearing a very becoming green velvet gown with a soft fur lining and a dyed woollen shawl. Rumour had it that the Queen must be very generous indeed, as people had noticed that Elizabeth had acquired plenty of stylish and expensive dresses recently. Some gossipmongers implied that this generosity might also stem from Sir Mortimer, as it was noticed that he followed Lady Elizabeth everywhere.

"I don't believe in this sort of coincidence, my lord," the lady replied, but the look in her eyes belied her cool tone.

"There is a chance that I might have been guided by destiny..." Armand smiled, making her heart beat faster.

"I'm not a great believer in destiny either, my lord, I rather believe that you've come here on purpose."

"Would I?" Armand was all innocence. "But I do remember now, I was looking for a lady of exceptional beauty to alleviate my mental sufferings."

"Keep looking then, my lord, maybe you'll find some lady who is kind enough to alleviate those sufferings. Although I rather doubt it."

"There's no need for me to continue searching, as I have found you!" Armand took her right hand and kissed the tips of her fingers gallantly.

What a difference from Mortimer, flashed through Elizabeth's mind. *Mortimer would have grabbed me already, covering me all over with his clumsy kisses.* "My lord, behave yourself," Elizabeth finally objected, but left enough time for Armand to plant the last kiss.

"Don't torture me. Lady Elizabeth, may I invite you for a short stroll in the gardens? I need urgent private tuition on the magnificence of English horticulture."

Elizabeth smiled, showing a row of perfect teeth. "Go and stroll through the gardens with the head gardener then. I have to go into the town on an errand for Her Majesty. I regret, my lord, I have no time."

"Coincidence – or destiny – is striking again, my lady. It must be my lucky day. I was just about to go into the town as well."

Gallantly he offered his arm, which Elizabeth accepted after brief hesitation, although she knew that she shouldn't.

***

"I think I'll need to drop a hint to Sir Mortimer." The Marchioness of Halifax watched the couple walking away in animated discussion towards the town from her window.

"I was always convinced that she was only playing with him, poor Mortimer, he's so naïve. Not a lot of brains in that handsome head. Elizabeth is aiming for an earl, that's obvious. But a Saint Paul will never marry a nobody like Lady Elizabeth, it would be considered a terrible misalliance, his family will see to that."

The Marchioness was smiling but those who knew her well would have been able to tell that this was no sign of kindness. The Marchioness was busily scheming when and how she could use this knowledge to her best advantage.

***

"What is it?" Pierre asked his friend, who stared with consternation at the message he had just received. Armand had just come back from town, in the best of spirits. But now he looked as if he had been struck by a bolt of lightning.

The message had been delivered by a dashing young musketeer, clad in his parade dress, hat crowned by a large feather. The young soldier had bowed deeply, as he had remitted the message addressed to the Right Honourable Armand de Saint Paul, Earl of Worthing.

"I've been appointed adjutant to General Forth, I can't believe my eyes. I'm to leave next week to serve in his camp."

Pierre read the short message and grimaced. "I'm starting to think that someone with a long arm wants to get rid of us. I was just going to tell you that I'm being sent on a royal errand to London. A special sign of royal appreciation, of course…"

"To London! They might as well send you to the gallows – or to the colonies. The Duke of Hertford riding to London as the King's envoy – straight into the arms of the King's enemies? That's sheer madness!" Armand was shouting now, forgetting his own summons.

"Madness wrapped in a royal wish – or command, whatever I prefer." Pierre sighed. "The Lord High Treasurer assured me that I'm going to receive a passport from Parliament to guarantee free passage and that I will have the status of a royal messenger. But I don't like it. To be frank, I had hoped to have you at my side."

"Someone is pulling strings to prevent this," Armand replied. "That's obvious enough. Too many coincidences happening at once."

After a pause he continued. "But let's remain optimistic. We still have some days left until we have to leave and there's a good chance that Charles and François will turn up in the meantime. I'm sure that they'll find a way to sort this out."

"Let's hope so," Pierre agreed, but he was far less optimistic.

"As there's nothing that can be done right now, let's practise our tennis skills. Jim found a shed and a pair of rackets, we have no more excuse."

***

160

Word had spread fast that Sir Mortimer had challenged the newcomers to play tennis, a tournament that promised a welcome change from the dull daily routine. Although the college tennis court was not as splendid as the one in Whitehall there was enough space for a good fifty spectators. Even the Prince of Wales had promised to appear in order to honour the match with his presence. Sir Mortimer was known to be a first class player, and if the two Frenchmen wanted to make fools of themselves, so much the better, it would be highly entertaining to watch them going down.

The great moment had arrived and the opponents met. Their greetings were polite but everyone could sense the barely hidden hostility beneath the polished surface. Everyone present knew of course that the reason for the discord could be found in the person of the lovely lady Elizabeth who sat in the first row, head erect, her beautiful face expressionless as a sphinx.

Pierre lost his match against a friend of the Prince of Wales – as predicted – but his style and posture were praised and the general feeling was – given the opportunity and a bit more training – he'd become a serious challenger.

The moment Armand and Mortimer stepped onto the court the atmosphere changed. Mortimer walked erect as a peacock and he let it be understood that he had arrived on court with the intention of destroying, nay, annihilating his opponent. Bets had been taken but the odds had been clear, generally the young Earl of Worthing was pitied – his defeat was a foregone conclusion. A French frog was obviously no match for one of England's champions.

The opening strokes confirmed this impression. Against Sir Mortimer's bravado, Armand's returns appeared lukewarm and powerless. Only Pierre frowned, as he knew that his friend could play much better – what was he up to?

Mortimer's face was flushed with triumph, he could smell an easy victory. He'd show Elizabeth who was the better man on the field; soon he'd step up the pace even more and crush this pitiful creature with his dark locks who had dared to challenge him.

But somehow his opponent managed to improve his play, first slowly, then faster and faster he drove the ball into dangerous corners, played it against the wooden walls so that the ball bounced back and took unpredictable directions.

What at first could have been explained away as beginner's luck soon started to put beads of perspiration onto Mortimer's face. A good fifteen minutes later he was dripping wet and realized that Armand de Saint Paul had been playing with him from the beginning, luring him into a false sense of security and was only now displaying his true face, the face of a master of the game of tennis.

The tension on the tennis court had become palpable, as the game turned into a merciless battle. The spectators watched spellbound, cheering and suffering with each point that was won or lost. The two opponents were both excellent players, who would tire first?

161

All of a sudden Armand's racket broke and the game came to an abrupt finish. The Prince of Wales, who had looked more and more worried about the open animosity displayed by the players, took this as a welcome excuse to end the game and declared a draw, a decision generally felt by all to be a wise one.

He called the players forward to shake hands as was customary but Mortimer smashed his racket to the ground, ready to storm out of the court. It took the firm intervention of his friends to avoid disaster and potentially snub the prince. Prince Charles pretended not to have noticed Mortimer's childish behaviour and even applauded him, before he found some gentle words for Armand. Then he put his hand on Mortimer's arm and led him from the court – thus skilfully separating the two opponents who were only too ready to get at each other's throats.

The court watched and relished this little scene. It had turned out to be just the kind of juicy scandal everybody had hoped for. Armand would be a rising star from today on, he had challenged and almost defeated the champion.

The lady Elizabeth kept her head erect. Only her tightly pressed lips showed that she didn't appreciate Mortimer's childish behaviour. Her true feelings were torn between pride for Armand – and cold fear. She had looked into Mortimer's eyes and had seen more than mere hatred – Mortimer was ready to commit murder.

"Congratulations, Armand, you planned this very skilfully," Pierre greeted his friend, who was rubbing his face with a fresh towel.

"Did I?" Armand was all innocence.

"You did! And don't be astonished if Mortimer is waiting with a dagger in some dark corner some time soon."

"Bah, that fool is nothing but an inflated scarecrow, let him frighten small children. I put him in his place, he needed a bit of a put-down. Did a nobody like Mortimer truly think that he could beat Armand de Saint Paul?"

"M. de Saint Paul is modest as always," his friend replied. "But not very wise."

But Armand wasn't listening; his eyes had been on Lady Elizabeth all the time. As she walked by, he whispered, "I played for you, you knew that, of course?"

Elizabeth allowed herself the merest hint of a smile. "Did you? I must admit that my attention was distracted most of the time, but I heard that some people around me were praising your skills indeed. Have a wonderful day, my lord."

She left Armand behind. He turned back to Pierre, "Isn't she magnificent? I swear, I'll make her beg on her knees to kiss me, this is a promise, the word of honour of a Saint Paul!"

Pierre gave up. He didn't need a clairvoyant to tell him that trouble was brewing fast. Maybe it was a good thing after all that they must leave Oxford soon. From today on, Armand didn't just have an enemy, Mortimer's pride had been bruised in public and the answer could only be a true challenge, ending in a deadly duel. Pierre knew his friend well enough. It would be useless to ask Armand to refuse the challenge or forget Elizabeth or just to be more careful.

If only Cousin Charles or François would arrive!

***

Cousin Charles was sitting in the library at Hertford House, close to the bright fire that burned day and night to fight the chill and humidity rising from the River Thames. Being close to the river was certainly an asset when it came to moving freely in and out of the city or visiting Whitehall Palace, but it brought the kind of freezing winter draughts that were a constant nuisance inside the house. Charles stretched his long legs and frowned, trying to sum up the confidential discussions and meetings of the past days – and to come to a final conclusion.

The kingdom was on the verge of disaster, there was no longer any doubt of that. The moderate members of Parliament had been skilfully silenced, bullied into submission by the cocksure members of the lower gentry. The lords Essex and Northumberland might still be under the impression that they held the reins in their hands, but clearly they did not, they had become puppets on the strings of the new majority – like so many others.

Charles frowned. He didn't like the prospect of becoming another puppet of the Puritans. But they had money, a lot of it, and their ranks were growing daily.

"The King is a sinking ship. Time to leave." He spoke aloud as the door opened. His last words must have been overheard as he was greeted by a cheerful voice.

"Better keep such thoughts to yourself, that's treason."

Charles jumped up. "François, how good to see you! Did you succeed?"

"Yes and no, my friend. I found traces of our friends, I certainly haven't lost all my skills." François looked rather smug; modesty had never been his favourite virtue.

"Pierre and Armand were held hostage in a forlorn and not very, how shall I call it, *reputable* inn, close to Dover. But when I arrived, our friends had already escaped, so let's be optimistic, my bets are that they've arrived in Oxford already."

"We should know by tomorrow as I sent a messenger to Oxford to enquire. I'm planning to ride to Oxford shortly and you should be joining me."

"My pleasure," François answered. "But now be a good host and get me a decent meal, I'm hungry. I've spent miles on horseback, I think I've earned a good meal and then M. Tavaillon can fall into his frugal bed."

163

"Don't forget your evening prayers, my dear Huguenot friend, or purgatory will be waiting for you." Charles grinned and helped himself to a handful of nuts.

Playing with Fire

"I've gone mad!" Elizabeth whispered to the reflection in the mirror, and a very strange reflection it was indeed. She had exchanged her usual riding attire, a rather garish velvet green dress with trimmings of dark mink, for a pair of velvet breeches, a lined waistcoat and a felt hat crowned by a large feather. The hat hid her chestnut hair, but nothing could hide her radiant blue eyes and her beautiful face.

Why on earth had she accepted Armand's invitation to ride out with him? It must have been those eyes, eyes that could melt ice and eyes that promised paradise on earth.

"I'm finished, my lady." The maid broke into her dreams, her voice petulant. It had taken a large bribe and the threat of dismissal to make her organize these clothes and help Elizabeth in a venture she clearly disapproved of.

"Thanks, Kate. You may leave now. I might be back quite late. And remember, not a word to anyone!"

The maid snorted and curtsied. She thought that she knew what her mistress was up to. It was no longer a secret at court that two men were battling for Lady Elizabeth's favour.

Not completely succumbing to madness, Elizabeth had taken the precaution of asking the Queen's permission to be absent for a day. The Queen had granted her request, but her mind had been distracted.

"Don't stay away too long, Elizabeth, nobody looks after me as well as you do." The Queen paused, and suddenly started to sob. "I'll need you when my time comes…" then suddenly she lapsed into French. "*J'ai peur, petite, je sais que la naissance sera très difficile…*" Two single tears rolled down the painted cheeks of Queen Henrietta Maria; her royal mask had slipped and suddenly the Queen looked frightened and fragile.

"I'll be at your side, Ma'am! Don't worry, my mother always told me that the last children are the easiest to be delivered," Elizabeth hastened to reply. More and more she had become the Queen's confidante, and at first she had been delighted, but lately she wasn't sure if she liked this role after all. Maybe the arrival of Armand had changed her mind, she felt more and more like a traitor.

"Elizabeth, you're such a pillar of strength for me!"

"Your Majesty is so gracious! I'll be riding out together with a group of friends, the weather promises to be wonderful tomorrow, a first glimpse of spring and the horses are yearning for a run. I'll be careful to be back early though!"

"Yes, go Elizabeth, enjoy your day, you deserve it. How I long to be back in Greenwich and to walk in my lovely gardens. Oxford is making us all gloomy, I think. You're right, you should profit from the first rays of sun. It has been a cold and miserable winter, we all need a bit of sunshine."

The Queen continued with reminiscences of her youth, years spent in the elegant and sunny royal castles scattered across the region of the Loire valley. Elizabeth encouraged her to tell those old stories again and again, as nothing pleased the Queen more than to relive her glorious past when she had been a beautiful and carefree royal princess of France.

***

But now the moment of truth had arrived. Nervously Elizabeth walked to the stables, nerves strung like a harp as she passed through the cavernous servants' wing of the building. It was still very early and the court nestled under a sleepy silence, but she must at all cost avoid encountering Mortimer, his friends, or anybody else who might recognize her, as this would spell disaster. There were already enough rumours circulating about her.

Elizabeth still vividly remembered her last encounter with Mortimer; it had ended in a terrible row. The only good aspect of their fall-out had been that he hadn't shown up since then. But she knew him well enough, and this kind of silence usually heralded a big storm. What was he up to?

Elizabeth's maid had bribed her boyfriend, a young groom in the royal stables. Would he be there as agreed? Would he be alone? Could he keep a secret?

But all worked according to plan. As Elizabeth reached the stables, trying hard to walk with long strides to look like a man, the groom was already waiting for her. He had a slight stutter and Elizabeth's smile almost knocked him out of his boots, creating even more knots in his tongue than usual. Even in her breeches and with her hair hidden by the large hat, she still looked stunningly beautiful.

Suddenly an idea flashed through her mind and she asked the groom, "Would you mind accompanying me to the city gate?" She suddenly realized that it would look far less suspicious if a gentleman and his groom were heading towards the city gates.

The groom flushed scarlet and nodded, unable to speak. Quickly he saddled a second horse and they left the stable compound. As it was early morning, the sun was just beginning to rise. She had chosen the time well; the courtyard was empty, as most servants would be gathering in the kitchen to start the day with a bowl of porridge.

Accompanied by the groom she reached the gate without incident. Here Armand was waiting for her already. Unusually for him he had dressed in a sober style with an inconspicuous hat, for which Elizabeth was thankful as she had the impression that the whole city must be staring at them.

If the groom found her behaviour strange, he didn't show it. He probably didn't even notice, as her dazzling smile and a shilling had numbed his mind to the extent that he'd have followed her to the ends of the earth if Elizabeth had asked him. But now he found himself dismissed and Armand took over.

"You're on time!" Armand smiled.

"I'm always on time," she answered.

"You might have changed your mind," he challenged her.

"I still might change my mind. I probably should."

"Don't! Have confidence in me," he pleaded. "Let's ride on!"

At a slow pace they rode to the gate where Armand greeted the guard with a vulgar jest. The guard answered back in kind and didn't bother to look too closely at the second horseman. As soon as they had left the fortifications behind, they let the horses run, enjoying the cool wind and the first rays of the sun that caressed their faces.

"I hate Oxford!" Armand cried out. "If it hadn't been for you, I'd have left already!"

Elizabeth breathed deeply, only now realizing how much she had missed her freedom. "It's oppressing, I admit, we're all crammed into this small city and see only the same faces day after day."

"A woman like you should sparkle at a court like Paris!" Armand answered.

Elizabeth made a face and quickly he added, "I'm not paying you some sort of fancy compliment, *ma chérie*, it's a fact. You shouldn't be imprisoned and chained to this crazy city."

They continued in silence, letting the horses run freely. Elizabeth enjoyed their ride, it was so much easier to ride like a man instead of having to sit side-saddle as a gentlewoman was supposed to do!

"Where are we going?" she cried. She suddenly felt as free as a bird.

"It's a surprise!" Armand cried back.

A good hour later they reached a thatched cottage that lay partially hidden behind thorny hedges, close to a lazy river. It was an idyllic spot, perfect for a romantic day. The banks of the river were partially overgrown by low-hanging trees that almost touched the stream of water that was gurgling peacefully at a slow pace.

They dismounted and Elizabeth suddenly started to feel shy. There was no more backing out now, the dice had been thrown.

Armand sensed that her mood had changed, and smiled at her. "Nervous?" he teased.

"What are we going to do here?" she asked, hating herself for asking this kind of silly question. She could only hope that her voice hadn't betrayed her nervousness.

"We are curious, aren't we? That's part of my surprise. But let's hide the horses first. I don't want a passer-by to find horses of such good quality close to this cottage, it might prompt awkward questions."

Once the horses had been looked after, Armand led Elizabeth inside. The tiny cottage was sparkling clean and a welcoming fire had been lit. A table had been set where cake, sweetmeats and mulled wine were already waiting for them. Elizabeth and Armand were greeted by a chubby young maid with glowing cheeks who curtsied deeply to welcome them, her face flushed with excitement.

Armand was satisfied. Jim had arranged everything to perfection, the golden louis d'or had been a good investment.

Silently they sat down at the table; Elizabeth's mind by now was in a state of complete confusion. So far she had really enjoyed this excursion, being coveted by a man whom all the women at court must fancy, reading in his glance how much he desired her. But sitting here, uncomfortably close to him, she realized that she must have been utterly foolish to have accepted Armand's invitation. But now it was too late to complain, she had crossed her personal Rubicon. Was she about to commit her biggest mistake ever, was she making a total fool of herself? Wasn't she discarding all of her principles – just for the magic of two brown eyes and the thrill of adventure?

The presence of the maid was reassuring, but Elizabeth was deeply embarrassed – what must the girl think of her? To cover her embarrassment, she took a deep sip of the hot wine and immediately the effect of the mulled wine spread in her body, and a feeling of warmth and comfort took over.

Armand sensed her agitation and kept a respectful distance. Sitting at the table opposite her, totally at ease, he kept an easy conversation flowing. Elizabeth listened spellbound to his dark melodious voice and the pictures he conjured of journeys and adventures in the remotest countries, countries she had only dreamed of so far. He took her travelling in her mind to sunny Italy, the snow-covered mountains of the Alps or the wonderful landscape of the Loire Valley.

How fascinating it was to listen to his stories about life at court in Paris, how entertaining and what a nice change compared to Mortimer's conversation – although lately they had barely talked at all – all Mortimer would do was grab and kiss her as soon as they were alone.

Elizabeth listened, laughed, had more wine, and before she could help it or fully realized what was going on, she was falling in love.

Armand filled her cup once again but this time he didn't sit down, he stepped behind Elizabeth and started to caress her neck and her shoulders. His touch was light and delicate and she closed her eyes.

How different and exciting was Armand's touch compared to Mortimer's clumsy moves. How could Armand's fingers convey the feeling of being so powerful and yet remaining so delicate? Enthralled she sensed that Armand was moving his face close to hers as he started to murmur compliments into her ear while his finger continued to caress her. Finally she felt his lips moving delicately from her ear to her shoulders, setting her body on fire.

"Do you want to follow me, *chérie*?" he whispered and took her hand.

She couldn't talk, she just nodded – how could she refuse? Her took her hand and led Elizabeth into a small bedroom where a bed covered with fresh linen was waiting for them. Burning beeswax candles spread their mild light and filled the air with their sweet scent mixing with the scent of the dried lavender that had been strewn lavishly onto the bed and the wooden floor.

Armand started to undress her, delicately, every move a caress. He kissed her deeply – but as she was about to answer his kiss, all of a sudden, the tiny remainder of sanity in her mind, dormant thus far, woke up.

Isn't it obvious that Armand is very experienced in this kind of situation? her mind whispered. *Aren't you giving yourself to him like a cheap chamber maid? Are you mad? Are you ready to sacrifice your future for a quick adventure, to be forgotten tomorrow?*

"I love you!" Armand moaned, almost tearing his breeches apart as he started to undress. She could see how excited he was.

But the spell had been broken and slowly she withdrew from his arms.

"If you really love me, I must ask you to stop here," Elizabeth whispered.

"What do you mean?" Armand answered crestfallen, panting hard.

"I mean that I adore you, Armand, but you're moving too fast. I'm a gentlewoman, not a cheap chambermaid."

Quickly she silenced his protest with a long kiss. "You know that I'm right," she finally said.

"Let me kiss you again. I promise I will behave like a gentleman," he pleaded, avoiding a straight answer, and she gave in.

He embraced her and kissed her passionately, but if he had hoped to make her change her mind, he was mistaken. Gently but firmly she rejected his advancing hands until he understood that she wouldn't waver and contented himself with keeping her in his arms.

Lying close to Armand she suddenly realized why everyone at court talked about love. Never having loved before, she had never understood what the fuss was all about. But now she started to understand, love was a glimpse into paradise.

"I love you, *ma chérie*, you're wonderful. One day you'll be mine."

"*Je t'aime*," she replied and kissed him.

"You speak French?"

"There's no better language when it comes to love!" she laughed.

They kissed again but slowly this time, until Armand started to disentangle himself from her limbs. "We must go back, *chérie*, back to reality." He sighed. "We must be back before the afternoon as the guards who take over the next shift are notorious for being difficult. They always suspect that some Roundheads will try to sneak through in the evening."

"I'm afraid you're right, darling. Let's ride back. I promise, I'll never forget this day."

"Nor will I, *chérie*! Why not ride out tomorrow again?"

Elizabeth shook her head. "You know that it's impossible, darling. We must be careful. Mortimer is waiting for his revenge and I may not neglect my duties with the Queen. She doesn't like it when I'm not around."

"Pah, who cares about Mortimer! But I understand that the Queen might be upset, she seems to be very attached to you. Let me find a place close to Merton College where we can meet from time to time, my love. Every minute with you is precious."

She kissed him passionately once again in answer and they dressed in silence, aware that any more words would only destroy the magic of the moment.

They rode back in silent companionship, but at a slower pace than this morning. Elizabeth was in deep thought – aware that this afternoon had changed her life. Her mind was made up, she was determined to marry Armand, he must be hers, nothing else would do. She'd keep him at bay until he moved heaven and earth to reach his goal – and the trap would close. This thought made her smile.

"You're smiling, my love?" Armand queried.

Elizabeth turned to him, radiating beauty and happiness that even her manly disguise couldn't conceal. "Yes, my love, don't I have every reason to smile?" – *as one day I'll make sure that you're mine*, she added in her thoughts.

Armand grinned back, carefree and very much unaware of Elizabeth's plans.

"Yes, my love, you have very reason to smile!" he answered. *But next time I won't accept no for an answer, no way will I let you off the hook again,* he added in his thoughts.

A Battle is Looming

The Marchioness of Halifax was looking out of the window, a letter from her cousin in her lap, stifling a yawn. It had been a particularly boring day and the letter in her lap was no improvement. Her young cousin had the annoying habit of starting sentences and forgetting the end – she was the epitome of a particular type of empty-headed female. The Marchioness had been looking forward to a bit of distraction this afternoon but the Queen hadn't been feeling well and had cancelled the intimate card party that had been planned. Her husband and son Rochester had left Oxford this morning– officially to go on a longer hunting foray – but of course she knew better. Sooner or later the house of Halifax would leave the sinking ship of the Stuarts and change allegiance, but as the stakes were high, such a move needed to be prepared with care and diligence.

Suddenly she noticed a lone horseman riding into the cobbled courtyard – nothing unusual. Just as she stifled another yawn and was ready to turn to the next page, sure of being confronted with yet another rambling tale by her cousin, she noticed something unusual. The horse suddenly lost its footing on the slippery cobbles and the horseman almost lost his balance. He finally mastered his horse, but he had lost his hat.

The Marchioness was suddenly wide awake. The horseman had long hair, unusually long hair, and what's more, hair of a colour that was unique at court. There could be no doubt of it.

I wonder if Sir Mortimer knows that his fiancée has been out riding disguised as a man. He's on duty today, therefore it can't be Mortimer she's been meeting. And it's not difficult to guess who she was meeting with... once again, she thought. What a juicy piece of news fate had handed her as a gift today. All boredom gone, the Marchioness weighed up the various unsavoury uses she could make of this scandalous piece of information, her fertile mind offering a wide range of options, whether blackmail or just the pleasure of lighting the tinder and watching Sir Mortimer go wild.

I will show this scheming trollop that she's taken a step too far, she thought, and went through the list of her female relatives who might be a handy replacement as maid of honour to the Queen. This opened completely new possibilities of potential influence at court and kept her busy until dinnertime.

In the meantime Elizabeth had quickly replaced her hat. Luckily the courtyard had been empty and her mishap had gone unnoticed. She stole back into her room where she dressed carefully. Armand should be dazzled by her beauty tonight, she had to keep the spell working. As she'd be on duty tonight, she was bound to encounter the Duke of Hertford and Armand later in the King's apartments where she was to wait on the Queen.

***

"You look like the cat that got the cream! You've heard the great news already?" Martin cried and waved as he detected Armand entering the courtyard that linked the college buildings with the royal stables.

Armand dismounted to greet his new friend, one of the few genuine friends that he reckoned to have found in Oxford. "What news? I have been out riding, I needed to get some fresh air, it was such a lovely day, not entirely to my taste, but lovely and very promising, very promising indeed. But tell me, what's going on?"

"Can't you hear? The church bells are ringing. Prince Rupert has won a great victory at Newark. The North is firmly back in our hands!" Martin beamed.

"That's really excellent news! Let's celebrate tonight, we could empty a bottle of wine and play dice together, Pierre will certainly join us."

"No time!" Martin's smile disappeared. "The downside is that I have to leave tomorrow morning for Kent to join General Forth. The King and his war council have decided to strike hard and fast in the South, now that the North is secure, and I'll have to leave tomorrow at sunrise."

Armand felt as if a giant fist had punched him in the stomach. "Who needs to leave?" he asked, trying hard to control his voice.

"Everybody who's got two legs and a horse to ride on."

"*Merde alors!*" Armand cursed.

"I have no clue what that means, but I can guess... You'll have to leave as well, I presume?"

Armand nodded. "I guess so. I was to join the general next week, but I now assume that I'll find a message telling me to leave immediately once I'm back in my rooms. Well, that's life. See you probably tomorrow on the way to Kent – or even better – let's ride together!"

"Agreed, I'll wait at the gate. I expect we'll be away just a few days, get rid of this Puritan vermin and be back," Martin said, hoping to console Armand. He could see from Armand's face that he didn't welcome the news at all and he had a suspicion that the reason for his displeasure might be the lady Elizabeth.

Armand tried to put on a brave face. "Yes, a matter of some days, you're right. See you tomorrow then."

By the time he reached the rooms he shared with Pierre, he had encountered at least five more fellow officers who were in a joyful, almost exhilarant mood. The atmosphere in Oxford, sober and bordering on the morose so far, had totally changed. People were cheering and laughing, the Lord had finally shown his Grace, divine justice had prevailed, and the enemy had been beaten.

Pierre was already waiting for him, looking decidedly crestfallen.

Armand greeted his friend. "You don't look particularly cheerful."

"I hope you at least had a wonderful day – so far. You've heard the news?"

Armand shrugged nonchalantly. "Yes, Prince Rupert had an astounding victory in Newark and now everybody, including myself, will be ordered to go South to make sure that Parliament suffers a second crushing defeat. You find me delighted, of course…"

Pierre nodded. "Yes, you have to leave for Kent tomorrow morning. I was told that General Forth is to block reinforcements arriving for Parliament from Cornwall. Forth is sharing command with General Hopton and they've sent an urgent plea to the King for more troops. But that's not all. I'm to leave for London immediately. The King wants to make sure that I'll profit from the victory in Newark to convince those members of Parliament who always support the winning side to change sides. Or should I talk about those vermin in Parliament?" he snorted.

"It's politics, what do you expect? A bunch of tame choir boys? Of course they're corrupt, they play foul and all of them are stinking hypocrites. Better be realistic when you deal with them."

Pierre frowned. "I presume you're right. I'm being naïve. How would you deal with them?"

"Promise them anything," Armand replied instantly. "Titles, land, influence, whatever they want to hear, just promise it. The King can deal with it later. But what about your own safety?"

Suddenly Pierre snickered. "A royal escort will take me to London. Handpicked by the Marquess of Halifax."

"That's madness!" exclaimed Armand. "Pierre, you can't accept this. Halifax hates you!"

Pierre remained unruffled. "It would be sheer madness, of course. Therefore I took the liberty of changing the plan a bit." He laughed. "Oh, and I may have forgotten to tell them, it's a surprise. I'll be safe, don't worry, Jim will also protect me. I only wonder why Cousin Charles hasn't sent word so far."

"Tell me more about your plan! Don't be coy!"

But Pierre only smiled like a sphinx and wouldn't reveal any more.

Seeing that his friend remained stubborn, Armand changed the subject. "Maybe Charles didn't receive any message after all. In these crazy times, nobody is certain that they'll be delivered. But you should meet him and François in London, they must be in the city by now. He'll be a great help."

Suddenly Pierre embraced his friend. "Be careful, Armand!"

Armand looked at Pierre in surprise. "What's going on, my friend, anything wrong?"

Pierre shook his head. "Nothing, but I suddenly had a strange feeling, as if a dark shadow had passed above us."

"That's the effect of staying in Oxford too long, invariably we've all become morose. Don't worry, I was born under a lucky star – you take care of yourself. You have an unhealthy habit of ending up in trouble. I'd feel much better if I could accompany you to London, but I can't! And I'd really like to know how you plan to escape Halifax's clutches."

***

Elizabeth soon realized that this evening wouldn't be following the normal dinner routine. The news of the royal victory had spread like wildfire and although the official celebrations were to follow only later, once Prince Rupert was back from the North, the Queen insisted on organizing a small dinner party to honour the victory – which in fact turned into a sort of improvised war council.

"Lady Elizabeth, may I be so bold as to say how magnificent you look!" The Lord High Treasurer eyed her from head to toe. Elizabeth was intensely uncomfortable under his covetous gaze; the man was known to be a particularly unfaithful sort and generally she avoided meeting him alone.

She sank into a deep curtsy. "I'm very much honoured, my lord. We've all heard about the great victory and thought that I should dress to suit the occasion."

The young Earl of Wiltshire who was also attending the dinner party looked at her and she could detect an appraising gleam in his eyes. Elizabeth noticed his look and smiled at him, fully expecting to be snubbed as usual – but this time he returned a shy smile before he turned his attention back to the King.

Maybe he doesn't detest me after all, Elizabeth thought. But the Earl of Wiltshire didn't matter to her anymore. She wasn't fishing for a rich marriage or a title like she had done before, she wanted Armand, she wanted love. Wiltshire might be considered handsome and certainly was rich, but his fair countenance couldn't bear comparison with Armand's dashing looks.

The Queen nodded. "You do look very well, my dear, indeed, you should wear the same dress when Prince Rupert comes back from Newark. You may even dance with our hero."

Only a week ago Elizabeth would have been thrilled to overhear all kinds of confidential information being exchanged during dinner, information that would have been worth a fortune to the Earl of Northumberland and his cronies in London.

But this had been a different life, a different Elizabeth. Had this really been her? A despicable woman who had traded news to the enemy and sold her kisses to Mortimer for money?

It was so hard to smile, to keep up appearances. The face with the dashing moustache she was yearning to see didn't appear – and worse, during the conversation it became more and more obvious that Armand would be among those who had been ordered to leave Oxford tomorrow at sunrise to join the armed forces in the South. It was the Earl of Wiltshire who let slip the news during dinner. He'd be among those to leave as well.

By the time she returned to her room, Elizabeth was desperate. The day that had started with such promise and had offered her a glimpse into paradise was ending in tears. Her maid helped her to undress but as soon as she had closed the door behind her and locked herself in, Elizabeth started to cry. She couldn't even remember when had been the last time that she must have cried, but now as the flood of tears started to flow, she simply couldn't stop them.

Elizabeth cried until she fell into an uneasy sleep, knowing that by tomorrow morning, Armand would have left – maybe forever. Love had come, finally, but not to make her happy. It had come to cause her anguish and pain.

***

The noise and the cheers of the soldiers leaving for the next glorious battle filled the streets of Oxford. Armand joined the excited crowd that was heading towards the fortifications, but he felt tired and listless.

The first time in his life when he had been called to arms, he had been excited and eager to earn his spurs, yearning to fight for the honour of his King and the House of Saint Paul and distinguish himself. The King might have been a different one – it had been Louis XIII back in France – but the scenario had been almost identical: the young laughing faces around him, boasting and gloating how fast they'd track down and annihilate the enemy. The pretty girls in the streets of Paris had cheered and blown them kisses. The young men had not been just riding, they had been flying out of Paris on the wings of glory to confront the enemy.

He remembered this well enough – but of course reality had been entirely different. The dirt, the mud, the crying of wounded animals – and the grim spectre with the scythe who passed without mercy through the ranks of the soldiers, carrying away so many of those laughing faces who thought that they were headed for glory. Instead early death had become their fate, with them all but forgotten by now and probably better off than those who had been left mutilated. But it would be useless to tell the truth to his fellow officers now. The older ones knew already, and the younger ones would discover the truth soon enough.

Maybe it's not so bad after all that I must leave, he mused. His mind had been dwelling on yesterday's adventure but had come to no clear conclusion. Yesterday's excursion had certainly not been the fulfilment of his dreams, but given another occasion, he was sure of making Elizabeth yield. Didn't they all in the end?

Elizabeth was passionate, beautiful, the perfect companion to make love with. But apparently she was still a virgin! When he had invited her, he had been convinced that he wouldn't be her first lover. In France at court, no maid of honour would keep her honour for long... sooner or later the King or the Queen would marry them off to an elderly provincial nobleman who would be happy to accept the fact that the effort of procreation had already been taken care of. England seemed to be different, yet again. Suddenly he felt a shiver: might she even be expecting him to marry her?

Armand didn't want to marry and he was doubtful that those qualities that made Elizabeth a perfect mistress would make her a good wife. He wanted a peaceful home life and a small fortune as a dowry would come in handy as well. Marrying Elizabeth would be like taming a tiger and his parents would be scandalized to see their son wedded to a lady from the lower gentry of Ireland.

Armand shrugged. Fate would decide for him, so why worry about it?

Soon he spotted Martin's grinning face.

"I've been waiting for you, my friend! I was worried that you Frenchies might never get out of bed on time!"

"At least the French know how to organize things properly, this is utter chaos, *quel bordel!*" he swore in French, as a passing horseman made his own horse shy.

They left the fortifications behind and somehow the chaos yielded to discipline as they rode on South where the next victory would be waiting for the Cavaliers.

Decisive Days

"Ready?" Charles asked François as he mounted his horse.

"I've been ready and waiting for you since dawn!" protested François, "but a certain Charles Neuville needed to partake of an extensive breakfast before he could even contemplate the daunting task of riding to Oxford!"

Charles grinned. "I wouldn't want to return to my dear wife Céline looking a like a hungry beggar."

"No chance of that," François replied, raising his eyebrows. "I pity your horse. You must weigh twenty stones."

"Spare your emotions for a worthier cause, my horse is solid enough, we get on very well." Charles patted his huge stallion who moved his head playfully. "See, he's eager to go. I'm not too heavy."

It took them almost one hour to leave London and its maze of streets, which were getting worse every year, as the city was growing fast without any visible organized planning. As usual a handful of coins provided smooth passage through the city gates and soon they were leaving London and its eternal foggy air behind, heading towards Oxford.

At noon they stopped for lunch at an inn (there had been no way of convincing Charles to skip lunch in order to reach Oxford earlier). Two weeks in the companionship of Charles Neuville had taught François that travelling with Cousin Charles was subject to its own rules and that any resistance would be futile. Partaking of long and extensive meals was one of the rules. François only sighed but used the stop to change his clothes and turn himself back into an elegant French aristocrat: Monsieur Tavaillon was forgotten – hopefully forever.

"Good to see you in clothes worthy of the name, finally. I had almost forgotten that you're quite a decent fellow actually," Charles exclaimed as François entered the private dining room. "Have a sip of this ale, it's not too bad. They wouldn't have a claret though, I mean, a claret worth drinking."

Charles shoved the tankard in François's direction and they ate in silence.

"What's your plan once we arrive?" Charles finally inquired.

"I haven't a clue. You told me yesterday in confidence that the royal troops have had an impressive victory in Newark – wherever that is."

Charles leaned back. "Yes, a crushing defeat for the Roundheads. Of course nobody in London dared to speak out loud of this battle. But Parliament was humming like a bee-hive, messengers being sent in all directions, members of Parliament being summoned back."

François nodded. "I thought so. I don't need a fortune teller to be aware that the Queen won't even listen to any of my suggestions of returning to France."

"Better be prepared to stay a month or two in England, but sooner or later, Her Majesty is bound to change her mind," Charles answered, after he had gnawed on a chicken leg until only the naked bone remained. "Not bad," he conceded and took another one.

"You mean the situation will get worse again?"

"Yes, most likely when the new army is trained and ready to fight. Unless your Mazarin opens his chests and sends the French navy, the King will be defeated. Time is running out for the Stuarts."

"We know that Mazarin won't send any troops or real money." François paused. "But why are you so sure that the King will lose in the end?"

"I haven't been idle. I know the details of the new army, they'll outnumber the royal forces by far – and I met the new leaders, among them this chap Oliver Cromwell whom everyone is talking about. He's got more charisma than the whole royal family combined... well, maybe with the exception of the young Prince of Wales, who might become a good leader when he's older. I think it'll become useful to let it be known in some weeks or so that the House of Hertford might envisage supporting Parliament, under certain conditions of course..."

"You won't!" François exclaimed crestfallen. "What about your honour and your sacred oath of allegiance?"

"It will be my honour to make sure that Pierre's son will become the next duke... And not some stupid Puritan who'll be appointed instead by the Crown, or by whomever will be wearing the English crown in a year or two. The House of Hertford, that's where my allegiance is – and that's where it'll always be."

Charles tackled a large piece of apple pie and his eyes were glowing with satisfaction as he discovered a jug filled to the brim with thick cream. He poured a generous helping on top of his pie and tackled it with gusto.

François needed a bit of time to digest Charles's last words. He had worked for Cardinal Richelieu long enough to know that politics and honesty were only ever matched by coincidence. But if the House of Hertford changed sides, the balance of power in England would never be the same. Charles was no fool, his instincts had always been right.

"Well, let's hope we meet Pierre and Armand in Oxford. They should be there waiting for us. I wonder why they haven't sent any message."

"I wonder why we haven't received any message," Charles replied, after he had swallowed the piece of pie he had been eating. "Delicious, you ought to try it!"

"Don't you ever think about anything other than food?"

"You're not listening, my friend. You should be. If I'm wondering why we didn't receive a message it means that I'm convinced that there's a great probability that some people at Oxford don't want us to know what's going on. I really do wonder…"

François sat silent as the implications dawned upon him. "You mean everything could have been planned from the beginning, even their being taken hostage?"

"I don't know, but we have dangerous enemies, enemies that are powerful and resent the fact that the Duke of Hertford has turned up in Oxford. We should be careful. That's one of the reasons why I shall let it be known that we might change sides, it's the best protection for Pierre I can think of."

Charles smiled, waving his fork at a silenced François. "But this doesn't mean that you shouldn't try the apple pie, you won't regret it."

***

"Hello, hello, Sir Mortimer! I was looking for you, I was hoping to have a little chat." Viscount Rochester blocked Mortimer's way into the stables by pushing his solid body directly into Mortimer's path.

Mortimer stopped, as snubbing Rochester was not an option – his family was far too influential. Rochester and his mother, the Marchioness of Halifax, besides having privileged access to all members of the royal family, had the reputation of being the masters of court intrigue. Rochester not only loved intrigues, but had a second pastime – he chased after almost any woman at court, lady or maid, he didn't make a distinction. Rochester was not a man of sophisticated taste, and any female open to a short amorous adventure would do. Elizabeth had sworn to Mortimer that she had rebuked him – but could Mortimer trust Elizabeth?

"Not going south?" Rochester continued, not in the least intimidated by Mortimer's silence and his belligerent stare.

"No, I'm waiting for Prince Rupert to come back, my orders have changed, I'm to serve under his Royal Highness." Mortimer couldn't hide his pride at being one of the select few who been chosen to serve under the conqueror of Newark instead of having to join Generals Hopton and Forth.

"That's a pity," Rochester smirked, while scratching his crotch.

Mortimer watched him warily, as something in Rochester's expression told him that he was enjoying himself enormously.

"Why should it be a pity? I take it as a special honour. There's no better general than Prince Rupert. He wouldn't choose you!" Mortimer answered, incensed.

Rochester shook his head. "Sir Mortimer, much as we know and like the prince, he is always exploding like a Chinese firecracker. Of course his Royal Highness is a gifted leader. But that isn't significant. Maybe I shouldn't share my news with you after all, I'm not sure that you're worth it."

"What news?"

Rochester grinned and continued scratching himself. Mortimer had swallowed the bait, the rest would be easy.

"My mother happened to see Lady Elizabeth." He gave a lengthy pause, watching with delight as Mortimer became tense.

"I'm sure she sees her frequently," Mortimer finally answered.

"That's true enough, but not coming back on horseback from a, hmm, should I call it an adventure? And you might be interested that she was disguised – as a man." Rochester smirked.

Like an angry tiger Mortimer jumped forward and grabbed Rochester's collar. "You're a damned liar! I challenge you!"

"You idiot, you've torn it!" Rochester cried out. "It's expensive Flemish lace. Why challenge me if my mother is telling the truth?"

"I don't give a shit for your Flemish lace!" Mortimer cried, but suddenly stopped as his mind started to digest Rochester's words.

"Your mother saw her? What do you mean, disguised as a man?"

"Let go of me, you fool, and listen to a friend's advice. If the lady Elizabeth was riding out secretly and it wasn't to meet with you, then there's only one person left she could have been seeing. It's an open secret at court that this Frenchman Armand has been casting mournful eyes at her."

"Armand de Saint Paul!" Mortimer howled like an injured animal.

"That's him. The same Armand who left for Kent this morning. As a friend, let me give you a hint: why not follow him? We all know that during war a lot of things can happen. My mother told me that the lady Elizabeth looked particularly smug, you should take care."

"You swear by the Almighty that it's true?"

"I swear to God. It's the truth," Rochester replied, his voice changing to a confidential whisper. "Listen to a friend, in truth you know already that you're losing her. Since the cursed day when that French snake entered our court, the lady Elizabeth has barely looked at you. He put a spell on her. These Frenchies, God only knows what kind of secret potions they're using to seduce our women. You must get

181

rid of him, Mortimer, or she'll never be yours and you'll be the laughing stock of the court. Your honour demands satisfaction. That's the advice from a true friend. Forget Prince Rupert, join Forth or Hopton, get your revenge!"

"Thank you, Rochester. I need some time to think. It's been quite a shock."

Mortimer staggered out of the stable building as if he had been blinded, unaware of the suppressed laughter behind him.

He returned straight back to the quarters he shared with his fellow soldiers and sat down on his bed, head buried in his arms. He wanted to cry, but he was a soldier, he couldn't sit and cry, he had to defend his honour. There was only one course of action possible. Rochester was right, he had to challenge Armand de Saint Paul.

Having taken a decision he felt better and he started packing. *You'll be the laughing stock of the court.* These words were still echoing in his brain, but he would show them that Sir Mortimer Clifford was no laughing stock.

He grabbed his belongings, he only needed a few things, there was no need for formal court attire in the field. He eyed the pair of duelling pistols that he had acquired some time ago. His face, frozen like a mask so far, suddenly became grim. Maybe he should even discard the idea of a duel. There could only be one solution, Armand must die. The looming battle would provide the ideal occasion. A stray bullet, maybe an accident. Armand de Saint Paul was not aware of it, but soon he'd be a dead man.

One hour later Sir Mortimer was already directing his horse through the crowded streets. He granted a short nod to the soldiers who were guarding the fortifications but as Mortimer was known to be a moody man, nobody took particular notice.

"Had a bad day, our Mortimer, did you see his face?" one of the officers remarked to his friend.

"He's known to be in love with the lady Elizabeth. Never court a redhead. They're only trouble," the other replied with a smirk. "Heaven in bed, hell in the house," my father used to say.

"How would he know?"

"My mother was a redhead." He laughed.

***

As many officers had left the city, an unusual atmosphere of calm reigned in Oxford. There was still the usual activity of an exiled government with continuous cabinet meetings, messengers coming and going, and still enough soldiers left to defend the city, but no grand activities like balls or dinner parties had been planned until Prince Rupert would be returning to Oxford.

182

As usual Lady Elizabeth was spending most of her time in the Queen's apartments. The Queen's pregnancy was becoming more and more difficult and the King had sent for her private physician, who had politely declined to attend.

"He won't come?" King Charles was lost for words.

"I'm afraid that he declined, Your Majesty."

"Why?"

"The physician is afraid to travel during war time, Your Majesty. He's devoted to Her Majesty but he won't come to Oxford as he has to cross territory held by Parliament and he's scared he might find himself arrested."

"In different times, I'd have him hung, drawn and quartered!" The King swore. "You may leave now, there must be other physicians in this kingdom who are more loyal to their sovereign."

The Queen was shattered. She had been clinging to the hope that her favourite physician would come soon, and so Elizabeth would need to muster all of her strength and optimism to avoid a disastrous breakdown. It was all the more difficult for Elizabeth as she was on edge herself. She was missing Armand badly, so much that it hurt. Time and time again she closed her eyes, trying to recollect those wonderful moments when they had been together in the cottage and she had been in his arms, forgetting the world around them.

She desperately longed for the comfort of Armand's embrace and she tried to fend off the black cloud of despair that engulfed her whenever she thought about her future – or indeed if there would be any future. She was only sure that she could no longer envisage herself living her old life, she'd rather die.

It was at the end of a very taxing day when she ran into the Viscount Rochester.

"My compliments to the beautiful lady Elizabeth!" he smirked. "You're looking lovelier day by day, my lady."

"My lord Rochester."

Elizabeth curtsied, immediately on her guard. Rochester's glance made her feel unwell, as if she had been stripped naked all of a sudden.

"You must be very lonely, my lady, I pity you," Rochester continued.

"Why should I feel lonely, my lord? I have the companionship of my Queen who is most gracious, Her Majesty looks after me like a mother." She hoped this would cool him down.

Rochester made a dismissive gesture with his hand. "I'm not talking about Her Majesty. I was just wondering…"

Her uneasy feeling intensified, but she couldn't help asking, "Wondering about what, my lord?"

"Now that Hertford and his French friend have disappeared, you might be missing some of your most fervent admirers. The same would apply to Sir Mortimer, whom I happened to meet earlier."

"I don't understand what your lordship is talking about. As a maid of honour, I only strive to serve my Queen, I certainly don't seek the admiration of any men."

Rochester laughed softly and came close, close enough that Elizabeth was forced to endure the stench of his breath as he grasped her hand. "I happened to meet Sir Mortimer, my lady Elizabeth, let me think... two days ago, or was it three days ago? I tried my best to convince Mortimer not to make a fool of himself, but he insisted on leaving for Kent in pursuit of Armand de Saint Paul. He's disgracing himself, the poor soul, no officer may leave during war time without permission from his commander, we all know the punishment for desertion."

Rochester saw Elizabeth's eyes widen in horror and he revelled at this sight.

"Yes, it's quite a shock, I was shocked as well. But he's always wont to take rush decisions, our Sir Mortimer, isn't he? He was babbling something about wanting to kill Armand de Saint Paul... You haven't been riding out with de Saint Paul recently by any chance, my beautiful Elizabeth? No, that can only be slander. There was, however, talk that you'd been seen out riding disguised as a man. But that's impossible, no member of the Queen's household would dare to do such a foolish thing."

Elizabeth gasped. Her worst nightmare had come true. "It's a blatant lie, of course, gossip to tarnish my name – as your lordship said yourself. Sir Mortimer has left, are you sure?" she finally managed to say.

"Yes, my beautiful lady Elizabeth. Look, Mortimer's friend is standing just over there, ask him, if you don't believe me. But it's true enough."

He lowered his voice. "You'll be very lonely now. They'll never come back, neither of them. This Armand will be a dead man soon enough and Mortimer will be sentenced and disgraced forever. But you can still count on me, I'm your faithful and loyal friend, you know this."

Elizabeth freed herself from his grip, fearing that she was going to vomit. Blinded by tears, she rushed back to the safety of her room.

Life can be so entertaining, Rochester thought to himself. *Give me a bit more time and the lovely lady Elizabeth will be mine, she has no other option.*

Elizabeth sat on her bed, trying to recover her senses. If Rochester knew her secret, the whole court would know it soon enough. Unless, of course, she became his mistress. "I'd rather be dead," she said to herself aloud.

The Queen needed her and was depending on her more and more. Rochester and his odious mother, the Marchioness of Halifax, had underrated their enemy. But remaining at court wouldn't help to save Armand. There could only be one way, but once she'd taken this route, there would be no way back. Not to court, not to her family, she'd become an outcast.

And yet she knew that she had no other option left. She must save Armand. She'd need two or three days to make her plans, but there was no alternative.

The dice had been cast.

***

Pierre's heart jumped for joy as the silhouette of Hertford Castle with its towers and crenellations came into view. He had insisted on a slight detour en route to London and was passing via Hertford. The officer of the royal guard hadn't liked the proposal, but he had no power to speak up against a peer of the realm and the duke's explanation that he must replenish his wardrobe sounded convincing enough.

The impressive castle lay in peaceful slumber – a war might be raging near-by, but thankfully and owing to the diplomatic skills of Cousin Charles, Hertford was thriving and had been kept out of this struggle. The fields might have been lying fallow, but this would change fast, as spring was in the air, the cattle were out on the pastures and the farmers would soon start planting the first crops. As soon as his tenants recognized the ducal coat of arms that preceded the horsemen, Pierre was cheered and warmly welcomed.

The castle doors were flung open as the cavalcade reached the outer gates. Word must have reached the castle bailiff already. Pierre asked the soldiers of his guard to dismount and left them in the capable hands of his housekeeper. They'd be staying for a day or two and only then would they continue on to London as planned.

As soon as Pierre had changed into clean clothes he sent Jim to fetch the bailiff for a private discussion. The good man arrived shortly, flustered and agitated: "Your Grace should have sent notice, I can only apologize, nothing is prepared. When Your Grace is absent we reduce the staff and close most of the rooms, my lord Charles keeps insisting that we shouldn't spend too much money when it's not absolutely necessary. Your Grace therefore may not find everything to Your Grace's liking."

Pierre smiled. "There's no problem at all, Stubbs. On the contrary, I appreciate it when my bailiff keeps the purse strings tight. Back in France I had to dismiss my bailiff at my castle Montrésor. It was a very sad story – for me and for him."

Stubbs changed colour as he got the hint and spluttered into explaining a long list of economies that he had either already implemented or was going to introduce shortly.

Pierre stopped him in his enthusiasm. "Can I count on your loyalty and discretion, Stubbs?"

"The Stubbs family has served the House of Hertford for several generations, Your Grace, we're not only servants, we view ourselves as your liege bound by sacred oath. We'll never betray your lordship," he replied simply.

"I trust you, Stubbs. Please choose twenty guards that I can trust completely, they must be armed and ready tonight as I'm going to dismiss the royal guard tomorrow morning and want to ride protected by my own men to London. Please only choose Protestants, you know the situation in London, I imagine."

"It will be done, Your Grace, let me add that we have no Catholics left in Hertford, all the families here converted to the true faith generations ago. I'll make sure with the housekeeper that the royal guards will have a good dose of ale and strong liquor tonight, this might help to convince them to leave the castle tomorrow without trying to pick a fight."

Pierre didn't have time to reflect on the fact that the true faith in Hertfordshire was definitely different from what was understood to be the true faith in France, as Jim suddenly intervened. "I'll help to get them drunk, don't worry."

The three men exchanged a long glance; they all understood what Pierre was intending to do.

As soon as the bailiff had left, Jim said, "A good decision, Your Grace, if I may take the liberty of voicing my opinion. I was downright worried, the guards are all Halifax men and it's common knowledge that the Marquess loathes Your Grace."

"Let me thank you, then, that you accompanied me, knowing that trouble was brewing."

"I'm not the one to leave my master when things get tight," Jim said. "Your Grace can count on me."

"I thought so, Jim. Now, let's get rid of the royal guard tomorrow and let's hope that we meet my cousin in London. He's a clever chap, I badly need his advice on how to deal with the fellows in Parliament."

***

The next morning the commander of the royal guard found himself confronted and largely outnumbered by a group of Hertford soldiers. All of them were farmer's sons, well built and well armed and in the highest spirits as adventure was looming – finally.

His own men were a sorry lot, as Jim had been true to his word and had initiated drinking game after drinking game until even the last guard had dropped snoring to the ground with the exception of those men who had spent their night inside the castle latrine, throwing up.

The commander of the royal guard listened to the polite but firm decision of the Duke of Hertford to dismiss his guards as he had changed his mind during the night.

"It's simply not right that I should deprive the King of such fine men as yours," Pierre explained with a faint smile, looking at the sorry lot. "I'll manage with my own men and you have my permission to return to Oxford. Oh, and please extend my compliments to the Marquess of Halifax, if you should happen to meet him."

The commander tried to keep a straight face but Pierre could see a flash of hatred in his eyes. "As Your Grace desires. But His Majesty may not be pleased, and I shall be held responsible for ignoring the King's orders."

"Don't worry. I have explained everything, please hand this message personally to the King. I also sent a messenger this morning to Oxford to announce your return to His Majesty, so you'll be expected. Better not delay your departure."

The hatred in the commander's eyes increased tenfold, but there was nothing that he could do, the duke had outmanoeuvred him. The officer bowed deeply and withdrew, knowing that a very unpleasant reunion with an enraged Marquess of Halifax would be waiting for him – and that the fat purse of gold promised to him on the execution of the Marquess's secret orders would become nothing but a dream.

"That's been dealt with," Pierre remarked with a sigh of satisfaction as soon as the King's guards had left the castle. "That went rather well, better than I thought. But now let's get to London as fast as possible before my friend Halifax can hatch a new plan. It's quite obvious that my presence in England has displeased some people greatly."

***

François and Charles reached Oxford after a surprisingly smooth journey.

"One wouldn't think that there was a war on at all," François remarked as they approached the fortifications around Oxford.

"You should have seen Oxford before, it never looked like a fort with all these moats and cannon, the army has made a remarkable job of it, actually," Charles replied, as he took in the picture of a totally transformed skyline.

They were admitted without any problem as Charles – as usual – happened to know the officer in charge.

"No need to give me directions through Oxford, I've stayed here often enough in the past," Charles said cheerfully. "Just tell me which college building the King is staying in and we'll find our way there."

This proved a little more complicated than Charles had foreseen as Oxford had turned into a gigantic and slightly chaotic camp of the royal army. Once they had found the King's new headquarters it still took considerable time until they were greeted by the royal servant in charge of housing the members of the aristocracy.

"Finding a needle in a haystack would have been easier," Charles exclaimed, not amused that he had been kept waiting.

"I very much regret the inconvenience and I do apologize, my lord. Why didn't your lordship announce your arrival in advance? I would have prepared everything and spared your lordship the inconvenience of searching and waiting," he exclaimed as soon as he recognized Charles Neuville, all the while wringing his hands in exasperation. It was well known that Charles was very influential and belonged to the elite group of royal advisors with permanent access to the King.

"I did in fact send not only one but *two* messages to announce our arrival." Charles wasn't at all pleased.

"I'm deeply sorry, my lord. But no message ever reached us. But we're living in difficult times, I have to admit. What a lucky coincidence, that I have available two empty rooms close to the King's quarters!"

He rang a bell to summon a footman and continued talking. "Your lordship's cousin, his Grace, the Duke of Hertford, left yesterday for London and his rooms are vacant at the moment."

"His Grace left?" Charles was dumbstruck. "For London, are you sure? What about his friend, Armand, the Earl of Worthing?"

"His lordship, the Earl of Worthing, has joined Generals Forth and Hopton in Kent, my lord. He left on the same day. Would your lordship mind sharing the rooms with the other gentleman…?" and he looked at François.

"This is Lord François de Toucy, a cousin of the Earl of Worthing. There's no problem with his occupying rooms together with me until the earl returns."

"Then everything is settled to the utmost satisfaction. I'll inform His Majesty immediately of your lordships' arrival and a lackey of the king's household will come later to organize dining arrangements."

Charles and François looked at each other. They didn't need words to express their surprise. On the one hand they were relieved to know that Pierre and Armand had reached Oxford as planned, but why had they left Oxford after only a few days, and why had Charles's messages been intercepted? Someone must have intervened to make sure that both friends had been removed efficiently and noiselessly from court before Charles could get there.

"Am I becoming paranoid, or do I sniff yet another court intrigue?" François whispered to Charles as they followed the lackey in his colourful livery to their appointed rooms through the endless corridors of the cavernous college building.

"Nothing paranoid about it," Charles answered gruffly. "Let me investigate tonight, maybe it's a coincidence, maybe Pierre simply thought he could meet me in London, but I don't like it at all. In fact that's an understatement, I dislike it very strongly. Forth will soon be engaged in a battle against the forces of Parliament and I don't like the idea of Armand being there. Pierre has gone into the lion's den – but why?"

"Let's hope that dinner will tell us more and that I can obtain a private audience with the Queen, after all, that's the reason why we're here."

The Lion's Den

The fortune teller was seated behind his desk. He was in an excellent mood. The blinds had been opened and the daylight streamed through the windows. In the light of day, the skull on his desk looked out of place, almost ridiculous.

"How much did the old battle-axe part with?" he asked Antonio while his fingers caressed the skull absent-mindedly.

"I made her pay five gold louis d'or, my lord. Five more when our predictions come true."

"They will, I presume?"

Antonio grinned. "Yes, the prodigal son will return to her house tonight. I dished out twenty shillings in the cheap brothel where her son has spent the last few weeks to get him sober and properly dressed. They'll bandage his arm to make an accident credible. He'll keep his mouth shut, he was pretty embarrassed once the effect of the booze started wearing off."

"How much money do we have in our chest by now?"

Antonio named a sum; it was truly impressive. He had an infallible memory for anything linked to numbers. Never having had any money before in his young life, he could sit for hours and sift through the coins and jewels that they had acquired during the last year.

"Have you heard anything about Hertford, by the way?" The fortune teller suddenly changed the topic.

"Yes, my lord. He did arrive in Oxford – nobody knows how though, he must have travelled in disguise. The Marquess of Halifax immediately set the wheels in motion to get rid of him. I know from Northumberland's secretary that Hertford is expected to arrive in London this week, if he reaches London alive, which – as he let me understand it – is not exactly Halifax's intention."

They exchanged a meaningful glance.

"Find out more, Antonio. As I said, I want to see him."

"Your lordship may see him in a coffin, as far as I understood the Marquess's plans."

The fortune teller smiled. "I think I'd rather fancy this kind of encounter. One should always treat members of the family with the greatest respect, even if they're bastards. Keep your ear to the ground, Antonio. If Halifax messes this up, we may need to intervene."

"Taking Providence into our hands? Indeed, we do this quite often, my lord. Don't worry, your wish is my command."

"I imagine a bit of sunshine will be beneficial after having spent more than a year in this miserable city. Sometimes I have the impression I can't even breathe here properly." The fortune teller continued, "What do you think about Portugal?"

"I have no idea, my lord, but I'll follow your lordship wherever your lordship chooses to go."

The fortune teller shot him an enquiring glance. "As obedient as a slave?"

Antonio suddenly fell to his knees and kissed his hand. "I'll never forget my vow, I'm your slave, my lord, forever."

"How touching. I think I may be becoming sentimental in my old age," he smirked.

Antonio kissed his hand again. "I'd go to hell for your lordship, if you commanded it."

He got up again and grinned, full of mischief. "But I admit that I'd rather follow your lordship to Portugal. I'll go to the docks tonight and find out which vessels are leaving this month, it shouldn't be too difficult. Spain would have been more of a challenge."

"Pick a ship owner who won't discard us the moment we reach the Channel, and one who's not too greedy or curious."

"Of course, my lord, I was born and raised in the docks, I know everyone and I know how to deal with them."

The fortune teller looked satisfied. "Spain is a beautiful country," he continued dreamily, "but I find their eternal obsession with spending hours in prayer and their habit of staging duels for matters of honour rather tedious. Portugal will be more entertaining. Don't forget Hertford though, or it won't be Portugal for you. You may imagine for yourself what your fate may be."

"Consider your cousin Hertford a dead man, my lord."

***

Pierre sat in the large drawing room that was used for formal meetings only. He had found Hertford House unchanged from his last visit, impeccably maintained and he'd need to thank Cousin Charles for looking after his English estates so well, as soon as the occasion arose. But he knew now that this occasion wouldn't come quickly. Upon his arrival in London, Pierre had found a note to say that Charles and François had left for Oxford. Truly a shame, as he must have missed him by only a day or two.

Charles had explained in his note that he had tried to contact Pierre and Armand, but in vain, which meant that someone must have intercepted all of their messages – and Pierre by now had a clear idea as to who this someone might have been.

Therefore Pierre had been compelled to find his own way in this maze called Parliament – but how to distinguish who was friend and who was foe? Luckily he remembered that the Earl of Sherwood was an old friend of Charles – and one of the few moderate members of Parliament who had succeeded in weathering all storms so far.

The earl accepted Pierre's invitation with pleasure and therefore this afternoon Pierre's attention was concentrated on the fragile man sitting in front of him. A man well into his sixties, he looked as shrivelled as a dried plum, but his eyes were lively, eyes that had witnessed many events and couldn't be fooled easily.

"I'm afraid that Your Grace might find Parliament grossly changed from what it was some years ago," the earl explained.

"Please talk freely, my lord, you may not know me well, but I'd be honoured if you would place the same trust in me that you extend to my cousin."

The Earl of Sherwood sighed. "Nobody trusts anybody these days, Your Grace. The world has changed. But as I'm an old man, I might be forgiven for making a fool of myself and being outspoken."

He paused, assessing Pierre once again and then finally made up his mind. "There's no more willingness in Parliament to come to an agreement with His Majesty. That's the simple truth. Old fashioned men such as I – who still respect the divine order of government – are the minority nowadays. The majority wants a radical change, some for the sake of religion, some for the sake of safekeeping the centuries-old prerogatives of the English aristocracy – but most are driven by a very simple and powerful motivation: they think that a new government will dispense land, new titles, new privileges – whoever will govern this country in the future will need to buy support from the members of Parliament. To put it bluntly: the gold diggers are out, Your Grace."

Pierre swallowed. "You mean, everybody can be bought, my lord?"

The earl shrugged. "Has politics ever been anything else?"

Pierre nodded. "You're right of course, my lord! I must sound very naïve. In fact your lordship is telling me – if I may say so – that King Charles is no longer considered a force to be reckoned with? Who might fill the void, the Prince of Wales?"

The earl shook his head. "I'm not a fortune teller, Your Grace, but the odds are that the Stuart dynasty will lose its throne. One of the options should be clear to Your Grace."

Pierre nodded. "Everyone knows that the Earl of Northumberland is hankering after the crown, the Percy clan has always considered itself above the kings of this country. Whenever the earl meets me he chokes on my title, he still considers himself far above the dukes of Hertford. But what about the new men?"

"These men may become our future, if truth be told. If they get their way, the King will not only be exiled – they're lusting for his head. Let me be open, this vision scares me, for several reasons. The country would never be the same. I'm not a Catholic, but this Puritan bigotry isn't to my liking. May the Lord spare us this adventure."

"Your lordship sounds resigned – why don't the moderate forces rally and consider an agreement to join forces with the King?"

"Because it's too late, Your Grace. Maybe Northumberland can still change the course of history, as he has his private army and holds large territories in the North, but he seems undecided himself as to what role he wants to play."

"You mean, while my lord Northumberland is still pondering about the future..."

"...the others are shaping it. That's the problem, Your Grace. By voting to create a new powerful army, Parliament has put the noose around its own neck. The future of this country will not be decided in Parliament, it'll be decided on the battlefield. The men who control the army will finally govern England – and we'll all have to dance to the tunes they'll be playing."

"It seems that I need to speak with the Earl of Northumberland quickly then," Pierre replied.

"Yes. Maybe Your Grace can open his eyes, if it isn't too late by now."

"Let me thank you for your frank words, you've saved me a lot of useless discussions."

The Earl of Sherwood smiled. "You don't need to thank me. Those were just the ramblings of an old man. The truth may be entirely different."

Pierre returned his smile. "It may be, but privately we both agree that it isn't. Have another glass of wine, my lord. I have no idea where my cousin bought it, but it's excellent."

The earl laughed. "I think your cousin makes use of the same smugglers that I do, we seem to share the same taste. I'll accept another glass with pleasure."

***

Elizabeth was checking her belongings and came to the conclusion that she lacked a pistol. It would be careless to travel through the countryside armed only

193

with the fancy dagger her mother had once given to her and that she kept safely hidden under her pillow.

"I hope you'll never need it," her mother had said, "but I've been to Whitehall when I was young and I remember never having seen so much splendour – and so much evil – in one place. Maybe King Charles is different but his father..." Embarrassed, she lowered her voice and crossed herself. "Rumour had it that he was in love with his minister Buckingham, can you imagine such a sin?"

Her mother had been right to warn her. The royal court was still a place where the greatest splendour met the worst evil.

Enraptured by Elizabeth's romantic story of wanting to join her lover, and sworn to utmost secrecy, her maid had bought yesterday on the market everything that she'd need for her escape: brown breeches, dark woollen stockings, a waistcoat and grey felt coat against the rain and the cold nights, a large hat and a leather bottle to carry wine and water. Elizabeth had a paid a small fortune for all of this apparel. She was aware that her maid must be cheating her by taking more than her fair share, but she didn't really care. There would be no way back once she had left Oxford, she'd be disgraced forever, and most probably she'd never set eyes on her maid again.

Tears welled up in her eyes, and annoyed with herself she brushed the tears away with a brusque gesture. But as her hand came down she failed to notice the bottle of precious perfumed oil that the Queen had given her as a present some weeks ago. The bottle fell off the mantelpiece and shattered on the floor into a thousand pieces, filling the whole room with the overpowering scent of roses.

Elizabeth cursed but didn't bother to clear the mess away. Her maid could take care of it when she returned. She had more important problems to deal with and her mind returned to her most pressing problem: What options did she have? Rochester had told her that Mortimer had left for Kent, incensed and ready to kill Armand. She hadn't seen Mortimer since – Rochester, for once, hadn't been lying. Therefore she must find Armand and warn him before it was too late... if it wasn't too late already. She couldn't dispel this thought, and it haunted her day and night.

Elizabeth was woken from her thoughts by the familiar scratching at the door and quickly covered the treacherous clothes with a quilt, although she hoped it was her maid returning early.

"Come in!" she commanded.

The door opened and the stout figure of Viscount Rochester entered, or rather fell into her room.

"May I pay my respects to the beautiful Lady Elizabeth?" he greeted her, closing the door behind him. As he spoke she noticed the sound of the bolt being drawn across as Rochester locked the door. She was trapped.

194

Elizabeth tried to ignore a mounting feeling of panic and spoke in a firm voice. "You may not! In fact, the Queen has forbidden any man to enter the quarters of her maids, you should be well aware of this rule, my lord Rochester."

"Should I?" he smirked. "But I have important news, my beautiful Lady Elizabeth, I'm sure the Queen will pardon my intrusion, it's done only with the purest of intentions."

Rochester came so close that she could smell a strong stench of liquor. He must have been drinking heavily since lunchtime. The stench mingled with his bad breath, as despite his young age, several of his teeth were turning black and rotten already.

She tried to pull back, but for every step back, Rochester moved forward and soon Elizabeth was uncomfortably aware of standing close to her bed. Rochester's eyes gleamed with a strange light, a mix of power and desire. Even worse, she could read the pleasure in his pale eyes that he derived from tormenting her.

"Don't you want to know what kind of news I have for you?" he breathed.

"Tell me and then leave my room, my lord, or I'll raise the alarm."

He laughed softly. "You underestimate me, I'm not one of those stupid boys who stare at you in mute adoration. I have paid the servants to stay away. We're all alone, my dear Elizabeth, nobody will disturb us for the next hour."

She stared at him in disdain. "Chivalrous as ever, my lord!"

"I have my own rules, Elizabeth, and maybe it's time you understood this.... and time you obeyed. But first let me show you these beauties."

He pulled a pair of duelling pistols from his pocket, true works of art with inlaid mother of pearl, gleaming dangerously in the light that penetrated the diamond panes of her window.

"I'll be fighting a duel in your honour, my beautiful Lady Elizabeth. Someone – consider him dead already – has launched a rumour that you are no longer a virgin. This kind of slander must be punished. I shall be the one to defend your honour, Lady Elizabeth, be thankful for it."

Rochester had pushed his body closer and closer. His sheer presence was nauseating.

"Stop it, Rochester!" she shouted, as loudly as possible. But nobody came to help, Rochester had been true to his word, all remained quiet, and they were alone.

The earl only laughed softly. "Go on, cry as loud as you like, my sweetheart, it's useless."

195

Elizabeth looked at her hands, but he only smirked. "Oh yes, you want to dig those beautiful nails into my skin, just try it... I like women with a bit of temperament."

His breathing came faster, her willingness to fight had only excited him. Then Rochester lunged forward, trying to pull her into his arms. Frightened, Elizabeth stepped back, closer to her bed. Her only remaining hope was the dagger that lay hidden under the pillow. She was ready to kill Rochester; she'd rather go to the gallows than become his mistress.

Her sudden retreat made him sway, as the heavy drinking had made him feel dizzy. As Elizabeth saw him teeter, instinctively she reached out and pushed him backwards as hard as she could.

Everything happened very fast: Rochester laughed, breathing hard, his desire only fanned by her resistance. But as he tumbled backwards he slipped and his legs suddenly gave away.

Elizabeth would never forget the muffled sound as his skull crashed against the marble mantelpiece of the fireplace; the puddle of scented oil on the floor had become a lethal trap. Rochester moaned only once, and then death followed instantly.

Elizabeth sank down on her bed, not believing that her ordeal was over. Strangely detached, she watched as the blood started to spill from the gaping wound in his cranium, dripping on the floor and mingling with the scented oil into a strange-looking red fluid. She sat there waiting, sure that royal guards or servants would turn up at any minute, banging at her door, and take her straight to the gallows.

But all remained silent. She must have been sitting on her bed like this for several minutes when she came back to her senses. *Don't be silly, Elizabeth, you can't stay here, you must leave! You must find Armand. That's the only thing that matters*, she thought.

Knees still trembling, she rose from her bed. Knowing that she had no time to lose, she forced herself to search Rochester's dead body until she found the duelling pistol he had pushed back into his pockets together with the small leather bag containing the powder and bullets.

Her search finished, she covered the dead body with covers from her bed. She could no longer bear the accusing look of Rochester's protruding eyes that seemed to be unable to comprehend what had just happened.

Quickly Elizabeth undressed and hastily got into the clothes that were lying on her bed. Then she took the money that she had been hiding inside her mattress. She had saved a small fortune, money that she might now need to rescue Armand. There had been a time when she'd have done anything to own such an amount, but now she didn't care. Only Armand's safety mattered, nothing else.

Quietly she opened the door and listened, but the corridor lay deserted. Rochester must have paid the servants handsomely indeed – including her own maid, as she should have been back by now.

Elizabeth knew that the next step would be the most difficult. She must walk down to the stables and get hold of a horse – but how? She didn't dare command a horse to be saddled in the name of the Queen when she was dressed like a man.

Still trying to figure out how best to outsmart the grooms and get hold of a horse, she approached the stables. All of a sudden she stopped, wondering what was going on.

"Yield to His Majesty, the King!" she suddenly heard the royal lackeys cry.

A swarm of lackeys and courtiers amassed in the courtyard, waiting for His Majesty to arrive. There could be no question of walking into the stables under the eyes of the King and his retinue. She might be disguised as a man, but Elizabeth had no illusions that she'd be recognized, creating a scandal. Thus she had no option but to back out of the courtyard, walking slowly, as if nothing special had happened, suppressing her feelings of panic and the urge to bolt like a rabbit. Only once the stables were securely out of sight could she start to walk faster until she had reached the centre of the city. Only here, in the shelter of the narrow streets lined by the typical whitewashed houses with their tiled roofs and black painted wooden beams, did Elizabeth allow herself to slow down. Remembering that she had to walk with long strides like a man, she made her way towards the south gates.

A new challenge would be waiting for her at the gates: she must pass the fortifications in her disguise. Not an easy task in such a small town where the guards would know most of the townsfolk. Unsure of how to proceed, she strolled across the market square where she spotted a farmer and his wife, preparing for their departure. Their wooden cart was hauled by two stoic oxen, solid and unprepossessing like their owners. The couple must have delivered poultry to the market as their open cart was covered in feathers and smeared with excrement.

"Where are you heading, are you going south?" Elizabeth cried out, trying to keep her voice as deep as possible.

"Yes, we're on our way to Wallingford, young man."

"May I join you? I have to visit my uncle in Kent but I couldn't find a coach or a horse at a price I could afford."

"Dear Lord, since our King moved to Oxford, everything has become outrageously expensive here, it's a disgrace! But all the good money goes into the pocket of these greedy merchants and the courtiers, don't think for a moment that they'd pay us a penny more for our geese – although we only deliver the best you can find around Oxford! Fat and plump, not even the King could ask for anything better," the farmer's wife exclaimed.

197

"They did offer us a fair price, Martha, don't exaggerate!" her husband intervened, pained by the public ramblings of his wife.

"Not as much we deserved! Greedy, filthy pack!" she continued but then, as changeable as the weather, she smiled. "If you can spare some pennies, you may join us, young man. You're so thin, you can't possibly walk to Kent. You'd be nothing but a skeleton once you arrive."

Elizabeth smiled back at the plump matron and squeezed herself between the farmer and his wife. A modest sum of coins changed hands and she was immediately rewarded with a large piece of cold pie that the farmer's wife had kept in her basket.

"You must eat, young man, you're far too thin! Your mother should have fed you properly!" The farmer's wife admonished her in motherly tones, immediately adopting the new companion who promised to be a pleasant alternative to her taciturn husband. Both the farmer and his wife were of ample proportions and Elizabeth was glad that she still could fit between the two on the coach box. As they reached the gates, Elizabeth sat between the couple eating her slice of pie, hat drawn deeply over her face. Her decision to join the couple proved fortuitous, as the guard waved them through, nothing unusual for a farming couple and their young son wanting to return to their village after the daily market had closed.

Elizabeth breathed deeply as the Oxford skyline receded behind her. Against all the odds she had left her old life behind, and was – admittedly maddening slowly – surely on her way south and, God willing, on her way to warn Armand.

***

Pierre smiled at the Earl of Northumberland.

"It's a great pleasure to see you so well, my lord. It's been some time since we last met."

"The pleasure is mine, Your, er, Grace." The Earl of Northumberland looked as if he had swallowed a toad. Pierre was amused, he knew that the earl considered himself to outrank anybody else and that addressing Pierre by his ducal title must cause him physical pain.

"No need to be formal, my lord. Just call me Beauvoir." He paused and looked at the secretary who was scribbling at a desk behind them. "But I'd prefer it if we could talk in private, my lord."

Northumberland nodded and gave orders to his secretary to leave the room. The secretary bowed stiffly and closed the door softly behind him.

"I trust Jonathan, this man is totally devoted to me. No women, no gambling, no wine, it's work from morning to evening, a typical Puritan. But you're right, Beaver, one must be cautious nowadays."

"Thank you, my lord. It's easier this way as our conversation has to be in the strictest confidence."

The earl nodded but he was on his guard. "I will not engage in any form of treacherous talk, Beaver!"

"Of course not, Northumberland. But don't we all know that the noble House of Percy is on a par with the royal house, if not superior in lineage? I should be addressing you as 'Your Grace' if times were different."

The earl started to thaw. Pierre had hit the right tone.

They were sitting in a small room, as the earl had proposed meeting Pierre in the cramped Westminster Palace which housed the House of Lords and the House of Commons, rather than coming to Hertford House. The earl had cited a lack of time, which meant that Pierre had been forced to visit the Houses of Parliament, or as Armand had called it, to enter the lion's den.

But everything had been smooth so far, Pierre had been received by Northumberland's secretary with all the respect that was due to his position and had been immediately led to the Earl of Northumberland, and had felt no animosity or particular tension, apart from the usual Percy arrogance.

"You are aware why I'm in London, my lord?" Pierre enquired cautiously.

"Yes, Beaver. Everyone here is." Pierre winced slightly as his French family name was massacred time and time again by the earl – why could the English never pronounce any French name correctly?

The earl continued. "But you can spare your efforts, Beaver, I'm certainly not interested in engaging in any kind of negotiations with a King who has continuously – for more than a decade – neglected the rights of his nobles and the prerogatives of Parliament that were laid down in the Magna Carta. His Majesty has bent the law and confiscated estates, levied taxes, dissolved Parliament to suit himself – let me be clear, His Majesty might try to come to an agreement because his situation is getting precarious, but the moment he regains power, we all know that he'll try to renege on any agreement he may have signed. And if it's not King Charles, it's his stubborn wife and greedy advisors who'll make him do it."

Pierre swallowed nervously. The earl was not known for his diplomacy, but even so, this answer sounded particularly harsh.

"The House of Hertford can have no interest in such a solution either," Pierre finally replied.

The earl looked startled. He hadn't expected this reply.

"I thought you were the King's man, Beaver?"

"We understand that our discussion is purely hypothetical, of course. But let's assume… in a given context… I'd have to choose. I'm just trying to understand the options. If the King were to lose his throne – an option that we all abhor of course – who'd take his place? One of the new military leaders, like Colonel Cromwell? Or would the head of one of the great houses of our kingdom decide to lead the nation? Naturally the head of the noble House of Percy would then come to mind in such a scenario."

Northumberland looked taken aback. Nobody so far had ever dared to formulate the options so crudely. He jumped up from his chair and strode through the small room, up and down like a caged tiger. Finally he answered, "It's hypothetical of course. A hypothetical question deserves an answer all the same, Beaver, but I have none. I cannot see a future in agreement with the King – but I doubt that Parliament should be ready to pass power into the hands of any individual at present, especially an individual from one of the old noble families. The Puritans are gaining influence daily."

They looked at each other, trying to read each other's thoughts, aware that their discussion would be qualified as treason by either the Puritans or the Royalists.

"I'm greatly worried, my lord." Pierre finally broke the silence. "Worried, because Parliament has placed too much power into the hands of the new military leaders. They might seize power and decide instead for themselves one day. I could therefore imagine supporting a solution that would avoid chaos. A solution where the House of Percy might take an important position. On the other hand, we must not forget Scotland – which means somehow the Stuart dynasty will need to be taken into account or the Kingdom of Great Britain will break apart."

The Earl of Northumberland looked at Pierre with a straight face. "Yes, it's a complicated situation. A situation that needs to be carefully assessed. I can't and won't give you an answer today, Beaver."

Pierre knew that the earl wouldn't dare to make any further move today. His cousin had warned him earlier that Northumberland was a slow thinker and very much set in his ways. But Pierre congratulated himself that he had sown the seeds of doubt – maybe the earl would choose his allies with more care in the future.

"I know that you're a busy man, my lord. I propose to leave now. I'd be honoured if you would join me for dinner at Hertford House – what about next week?"

"I'm honoured and will consider it, Beaver. I'll let you know when I shall be available."

There was nothing else to be said and the earl rang a bell.

His secretary, having listened to the conversation from behind a hidden door, immediately left his hiding place and reappeared, every inch the trustworthy servant.

Pierre felt much relieved the moment he was allowed to recover his arms from the yeomen of parliament and could return to Hertford House, well protected by his own guards. He hadn't sensed any tangible danger, but the Earl of Sherwood had warned him: Parliament was full of zealots and hypocrites. The latter would be prepared to sell their grandmother to the devil himself – if he paid in gold.

Northumberland's secretary, Jonathan, was having a hard time not showing how jubilant he was feeling. Today's eavesdropping would certainly earn him a golden louis d'or from his new friend. How could Northumberland be so foolish? Nobody of sane mind should ever discuss confidential matters in Westminster.

His mind went back to his new friend. A few months ago Jonathan had met a charming yet very secretive young man. The young man had called himself Tony and had invited him for a drink. Another drink had followed and finally they had visited together one of those infamous taverns in the London docks he had heard so much about, but had never dared to enter. It was Tony who had opened a new world to him, a world he had only dreamed of before.

Since that day they had met more and more often. Curious, Jonathan had tried hard to get to know more about Tony – but Tony had never divulged his true identity – nor the identity of Tony's master. Jonathan only got to know that this master must be severe and very demanding, and that Tony was obliged to give him news about anything that happened in Parliament. The master would pay well for this information – but whenever Tony would come home without any interesting news, he would be beaten and whipped and sent to bed without a meal. A single tear had rolled down Tony's cheek when he had told him the sad story. Since that day Jonathan had made sure never to come to their meeting without a story that would be of interest for Tony's master – and thus save Tony from his master's wrath.

Jonathan's heart beat faster as not only had Tony become a regular source of considerable income, but Tony was exceptionally beautiful, in a boyish way, with soft skin and a smile that showed a row of impeccable teeth. Jonathan was aware that his desire must come from the devil and that he was supposed to fight it. Dutifully he had tried to chastise himself and to purify his soul. He had tried all possible means: prayer, fasting, even flagellating himself – but to no avail. Whenever the young man with the soft skin and deep blue eyes looked at him, Jonathan was helpless, the world around him ceased to exist. Overwhelmed by a so far unsated desire, wanting to please the young man, Jonathan continued to spy for him and report every detail – just to be tortured by his conscience immediately after Tony had left and the spell would be broken.

Jonathan knew that today's information would be exceptionally valuable. The Duke of Hertford was trying to rally allies for what could only be qualified as a coup d'état – treason in the eyes of either the royal or the Puritan faction. This was worth a special reward – and more than the chaste kiss he had received from Tony so far. The secretary's heart was beating faster and faster as he finished his crucial notes of the discussion he had overheard.

Suddenly he was awoken from his daydreaming. "What are you scribbling there, Jonathan?" thundered the voice of the Earl of Northumberland. "Are you listening to me, show me what you're writing!"

The secretary came back to earth and blushed. "I apologize, my lord, but you instructed me to draft a deed for your estate on the Scottish border and I'm trying to note the essential points before I start drafting the final version, it's very technical."

The earl was immediately mollified. "Indeed, I had forgotten about this. But leave this for now. We have a more urgent matter to attend to as I need to prepare a speech. Hertford said a lot of nonsense but he was right in one thing, I must make sure that this Cromwell does not steal all of the attention."

***

"Well, you've looked better." The fortune teller smirked and looked at the swollen eye of Antonio who had returned from a day excursion.

"I know, my lord. It doesn't just look terrible, it hurts like hell. Cook has helped me to put a balm on it, but she told me that it's going to take some time before I'll be back to normal. It stinks like hell, at least." Antonio's voice was miserable.

"What happened?"

Antonio suddenly dropped to his knees. "I have failed, my lord, I'm not worthy to be your trusted servant."

The fortune teller frowned. "That's up to me to decide. Don't act the fool, tell me immediately what has happened."

Antonio swallowed. The fortune teller had not raised his voice, but a note of steel had crept into it.

"I presented myself at Hertford House and pretended to be searching for work as a servant for the duke, preferably as a lackey. The major-domo didn't even take the pains to receive me, he sent a footman to chase me away, an arrogant lad who told me that they only employ people from families that have been serving the duke's household for generations. I didn't want to give up and offered him ten shillings if he'd get me in somehow and..." Antonio's voice faltered. "This was his answer. He threatened to call the sheriff if I didn't get out of his sight immediately."

"That wasn't very astute of you, normally you're smarter than that. That's why I employ you, not to get into stupid brawls."

Antonio had feared worse and took the mild reproach as a sign of absolution.

"My lord might be inclined to forgive me though as I do have important news – and I'll find a way to get rid of Hertford, I promise."

"Again, that's for me to decide if I wish to forgive you. Give me the news."

Antonio had regained his usual cheeky demeanour and continued with a broad grin. "Northumberland's secretary is eating out of my hand now. He told me that Hertford met the Earl of Northumberland yesterday in Westminster Palace. They sent him out of the room but he could listen in and heard that Hertford was proposing that Northumberland should become a sort of regent. The secretary noted it all, but as I can't read, I kept the notes for you, my lord."

He handed the precious document and the fortune teller started to decipher the notes that the secretary had quickly scribbled down. As soon as he had finished reading, he looked at Antonio. "I forgive you. Oh, and there's no more need for you to assassinate Hertford. This piece of paper will be his death sentence. Now let me handle this."

"I don't understand, my lord."

"Did I ask you to understand?" the fortune teller replied softly.

Antonio opened his mouth to reply but the piercing glance from icy blue eyes made him change his mind. "No, my lord. As you please, my lord. Is there anything I can do for you, my lord?"

The fortune teller chuckled. "That's a lot of 'my lords', Antonio. Yes, there's something you can do. We need to get Cromwell here, as fast as possible. Is he still in London or already on his way to the troops in the North?"

"He must be in London as he's expected to hold an important speech tomorrow in parliament. The secretary mentioned it. Shall I go and ask him to come?"

"With a face that looks like it's fresh out of a battle?" The fortune teller frowned. "We're supposed to know the future, so how can he confide in you if you can't even avoid getting into a brawl?"

"I didn't think about that," Antonio replied meekly. Then suddenly he grinned. "I have an idea. Couldn't I hide behind my lord's famous red mask when I talk to Cromwell? Northumberland's secretary will help me to get into Westminster Palace and make sure that I can meet the colonel there."

"That's a good plan. Make sure that it happens – are you sure that this secretary will smuggle you in? Why should he do this, it's quite a risk?"

Antonio showed his bruised eye and grinned. "That's fairly simple. I'll tell him that you beat me today and that I must see Cromwell or I'll be a dead man by tomorrow."

The fortune teller was not amused. "You're far too sure of yourself, Antonio. I might indeed beat you if you fail again."

203

Antonio fell to his knees and kissed the fortune teller's hand. "Beat me, my lord, if it pleases you. But don't send me back to my old life. I'd rather die."

***

Armand tried to find some sleep in the miserable bed that had become his new home since yesterday. He knew that he should be happy, as most soldiers or even officers had to sleep in draughty and leaky tents, which was no fun in the damp and cold March weather.

But in reality he didn't care too much about a damp bed, or the strange smells wafting over from the kitchen with the open hearth where a fellow officer, the farming couple and their numerous offspring would be sleeping at night, together with their treasures: two goats, a pig and their poultry.

Armand was worried. The strange thing was that he seemed to be the only one to share this feeling. His fellow officers were still bathing in the glory of the recent royal victory at Newark – and repeating such a victory in the coming days here in Kent was a foregone conclusion. Whenever he had uttered a word of caution his fellow officers had immediately denounced him as a wimp, or even worse, as a damn French traitor and Armand had quickly understood that keeping his mouth shut was the only option.

His fellow officers were parading like peacocks in the small village where the army was camped out, boasting aloud of the superiority of the royal troops compared to the 'peasants' that were known to be fighting for Parliament, born losers, all of them.

Armand had enough experience to know that discipline was the core of any military undertaking and this conceited assembly of aspiring heroes was anything but the well-oiled military machine that was the pride and the success of France. It had taken a genius like Richelieu to create this machine and as far as Armand could judge, there was no man like Richelieu holding the reins in England.

The battle was known to be imminent. Part of the enemy's troops, General Waller's army, were arriving from the west and it would be crucial to keep Waller separated from the enemy troops led by the earl of Essex who'd be arriving from London. Both armies combined would be a much more difficult prospect to beat.

Armand blew the stinking tallow candle out. Maybe he was starting to imagine problems where there were none. As he listened to the noise of the combined snores of humans and animals close to him, he suddenly heard a faint rustle.

Automatically Armand grabbed his dagger, a sixth sense telling him to be on alert. But as the unannounced visitor came closer Armand relaxed as soon as he felt the furry warmth of a cat caressing his cheeks.

"Am I using your bed?" he asked the cat in a low voice. The cat purred in answer and cuddled close to him.

"I hope you're a female," he yawned. "Don't take it the wrong way, but I prefer to have a female companion in my bed. But even if you're a tomcat, there's a clear advantage if you stay with me, I won't have to worry about rats now."

Soon both of them were deeply asleep. If only Armand had known…

Mortimer had been lucky. Not only had he been able to locate the royal troops fairly quickly, the adjutant to General Forth didn't ask too many inquisitive questions as to why and for what purpose he had turned up. In fact the adjutant was congratulating himself that a trained military man like Sir Mortimer had joined them. He had enough Cavaliers to deal with who seemed to view this campaign as an excursion and attached more importance to the feathers on their hats than the daily worries of having their muskets well oiled and keeping their powder dry.

Mortimer blended into the army as if he'd been there forever; he just made sure to keep a low profile. When the day of revenge came – and this day would come fast – he'd strike without warning. Rochester was a pig, but he had been right, it would be silly to play the honourable gentleman and stage a duel. Death must strike fast, in the darkness. Then Mortimer would ride back, marry Elizabeth and remove her from court, sire a son and keep her at home. No other man should ever touch her, this was his holy vow.

How proud this Armand de Saint Paul was riding on his stallion, how arrogantly he looked down on his fellow officers! Soon, very soon, Armand would be dead and cold like the earth, forever forgotten. He'd see to that!

***

Back in Oxford, François had done his best to turn himself into the shining example of elegance that he normally was, an exercise that always gave him the greatest satisfaction. His hair had grown a little, but his haircut still reminded him painfully of his disguise as Mr. Tavaillon, the Huguenot merchant. But the dark blue velvet outfit he had acquired in London could pass even the most critical examination, as did his Flemish lace collar, silk stockings and elegant buckled shoes.

Obviously the Queen didn't seem to mind his haircut. She was delighted to receive a fellow countryman from France, especially a man who was not only exceptionally handsome but also closely related to half of the French nobility and likely to know the latest rumours circulating at court in Paris.

"*Vous êtes ravissante, majesté, votre servant toujours.*" François greeted the Queen with his typically elegant bow speaking in his most refined accent.

The Queen dived behind her painted fan and she smiled graciously, hoping that the elegant visitor wouldn't notice that she had recently lost a tooth, another one.

François had requested a private audience with the King and the Queen, and much to his surprise his request had been granted with only a few days' delay. Having dutifully greeted the King and after having exchanged the usual small talk prescribed by protocol, the doors closed behind the royal lackeys and they could talk in private.

"We gather that you have news from our sister-in-law, my lord?" The King came straight to the point.

"Yes, Sire, Queen Anne sends your Majesties her sisterly regards and her assurance that her support will never waver."

"That's very kind, she's such a dear!" the Queen added.

"You may have noticed, Marie, that M. de Toucy has mentioned her support – but nothing concrete. Are we right?" asked the King, looking quizzically at François.

François cleared his throat. The King had immediately seen through his words. The Queen had sent warm words of support, but was far from being prepared to send money, ships or troops.

"It's a difficult period in France," François hastened to explain. "King Louis XIV enjoys excellent health but he's only six years old and the Queen is constantly fending off all kinds of attempts to wrest control of the government out of her hands. There are uprisings in the country instilled by Huguenot powers who seek to weaken the French monarchy as long the rightful king is still an infant. France needs to keep her troops at home and on constant alert, Your Majesty."

The King pressed his lips together tightly. He was less than pleased. François suddenly had the feeling that his new velvet coat had become too tight.

"That's understood then, my lord. But let's come back to the subject: you've requested a private audience, de Toucy; if it isn't to tell us that the Queen is pledging troops or money, what is that you wish to discuss?"

Queen Henrietta Maria had only now grasped the terrible truth, that no real support would be forthcoming from her sister-in-law.

"But Anne *must* help us!" she cried out in distress. "You *must* tell her, my lord, how difficult things are over here! She obviously doesn't understand our plight."

"I shall do all in my power to enlighten Queen Anne," François replied, wishing fervently he was elsewhere. "But I still owe an answer to His Majesty. In fact I was sent by His Eminence, the Duke Cardinal Mazarin to England. His Eminence and Her Majesty, Queen Anne, are worried about Your Majesty's safety. They'd be delighted to welcome Your Majesty back in France until His Majesty has claimed the victory we're all praying for over the rebel forces."

The King turned pale. He had immediately understood the implication.

"So they sent a smooth talking messenger instead of an army, my lord," he replied, his tone flat.

François had known that this audience wouldn't be an easy one and braced himself for a major tantrum and insults, but the King only stood up and walked

207

slowly to the window. A leaden silence reigned in the room. Tears rolled down the Queen's cheeks, ruining her make-up and leaving dirty stains on her collar.

Finally the King turned around. "I too am concerned for the Queen's safety, de Toucy. But not because of the war, we'll defend ourselves, whatever people might say. I have excellent generals – we did win the battle of Newark after all. I swear to God that there'll be a Stuart on this throne generations after me. But the Queen's delicate situation calls for an excellent physician and I might consider sending her to Bath to improve her health. Tell my sister-in-law that we thank her for her concern but it would give the wrong sign to our enemies to send the Queen to France at this moment."

"To Bath, you never told me!" the Queen protested, totally taken by surprise.

"It's not yet been decided, my dear, but I'm not blind. You try to make me believe that you're fine but we must be careful. Bath has wonderful waters and your private physician could look after you. It would make me feel much better to know that you're in the best hands. Now that the lady Elizabeth has suddenly disappeared, you urgently need someone capable of looking after you."

He had moved back to the Queen's chair and patted her swollen hands.

François hadn't been expecting any quick decision, but felt relieved all the same. The King had shown masterful control of himself and had received the bad news with dignity. If the Queen was to move to Bath, it would be much easier to bring her to safety if events were to spin out of control. Unluckily Mazarin rarely erred, things were bound to get worse. The King had said that nothing had been decided yet, but François was almost sure that he was only waiting for the right moment to tell his wife that she'd need to leave Oxford.

François looked at the royal couple and suddenly he felt sorry. No royal title or privilege could make up for the disasters they had faced during the past year. They might be clad in silks and velvet, covered with jewels but François saw an ageing couple, tired and at a loss as to how to navigate those uncharted waters that were waiting for them.

***

"How did it go?" Charles asked François and thrust a glass of wine in his direction. "You look as if you need it."

"Do I? I must be losing my touch then," François replied and emptied the glass. "But taking into account that I had to confess that there'll be no support at all from France and that my government judges the situation desperate to the point that the Queen should be heading for exile, I think I accomplished my mission in style. At least I wasn't executed on the spot."

"The old Roman emperors did this," Charles replied good-humouredly. "It had some merit, I should propose it to King Charles. At least it granted the emperors an immediate feeling of relief and gratification."

François pulled a face. "I'll never get used to your sense of humour."

Charles laughed. "My wife keeps telling me the same. But let's be serious again. I sense problems are on the way. The Marquess of Halifax is far too friendly towards me, that's very dangerous, he's a vile snake. His wife's gone out of her mind as her oldest son, Viscount Rochester, was found dead in the abandoned room of one of the Queen's maids of honour. All the elements necessary to create a perfect scandal at court! The Marquess is less stricken by this bereavement. He never got on with his son, they quarrelled daily. He prefers his younger son, who's serving under Prince Rupert."

"Dear me! Accident or murder? Here in Oxford – any idea what was going on?"

"It looked like an accident – but who knows? The scandal has been hushed up in order not to upset the Queen but everybody else knows…"

"What a scandal! Which maid of honour is involved? I guess she's just a maid now, no more honour attached to her name…"

"Lady Elizabeth Huntville. She's disappeared without a trace. It must have been quite a scene. My groom told me that Rochester was lying in a pool of his own blood. Lying next to him, Lady Elizabeth's blood-stained dress was found."

"Maybe she did murder him after all, trying to defend her honour?"

Charles made a face. "Lady Elizabeth was never reputed to be meek and mild, but I simply couldn't imagine her murdering someone, that's going too far. I guess it was an accident and she fled in panic."

François shrugged. "Not our business, on any account. What's bothering you then?"

"I think Halifax was behind the idea of sending Pierre to London and that he's been intercepting our messages. If that's true, there can be only one reason why he wanted Pierre to be removed from court."

"Why is that?"

"He wants to retain his grip on the King. Halifax and the ministers are the true government right now, the King might think that he governs, but that's an illusion. As Halifax is bargaining to change sides, he must stop Pierre filling the void. Pierre was the King's only ace in this game."

"Clever, most devious," François murmured.

"Yes, Halifax and his wife are very dangerous. Sometimes I think she's the worse of the two, totally ruthless. In any case I've decided to go back to London urgently, but I won't inform anybody else for obvious reasons…"

"I'll need to stay here, to make sure that the Queen really does prepare to move to Bath and I will then report back to His Eminence. The Cardinal told me that he'll be keeping a ship ready, but the sly fox wouldn't give me any details. On what date will you travel to London, Charles?"

"Today is March 27th, let's say tomorrow, or latest, the day after tomorrow."

***

"Any news of the Roundheads?" Mortimer asked a fellow soldier.

"Yes, I have a friend serving under Hopton. He told me that the enemy is no match for our forces, unless we allow them to combine. The strategy will be easy: beat the Cornwall battalions first and then attack the forces coming from London."

"Which Londoners?"

"The 'London Lobsters', you should know them."

Mortimer grinned. "Sure, everybody knows them. Armed to the teeth. But we'll crack them! That's a promise!"

"That's the spirit!"

Privately Mortimer was less pleased about this news. The London Lobsters, thus nicknamed for their heavy protective armoury, were a difficult enemy to tackle. But in the end he was here not to win a battle, he had come to take his own private revenge, that was the only thing that mattered to him. As soon as he had reached the headquarters, he tried to single out a guard who looked bored and happy to find someone to chat with.

"Filthy weather, mate," he greeted the guard.

"Isn't it always? Time spring was here."

The guard looked at Mortimer. "I can't let you pass, mate, unless you're on an errand for the HQ. The big shots don't want to be disturbed."

"Do they ever want to be disturbed? Don't worry, I'll be gone in no time. By the way, have you heard of a French officer serving under General Forth?" asked Mortimer, trying to appear as casual as possible.

"Why would this be of interest for you?" asked the guard suspiciously.

"If it's him, we played dice together up in Oxford and he still owes me. He's got dark curly hair and brown eyes, you know the French, they always promise to pay later..."

The guard spat on the ground. "Scoundrels, all of them, if you ask me. Snail and frog eaters, what can you expect? Yeah, there's a man called Armand Sint Pol that fits your description. A French noble, he's got all the airs and graces, thinks he's superior to us English. Serving in the cavalry under Forth. But all the officers are in the tent over there, I told you, nobody is allowed to disturb. Your money will have to wait."

Mortimer thanked the guard profusely and left. He knew where he'd need to be tomorrow. Victory or not for the royal forces, Armand would be a dead man by tomorrow evening.

Cromwell Steps In

Oliver Cromwell stepped down from the rostrum, still elated, face flushed, as he had just ended his speech invoking the judgement of the Almighty, for the good Lord was known to be on the side of the Righteous.

In his long speech he had crushed his enemies, ranging from the bigot Stuarts to the treacherous and scheming Papists. Finally he had painted a rosy picture of England's future: a safe country protected from evil and vice, glowing and striving under the blessing of our Lord in Heaven. Then he had mentioned the necessity of levying new funds to support this crusade – admittedly this had been the most difficult part. No Parliament liked to vote for new taxes. But at the end of his speech there were loud cheers, and applause echoed across the benches. Only those members of Parliament known to be close allies of the Lords Essex and Northumberland sat quietly, clapping their hands in a polite but not *quite* enthusiastic manner.

As such their reaction wasn't surprising. The wealthy landowners would have to bear the brunt of the new taxes, taxes that were needed to fund the new army. Cromwell knew that he'd need to be careful. During the next months, support from Northumberland and his allies would be vital, but later… Later a new England would take shape, a pure country, devoid of the sins and vices of the past. And if the fortune teller was right, it would be his destiny to lead this new and pure country into a dazzling vision of the future.

Oliver Cromwell walked down the aisle greeting acquaintances and talking to the back benchers, greeting each of them by name, taking each of them seriously. He was fighting hard against the sin of vanity but he couldn't help but notice how much his position had changed during the past months. From an almost unknown member of the lower gentry he had become one of the accepted leaders of the Puritan faction, a man people looked up to. He would show them the path to enlightenment.

Cromwell had already left the central nave when a clerk tugged at his sleeve. He looked down and frowned, he didn't appreciate this kind of intrusion. But he recognized the face of the man, he had met him several times already, as he was the private secretary of the Earl of Northumberland.

"What is it, man?" he hissed, not wanting his fellow peers to notice, and wondering why Northumberland wanted to see him.

"Colonel Cromwell, there is a man who wants to speak to you, in private."

Cromwell frowned. "Who is he, if he's not your master? Why has this man sent you? Why doesn't he dare to show up himself?"

The secretary seemed to shrink before his eyes. "I apologize, sir, but the man was very insistent and told me that you'd be eager to meet him. He has news of the man with the red mask."

Cromwell was dumbstruck. Never had he anticipated this response. Quickly he looked left and right to make sure that they wouldn't be overheard. "Shh!" he commanded. "Where is he? Does anybody else know? What about the earl?"

"Nobody knows, sir, not even his lordship. The man insisted on absolute secrecy. He's waiting in a side room."

Cromwell hesitated, not knowing what to think. Finally curiosity got the better of him. "Show me to him."

Cromwell was unsettled. Nobody should ever find out about his involvement with a fortune teller, the consequences would be disastrous. But it seemed improbable that the fortune teller would have contacted him here, right in Westminster Palace, without having an urgent and genuine reason, and this reason could only be another vision – or a warning.

The secretary seemed to be as keen to keep this meeting secret as was Cromwell. He ushered him out of the great hall, led him up some creaky stairs and soon the noise and the chatter so typical of Parliament receded and they reached a secluded part of Westminster Palace Cromwell had never seen before.

Suddenly he felt ill at ease. Here he was, following a man he barely knew, and he was unarmed, as the rules of Parliament demanded that no arms could be carried inside. But before he could reflect further upon the danger and folly of having accepted this summons, the secretary opened a door and led him inside.

A man of slight, boyish build was waiting for him, his face hidden behind the red mask he had seen before. The secretary withdrew in order to wait outside. Cromwell breathed deeply as the door closed behind him.

"Greetings, Colonel," said the voice behind the mask. "My master is expecting you tonight. The future of this country is at stake, the forces of evil are awake. Be at his house no later than eight pm."

The man bowed theatrically and before Cromwell had fully grasped the content of the message or could find the words to accept or decline, the messenger disappeared through a door behind him. Cromwell was alone now.

The door opened again and the earl's secretary appeared.

"May I lead you back, sir?" he asked politely.

"Yes," Cromwell answered curtly, and added after a minute's silence, "this encounter has to remain secret, you understand?"

The secretary looked at him. "What encounter, my lord? I haven't seen or heard anything, I do apologize."

Cromwell laughed softly. "That's correct. If the Earl of Northumberland should ever no longer require your services, you may always come and join me!"

The secretary bowed deeply. "It would be an honour, sir."

He knew that Cromwell represented the future. Northumberland was an old fool.

***

"Will he come, you didn't fail?" asked the fortune teller.

"I'm certain that he'll come, my lord. I acted exactly as your lordship had instructed me to do and I left him dying of curiosity."

Antonio replayed the little scene in Westminster Palace and the fortune teller nodded with satisfaction.

"Yes, that should have done the trick."

As soon as dinner was finished and the candles in the fortune teller's reception room had been lit they heard a coach drawing up in front of the house, followed by a forceful knocking on the door. The clock was just chiming the eighth hour.

"That sounds rather impatient," remarked the fortune teller with a wry smile as he limped to his desk.

"It does indeed," Antonio replied. "I'll let him in."

He hurried to the door where Oliver Cromwell was waiting. Antonio had covered his bruises in the meantime by means of skilful make-up and looked every inch the dignified servant of a man of importance. But it was doubtful that Cromwell would have even noticed any of his injuries. He stormed inside and bellowed, "Why has your master asked me to come at this unusual hour? I don't care for this at all, I don't have much time, don't keep me waiting."

"Welcome, Colonel, the master is expecting you already."

Antonio bowed reverently and led him straight into the fortune teller's room, lit as usual by a single bright candle inside the skull that seemed to be grinning at Cromwell, even more brazenly than he remembered from last time.

"I don't appreciate being disturbed in Parliament, never do this again. Our dealings must remain secret." Cromwell opened the discussion in a belligerent tone, skipping greetings and all conventional niceties.

214

"It won't be necessary again, my lord," the fortune teller answered, not at all intimidated by the colonel's blustering tone.

"Why is that? And why the 'my lord'?" Cromwell replied, raising his eyebrows. By now he was furious with himself that he had given in to curiosity and come at all.

"Because this will be my last guidance. I shall leave this country very soon. I want your lordship to know that I have received a warning – a warning that fits perfectly the vision I shared with you before. The stars tell me that you'll be elevated soon and will become a lord, the greatest lord of this country, but only on one condition."

Cromwell swallowed hard, his heart racing. Could it be that his most secret wishes would come true soon?

"What condition? Another louis d'or?" he replied, trying to hide his embarrassment behind his sarcasm.

The fortune teller shook his head and replied softly. "How wrong you are. Tonight my advice will be for free, as the future of this kingdom is at stake. But if you don't trust me, leave now. Our ways will part tonight."

Cromwell swallowed a curt reply. After a moment's deliberation he spoke again. "I apologize, sir. I'm surrounded by hyenas, sometimes I don't know anymore whom to believe and whom to trust. But I came tonight, that's proof enough that I'm willing to listen. But I have to leave tomorrow morning for the North, I don't have a lot of time. Tell me first: will there be a battle in Kent?"

The fortune teller generally avoided such kinds of concrete statements, but he had heard enough from Antonio to be confident. "You know better than I do, that a battle is imminent, my lord," he answered. "But I can tell you that the stars are favourable towards your forces."

Cromwell started to relax, and eased himself into the armchair reserved for visitors, opposite the fortune teller.

"Tell me then, why you wanted to see me, if it isn't to warn me of another defeat?"

"What difference will one or two battles make as long as the King's position weakens month after month? I asked your lordship to come as the stars have spoken to me: this time a true menace is looming. Danger to you, danger to Parliament, danger to the Puritan faith as a new force has entered the game. A force that can breathe new life into the Royalist cause."

Cromwell's eyes opened in alarm. This was worse than anything he had expected to hear, a nightmare come true.

"What do you mean?" he finally replied. "Who's the new force? Will the French invade this country?"

"The French won't move. A weak England is their dream come true. The danger comes from the Duke of Hertford. He has joined the ranks of the King. He's young, he's rich and..."

"And? Don't keep me in suspense!"

"... and the duke is negotiating a secret alliance between the King, himself and the Earl of Northumberland. If you don't take care, my dear Colonel, you may soon find yourself in the Tower of London, disgraced and disposed of like a useless toy. The game of power is a dangerous one, never forget that."

"I can't believe this!" Cromwell finally answered. "Northumberland is one of my closest allies. Your stars may say a lot, but I need proof."

"The stars..." the fortune teller shrugged, "may guide us, but the danger is imminent. Genuine danger. Here is the proof, take it – but use it intelligently."

Slowly he opened a leather casket and removed a sheet of paper, on it the notes that Antonio had received from Northumberland's secretary. Cromwell grabbed the paper and started to decipher the scribbled words as the fortune teller continued, his voice now hard and determined. "As I was warned by the stars, one of my men has shadowed the duke and these are the notes taken during a meeting between the Duke of Hertford and the Earl of Northumberland, a meeting held only recently in Westminster Palace. The notes prove beyond any doubt that the duke is wooing Northumberland to change sides, to become a traitor to the Puritan cause. I leave the consequences to you – but the stars have warned me. A bright new star is ascending, threatening to overshadow your light! Either you let him shine or..."

Oliver Cromwell jumped up. "I'll squash him! This, this – dukeling, what does he think? Does he think he can come over from France and dabble in English politics?"

"Don't forget, Colonel, that the duke was brought up and educated in a monastery. He may have sworn to become a Protestant, but isn't this rather doubtful? His wife is Catholic... it's more than probable that Rome and the ugly face of the Inquisition are hiding behind his youthful façade..."

"I know these Papists, they're cunning and treacherous. Leave this to me, the duke's star will shine no longer as of tomorrow. I'll have him arrested tonight!"

The fortune teller cleared his throat. "May I offer you some advice, my lord?"

Cromwell paused and frowned. "Yes, of course. But I can sense that you don't agree?"

"The enemy must be crushed, I fully agree. But you have to deal with an enemy who's cunning, my lord, so you should fight him with his own weapons. If you arrest

Hertford, all the lords in Parliament will be alarmed, and fear for their own lives. The Neuville clan will move heaven and earth to try and remove you."

The fortune teller let the message sink in and reluctantly Cromwell admitted, "I'm afraid I was a little rash, you're right, one needs to be more strategic."

The fortune teller nodded. "Exactly, my lord. But if it, ahem, happens that the young duke should disappear, let's assume into some remote and silent chambers of the Tower and should never be seen again, it will take a long time before your name might be linked to such an episode. In the meantime your lordship can warn Northumberland, as a friend, in private, that the accusation of treason is hanging over him from now on. As a Percy he won't risk being hanged, or boiled in oil or torn apart by horses – although being beheaded in public is disagreeable enough, one might say. Northumberland is a coward. He'll be eating out of your hand for a good while yet, and your lordship can take the reins of power and lead England to new glory."

Cromwell bowed. "I'm indebted to you, sir. When you read the stars next time, you'll see that the ascending star is extinct and mine will be rising, you have my word on that." He strode out of the room and minutes later his coach was gone.

"What did he say?" asked Antonio.

"Don't take me for an idiot," replied the fortune teller coldly. "I know that you listened to every single word, I know you too well."

Antonio laughed softly. "You're right, my lord, I couldn't help it. What is our colonel going to do?"

"If the duke doesn't wake up soon in the Tower of London and end up being executed by the end of the week, my name's not Henri de Beauvoir! And he'll listen to our advice, and pay handsomely for it."

Antonio laughed. "My lord was masterful. The righteous colonel stormed out like a raging bull and will do the dirty work for us, all we need to do is stand back and watch!"

Henri de Beauvoir smirked. "Yes, watching my bastard cousin's demise will be my pleasure. How sad that dear Colonel Cromwell will never make it to paradise in the end, but he'll only become aware of this once the doors of heaven open and the devil is there waiting to get hold of his soul."

Lady Elizabeth's Journey

Elizabeth had reached the isolated farm, home to the friendly couple that had allowed her to escape Oxford in safety. The journey had been extremely slow as neither the ox nor his masters had been pressed for time. Thus the wagon had rumbled peacefully along bumpy roads and through picturesque villages while the farmer's wife had chatted incessantly – despite the fact that neither her husband nor the presumed young gentleman ever answered. Here in the peaceful countryside surrounding Oxford the ravages of civil war were still far away, at best only a distant rumour.

They arrived in the early afternoon but it would have been too late to leave for Kent the same day, especially as Elizabeth had never been there before. Never in her life had she been further south than London.

She therefore gladly accepted the couple's invitation to sleep overnight in the haystack above the stables and after some friendly bargaining she bought a gentle mare from the farmers that looked sturdy enough to take her south.

As soon as the cocks greeted the first rays of sunlight Elizabeth left the farm, following the directions given by the friendly couple the day before. She knew that she'd need to ride south, heading in the direction of Canterbury as the royal army was stationed there. Elizabeth calculated that this should take her two good days of travelling – which meant two days of worrying, two days of longing to see Armand again.

But how to develop a plan of action? She couldn't simply ride into the army camp, her disguise was sure to be uncovered. She might have fooled the short-sighted farmers but she wouldn't be able to fool an army of men. Bribing her way into the camp might be an option, she knew only too well the power of gold to open doors. But who would she pay and how then could she be sure of finding Armand? How would she convince him to swallow his pride and leave the camp with her?

She cursed, as she realized all of a sudden that she had completely overlooked an important obstacle: the concept of male honour. She'd need to deal with the fact that Armand would most probably insist on staying and challenging Mortimer. Why were men always so stupid?

In the end she gave up, there was no solution she could think of. Fate would need to show her a way. Hadn't her life been completely turned upside down in a matter of a fortnight only and shown her the irrelevance of foresight and planning?

As she trotted along the road at a pace determined only by her gentle mare, who was unwilling to change speed, Elizabeth had ample time to indulge in daydreaming. She remembered and relived again and again every precious second she had spent in Armand's arms while her mind dwelled on the picture of a bright future.

She imagined herself in vivid colour living somewhere in France, in a country where the sun shone every day. There'd be beauty and laughter – and she'd be far, far away from the pitfalls of her previous life.

But fate is as capricious as a butterfly....

The London Trap

"There's an urgent message for you, Your Grace." Jim bowed. It had only taken a few days for him to turn into an almost perfect valet. Jim handed an envelope to Pierre. "The messenger told me that he'll be waiting downstairs for Your Grace's answer."

Pierre frowned and opened the document. It carried the elaborate seal of Westminster Palace, which was unexpected. He'd rather been expecting a reply from the Earl of Northumberland but the earl would certainly use his own coat of arms.

"An invitation from Colonel Oliver Cromwell to see me in private?" he spoke more to himself than to Jim. "That's strange – but of course very interesting. The good colonel might want to seek a truce with the King after the recent defeat in Newark, perhaps?"

He turned to Jim. "Tell the messenger that I'll come to Westminster Palace this afternoon as requested. Give orders for my barge to be made ready, that will be much faster than taking a coach. Ah, yes, ask two of my men to accompany me, you never know what might happen in London."

Pierre spent the morning in the company of his bailiff poring over the accounts of his vast English estates. It was a tedious task and he could only feel extremely grateful that Cousin Charles usually looked after his British affairs; he also discovered that Charles had acquired large stretches of land in the colonies in his name, in Virginia, a colony he had barely heard of.

Later he dressed with care but in the most sober colours, so as not to irritate any of the zealous Puritans. Only the velvet-lined waistcoat with sable fur trimming would underline his ducal status.

The Hertford barge with its bright golden trimmings and his coat of arms at the stern was waiting for him at three o'clock. His oarsmen gave of their best, and soon Westminster Palace with its private jetty came into sight. Pierre disembarked, followed by his private guard until they entered the old palace building that housed the two chambers of Parliament. As soon as they entered the grounds of the revered institution, his guards were obliged to wait outside. It was a centuries-old tradition that no gentleman was allowed to enter parliament armed or accompanied by his own guards. A wise rule, as deadly brawls had once been a part of life in Parliament.

Pierre's arrival had been expected and with all the respect due to a peer of the realm he was led through the cavernous building until he reached the small office that Cromwell must have chosen for their private discussion. But all of a sudden Pierre sensed that something was wrong. Inside the small room a person was waiting for him, but it was not the Colonel. He had never seen the man who was sitting there – and yet – something in his face appeared disturbingly familiar.

He waited, but nothing happened. The man didn't move and remained silent. Finally Pierre decided to speak as the silence was unnerving him.

"Colonel Cromwell invited me to come to speak privately with him, why do you keep me waiting?" He signalled to the two Parliament guards standing behind him.

"I can assure you, that we won't keep you waiting, Your Grace."

The man gave a sign to the guards and suddenly Pierre felt the blade of a dagger pointing at his back, cutting through the velvet material of his waistcoat.

"I hereby inform Your Grace that you are under arrest, as you have been found guilty of engaging in acts of treason. Your Grace is aware of the punishment inflicted by English law on those who dare to break it?"

The man had a strange accent, but Pierre didn't notice, he was furious.

"That's a lie. The law in this country is not in the hands of people like you or Colonel Cromwell. You may not like it, but the law may only be spoken in the name of the King. You will regret this impertinence, you must be totally mad!"

But the man only smiled. Slowly he removed the large hat that had hidden most of his face, then he removed his false moustache.

Pierre gasped. He knew this face so well – it was the face of his cousin. Pierre swallowed hard. "Henri de Beauvoir!"

This must be a nightmare, this couldn't be true! But as Pierre's arms were brutally bent backwards and bound, there could be no denial. He had delivered himself into the hands of his murderous cousin.

"Yes, it's the rightful Marquis de Beauvoir who's standing here. My dear bastard cousin, don't gawk at me like a simpleton – but then, you were never that bright, *n'est ce pas?*"

Henri laughed softly. "Isn't it nice to have a family reunion? But you don't look particularly pleased, do try harder."

"What's going on?" Pierre finally demanded, having regained his voice.

"You've been stupid enough to get involved in politics in this strange country and Mr. Cromwell, a good friend of mine by the way, doesn't appreciate your amateurish meddling at all."

He paused, relishing Pierre's consternation.

"This here," he waved a document, "is an arrest warrant issued by Parliament to hold you for acts of treason and I thought that you might appreciate it if these bad tidings were brought to you by a relative rather than by some unknown stranger. Let me kiss you goodbye – the sentence for treason by the way, but you'll know this, I guess, is beheading."

Henri stepped forward as if he wanted to kiss him. Pierre couldn't retreat, the blade of the dagger was cutting into his shoulder. As Henri came closer Pierre could see new scars marring the former beauty of his face from a close distance. Henri stopped, spat at Pierre and then he turned to his men. "Take him to the Tower, everything has been prepared."

Before he could respond, Pierre was gagged and his eyes blindfolded with a cloth. There would be no trial, no public assembly. He realized that he had walked into a trap like a blind mouse. It didn't matter in the end if the trap had been set by his cousin Henri or by Cromwell. He was to be removed, silently, efficiently. A pawn in the game of chess they call power, a pawn that had been careless enough to get in the way of a cousin he had believed to be dead and a ruthless colonel who aspired to become the new ruler of England.

Pierre was tossed into a barge, this time not his own comfortable one but a stinking barge, with a malodorous mix of sweat, mould and sewage. As soon as he had stepped inside the barge, a musket was pushed into the hollow of his knees from behind and like a heavy bag Pierre slumped on the hard bench wincing in pain as he hit the wooden planking.

He heard the familiar sound of oars dipping into the River Thames, until they reached an underground access or canal that must link the river Thames with the Tower. Down here it was biting cold, and he could hear the hollow echo of the men's rough voices and the oars dipping into the water. How many famous people had taken this way before him? How many had ever left these walls alive?

"Move your arse!" a stern voice commanded.

"You must say: move your arse, *Your Grace*." The guard's friend giggled. "Didn't your mum teach you good manners? Maybe we should carry his Grace – it might just happen though that I should slip and drop our precious cargo in the river."

"That might earn us an extra shilling," joked a second voice, followed by the rough laughter of the others.

"Move you arses, men, or you'll be taking a swim in the river. We have a prisoner to deliver and that's all," answered the stern voice of their commander. Immediately the men obeyed and fell silent.

Pierre stumbled to his feet and was dragged up a mossy and slippery jetty. He walked awkwardly, knees still hurting while he was pushed up several steps, and heard doors open and shut. They climbed a flight of stairs upwards, then they went down until he lost count of how many stairs he had mastered. As he was still blindfolded, he slipped several times and banged his head against the low ceilings

222

and bruised himself, until finally they reached his destination. Only now as the cloth was removed from his eyes could Pierre set eyes on his final surroundings.

There was not a lot to see though. Colonel Cromwell had not deemed it necessary to follow the tradition that members of the high aristocracy had the privilege of being brought to the upper part of the Tower, the former royal palace. He had been brought down to the dungeons normally reserved for the lowest scum.

In the flickering light of the torches and the few rays of light that found their way through the tiny barred window, he realized that he had been brought into one of the damp prison cells that must be adjacent to the River Thames. The light of the torches was reflected off the wet limestone walls. His prison cell was totally empty with the exception of a wooden bed that had been placed in a corner. Pierre reflected – in a strangely detached manner – that if Cromwell or his cousin didn't kill him, the cold and the damp from the river certainly would.

The heavy oak door fell shut uttering a sorrowful creaking noise, followed by a loud bang as if even the door wanted to protest against the injustice it had to witness. Once the door was closed, everything was dark and silent and Pierre crumpled upon his bed, giving up any proud ducal airs as finally he succumbed to the abyss of misery and despair that was engulfing him.

***

"Excellent, brilliant!" The fortune teller had never been in such a good mood before. "This was really excellent. Everything worked to perfection, my cousin will never see daylight again and Cromwell paid us a fortune, as I worked out a plan that will leave him with clean hands. You're sure he'll never come out alive?"

Antonio nodded. "Yes, my lord. I promised a lavish bribe – but have paid only a part so far. The rest will only be paid when the duke is dead. They'll forget to bring him food and he's mentioned nowhere in the records of the Tower, so he doesn't exist. It's as simple as that. Such things can happen in a big prison. There's no heating, give him three of four nights and he's a dead man."

"You have no compassion?" asked Henri de Beauvoir, the fortune teller.

"I have only one passion, my lord." Antonio sank to his knees and kissed Henri's hand.

"How endearing," murmured the fortune teller. "A new experience, indeed. Let's go home now, I feel like celebrating."

Jean Steps In

A fortnight before, Pierre's faithful servant, Jean, had taken his leave from a buoyant and heavily pregnant Marie and a very thoughtful Céline in Reims. Travel to Calais had been smooth and fast but he had been compelled to stop and wait almost a week in the port of Calais until the stormy weather had cleared and the captain had been willing to set sail for Dover. During this time, night after night, Jean had been haunted by strange and most terrifying nightmares. Therefore it was with trepidation rather than relief that he set eyes on the skyline of London, having ridden the last miles as if the very devil were pursuing him.

Jean was immediately recognized by the staff at Hertford House but he entered a palace in a state of turmoil. "Jean, it's so good to see you again, you must help us!" wailed the major-domo.

"What's happened, can I greet my master first, is he here?"

"Oh Jean, I don't even know how to tell you! It's a disaster, I'm shattered! His Grace has been missing since yesterday, we have no idea what's going on or where he could be." The major-domo tried hard not to weep, but this rock of dignity had become a bag of nerves.

Jean stiffened. His worst fears were becoming reality. "Is there anybody who can tell me something clear and concise?" Jean demanded of the major-domo.

"Let me explain, I'm used to managing in a crisis," came an unfamiliar voice suddenly from behind. "How do you do? I'm Jim, I've been his Grace's valet during the past weeks. I met the duke after he arrived together with my lord Armand from France. I won't go into details, but they had a sort of, well, let's call it a disagreement, with a bunch of thugs and I helped them out. Well, now it seems that his Grace is in trouble again. Who are you, by the way? From the way the major-domo was greeting you, you must be the Messiah himself...?"

Despite his worries, Jean had to laugh. "I'm Jean, I'm the French valet of M. le Marquis, I mean his Grace, in France." Jean sighed. "My master is prone to ending up in trouble, that's why I rushed to England, I simply knew that something was wrong. I should never have let him travel alone."

They shook hands, having taken an instant liking to one another.

"His Grace has been talking a lot about you, mostly as he was missing your talents when I was looking after him. He told me that you were supposed to be looking after his wife. By the way, I'm not a valet by training at all – as his Grace never stops reminding me," Jim grinned, full of mischief.

Jean smiled back. "I simply had to come, I had nightmares that something might happen to M. le Marquis. Apparently I was right. Tell me all, Jim, what happened, what can we do?"

"His Grace set off in his barge and with two of his guards for Westminster Palace yesterday afternoon, as he had received an invitation to join Colonel Cromwell in Parliament. I don't know if you've heard about Cromwell? He's a military leader, one of the new powerful men here in London. I know about this meeting as his Grace read the message aloud when I was still in the dining room. His Grace was expected to return home before nightfall but nobody came, no message, nothing. Only the empty barge returned the next morning, the oarsmen had been searching for the duke the whole night. The major-domo informed the sheriff, sent a messenger to Westminster Palace but word came back that Cromwell had left London two days ago, they claimed that nobody has even seen the duke, his two guards have disappeared without a trace."

"Is Mr. Charles Neuville in London? He would know what to do!"

"The major-domo sent Lord Charles a message. I've never met him, but I've heard a lot about him. Lord Charles is in Oxford though, we'll need to come up with a plan ourselves. You look totally exhausted. May I suggest that you freshen up, have a meal and let's sit down to do some thinking together. There must be a way to bribe our way into Westminster Palace," Jim suggested.

Jean raised his eyebrows. "You don't sound like a servant at all, Jim."

"Oh, I forgot to introduce myself properly!" Jim bowed elegantly. "My name is Jim and I'm probably one of the most astute smugglers of fine wine and liquor this kingdom has ever seen."

Jean grinned. "You sound like just the right man in these circumstances. Let me change my shirt and let's talk over a meal in the kitchen and see what we can do. I know that my master is in trouble, but he isn't dead yet, I'd feel it if he were."

"Then there's still hope – let's go find him and make minced meat out of his enemies!"

***

Cousin Charles had shrouded his plan to leave Oxford in total secrecy. Only François knew that his early morning hunting foray – accompanied by a single groom – would be an excuse to mask Charles's immediate departure to London.

Charles knew the region between Oxford and London like the back of his hand, therefore he had no difficulties avoiding the patrolling soldiers from both sides and arrived at the gates of London without being noticed or having encountered any major incident. There had been a small incident en route, but the two highwaymen who had anticipated an easy prey on seeing a lone horseman travelling to London

225

accompanied only by his groom had paid dearly for their insolence and were now awaiting the last judgement with a neat bullet hole in their heads.

Charles had the skill of being able to take on any identity – nobody would have suspected that this giant of a man in suede breeches and simple waistcoat was in truth a member of one of the leading families of the kingdom.

"Hello Elias," he greeted the officer, who was trying to cope with the never ending influx of travellers through the western gate into London.

"Is that you, Charles?" exclaimed the young officer. "You look like a damned poacher!"

"Do I? You look worse, if that's any consolation, you look like an idiot Roundhead!"

Elias made him a sign for him to be quiet and move to one side. "You know, Charles, I have only a small barony to inherit – and only if this stubborn uncle of mine finally makes it to the grave. Met him last week and he still looks disconcertingly healthy, how can he be so inconsiderate! Therefore I can't afford to lose my position in the guards and I have to pretend that I'm a Puritan at heart. All this bullshitting, I'm so fed up with it. You're a lucky man though."

"Why am I lucky?"

"That you ran into me. We've received secret orders that you're to be arrested. Treason…"

Charles whistled. "You could make a fortune by delivering me into the hands of justice," he remarked casually.

"Deliver the bloke who rescued me from London's worst gambling den? Of course not!"

"That's the spirit!" Charles grinned. "I'll never forget the eyes of that charlatan when I visited his establishment."

"Visited his establishment!" Elias exclaimed. "You entered like the devil in person, sword drawn and pistols loaded. His eyes almost popped out of their sockets."

"Yes, I think I looked pretty convincing." Charles looked smug. "Those old times, now I'm a married man, what has time made out of us?"

"You may well say so," Elias sighed. "I'm going to be married soon. A good match, but she's so… Puritan, know what I mean?"

"Yes, I see. But back to the present, what should I do?"

"Don't let anybody who you wouldn't trust with your life know that you're back in London and certainly don't show up at Hertford House, they're waiting for you!"

"They're waiting? How can they know?"

"Halifax sent a message that you're no fool and would probably come back to London in the next few days."

Charles eyebrows just moved a fraction upwards. "Halifax said this, how interesting, always good to know who one's friends are... thanks a lot Elias, you've probably saved my life, I won't forget this."

"I'll remind you of it, Charles. At least you owe me some of those bottles of French wine you smuggle into London."

"A barrel, my friend, a barrel, it's a promise."

Elias, aware that they were being watched by the other soldiers, then made a show of searching the two horsemen thoroughly. Finally he waved Charles and his groom through and Charles, keeping a leisurely pace, directed his horse in the direction of one of those suburbs of London where nobody would ever search for a knight of the realm.

Here he found a room that would have horrified his valet, but at least the bed seemed solid enough and finally Charles explained to his groom, "They're searching for us, Chris. You have to find a way to get into Hertford House without being seen and inform them, I need to know what happened to his Grace. I'm fearing for the worst. Try to come back with as much information as possible."

"I listened while you were talking to Sir Elias. Let me tell you, it's no problem for me to enter Hertford House, my lord."

"Why 'no' problem? The Roundheads are dangerous, they want to see us hanged from the nearest tree. Be careful, it's no time for bravery."

His groom blushed. "I happen to know the daughter of the butcher quite well, my lord, one day we plan to get married. I'll join the daily meat delivery early in the morning, dressed like a butcher, nobody will ever suspect that I'm your groom."

"Chris, you're a gem. Remind me if ever I should forget. That's worth a very nice wedding present."

Charles retired to his room, pretending to be too tired to have his evening meal in the noisy tap room and prepared himself for hours of waiting. Although he tried very hard not to imagine what could have happened to Pierre, he failed, of course, and a series of scenarios, each worse than the other, came into his mind, making it impossible to close his eyes and get the sleep his body so longed for.

**

Breakfast in the vast kitchen in Hertford House was normally a boisterous and very noisy affair, a cacophony of clinking dishes, pots and pans, snippets of conversation, laughter and jokes, turning salacious as soon as cook or the senior servants stopped listening – or pretended not to listen.

But today an unusual silence reigned in the cook's kingdom and the arrival of the butchers' delivery was greeted with doom rather than the usual excitement and curiosity.

"Leave the baskets in the larder, lad," Cook sighed. "I'll have a look later." She started to cry.

"I had ordered lamb, especially for his Grace. His Grace had congratulated me several times on how tender my roasted lamb was."

"Stop crying. It's me!" the butcher suddenly said to her.

"My goodness, it's Chris!" she cried. "Why are you delivering the meat this morning?"

"Oh, dear Lord, don't be so stupid, mistress Mary. I'm here in disguise sent by my lord Charles. Go and fetch the major-domo, I need to talk with him!"

The two valets turned their heads in unison and Jean jumped up as if he had been stung by a wasp.

"You've been sent by my lord Charles? Where is he? We need him urgently!"

"It's Jean, isn't it? I thought you were in France! Good to see you again. But who's the man next to you?" his suspicious glance fell on Jim.

"That's Jim, he's been serving as his Grace's valet while I wasn't available. He's all right, not one of those weaklings who drop to the floor when they see a pistol."

Chris shook hands with Jim, assessing him at the same time. Apparently he was happy with what he saw, as he sat down at their table and told them the story of their arrival in London.

"That's the background then." Jim whistled.

"Cromwell and Halifax have declared war on the House of Hertford. Can Lord Charles help us?"

"He's the best!" Chris answered immediately, ever ready to start a eulogy about his master.

"Charles Neuville is the right man if you're in trouble," Jean conceded. "I'd rather have him with us than against us."

228

"That's the plan then, let's go and meet him. Where is he?"

"My lord Charles is hiding an in inn, 'The Black Sparrow'."

Jim grinned. "Excellent, nobody would ever think that a gentleman would hide there, it must be one of the worst inns in London."

"You seem to know London quite well!" Chris grinned. "Interesting...."

"They happened to be one of my customers – in a former life of course," he hastily added.

"Don't talk, let's just go!" Jean admonished them.

But all of a sudden Cook stood in front of them, and although she wasn't very tall, she was a person of considerable authority.

"Nobody is going to leave without a basket of food for my lord Charles. He must be suffering in that terrible inn. I'll prepare some of his favourite dishes and don't you dare leaving without them!"

The three men nodded meekly and Cook waddled off to the larder where she busily started packing things.

"We need to leave separately and meet only after we're sure that nobody is following us," Chris remarked.

"You're right, Chris told us that Hertford House is guarded by the Roundheads. Where can we meet?"

"Let's meet in the butcher's shop. Jean and I can leave together carrying the empty baskets and of course the full one for my lord Charles. Jim can come and visit our shop half an hour later, nobody will find that suspicious."

"Chris, you're a genius," Jim beamed.

"It has been said before, and not that long ago, actually," Chris smiled back.

Their plan worked to perfection; the guards hanging around outside the building didn't notice the butcher's apprentices who heaved the heavy basket back onto the wagon and left Hertford House. Soon the three men were on their way to the Black Sparrow and encountered a Lord Charles who rather resembled a dangerous tiger in a cage. He could only be mollified once he spotted the basket full of delicacies that cook had packed for him.

"That's excellent." He sighed with satisfaction. "They can't even cook porridge in this miserable inn. Can you imagine?"

"Of course they can't. The staple breakfast in this part of London is gin," Jim replied.

"You've got a point there," Charles conceded. "Now, who's going to tell me what's going on. I guess Pierre has been arrested? And who are you?" he said, pointing at Jim.

Jim repeated his story and Charles had to laugh as heard the story of how Pierre and Armand had been able to wriggle themselves out of the first trap in Dover.

"Excellent!" he wheezed. "I wish I had seen the innkeeper's face."

Jim continued the story, finishing with the sudden disappearance of the Duke of Hertford, and the mood swung back to being sober again.

"Let me recap, then," said Charles, taking the lead. "We know that Cromwell – or somebody else in his name – has issued a secret arrest warrant for Pierre. He was last seen at Westminster Palace, the oarsmen have sworn that he went inside. After that we have no trace. What are we to make of this?"

"It seems simple enough, we need to find someone in Parliament who has either seen the duke or who can tell us who's behind this warrant. Once we know, we can try to trace the duke," Jim replied.

"Yes, but do you have any idea how to do this?" Charles asked. "I'm wary of contacting the men I know well in Parliament. Many of my so-called friends might be tempted to forget any notion of friendship the moment they think they can betray me for a good price. I don't want to present myself on a golden platter."

"I know that the duke visited Westminster Palace some days earlier, my lord," Jim intervened. "He met the Earl of Northumberland. Maybe I can try to get close to someone in his retinue and get some information. It might just be a coincidence, but I'd swear that there's a link somewhere…"

"Yes, do please. Northumberland is a toad. He'd gladly deliver my cousin and me to the gallows. I do know that he has a private secretary, however. He's his right hand man, Northumberland leaves everything to him, he writes his speeches and arranges all his meetings. Try to speak to him."

"I'll do that immediately. Would your lordship know anything about this secretary?"

"He's reputed to live like a monk. Northumberland likes to joke about it in private that he's the only man he can leave alone with his sister. Ahem… Lady Lucy has, umm, quite a reputation."

"That's always suspicious. When men are reputed to have no vice at all, they usually have plenty. Maybe he likes to gamble? I'll find out."

"Anything I can do to help? I can't just sit here and do nothing," Jean pleaded.

Jim shook his head. "Don't take this the wrong way, Jean, but with your French accent and your dark skin, you'll be spotted miles away. I might need you later to help me. The odds are that the duke is mouldering away in some prison, they wouldn't issue an arrest warrant if they were to kill him immediately. But we have to hurry, London prisons are not comfortable places."

Jean swallowed hard, but he took the point.

Charles simply said, "What are you waiting for? Go! I'll wait here. Jean, Chris, tell Cook that her food was excellent – as usual. Bring me another basket tonight unless you want me to starve to death in this horrid inn."

***

"You have a petition for his lordship, the Earl of Northumberland?" The arrogant clerk frowned. "There can be no question of having it delivered for at least a fortnight – most probably a month or more, his lordship is a very busy man. In any case you'll need to receive the approval of Mr. Jonathan, his private secretary first! Only he will select those petitions that his lordship may condescend to read."

"I know, sir. Take this as a humble token of my appreciation for the heavy workload you must be under. I'm aware that it must be extremely arduous to work for an important man like his lordship."

Jim slid a shilling over the desk and the haughty face of the clerk softened. "As you have just pointed out, I'll need to talk urgently to his lordship's private secretary. The guards have told me that he's in today, so maybe you would be so kind as to throw in a good word for me about seeing him today? I'd be ever so grateful and be your servant forever."

Two more shillings followed.

The clerk hesitated. This encounter was becoming very lucrative, much better than he had anticipated. Often enough petitioners would insult him with tearful stories and pitiful copper pennies – but there was always a risk to disturbing the private secretary of his lordship, as his temper was legendary.

"I'm not sure," he finally answered. "Mr. Jonathan is a very important and very busy man, he has many things to look after. Come back tomorrow."

"Five more of those, if you can convince Mr. Jonathan to see me today." Jim heaped five silver coins onto the table. They disappeared with amazing speed.

"I can't promise," the clerk whispered, "but let me see now what I can do for you. Jonathan loves money. Do you have any more in case he does agree to receive you?"

231

Jim nodded and revealed a leather bag filled with clinking shillings. The eyes of the clerk almost popped out of their sockets and he licked his lips. "That's a small fortune, I'll inform Mr. Jonathan right away."

Jim was made to wait, but he had been prepared for that. Finally, after what seemed like an eternity, he was received by the private secretary, a man even more arrogant and filled with his own importance than the first clerk he had met.

"What's so urgent that it can't possibly wait?" the earl's private secretary scolded Jim as soon as he set foot over the threshold.

Jim bowed reverently and watched the clerk closing the door.

"Can't you speak?" The secretary was now shouting at him. "What kind of simpleton are you? I don't have any time to waste, tell me why you've come and why you told the clerk that the world would end if I didn't see you today."

Jim approached him, bowing deeper and deeper, the incarnation of a humble and shy petitioner. Once he was standing close to the secretary his hand suddenly reached out and before Jonathan had understood how it had happened, and indeed what had happened, he found himself in an iron embrace with a dagger pointing at his heart.

"Let's talk for a moment," Jim breathed. "Like good friends would."

Jonathan inhaled, ready to shout for help, but his throat was pinched by a hand of iron until the blood was pounding in his ears.

"Let me live," he croaked.

"Maybe," Jim answered. "I could consider it... but only if we talk like good friends, like brothers. You were the last one to see the Duke of Hertford alive! Where is he now?"

Jim had no idea if this statement was true at all, but his gut feeling had been to give it a try. It had only taken minutes for him to understand that not only was the clerk corrupt, but that everybody here was selling himself to the highest bidder. If anybody knew something about the duke's whereabouts, it must be the secretary – the man closest to the fleshpots of power.

"How do you know?" Jonathan replied, taken aback. "Who talked?"

"That doesn't matter, my friend. Where's his Grace now?"

"I can't tell you! It's a secret."

The fingers of iron pinched Jonathan's throat again, it hurt like hell. Fast, very fast, Jonathan came to the conclusion that he was no born hero. "In the Tower," he croaked.

Jim let his hand sink down, giving some respite. "That's a good boy, we're quickly becoming best friends, I can feel it already!" Jim complimented him. "Now, take me there!"

"Certainly not!" the secretary shouted and lunged forward towards his desk, aiming at the knife he used to sharpen his quill.

"Who's the simpleton here?" Jim commented, as he planted his dagger straight into the secretary's breast. Like a deflated bag the latter slumped forward onto his desk. A random visitor might think that he'd suddenly fallen asleep.

"Maybe that's the best solution after all," Jim muttered under his breath. "It would have been quite a challenge to walk through Westminster Palace with this madman and not get noticed. But I'd better leave now, I think."

Cautiously he opened the door but his luck held; the corridor was deserted. Seconds later, Jim had disappeared into one of the numerous galleries and courtyards, melting into the mass of anonymous guards and servants whose presence was taken for granted and nobody ever really noticed.

The Tower of London. That'll be a real challenge. Lord Charles will not be amused. Everyone knows it's much easier to get into the Tower than out, that's for sure, Jim said to himself. *And I'm not certain I like the idea of going there either. I've had more pleasant assignments, I must admit.*

The Battle of Cheriton

The thunder of cannon fire filled the air above the plains, only to be interrupted by the sharp rattle of hundreds of musket shots, mixed with the excited whinnying of horses, their hooves pounding on the ground as they sped forward, scenting victory.

But as soon as the wave of approaching foot soldiers met the cavalry, the grand slaughter began. Bellies of soldiers and horses alike were slit open without mercy, making them scream in their hour of death. In no time the soil was drenched in blood, a stinking, slippery mess of mud, blood and spilt guts.

Quickly the drums kicked in, dark, menacing and relentless, drowning the cries of the wounded, and leading the soldiers further into battle, numbing the mind and driving them forward. Clouds of dark smoke hung over the rolling contours of the battlefield, creeping far into the surrounding forests like shapeless ghosts, blinding Mortimer and making his eyes sting and his nose run with the acrid smell of burnt gun powder.

And yet, there could be no doubt, the battlefield was his world, the place where he belonged. Why had he ever left active duty to join the court in Oxford and become one of those damned courtiers he detested so much? It was here, in the heat of the action on the battlefield, that he felt alive again. His heart was throbbing, beating faster and faster as he scanned the field for the approaching enemy, shouting commands, all the while encouraging his men. In the heat of the battle it was quickly forgotten that Mortimer should never even have been here. As soon as the tide of the battle had threatened to turn against the Royalist troops, Mortimer had taken command and gathered a flock of soldiers around him, leading his small group against the enemy.

Mortimer had no means of following the exact course of the battle from his position among the foot soldiers. At first it had just been a feeling of unease, a mere suspicion that things might be going wrong, but soon the bitter reality became clear: the victory that had seemed a foregone conclusion only yesterday evening was turning not only to defeat but into a fully blown disaster for the Royalist troops.

Things had gone well for the royalists until crazy Sir Henry Bard had decided to show off his bravery and launch a lone attack with his own regiment, having totally misread the enemy's intentions. His opponents, the London Lobsters, did not have the slightest intention of surrendering and, furthermore, they were superbly armed.

Bard's looming defeat had triggered the need for reinforcements, weakening the Royalist forces elsewhere and destroying Hopton's and Forth's careful master plan to keep the Roundheads divided. By the afternoon defeat for the Cavaliers was looking ever more likely and Mortimer could no longer ignore the urgent signals to withdraw in order to avoid a total annihilation of the Royalist troops.

By sunset the remains of the royalists were trying to gather outside Cheriton forest and regroup their position, but they were a pitiful lot by now, no comparison to the proud Cavaliers they had been only hours before.

As Mortimer found himself reunited with the remains of the Royalist cavalry he quickly scanned the rows of remaining officers with his stinging eyes. It was only now that he remembered why he was here at all. Mortimer squinted to try and recognize the face of the officers on their horses, but he couldn't make out the face of Armand de Saint Paul.

Maybe the bastard is dead. Hope welled up and his heart beat faster. *Praise the Lord, and may he rot in hell.*

He scanned the ranks of officers once again until he detected some familiar faces, one of them being Sir Martin. They had played cards together only a fortnight ago. Better make sure that Armand really was dead and forgotten.

Mortimer walked over. "Your servant, Sir Martin, I hope you recognize me?" he shouted.

Martin looked at him, completely at a loss, unable to place the man with his besmeared face and the uniform of the foot soldiers.

"It's Sir Mortimer, we played cards together in Oxford, it is Sir Martin, isn't it?"

Martin suddenly recognized the tall blond man and greeted him with a crooked smile. Like all of the officers, he looked utterly exhausted.

"Oh dear Lord, Sir Mortimer, at least you survived this carnage. Since when did you join the footies? Hey, aren't you wearing the wrong uniform! You should have been with us! Maybe things would have been different then."

"That's too long a story to explain, Sir Martin. The Marquess of Halifax sent me with an urgent message for Armand de Saint Paul; I was supposed be serving up in the North, actually. But as the battle started I couldn't resist joining and serving my King. But how can I find Saint Paul now, I hope nothing has happened to him?"

"No, don't worry, Sir Mortimer. Armand de Saint Paul has already left the battlefield. General Forth sent him to Wintershill, from where he's going to try to find a boat to France. Forth sent him on an urgent mission to organize reinforcements from France. His father is a big shot there, maybe he can be more successful than we have been so far. It's our only remaining hope. He shouldn't be too far away." Martin shrugged and sighed. "We lost a huge part of our Southern territories today, there's no doubt. Not a good day for the King's army."

They exchanged some more words, trying to console each other, making such platitudes as 'a lost battle doesn't mean a lost war'.

"I have to go, otherwise the Roundheads will catch up with us," Mortimer finally said. "I need to look after my fellow soldiers."

"Good luck, let's hope all of them survived."

Martin waved goodbye and Mortimer joined the steady trickle of foot soldiers spilling into the surrounding forest, trying to leave the battlefield as fast as possible, for soon the enemy would start hunting down the remains of the King's army. No time must be lost.

Mortimer joined the long trail but his mind was working feverishly. *I need a horse*, he thought, *I must follow that damned Frenchman to Wintershill.*

Providence appeared in the form of a group of horsemen who were speeding through the woods with a spare horse in tow.

"Lord Hampton, you're Heaven sent, I need your horse!" he cried out.

The horsemen stopped, bewildered that a simple foot soldier should have recognized Viscount Hampton and mustered the courage to address him.

"Who the hell are you?"

"Mortimer Clifford, Hampton. I lost my horse in the battle," he lied.

Viscount Hampton was known to be too vain to use an eye glass although he was as short-sighted as a mole. But the voice rang a familiar bell and Sir Mortimer's speech was too educated to belong to a commoner.

"All right, Sir Mortimer, take the horse. But return it to Oxford, His Majesty has lost many horses today, we need every single one!"

"On my word of honour, my lord. But we only lost a battle, we didn't lose the war!"

"That's the spirit, Sir Mortimer, that's the spirit, see you in Oxford!"

The group gathered speed, now no longer hampered by the spare horse while Mortimer lingered behind. But as soon as possible he disappeared into the forest, while the remains of the King's army fled northwards.

Mortimer dimly remembered that Armand would need to travel along major roads via Winchester further down to Southampton or cross the vast forest that stretched from Cheriton down to the coast. As the roads must be swarming with enemy Roundhead soldiers by now, Armand would need to go through the forest. But Mortimer's first priority would be to search for a dry shelter tonight. As soon as the sun rose, he'd be on his way to search for Armand, and if need be, he'd follow Armand to France and beyond.

236

Elizabeth was awoken by a cry, her own cry. Her heart was racing – where was she? She opened her eyes, but there was only darkness around her. It must have been a nightmare that had woken her up in the middle of the night, once again. She remembered every detail of her dream: Rochester grabbing her, heaving his stinking, heavy body on top of her, his face covered in blood. Hadn't her grandmother told her that the souls of the murdered came back at night from their graves to haunt the living?

Not knowing any better, Elizabeth had been travelling on the main roads to Southampton and it was a sheer miracle that she hadn't fallen into the hands of thugs or either one of the warring factions. Very much aware that her masculine disguise wouldn't fool anybody who got too close to her, she kept her distance and spent a considerable amount of money in order to ensure that she'd be able to sleep in a room by herself and dine in a private parlour.

Tonight's landlady, a stout person with glowing cheeks, might have been surprised that the unassuming young gentleman who had arrived tired and late in the evening had been prepared to pay any price. Overriding the reserve of her husband, Raymond, who had looked suspiciously at the stranger, she had been happy to let the most expensive but last available private room. In no time some silver coins had disappeared into the cleft of her ample bosom and she had ushered the presumed young gentleman upstairs.

"Your responsibility, Cathy," Elizabeth heard the landlord mutter. "Don't forget the other guests…"

But Cathy had seen many people in her long career and as long as they paid and didn't make too much fuss, she'd gladly welcome them. And she had immediately taken to the fragile looking young gentleman who had looked at her with brilliant – and yet so sorrowful – blue eyes. Maybe the young man had fallen hopelessly in love? Well, she couldn't help him in that case, but at least she could provide him with a decent dinner and a warm bed.

The next morning Elizabeth waited in her private parlour for breakfast to be served. She must have looked dreadful, as it had taken her a long time to get back to sleep after the nightmare had woken her up. Next to being able to ride in a normal saddle this was probably the second advantage of pretending to be a man: nobody cared if she looked beautiful or not.

The door opened and her landlady appeared, cheeks glowing even more than yesterday, if at all possible. She was bursting with news and as she placed an earthenware bowl filled to the brim with hot porridge she started chattering. "I have news, my dear sir, but not good news, by any account. Didn't you want to ride further south today?"

237

"Yes, my good woman, I need to visit my uncle who owns a farm close to Cheriton. He's sick and we fear the worst. I promised my mother to go and see him, I have no choice."

"Oh dear Lord, I have truly bad news then. This morning some horsemen from the royal cavalry came to our inn. They told us that yesterday a big battle took place in Cheriton and…" Her voice faltered. "The King's troops are in retreat." She opened her eyes wide. "Thousands are feared dead, poor souls who gave their lives for our King. The rest of the troops are fleeing North even as we speak."

Suddenly the landlady started to sob. "Poor King Charles, poor England. Will we now all be governed by these Puritan zealots? No more music, no more laughter or merry games in my inn?"

Elizabeth was frozen. She didn't know what to say and had to fight hard in order not to join in with the free-flowing tears of the landlady. But she wouldn't give up, she simply had to go and see for herself what had happened. Maybe Armand was wounded and needed her help? She must warn him, if Mortimer was still alive. Had Mortimer been drawn into the battle? Had he survived?

Pulling herself together she comforted the landlady. "Don't worry too much, dear lady, I'm sure the King's generals will win the next battle! All is not lost yet."

The landlady wiped her eyes with the hem of her apron, sniffed, and then firmly ordered her guest to eat heartily as the young man looked far too thin for his own good. Feeling much better after having delivered this stern lecture, she left the room.

Elizabeth forced herself to eat some spoonfuls of the porridge, knowing that she couldn't possibly spend the whole day on horseback without a meal. But how could she find Armand? If she rode to Cheriton, she'd ride straight into the arms of the enemy and she didn't even want to imagine what would happen if she got caught by the Roundheads. She went into her room and suddenly did something that she hadn't done for a long time. She knelt down and prayed.

***

Mortimer left his hiding place early. Luckily he knew this part of the country well. The Earl of Wiltshire was one of his closer friends and his castle Wintershill was one of the larger great estates. Last year Mortimer had been invited to stay in Wintershill Castle with a large party of young Cavaliers when they spent almost three weeks riding and hunting in the vast forests close to Cheriton.

Although Mortimer had been convinced he would never find sleep after the dramatic defeat, not only did he doze off immediately after finding dry shelter, he had slept like a log the whole night and now felt ready to face the challenge awaiting him.

When he reconsidered his plans in the cold light of day, his initial plan to roam the forest and search for Armand struck him not only as complete nonsense, but sheer madness. He'd ride on to Wintershill Castle and decide there what to do. If Armand should turn up there as well, Mortimer would be careful to remain hidden, nobody must ever know of his presence until he had been able to carry out his plan. Worst case, he'd ride on to Southampton. Armand would certainly try to take a boat from the port and it would be much easier to search for Armand in Southampton than to follow him to France.

Mortimer felt relieved. He now had a plan of action, one which made perfect sense. Wintershill Castle was only some miles away and even though he must take care to avoid public roads, he should arrive at Wintershill Castle in a matter of hours only.

***

Still pondering where to go and what to do next, Elizabeth left her room in order to walk to the stables and order the groom to saddle her horse. As she walked through the dark corridor downstairs she could hear that the private parlour was now in use by a boisterous group of officers who must have ordered a late but extensive breakfast. A young footman appeared with a tray filled with dirty dishes; the gentlemen must have been very hungry. As the footman trotted out of the room, he left the door slightly ajar and Elizabeth could hear the voices very clearly.

"All lost because bloody Sir Henry wanted to put on a show." The voice was trying to sound sarcastic but it was clear that the speaker was tired and annoyed.

"No doubt about it, Murray, but Hopton should have moved the cavalry early enough to a different position," a second voice answered. "You can't put it all at Sir Henry's door. The generals underestimated the force of the London Lobsters, well, now it's too late anyhow, we paid dearly for our mistakes."

"That's true," the third voice cut in. "The King and his generals have to wake up, the Roundheads are no longer just some loose cannons, they've become an army we must reckon with. We must change our strategy, it's turning into a bloody serious war!"

"How do we change strategy if we have no money, almost no soldiers, and nowhere near enough horses?" another voice cut in, and a silence ensued as the truth of his words dawned upon the others.

"I'll have to leave you now," said the second voice finally. "I need to ride home, make sure that the Roundheads don't loot my estates. Forth told me that I'm to meet a Frenchman there, he has given me orders to find a ship in Southampton and get him safely to France to organize reinforcements from there. Not that he'll be able to achieve anything, this Mazarin is leaning back and watching with delight as his old enemy England tears itself to pieces. Bloody French!"

"Yeah, I guess you mean Armand de Saint Paul, the Earl of Worthing. Never trust the French, I always say. Better keep an eye on your home though, Wiltshire.

239

So far the Roundheads haven't done anything nasty, they might still try to get us on their side, you never know."

"Yes, I mean Armand de Saint Paul. Forth sent him down south straight from the battlefield. What a crazy idea! I wonder how Saint Paul will ever find Wintershill. He's never been in this part of England before, as far as I know. I wouldn't be surprised if he's been caught by the Roundheads – or maybe worse – got lost somewhere in the forest. Finding him will be a whole lot of fun."

Elizabeth sent a prayer of thanks to her guardian angel. Now she knew what to do. The Earl of Wiltshire had never addressed more than a few formal words to her. Maybe the earl was too shy, but most probably he had not been willing to speak to her because of her lower rank – the Wiltshires were reputedly one of the oldest families in England, their first barony could be traced back to the time of William the Conqueror. But all of this didn't matter, she'd find a way to speak to the earl – Armand must be found and rescued!

Elizabeth hastened to the stables as her horse must be saddled quickly. The easiest solution would be to follow the earl from a safe distance. Once arrived in Winchester, she'd decide what to do next.

The only thing that mattered was that her prayers had been answered. Armand was alive!

The Tower of London

Was it night or day? Down here, it didn't make a lot of difference. The dampness and cold had crept into his body, numbed his feelings, and paralysed Pierre's mind. Was this the end? Yesterday he had been hungry and thirsty, now it didn't matter any more.

Lying in his bed he heard the bolts of the door slide open and hinges creak, as steps came closer. These were not the nailed boots of the guards, but soft leather shoes, stepping carefully on slippery stones. Had they sent an assassin to finish his sufferings? Then so be it…

Antonio approached the bed and looked thoughtfully at the prisoner who was lying there, hunched like a frightened animal. He stepped closer and held a candle to the face of the prisoner, his breathing barely audible.

Excellent, he thought. *Our little duke is almost dead, my master will be content. A few more hours – another day at most – and the duke will be no more.*

Suddenly Pierre opened his eyes and saw an almost angelic face hovering above him, an appearance rendered even more saintly by the light of the candle that surrounded Antonio's head like a halo.

"Am I in heaven?" he asked.

"Soon, Your Grace," Antonio answered softly. "But maybe it will be hell, who knows?"

Pierre sighed and closed his eyes. He didn't hear the bolts sliding back into position, nor the rough laughter of the guards as Antonio gave them the next golden Judas coins that they had been waiting for. They promised to forget the prisoner for yet another day – who could tell later why the prisoner had died, a prisoner who didn't even exist?

In London people died every day, young and old, rich and poor. One more or less wouldn't make much difference.

***

"You're aware what you have done, my lord?" Charles thundered. "You, the head of the Percy clan, a peer of our realm, you allowed that a fellow peer should be arrested like a common thief?"

The Earl of Northumberland seemed to be shrinking in his boots. Cousin Charles was always a force to be reckoned with, but when he was furious, he was wrath personified.

"It's not of my doing!" Northumberland protested meekly. "Colonel Cromwell's messenger informed me that Hertford had been sentenced, a case of treason, there was no ambiguity. He showed me the written warrant sealed by Parliament." His face was pale, and he felt cold sweat running down his spine. Where were his guards? What had this furious giant done with them?

"The head of the House of Percy a puppet on the strings of a bigot Puritan? Are you aware that one of the peers of our realm has been imprisoned in the Tower – against all laws, not even heard by his fellow peers, as is our centuries' old prerogative? And you allowed this precedent? Why not hand the English crown directly to Cromwell and his Puritan cronies and kiss their unwashed, stinking feet? But don't forget that you, and maybe your children, could well end up in the Tower if you, my lord, allow such precedents to happen."

Charles almost spat out the last words.

The Earl of Northumberland swallowed hard and his face changed colour to an unhealthy deep purple. He wanted to reply but as he noticed the bolts of lightning coming from Charles's eyes, he shut his mouth quickly again. Automatically his hand moved to his left side to draw his sword, but there was none, as the rules of Parliament forbade anyone from being armed.

There was a minute of silence as the earl tried to come up with an explanation, but he found it impossible to confess what had really happened. Cromwell had played his game with the greatest skill. He had been subtle and persuasive, describing the warrant as a means to make the duke spend some time in the Tower suites – just enough to make him change sides and embrace the cause of Parliament. Letting the Duke of Hertford rot in a damp prison cell in the Tower was an entirely different story and Charles Neuville was right, if Cromwell succeeded, there'd be no safety even for the highest peers of the realm, including himself. The sober truth was even worse. He'd never be safe again. Cromwell still had the incriminating document – but he didn't dare tell that to the giant in front of him who'd gladly kill him if anything happened to the Duke of Hertford. To make things worse, Cromwell had been cautious enough to avoid signing the warrant himself, nobody would ever be able to incriminate him.

"What can I do?" he finally stuttered. "I was misled."

"We'll leave for the Tower together, and now."

The earl changed colour again. "But the Tower is in the hands of the London garrison, Cromwell's men."

Charles shrugged. "Everybody knows that. But everybody also knows that one of your nephews is serving there as well, he's in command today. You'll make him open the prison cell."

"I can't!" Northumberland croaked. "It could mean my death warrant."

Charles gave a sign and Jim, who had been lurking in the corner, stepped forward with a gleaming blade in his hand.

"It's your choice," said Charles, his voice like steel. "Either you're a man and you set my cousin free today or this blade will cut your balls off, here and now, as you're not worthy to be called a man or a peer of the realm. Choose!"

"Let me do it, my lord!" Jim pleaded. "This whimpering pudding of a man delivered the duke to the gates of hell. He deserves to lose his balls. I'll get his Grace out of the Tower somehow, I promise." He moved closer, murder and revenge in his eyes.

"Stop this crazy servant of yours!" screamed Northumberland. "I'll find a way to get Hertford out of the Tower. But promise never to tell anybody that I was involved."

"Once a coward, always a coward. I promise, don't worry. But if his Grace is harmed in any way, consider yourself and Cromwell dead men, if this is the last thing I do in this world. Now let's go."

Jean had been keeping watch together with several Hertfordshire men, handpicked by Charles. If Northumberland had hoped to raise the alarm or receive help from his own guards, he was to be disappointed. All of his men had been skilfully removed and in no time he found himself packed into a barge, one of the many that shuttled up and down the River Thames on a busy day.

At the Tower it was the same scenario: no guards were to be seen outside, as Charles's bribes and, where necessary, Jim's dagger had removed all obstacles.

At the gate the Earl of Northumberland was greeted reverently. His demand to see his nephew might be a little unusual but didn't raise any particular curiosity or concern. They were led up steep stairs to the royal apartments, no longer in use by the kings and queens of England but home now to the officers of the London garrison. Northumberland was only too aware of the dagger at his back, and however hard he had tried, there was no way to escape the iron grip of the two servants behind him. They resembled two dangerous snarling dogs rather than human beings.

"Uncle Percy, what a surprise, what brings you here? I hope that it's good news?"

The nephew sank to his knees and kissed his uncle's seal. In the Percy clan, Northumberland was the undisputed ruler.

"Yes, Henry, I have excellent news. Our forces have beaten the King's army in Cheriton. That's the reason why you may free the Duke of Hertford now, we need him to return to Oxford as now Parliament can dictate the conditions of a truce, there is no need to detain his Grace any longer."

"That calls for a celebration indeed! General Hopton had been bragging that he'd walk into London by summer, and now he'll be toadying to the Scottish borders instead, I presume." The nephew beamed. "But I have no idea what you're talking about, uncle. There's no Duke of Hertford in the Tower, I should know. If there were, he would be in the royal apartments, but they're not in use, no prominent prisoners are here at present, thank God."

Northumberland was confused. He looked to Charles, hoping for a clue.

Charles confirmed it. "There's absolutely no doubt that the duke is being held in the Tower. It is indeed most regrettable that my cousin, the duke, is here, lieutenant; somehow it seems that a terrible mistake has been committed. His Grace must have been imprisoned in the cells downstairs in the dungeons, you must free him immediately, no doubt you understand the implications of all this…"

The lieutenant looked puzzled. "That's impossible. No peer of the realm may be imprisoned without a warrant signed by the king or his own peers. Those are the rules and I'm here to make sure that the rules are respected. At least as long as Parliament doesn't decide to change them."

"That's correct, lieutenant. Let's go down immediately and if such a mistake has been committed we must set the duke free immediately; this is why your uncle insisted that we come urgently, no injustice may be done in the name of Parliament. As commander on duty, you'd be personally liable."

The nephew went pale and looked at his uncle, questioningly. The earl nodded. "Yes, my Lord Charles is correct, a terrible mistake must have occurred and I have to request that you, nephew, treat this issue with the highest confidentiality in the interest not only of yourself but of this country. Nobody must ever come to know of it, you understand?"

The lieutenant nodded. He was a simple soldier, but the idea that a duke could rot away in the damp prison cells had all the hallmarks of a major political scandal and must be hushed up at any cost. If a scapegoat were to be sought, it might well be him. He didn't like this idea at all.

"I understand, uncle. Let's go downstairs, but I'll pick two men from the North to accompany me, you cannot trust these Londoners."

"That's true enough," Northumberland sighed. "A nest of poisonous vipers, the lot of them."

It took some time to find two guards from Northumberland, maddening minutes while Charles contemplated whether wringing the earl's neck wouldn't give him the satisfaction and relief he so craved.

Finally the small group descended to the prison vaults – or down to hell as it seemed to them. The royal apartments upstairs might not be the most cheerful place, as too many tears had been shed here by previous occupants before the poor souls had been led to the scaffold on the whim of their sovereign. But as the small group stepped down the narrow staircase it seemed that Hades itself was waiting for them, a dark hell, stinking of sewage and mould, slippery and wet from the dampness of the river.

The sound of hobnailed boots echoed through the century-old vaults built of limestone on the orders of William the Conqueror almost six hundred years ago. Finally they entered the prison, where a forgotten tallow candle spread its dim light. The lieutenant searched frantically through his bunch of keys until he found one that fitted, just as Charles was coming to the end of his patience – a quick glance at Jim and Jean showed him that they were just about ready to commit murder as well. After what seemed like an eternity, the door was opened and Charles rushed forward, almost falling over on the slippery stones. He lunged forward and embraced Pierre. "Thank God, he's still breathing!"

"I have no explanation at all for this!" Northumberland's nephew was flabbergasted. "I can't even apologize, my lord. I have no record of this, nobody informed me that we have a prisoner down here." He turned to his two men and shouted, "Bring the duke to my room, he needs warmth and hot broth, quickly! Bring the guards responsible for this to my rooms, I want to interrogate them myself."

Charles insisted on carrying Pierre upstairs himself, his cousin lying in his arms like a lifeless doll. Once they were back in the royal apartments a frenzy of activity was set in motion to bring Pierre back among the living. The two valets competed against each other in earnestly attending to him until Cousin Charles ordered them to step back and took matters into his own hands.

Half an hour later two guards were brought forward and it only took a few seconds of questioning by their furious commander under the threat of having them staked and torn to pieces in the public marketplace to make them confess every detail. They had taken orders from a stranger to make sure that the presence of the prisoner would remain a secret – even from their commander. The stranger had told them that it was secret order signed by Parliament, and had shown them a document with a seal they knew so well.

"We believed him!" wailed one of the guards. "We're innocent! I swear to the good Lord."

"Let me search him, sir!" Jim pleaded.

"Go ahead!" answered the lieutenant curtly.

Jim searched the filthy pockets of the guards, then his stockings and boots – finally he found a golden louis d'or hidden in the stinking leather sole of his boots.

"That's proof enough," Jim remarked with satisfaction.

"Say your prayers," the commander replied to the prison guards. "Tomorrow the Tower ravens will have a feast."

Under howling protest the guards were led out of the room.

"What are we to do with them?" The lieutenant was nonplussed. "I can't have them sentenced to death as we want to keep this secret. But we can't keep the guards here either, this crime asks for some type of severe punishment."

"Let me take care of this," Jim offered. "Nobody will ever know a thing, they'll simply disappear."

The lieutenant looked at his uncle. Northumberland nodded. "I agree, that's the best solution."

Suddenly they heard a moaning sound. "Pierre's waking up!" exclaimed Charles, and rushed to his side.

Pierre opened his eyes, unable to understand where he was.

"Charles?" he asked, delighted.

"Yes, my little cousin, it's Charles. It seems to be my fate to rescue you again and again."

"Not me." Pierre whispered. "You don't understand. It's Armand, he spoke to me, if you don't help him fast, he'll die."

Pierre sighed again and before he closed his eyes he stammered, "Don't delay. Help Armand!"

Three pairs of eyes met each other in total consternation.

"Damn!" Charles cursed. "I expected gratitude – and what do I get?"

"Our next task," Jean replied with a sigh. "But where the hell do we find Armand?" he added.

"Maybe I can be of help here," Northumberland suddenly intervened. "Armand de Saint Paul was to serve under General Forth. He fought in Cheriton."

"Well done, indeed, Northumberland, you've got excellent spies in Oxford, I can see. Thanks for the information. We'll bring the duke back to Hertford House, and then," he sighed, "it's time to ride south. Did I ever say that I felt bored? Remind me never to say such nonsense ever again!"

"We lost?" The King was speechless. "But my generals told me that victory would be certain, easy!"

King Charles's face looked ashen, his hand gripping his armchair hard as if he wanted to reassure himself that the world wasn't falling apart.

The Marquess of Halifax bowed deeply. "That's what they said indeed, Your Majesty. We'll certainly learn later what happened and will have to decide how to discipline the men, but for now the messengers just tell us that we lost the battle and the generals need to evacuate Hampshire and the bordering counties as we have no more troops available to secure them."

The Marquess bowed again deeply and left a king who was devastated. The victory of Newark had looked a like a new beginning, a silver cloud on the horizon. Tactics had been discussed in detail and at length with Prince Rupert: first they'd secure the North, then the South, then launch the final assault on London. Now this careful master plan was nothing but a dream, his kingdom shrunk in a matter of hours to some loyal counties close to Cornwall and those in the North. By name he was still the King of Scotland and Ireland – but would his subjects in those remote kingdoms respect their oath of allegiance when things were dire? It was doubtful at best, as no king had ever ruled the Scots – rather the Scots had a bad habit of ruling their kings.

Another truth dawned upon him. Oxford would no longer be safe, he'd need to evacuate the city, and this meant he'd need to send the Queen to safety in Bath. How would she take the news? He feared the worst. He simply couldn't tell her. Suddenly he had an idea – at least this problem could be solved.

"Call me this Frenchman, this François de Toucy! I need to talk to him quickly," he ordered his lackey.

"Immediately, Your Majesty!"

As François had been riding out, it took more time than foreseen to bring him before the King. Deaf to the urgent pleas of the desperate servant, François had insisted on returning to his room first to dress correctly to meet the King of England. These English peasants might think it appropriate to meet their sovereign in their dirty riding attire, but he, François de Toucy, knew better than to lower himself to such standards.

Therefore a very elegant and impeccably dressed François de Toucy, skin still glowing from some hours spent in the saddle, met a King who looked ghastly, the mere shadow of a powerful sovereign. But years spent at court had taught François to keep his face under complete control. The King appreciated that François was going through the reassuring motions of royal protocol, a centuries-old routine that helped

King Charles to regain his balance and come to grips with the difficult tasks that fate had decided to lay on his shoulders.

"How can I serve Your Majesty?" François finally asked.

"We may need to retreat shortly to our Northern territories," the King replied haughtily, making it sound as if he were planning a lengthy hunting foray.

François raised his eyebrows and waited. Finally the King cleared his throat and continued. "You'll hear it soon enough, de Toucy. Hopton and Forth allowed themselves to be defeated. We lost a battle and a considerable part of our southern troops. Oxford may not be safe in the future. We want you, therefore, my lord, to inform Her Majesty, the Queen, that it's our wish and royal command that she is to take up residence in Bath where she'll be safe and can be treated by her private physician."

François knew how difficult it must be for the King to speak those words. Once again he felt sorry for this man whom luck had abandoned. "It will be done, Your Majesty. I'll inform the Queen and I'll gladly accompany her to Bath if Your Majesty would kindly grant me this request."

"We not only grant this request, it will be a relief for us know that Her Majesty has a compatriot and friend to bring her to Bath. The Queen is in a delicate situation, as you may know."

Their eyes met, no further words were needed. François bowed deeply, his face set in the mask of a non-questioning courtier. Only his wife and closest friends would have known how much he detested the task that lay before him: to inform the pregnant Queen that she was to leave her husband and court in order to live in a small provincial city, far away from anybody she knew and liked. Her only companions would be constant worries and concern: about her own health and safety, the growing baby in her belly, her husband, the children she'd have to leave behind, not to forget her kingdom that was in a state of dissolution.

But to his total surprise, the audience with the Queen turned out to be entirely different from his expectations. François had been prepared for tears, her legendary tantrums, dramatic scenes. But the Queen listened politely to his polished words and cut him short. "I know why His Majesty sent you. I shall have to leave for Bath. You can tell His Majesty that I'm ready and that I appreciate his kindness and consideration."

The Queen rose from her armchair and immediately François jumped up to follow her example.

"I was born a *Princesse Royale*, a *fille de France*, Monsieur. I had to learn as a young girl that a royal princess, and later a queen, has no right to a private life, we belong to our country, we're married to our country and we'll die for it. If the Lord wants to test my resilience, so be it. I'm ready."

François sank to his knees and kissed her hand. "Your servant forever, Ma'am. You are truly a great Queen."

"I don't consider myself a great queen, but I know my duty, Monsieur. A pity that the great majority of people at this court don't. Things might have turned out differently if they did."

Lady Elizabeth Continues Her Journey

Elizabeth urged the inn's groom to saddle her horse quickly and added a fat gratuity to silence any protest that other guests had requested his services earlier and should be served first. In due course her horse was saddled and ready to leave, and just in time, as the Earl of Wiltshire appeared, accompanied by his groom and a fellow officer she hadn't met before. Hearing them enter the stables Elizabeth ducked into a corner and made herself invisible.

As the groom untied their horses, Wiltshire said to him, "You must guide us, Harry. You were born here and you know this region in and out. How can we best ride home without being caught by those bloody Roundheads?"

"The only way is to ride straight through the forest, my lord. Most people won't do it, the folks here say it's haunted and sometimes I think they're right. My father was one of the forest wardens. It's a weird forest, he always said. But we have no choice. All the roads will be blocked and controlled by the enemy."

"Yes, that's true. You're sure you'll find your way in the forest? I have no desire to get lost, I remember I lost my way once, I was a young boy then, but it was quite an experience."

"I'm sure to find the way, my lord. I know the forest like the back of my hand."

His fellow officer laughed. "The famous Earl of Wiltshire, decorated with the highest medals for bravery in the field, frightened of getting lost in a forest?"

The earl grinned, his boyish face full of mischief. "Yes, I was scared stiff. I was on a young, untrained horse I wasn't supposed to be riding. I was expected to be spending my day at home, studying diligently with my tutor – and I knew that my father would be waiting for me with a whip, he never shared my idea of fun and wasn't known for being very compassionate either."

"That's frightening, indeed. Did he use the whip in the end?"

The earl laughed. "He wanted to, but my grandmother saved me. She put him in his place and started to remind him of a string of stupid things he had done at my age. The punishment was reduced to confinement in my room, and I was sent upstairs without dinner."

"A bit of suffering then all the same!"

"Not really," he winked. "A parlour maid brought me dinner secretly later at night, we were about the same age, and… But we shouldn't be standing here exchanging reminiscences. Let's go. Do you think the weather will hold, Harry?"

"I think so, my lord. But tomorrow we should expect some really nasty thunderstorms." He pointed at a scar on his cheek. "Whenever my scar is itchy, it's a sure sign that the weather is going to change. We'd better be home by tonight."

Minutes later the small group left the inn, and guided by Harry they immediately turned towards a narrow path on the left and were swallowed by the dense forest. Elizabeth watched them leave and quickly steered her horse onto the same path. She'd rather have left a much bigger distance but she was terrified at the thought of losing sight of them. Elizabeth knew that she had no choice: either she followed the three men through the forest to Winchester or she'd risk running straight into the arms of the Roundheads who were swarming all over the region in pursuit of the last remaining Cavaliers.

Better the forest then.

The plan had appeared simple enough but in reality it turned out to be quite different. Elizabeth was constantly torn between feelings of despair – once she was convinced she'd lost trace of the three men – or bouts of panic when she almost bumped into them.

On one occasion the horsemen stopped close to a small stream to water the horses and to give Harry the opportunity to decide which direction to choose.

Elizabeth managed to rein in her horse just in time when she caught sight of the men, but she couldn't stop her mare from snickering in protest. Luckily the three were diverted and didn't notice as Elizabeth quickly steered her horse into the dense undergrowth that offered the perfect hiding place. From her safety she watched them, envious and thirsty, as the men had thought about taking a flask of wine with them, until they mounted their horses again. The group rode on, guided by a confident Harry. "We're close to Winchester now, my lord. Another hour or so and we should cross the boundary of your lordship's estate."

"Excellent, Harry. The last few days have been exhausting, I can't tell you how happy I'll be to get those boots off my legs and burrow into my bed for at least two full days!"

"That's exactly my plan as well," cut in the second voice. "If I've managed to get three hours' sleep during the past two days, it's a miracle."

The last words that reached her were already indistinct as the horsemen had gathered speed and Elizabeth lost sight of them once again. She forced herself to let some time pass before she left her hiding place and continued in her pursuit. She knew which direction the men had taken and therefore wasn't particularly worried that she couldn't hear or see anybody. But after some time she started to wonder when she'd be able to see a fresh sign of the group. You never knew, maybe they had turned left – or perhaps right? Had she missed a turn?

Elizabeth rode on, but the forest remained silent and suddenly appeared foreboding, threatening. At first all she had was a vague feeling of unease but this soon grew to a palpable anxiety. Elizabeth slowed down and listened. Nothing – apart from the sound of the wind tearing at the barren trees, the lonely cry of a bird, the random noise of creaking branches and trees.

Listening to the sounds of the deserted forest, the truth dawned upon her: she was alone. The men had disappeared as if they had never existed. Fighting back tears, Elizabeth stopped her horse as her path ended in a fork – which direction should she take? She was lost.

Still unable to decide which direction to choose, the sound of pistol fire echoed through the wood, making her mare rear in panic. Elizabeth was an excellent horsewoman, but this assault came as a total surprise. As she fell off, she screamed, fearing the worst. Luckily the ground was cushioned by moss and dead leaves, but her fall had been abrupt. Still dazed from the shock she looked around, trying to find out what had happened and from what direction her assailants must be coming. Her instincts told her to get up on her feet as fast as possible but maybe it was shock, maybe the pain, she simply couldn't move. Hating herself for her weakness, tears welled up in her eyes. The last days had been a very trying combination of fear, pain and exhaustion – this last incident was just too much for her to endure.

"Don't move!" commanded a stern voice and a man stepped forward. It was the Earl of Wiltshire holding a pistol in his hand. His groom Harry and the third man followed, all of them pointing their weapons at her. Elizabeth watched the earl moving closer, ready to fire his pistol again. She didn't dare move. The earl's attractive face no longer showed a boyish look of mischief – this time the earl meant business.

As soon as he was close enough to examine his prisoner and look into her eyes, a look of utter surprise changed his face completely. "Who are you?" he exclaimed.

"Lady Elizabeth Huntville, my lord," she answered, and despite the pain from her steep fall she had to suppress the urge to laugh out loud as his face changed to an almost ridiculous expression of shock.

"Lady Elizabeth!" he exclaimed "What on earth are you doing here – disguised as a man? We thought you were a poacher."

"Wouldn't a gentleman first offer to help a lady get back on her feet?" she suggested.

"Of course, I do apologize." He was totally confused now. "I really do apologize, I didn't know… does it hurt very much?"

"Of course it does!" she answered as he helped her back on her feet. But as she noticed the true concern in his eyes, she softened. "You couldn't possibly know that it was me, I guess I should be the one to apologize. Let me explain to you later why I had to choose this ridiculous disguise."

"Can you mount your horse?" he asked.

"If you help me, yes, I think I should be able to do so," she answered, suppressing a moan as a he took her in his arms to lift her up. Once she was securely seated in her saddle she said, "Let's go!"

The group of four rode on and Elizabeth clenched her teeth in pain at every move. She could read from the groom's expression that he thought it utterly scandalous for a woman to ride and dress like a man, but Elizabeth couldn't care less about his obvious contempt. All that mattered was that she'd be in Winchester tonight and – God willing – would meet Armand there and could warn him. All concerns as to how to present herself at Wintershill Castle and what kind of story to invent didn't matter any more – fate had answered this for her now. Relieved, she sent a small prayer of gratitude to her guardian angel.

Harry was true to his word, and a good hour later they crossed the estate boundary and soon the silhouette of the stately castle came into sight. By now every single bone in Elizabeth's back was aching. Elizabeth bit her lip and kept a straight face but she could see that the Earl of Wiltshire was looking at her with a worried expression, very much aware that she must be suffering.

Once they had arrived, she tried to dismount but she simply couldn't. Gladly she allowed the earl to take her into his strong arms and carry her inside where he placed her tenderly on a sofa. Elizabeth wanted to speak but he made a sign for her to remain silent.

"You need to eat and drink something first, Lady Elizabeth. I know I shouldn't say this to a lady, but you look ghastly."

Despite her pain, Elizabeth had to laugh. "I'm afraid 'ghastly' is an understatement, I know. No need to pay me any compliments, my lord. Let me thank you first for not shooting me – I think I would rather an aching back compared to the alternative of lying in a coffin."

Wiltshire had to grin. "It was pretty tight, wasn't it? I was convinced that you were a poacher or worse – a damned Roundhead."

Elizabeth gladly accepted the mulled wine and cake that were brought by a scandalized butler, full of indignation now that the groom had spread the story in the servants' quarters about the lady dressed as a man. The earl took a glass for himself but then dismissed his servants. They were alone now and looked at each other, suddenly shy and unsure how to go on.

"I guess I owe you an explanation, my lord," said Elizabeth, in an attempt to break the ice.

253

"I'm curious, I must confess. Why do I have the pleasure of your company and why are you travelling in disguise? You should be in Oxford, looking after Her Majesty, if I'm not mistaken?"

He spoke lightly but Elizabeth could see in his eyes that he was truly concerned about her well-being and this took her by surprise. Never had a man looked at her with real concern in his eyes. Many men had admired, even worshipped her; Mortimer had watched her like a jealous dog would watch a precious bone. She was his prized possession – but had Mortimer ever cared about her as a person?

Until this moment she had simply assumed that Armand loved her like she loved him, but did he really? He had never looked at her like this. It dawned on her that she might have been living an illusion, had she made an enormous and utterly stupid error? In truth, Armand had never talked about love, about herself or her feelings. Had it not just been elegant and refined courtship and pure desire, skilfully wrapped up to resemble love by an experienced master of seduction – a make-believe to make her fall in love?

Suddenly she was overwhelmed by the need to have someone to confide in. For a reason she didn't understand, she couldn't lie to the earl. Maybe for the first time in her life, she felt an urge to be open and sincere.

"Lord Richard, I'm not worthy of your concern," she finally answered, trying to find the right words.

"Let me be the judge of this, Elizabeth. Please trust me and tell me the truth." The earl cleared his throat. "Maybe it would help if I were truthful with you as well. I never dared to tell you, but I have always admired you. If it hadn't been for Mortimer, I think I'd have spoken to you before about my feelings. I'm sorry to blurt this out, but somehow the usual conventions don't seem to matter tonight."

Elizabeth smiled. "Yes, it's a strange situation. But you'll change your mind about me, once I tell you the truth."

The earl didn't move. "Don't diminish yourself, Elizabeth. Just tell me everything. Consider me your friend. A friend you can trust."

She couldn't resist, all she wanted for once was to share her feelings. She suddenly realized that she didn't have a friend – shouldn't everybody have a friend they could trust?

"Everybody at court thinks that I'm betrothed to Sir Mortimer, but that's not true. He's been spreading this rumour to make sure that no other man would talk to me," she began, looking out of the window, not daring to look into Wiltshire's face.

"Sir Mortimer had indeed proposed marriage to me – several times. But I refused his proposal. I was not completely truthful with Mortimer, though. I told him that I couldn't marry him for a lack of dowry. The truth is I never loved him, I don't even know if I like him. But I have no family at court, nobody to protect me. What could I do but to invent some story? Furthermore, Lord Rochester was pursuing me, he tried to make love to me, force me to accept his unsavoury attentions – Sir Mortimer at least offered me his protection."

"If I had only known that Mortimer's motives were entirely selfish," Wiltshire murmured. "He told me that you were deeply in love, both of you."

Elizabeth shrugged. "Maybe that's what he wanted to believe. Mortimer is not a bad man, I don't want you to misunderstand me. I won't pretend that I was completely innocent – as Mortimer was insistent that I should marry him, I accepted his gifts, and even money – I must have been mad, there's no excuse."

It was difficult to speak those words. Had this really been her, Elizabeth, the proud Lady Huntville who had accepted payment like a cheap maid in a run-down inn?

"One day everything changed. Armand de Saint Paul arrived in Oxford – and I fell in love, hopelessly, like a young girl. For the first time in my life, I suddenly knew what this strange feeling was. I couldn't sleep, I couldn't eat. Does this sound strange to you?" She looked at him with wide eyes.

Elizabeth was not aware how beautiful she was, despite her strange haircut and the male riding attire. Bizarrely it made her look even more fragile and desirable in Wiltshire's eyes. He swallowed deeply before he replied, "I know what love is – I think I can understand, go on. Love can be heaven … and can be hell."

"Mortimer of course realized that I had changed and he didn't take it lightly. He sensed that I was in love with Armand – and threatened to kill him and have me removed from court, by force if need be. I only found out later that it was the Viscount Rochester who was playing a foul game behind the scenes, inflaming Mortimer and making sure that Armand would be sent to serve under General Forth in Cheriton. As soon as Armand had left, Rochester told Mortimer that I had been seen … accompanied by Armand. Mortimer immediately vowed to get revenge and left Oxford – ready to murder Armand."

There was an uneasy silence. Finally Wiltshire asked, "How did you come to know this? And did you, ah, spend, ahem, time with Armand de Saint Paul?"

Elizabeth looked straight into his eyes. "I won't lie to you, Lord Richard. I did spend time, as you call it, with Armand. But although I was in love for the first time in my life, I wasn't foolish enough to throw away all of my dignity."

Did she detect a sign of relief in his eyes?

"As soon as Mortimer had left court to pursue Armand, I was alone and Rochester waylaid me. How much he cherished telling me how clever he had been to play both men against each other, to show me how cheap and despicable I was in his eyes. Then, it happened."

She started to sob as the whole scene came back to her – would she ever be able to forget the smell of the perfumed oil mingled with the scent of fresh blood?

"You don't have to tell me, Elizabeth," Wiltshire replied, his voice surprisingly tender. "I think I know enough."

"You don't. Rochester trapped me in my bedchamber, wanted to throw me onto my bed. But he had been drinking heavily and was unsteady on his feet. As I noticed this, I pushed him backwards. He slipped and fell on puddle of scented oil, crashing his skull against the mantelpiece. Rochester died instantly. I do feel sorry for this – but I must take responsibility for his death. I grabbed my clothes, my money and I ran away."

Elizabeth stopped, scared to look into Wiltshire's eyes. What must he be thinking of her?

"To put it crudely, I killed Rochester, and whatever I do, I shall never be able to free myself from this knowledge. I packed my clothes and I left Oxford disguised as a man to warn Armand. I didn't want him to be murdered by Mortimer – to know that another man might lose his life because of me. But I'm an outcast now. All I can do is save Armand and then go back to Ireland. I don't need judgement, I know what I have done. I'll have to live with this memory."

Her tears had stopped, she was speaking in a detached, composed manner. The fact that Elizabeth calmly assumed her responsibility and didn't dramatize facts that would have driven most women to insanity moved Wiltshire even more than if she had thrown herself at his feet to ask his forgiveness. She was a remarkable woman. He looked at her pale face and couldn't but admire her courage. The courage to have told him a story that might ruin her reputation forever, the courage to take enormous risks to save the man she loved – or thought she loved.

"You're a redhead," he replied softly. "My mother is like you. She can be the gentlest person in the world, but when she's irate, better not to cross her, she'd kill you soon as look at you! She'd be a better soldier than I'll ever be. Rochester – I know him only too well – he was a pig, always trying to play people against each other. We all hated him. You defended your honour, Elizabeth, this has nothing to do with killing him, he deserved his fate."

He suddenly laughed. "That great bully Rochester, felled by a fragile lady and a puddle of scented oil, who could have imagined this?"

He took her hand. "You were frank with me and I'll be honest with you. Your behaviour with Armand was scandalous. I should be shocked. I should tell you to leave, but I can't. It's a strange moment for me to tell you the truth: I've been in love with you, Elizabeth, desperately in love for months. But I had sworn to myself never to betray a fellow officer. This is why I never approached you, this is why I avoided speaking to you. I believed that both of you were in love and that you had accepted Mortimer's proposal. If it's Armand you truly love, I'll not stand in your way, I even promise to help you. But your story has given me hope, if you're looking for a true friend, a man who's not only smitten by your beauty – give me a chance, Elizabeth."

It would have been so easy to say yes, to sink into his arms, but resolutely she shook her head. "You deserve someone better than me, Richard. Believe me. But thank you, for the first time in my life, I think I've found a true friend. As for Armand, I realized all of a sudden that it's over. It wasn't love after all, it was an illusion. I was smitten, a young girl who had never encountered a man of his charm and looks before."

She kissed his hand and closed her eyes, she would remember this moment forever. Suddenly she opened her eyes and exclaimed, "But for heaven's sake, where is Armand? He was supposed to be coming here!"

***

"Where can we find Monsieur Armand?" Jean didn't know what to do. "Usually he's never far from my master, the Marquis."

"Remember, Jean, Northumberland told us that he had been assigned to serve under General Forth in Cheriton. This is why he couldn't join Pierre in London." Charles was looking worried.

"Didn't the Earl of Northumberland mention that the royal troops were beaten yesterday at Cheriton?"

"Yes, Jim, he did. I can only hope that everything is alright. Luckily Armand is like a cat, he has nine lives. Anyhow, I'd better saddle my horse and ride down to check what's going on, I can be there by tomorrow."

"May I voice an objection, my lord?" Jim asked cautiously. You never knew with these nobles…

"Of course, Jim. What's the matter?"

Jim cleared his throat. "I don't think it's a good idea for your lordship to ride down to Cheriton. As a close relative of the duke your lordship should be very careful. Your lordship might be in peril as well."

Charles was thunderstruck. "You're absolutely right, Jim. In the heat of the moment I forgot, but there's been a very careful master plan behind all of this, Pierre's disappearance in London, Armand's urgent order to join General Forth – if that's not the long arm of the Marquess of Halifax… Or of Colonel Cromwell," he continued. "There must be a link, somehow."

Charles pondered his last words and went on, "A week ago I'd have told you that you were barking mad. But since then a lot has happened, I may well be in danger as well. I can only guess that the Marquess is about to change sides. I think I'd better make sure I have enough friends left in Parliament who'll cover my back – but I must also rescue Armand. Pierre and he are like twins, if Pierre tells me that he's in danger…"

"… something serious must have happened," Jean cut in. "I believe this too, we must do something, my lord. And as fast as possible."

Jim interjected, "May I propose a plan: What if Jean and I rode down? I'll dress like a Roundhead and Jean can play my mute servant – otherwise his French accent will give us away. But I'd like to have Jean at my side, if we do have to do something to get Monsieur Armand out of some nasty situation… it's better to have a helping hand."

He looked at Jean. "You look like a man who hasn't just been a valet all his life…"

Jean grinned. "That's correct, Jim. In my previous life I was a pirate, quite a different kind of occupation, I can say."

"That's perfect then, Jean, a bit of pistol fire won't send you into hysterics!"

The two valets shook hands. Charles told them it would be as well to keep their mission secret, then advised them to be careful and wished them luck. As the two left, he could hear them talking to each other in the corridor. "What does this giant master of yours think? That we're rank amateurs?"

"My lord Charles behaves like a clucking hen when it comes to his cousin and his friend," Charles heard Jean answer.

"A clucking hen, really!" Charles exclaimed. "These servants nowadays consider themselves equal to their masters, what is the world coming to?"

***

The Earl of Wiltshire rang a bell and the butler appeared on the spot; most likely he had been listening at the door.

"Has anybody arrived today? I'm expecting the Earl of Worthing, but he often uses his French name, Armand de Saint Paul."

"Nobody has called, my lord. Only a delegation of the local Roundheads but I thought it appropriate to inform them that your lordship had gone out hunting."

"Well done, Thomas. In the meantime will you please prepare a room for Lady Elizabeth upstairs. As rumours are flying fast, you will no doubt have already heard that the royal troops lost a battle in Cheriton yesterday. This is why her ladyship had to flee in disguise. She wishes now to change back into more ladylike attire."

Elizabeth saw the butler's look change from contempt to surprise and then awe. "Of course, my lord. It will be done immediately."

258

Elizabeth was sure that tonight tongues in the servants' quarters would be wagging – but did she care?

The earl walked to the window and frowned. "It's dark already. We can't do anything today to find Armand. Tomorrow morning we'll organize a search party if he doesn't arrive."

Elizabeth tried to get up, but she couldn't suppress a moan. Every bone in her body seemed to hurt.

The earl looked at her. "I am so sorry, I forgot that you're indisposed."

He turned to the butler and said, "Lady Elizabeth had a riding accident," then he looked back at her, his voice dripping sarcasm like honey, "Maybe you overrated your riding skills, Lady Elizabeth?"

"The moment I can sit on a horse again, I'll show who has the better skills, my lord," she hissed back.

The butler watched this exchange with interest.

"You may go, Thomas, what are you waiting for?"

"Immediately, my lord," and Thomas withdrew, the epitome of dignity and diligence.

The Earl of Wiltshire turned back to Elizabeth who looked at him with eyes that sparkled with indignation. "First you shoot at me and almost kill me, then you make me a laughing stock in front of your butler – but I'll show you!"

Wiltshire laughed as he lifted her up. "Excellent, Elizabeth, you're back to your true self. I was concerned that you might be turning into a saint. I should have known of course that I shouldn't worry too much about that."

Before Elizabeth could answer this latest insult the earl kissed her.

I shouldn't! Elizabeth thought, then closed her eyes and kissed him back.

"You're insane," she finally said.

"I know, but are we not living in crazy times? Let's make the best of it." And hungrily he kissed her again.

***

Later, after dinner, the earl called his groom Harry and the warden of the forest. "It looks like we need to organize a search party. Armand de Saint Paul must have lost his way in the forest, he should have arrived before I did, in fact."

259

Harry frowned. "We'll see some pretty heavy thunderstorms tomorrow, my lord. The weather will be awful – and that's an understatement – it's going to be very dangerous in the woods."

"I know, Harry, but we have no choice. We can't leave Armand alone out there."

"We'll need dogs for the search," the warden said, accepting the verdict. "Only dogs will be able to find him. I propose setting up three parties, to cover a large section. Where is this person supposed to be coming from?"

"From Cheriton…"

They looked at each other as Harry and the warden immediately understood the implication. "Your lordship should be aware that the Roundheads are already swarming all over the estate. If they can prove that your lordship is siding with the enemy, you might get into trouble."

"Yes, that's the only advantage of the bad weather, none of the Roundheads will be putting their dirty noses into our affairs," the earl replied.

"Yes, they won't want to risk getting their beautiful hair wet," Harry grinned. "What a bunch of conceited hypocrites, let's hope that our troops win the next battle, my lord. If we do run into one of them, we'll pretend that it's a hunting foray, let them prove that it's not true. My people will keep their mouths shut, I can vouch for them."

Wintershill Castle

Sir Mortimer's face was set in a grim mask. He tried to paint a picture in his mind of the various possibilities for Armand's demise – a traitor's end must be painful and slow. Mortimer was looking forward to it, he'd savour every single second. Shortly before he reached the city of Winchester, a peasant riding on a donkey made a sign for him to stop.

"You look like a decent fella," the old man said to him in greeting, baring a smile with only two teeth left. "A mile down south, those bloody Roundheads have blocked the road. I thought it might be useful for you to know about it..." he mumbled.

"Very useful, thank you. May the Lord bless you!"

Mortimer dived quickly into the shelter of the forest, thankful for the old man's advice. But the way through the forest took him considerably more time than anticipated. He heaved a sigh of relief when finally the towers and turrets of the stately castle came into sight against the twilight of the setting sun. Not that there was a lot of sun to see, as heavy clouds obliterated the sky, harbingers of an approaching thunderstorm.

Mortimer had been pondering for hours how best to set his plan into motion. The Earl of Wiltshire wouldn't help him; on the contrary, any such motion would be strictly forbidden by the sacred code of honour. Armand would be considered a guest and would be staying in the castle under the earl's special protection. Secrecy and swift action would be the key to success.

It might not be the behaviour expected of a gentleman, but Mortimer had no option but to lurk around and peek through the windows to ascertain if Armand was already here. Later he must wait for the best opportunity to waylay Armand at a time and place where the earl wouldn't be able to interfere. Armand should know of course who his adversary was – but it would be stupid to let anybody else know. Armand would be removed from the realm of the living, and Mortimer would then ride back to Oxford, invent some excuse for his absence and marry Elizabeth. The plan was simple; it couldn't possibly fail.

Mortimer entered the vast Wintershill estate via the woods, avoiding the gatehouse and its noisy dogs. Here, he tied his horse to a tree and walked the last yards towards the castle. After hours spent in the saddle, his first steps were awkward and painful.

During sunset the servants would be busy preparing dinner, therefore Mortimer was fairly confident of being able to look around without being noticed. He still remembered that the stately drawing room was located on the left, next to the library with its leaded windows granting a beautiful view over the rose garden, now still in a state of hibernation. From there the garden stretched hundreds of yards further towards the forest. But now all was quiet and the garden terrace lay quiet and abandoned.

Silently Mortimer tiptoed to the window of the drawing room. He found it empty with only a lone candelabra spreading its light. Mortimer then moved on towards the library, careful to remain hidden in the darkness.

He found the curtains only partially drawn and he could clearly discern three persons inside. It was easy enough to identify Lord Richard and his butler – but who was the young man resting on the sofa? The butler bowed and left, and the earl and the young man were alone now. Mortimer saw the earl moving closer to the sofa, he was speaking to the young man, and suddenly, Mortimer couldn't believe his eyes – the young man seized the earl's hand and kissed it!

Sir Mortimer was horrified. Of course he knew that those kinds of relationships existed, a drunken officer had once tried to approach him in Oxford with an unsavoury proposal – but surely not the man he believed to be his friend, the Earl of Wiltshire! Lord Richard couldn't be romantically involved with another man! The idea was simply disgusting!

Scandalized, Mortimer watched the earl lifting the gentleman up from the sofa. A gentleman who must still be fairly young as he was of very slight build. But if the kissing of the hand hadn't been bad enough, the earl bowed his head and suddenly kissed the young man passionately on the lips. After only a second's hesitation, the young man gave up his reserve and returned the kiss. Mortimer expected the trumpets of Jericho to sound any minute and announce the last day of judgement, was the world going crazy?

The earl, still carrying the young gentleman in his arms, moved closer to the window. As he entered the halo of light cast by the candelabra on his desk, Mortimer suddenly discovered that the face of the young man looked strangely familiar, but how could this be?

The Earl of Wiltshire stepped forward and now Mortimer could clearly see the colour of the young man's hair. Mortimer suddenly felt hot and cold simultaneously – there was only one person in England he knew who had this particular hair colour, resembling flames of copper. And if he needed one last piece of proof, Elizabeth now opened her beautiful violet eyes, looking at Lord Richard in a way she had never looked at Mortimer before.

Mortimer felt as if the world was collapsing right at his feet. He felt sick with hurt pride, anger, disgust and burning jealousy.

Elizabeth must have travelled to Wintershill Castle disguised as a man – Rochester, the swine, must have told her everything. Sick with anger Mortimer raced back to his horse, he needed to think. Well, not really, as his mind was already made up. The root of all evil had a name: Elizabeth. She had betrayed his pure and selfless love – yet again. She had made him lose his honour, betray his king! Elizabeth must pay for this, pay with her life. Armand had in fact been nothing but a blind fool in love, just as he had been.

But now Mortimer was in love no more. Love had turned to hatred.

Mortimer remembered that there were several barns located close to the stables. They would provide shelter and a warm bed for tonight. Tomorrow would be the day of judgement for Lady Elizabeth. This was his sacred task now, the evil had to be rooted out – even if afterwards life would hold no meaning for him.

Elizabeth had to die, although he knew that he'd die with her. First his soul, then his body. If this meant burning in hell forever, so be it. Mortimer was ready to pay any price but he'd never leave Elizabeth to another man.

***

The clock, a marvel of craftsmanship and sophistication created by a goldsmith in the southern parts of the German Empire and acquired by the late earl at great expense struck eight in the morning. The present Earl of Wiltshire sighed. He had no more reason to wait inside. Grimacing at his own image in the mirror he heaved a last sigh and stepped out of the door where his men were already waiting, waiting in vain for the sun to rise.

Instead of playful rays of sunlight, there were only freezing gusts of wind, tearing at the tiles on the roof, the barren trees and the naked rose bushes. A steady rain was drenching men and horses; no coat, leather jacket or felt blanket could withstand the torrents pouring down from the sky, and according to his groom Harry (who rarely erred), worse was still to come.

The earl gave the expected sign and the men set off silently. There was no need for the bellowing of commands, as every detail of their search had been discussed and decided beforehand. Only the dogs were barking noisily, excited at the prospect of getting out and hunting – they didn't care about the weather. At least they were having fun, the earl concluded, but they must surely be the only ones.

If he was honest, the chances of finding Armand were almost non-existent but he owed it to Lady Elizabeth and General Forth to search for him. No human deserved to be lost and lonely in the dense forest as the apocalypse approached – at least that's what the sky seemed to be promising this morning.

The next hours were an experience the earl would have forgone with pleasure. They were riding through the forest bordering his estates, a forest that he thought he knew well. And yet today the forest reminded him of the very antechamber of hell. A vicious wind was howling brutally through the trees and branches, making them sway like pikestaffs on the field, a constant danger for the horses and the men passing below.

In this darkness it was impossible to spot treacherous roots, potholes or low-hanging branches and thorny tendrils that were strewn across the path, and very soon they were forced to dismount and lead their unwilling horses along narrow paths as the rain kept pouring down from above. Boots, stockings, breeches – every single piece of clothing was soaked through. Soon the earl lost all sense of time or even pain as his feet and hands were numbed by the cold to the extent that could barely hold his horse's reins.

They dragged on until the first thunderstorms were unleashed, more ferocious and wild than he had ever seen before. The horses panicked as bolts of lightning struck all around them, and rolled their terrified eyes, trying to escape. Even the dogs sensed the danger now and it took all the experience of the kennel master to keep them under control.

"Let's try this way, my lord," Harry suggested, "that's the last option. Further behind there is the river, it's unlikely that the gentleman should have crossed it. Coming from Cheriton, he must have taken this way – or if he lost his way much earlier, then let's hope that the others find him – if anyone finds him at all," he added gloomily.

"All right, let's check this way and then return. If I'm not back in my bed with a hot brick soon you may find Armand de Saint Paul but you'll have lost your master in so doing," and the earl sneezed loudly.

"Take this, my lord, it usually helps." Harry offered him a metal flask and the earl took a large gulp.

"Gosh, what's that!" he croaked after he had regained his senses.

"My ma brews it, it's her secret." Harry grinned and took a deep gulp himself.

The earl suddenly felt the warmth creeping back into his limbs and nodded enthusiastically. "Whatever it is, it's amazing, a veritable magic potion. I think you may just have saved my life. Look, even the weather is improving; the first clouds are breaking up. Give me another sip."

"Yes, it's a very special brew," said Harry, with a grin. They trudged on, leading the horses behind them, relieved that the floods coming from above had stopped as abruptly as they had started. The dogs were still swarming around them, calmer than in the beginning – but never tired of circling around the horses and taking in the scents of forest.

As they started to bark and sniff excitedly, the earl was convinced that they must have spotted a fox or even a boar. Then the dogs started barking and the pack stormed into the undergrowth, their barking culminating in hysterical delight.

"They must have found something, let's have a look," Harry commanded the footmen and they followed the dogs' lead into the dense undergrowth.

There, lying a in pool of rainwater, unconscious and surrounded by the excited pack of dogs, they found Armand de Saint Paul.

"I can't believe my eyes!" the Earl of Wiltshire exclaimed.

"That's all due to ma's secret potion," Harry grinned.

"I'm inclined to believe you, but why didn't you offer it to me earlier, it would have spared us a lot of effort!" the earl replied.

***

From his hiding place, Mortimer watched the drenched men coming back from their excursion. The earl was one of the last to arrive and as soon as Mortimer caught sight of the makeshift stretcher, he knew that Armand had been found.

Dead or alive, he didn't care anymore. He knew now that Elizabeth was the root of the evil and the cause of his anguish.

Mortimer crept back into the barn and unpacked the rest of his provisions: a slice of smoked ham, a piece of rock-hard bread and a shrivelled piece of goat's cheese. He dipped the bread into watered wine to make it edible and while he chewed on the bread, the cheese and the tough ham he tried to figure out when and how to strike.

Tomorrow at the latest, that was for sure.

Revenge

"We can't go on, Jean! Look, there's a farm not far away, let's stop here for the night."

Jean looked at the sky and saw the first bolts of lightning flash across sinister looking clouds. The thunderstorm was still some miles away but they could already hear the remote rumblings of the thunder, growling like a tiger preparing to pounce. Reluctantly he gave in. Jim was right, they couldn't possibly continue on their way when a thunderstorm of biblical dimensions was going to break right above their heads.

"You win. Let's look for shelter," Jean replied.

It took a certain resolve to pass the snarling dogs (luckily chained to their kennel) and considerable time to convince the farmer and his suspicious wife to let them stay. Maybe it was due to Jean's silver shillings or Jim's silken tongue, or possibly both, but in the end they were not only allowed to sleep in the stables next to the horses, but the farmer's wife, a woman of remarkable proportions, provided them with a very edible dinner, along with a tankard of home brewed ale.

"See, I was right to stop here," Jim mumbled whilst devouring a hunk of cheese. He looked with admiration at the cheese. "Delicious, I wonder if they'll sell me another piece tomorrow?"

"How can you think about food right now? I never disputed that we should stop here, but we're losing precious time!"

"Maybe – but you have to admit that we made progress much faster than anticipated. That's the only advantage of the thunderstorms, none of these idiot Roundheads dared to show up on the roads."

Jean had to agree, and indeed they had reached Winchester city in only one day.

"How do we find out what has happened to my lord Armand?" Jean asked. "It's good that we'll be in Cheriton tomorrow, but where do we go from there?"

"When you're a smuggler, you get to know your customers very well," Jim replied, looking smug.

"What do you mean?" Jean didn't understand a word.

"Close to Winchester there's an inn, the landlord and his wife are known to be loyal to the King. The landlord was always a good customer of mine. I'm quite sure that he'll know all about the battle, I'd even bet that some Royalist officers will still be hiding there. If we're lucky, they might have heard something about Armand – worst case the landlord can tell us where to find some more Cavaliers. It's impossible that everybody should have disappeared in a matter of a day or two."

266

Jean was impressed. "You seem to be quite sure of yourself, let's hope that you're right. Now let's get some sleep, I'm totally exhausted."

Jim laughed. "And you tell me that you were a pirate in your youth? A bit of riding and you're exhausted already?"

"We didn't ride, stupid, we sailed. But we used our considerable skills to silence people who talked far too much. Seems that I may need to brush up on my skills once again."

Jim got the hint. "Alright, pirate, I'll shut up," and extinguished the wick in the lantern.

***

The next morning brought an unpleasant surprise. The weather was still abominable and they were forced to stay inside.

Jim looked out of the stable door and closed it immediately. "If we want to leave right now, we'd better look for a boat. You can't see where the moat ends and the farmyard begins. I'm afraid that we'll need to wait until we can see our way."

Jean was on tenterhooks but a quick glance outside confirmed Jim's assessment of the situation. By noon the miracle Jean had been praying for happened and the clouds started to break up. "How far is your inn from here?"

"Less than an hour's ride – unless we need to swim there," Jim answered, as he finally mounted his horse.

But they were lucky. With the exception of a single road that was blocked by a fallen tree, they were able to ride directly along the muddy roads to 'The Horse With One Leg', a strange name for an inn, especially as no one had any idea where the name originated from.

"Maybe it was a joke," Jim suggested.

"Maybe, after all, you English are known to have a strange sense of humour." Jean grinned.

"Maybe, but others are known to have none," Jim replied, and grinned back.

***

'The Horse With One Leg' was a well-kept inn, neat and tidy, and a wonderful smell of roasted lamb seasoned with rosemary reminded the two horsemen that lunch time was approaching.

They left their horses in the hands of a capable-looking groom and entered the tap room where the landlord was leaning over the counter, in animated conversation with

267

a local guest. As soon as he recognized Jim, he excused himself and greeted the two new guests with great enthusiasm.

"Praise the Lord, Jim! You're just the man I need. I was talking with Cathy only yesterday, saying that I must find you. My Spanish wine is almost finished, I need two vats of brandy and five dozen bottles of a decent claret wouldn't go amiss."

He paused and looked at Jean. "Is this your new partner? I can see he is from the colonies. That reminds me, I need rum – the last barrel I bought was rubbish, I could only use it to make punch, and the next day my guests complained that they had a splitting headache."

Jean laughed. His dark skin ensured that most people treated him like a slave; being taken for a smuggler made a pleasant change.

Jim shook his head. "No, Jean did come from the colonies, but he's not in this kind of business. He's a duke's valet now, you need to be respectful."

The landlord's eyes opened wide. "Oh dear lord, you must be joking! A real duke?"

"Yes, my master is his Grace, the Duke of Hertford and he's a French Marquis as well," Jean answered proudly. He simply couldn't resist the temptation of showing off a little.

"The Duke of Hertford, indeed, only serving a royal would be more prestigious! That calls for a drink on the house! Cathy, bring us the Spanish wine, the good one!"

The landlord turned back to Jim. "When can you deliver? You know that I pay a good price, real silver money, not these new shillings minted by Parliament where the Lord only knows how much silver is still in them."

"I know, Raymond, but I'm not here on business. If you help me though, I might give you a hand finding a decent wine, I still have a source in Plymouth…"

"What can I do for you? Let's have something to eat and you can tell me all."

They settled at the table and, as Cathy arrived with trays loaded with delicious dishes, Jim continued. "We're looking for a French man, he's an earl, and we know that he served under General Forth in Cheriton this week. Do you know what happened?"

"Who doesn't!" exclaimed Raymond. "Sir Henry screwed it all up. What a shame!"

"Did you hear about the French man, or do you by any chance still have some of the royal officers as, ahem, guests in your inn?" Jim asked him.

"Are you crazy?" Raymond whispered back. "Far too dangerous. The Roundheads have got into the habit of searching my inn at least once a week, everyone here knows that I'm loyal to the Stuarts. All they want is to find some excuse to hang me."

Jim was disappointed. "You didn't see any officers after the battle then?"

"I didn't say that! I only said that they don't stay here and that nobody mentioned your French earl."

"How and where can I find someone who might be able to tell me?" Jim finally asked, less confident than before.

"Oh, that's an easy question," Raymond beamed. "The Earl of Wiltshire passed here on his way back to his estate. He was serving under Hopton and he should know what happened to your French earl. These fellows always know about each other."

"You're our saviour!" Jim shook Raymond's hand enthusiastically. "Wiltshire Castle doesn't ring a bell though with me, where is it?"

"Wiltshire Castle doesn't exist and Winchester Castle is a ruin, Jim. His lordship's estate is called Wintershill Castle, it's not too far from here."

"What do you mean by 'not too far'?"

"Three or four hours via the forest, half a day if you take the road. But you couldn't really take the roads though," Raymond added after short reflection.

"Why not?"

"Because you'd run straight into a battalion of the London Lobsters. They're probably completely drunk by now."

"I agree, that's not a good idea! They'd skin us alive," Jim exclaimed.

"That's what I'm thinking as well. But if you promise me to find some decent barrels of wine – at a price I can afford, that is – I could ask my groom to guide you to Wintershill Castle. He knows his way through the forest."

The landlord looked decidedly sly; he knew that Jim couldn't possibly refuse such a generous offer.

"You've beaten me." Jim shook his hand. "You'll get your wine. But give me a fortnight, first I need to find this Frenchman and get him back to London."

After a sumptuous meal on the house, they parted as friends. When Raymond called their guide-to-be, the same capable groom who had looked after their horses appeared.

"His parents live on the Wintershill estate, that's why he could find the way in his sleep," Raymond explained as he waved goodbye.

"We're in good hands then."

"You couldn't ask for any better!"

***

Mortimer was bored to death although he tried to keep the flame of his hatred burning, but one couldn't go on hating for hours while sitting in a dark barn waiting for something to happen. He hated every second he had to sit there idle but knew he had to wait for the servants to be out of the way. If necessary, he'd wait until they were in their beds tonight.

Finally something interrupted his boredom as Mortimer heard the sound of an approaching coach. Curious, he peeped out and saw a man clad in black with a large leather case in his hand who descended from the coach and disappeared inside Wintershill House. This could only be a physician, which implied that Armand de Saint Paul must still be among the living.

The doctor had arrived at lunchtime and most servants, with the exception of those on duty in the dining room, would be gathering in the great kitchen, their minds focused on lunch and nothing else. Mortimer simply couldn't endure remaining inactive inside the dark barn any longer. As soon as he had made sure that all was quiet in the deserted courtyard, he sneaked into the house through one of the back doors. Using the servants' staircase, he climbed to the first floor where the earl's bedrooms and those of his guests were located, most rooms being empty at this time of the year and therefore providing a perfect hiding place.

Mortimer slipped into one of the empty bedrooms, taking care to leave the door slightly ajar and he was not to be disappointed. Not much later he would witness a hustle of activities concentrating in one of the neighbouring rooms. Finally the physician, clad in the darkest of black, left the room, accompanied by the Earl of Wiltshire.

"Your lordship doesn't need to be worried. The patient's fever is receding and although the cough may sound worrying, I don't think that's there's a dangerous inflammation of the lungs – the young man appears to be particularly robust and should be out of his bed soon."

"Thank you, sir, we were very worried indeed."

"He has an excellent nurse, the young lady…?"

"Lady Elizabeth Huntville."

"Yes, Lady Elizabeth, she seems to be very dedicated to the young man."

"Lady Elizabeth's mother is French actually," the earl improvised. "Monsieur Armand is a distant cousin of hers."

"That explains it, a very handsome pair, both of them, if I may say so."

Mortimer didn't hear the earl's answer but he had heard enough; the flame of hatred reignited and was burning brightly again. Strangely, that felt really good. A handsome pair, the doctor had said, but no more by tomorrow. A pity that he had forgotten to take his pistols – revenge would have to wait a few more hours.

The earl went back into the sickroom and found Elizabeth leaning over Armand, dabbing his forehead with a perfumed cloth. Elizabeth was even more beautiful today, as she was now wearing a woman's dress which showed her slender figure to her best advantage. The earl had a question in his eyes that he didn't dare to ask. Elizabeth looked back and smiled at him, a smile that went straight to his heart.

"Shhh," she whispered. "He's sleeping, don't talk now."

The earl took her hand, his eyes still asking the same question.

Elizabeth finally gave in, unable to resist this pleading glance. She shook her head and whispered, "I haven't changed my mind. It's over, Lord Richard, it was an infatuation only. I'm still very fond of Armand, but I know now it was never love after all. Do you believe me?"

The earl didn't reply. Pulling her gently into a corner, he kissed her as if there were no tomorrow.

Both of them had no idea that fate was waiting in the next room.

***

"Impressive!" Jim whistled as Wintershill Castle came into sight.

"Hertford Castle is bigger," Jean replied with a critical look.

"Don't be so blasé, Jean, Whitehall Palace is even bigger, I'd bet. You must admit that Wintershill is a nice estate."

"To be honest, I don't care about towers and turrets, I would love simply to have a decent bed and be sure that my lord Armand is alive and well. That's all I'm interested in for the time being."

"We'll know soon enough. Can you lead us to the entrance and call the butler?" Jim asked, turning to the groom.

"Aye, sir. Whom should I announce?"

"Tell the butler that the valet of his Grace, the Duke of Hertford, is requesting an interview with the Earl of Wiltshire."

The groom nodded, suitably impressed, and dismounted.

"Nothing better than a duke's title to gain entrance anywhere," Jim remarked. "I shall miss this when I go back to my old business."

"You've decided to go back?" Jean asked.

"Yes, too much of 'your lordship' here, 'your lordship' there for my taste. I like to be my own master."

They were kept waiting for almost fifteen minutes until a haughty-looking butler condescended to address them.

"You have made it known that you wish to speak to his lordship, the Earl of Wiltshire?" the butler asked, looking at them if they were some strange kind of vermin to be removed as fast as possible from these noble surroundings.

"Yes, we urgently need to speak to his lordship," Jim replied, eyeing the butler in a bellicose manner.

"May I see your credentials, please? You must understand that his lordship's time is precious, but maybe I can arrange for his lordship to be free some time later today."

"You dried old prune, move your rattling bones and tell the earl to come here, it's urgent!" Jim shouted, visibly upset.

Jean shook his head. "I do apologize, sir, my groom spoke a little roughly. It's been a tiring day."

Jim wanted to protest but Jean continued smoothly, "Of course I understand that the Earl of Wiltshire is a very important man and may not be disturbed without good reason. I'm the valet to his Grace, the Duke of Hertford, and would ask you to show this document to his lordship. As my groom mentioned, we have an urgent matter to discuss and his lordship's immediate attention would be greatly appreciated."

Jean unfolded a letter signed by Lord Charles, congratulating himself that he had reminded Cousin Charles to sign a letter of recommendation for him.

The butler took the document as if it were tainted and eyed it sceptically. But the Neuville seal and ducal coat of arms didn't fail to impress. Reluctantly he agreed to inform the earl and withdrew upstairs.

"Sometimes a bit of diplomacy works wonders," Jean said, looking smug.

"Maybe." Jim was still sulking. "I'd have taught this inflated bag of scum that he'd better let us see the earl fast…"

Only minutes later the Earl of Wiltshire entered the hall.

"You want to talk to me?" he addressed Jean. "This is rather strange, though? Why would his Grace's valet be asking to see me?" and he raised his eyebrows.

"I apologize, my lord, for the intrusion, but this is a matter of pressing urgency," Jean answered.

The earl looked surprised. "You have a French accent, and I can see that you come from the colonies?"

"My master, the duke, is also a Marquis de France," said Jean proudly. "He was born in France. I've been his private valet for more than three years."

"Yes, I remember now. Hertford was born in France and inherited the title from his grandfather. What can I do for his Grace?"

"My master is staying in London but he sent us down to Hampshire to investigate, as his best friend is missing. He served under General Forth in Cheriton. We wonder if your lordship could give us some information, his Grace is greatly worried that his friend might be wounded."

The earl looked at him. It was difficult to read his face but his eyes were alert. "Why should I know something about Cheriton?" he finally drawled.

"We know that your lordship fought in Cheriton," Jim intervened.

"Why should you know that?"

"We passed through 'The Horse With One Leg', and the landlord told us that your lordship and other officers passed through after the battle," Jim replied promptly.

"Great to have friends like Raymond," the earl murmured. "Why didn't he simply tell the Puritans to come along and arrest me."

"There's no danger, my lord. Raymond and I are old friends. In the strictest confidence, I can tell your lordship that I am the, ahem, man who provides Raymond with his best wines. I believe that your lordship is a good customer."

"Nothing ever stays secret here in Wintershill, I see that now. Even my drinking habits are public knowledge." The earl shrugged but a faint smile was playing around his lips. "As it's no secret anymore, I admit, I fought in Cheriton. What's the name of the duke's best friend? Maybe I can be of help."

"Armand de Saint Paul, Earl of Worthing, my lord."

273

The earl smiled. "I think I may be able to help you, indeed. A last question, how could I identify this Monsieur Armand?"

"He's of medium height, muscular, with brown, curly hair, a moustache, brown eyes, a small mole on his chin. His lordship always wears the seal given to him as a gift by his father, the Marquis, with the Saint Paul coat of arms. And, oh yes, M. Armand never succeeded in speaking English without a very pronounced French accent," Jean replied immediately.

"Well, that's accurate enough. It might be of interest then for you to know that his lordship is upstairs. We discovered him yesterday in the forest, luckily early enough before the cold could take hold and kill him. He's conscious now and is already speaking about wanting to leave his bed."

"Praise the Lord!" said Jean, crossing himself, forgetting that he was supposed to be a Protestant servant.

They went upstairs where they found Armand propped up against several cushions and protesting at the administrations of a servant.

"Wiltshire, tell this idiot that I want my breeches and what I definitely do not want is this strange kind of broth he wants to serve me instead of a decent dinner. I don't eat slime. No wonder I have a splitting headache with this idiot here fussing around me and getting on my nerves."

"Try to behave, Armand, we have visitors," the earl laughed.

Armand squinted and spotted Jean and Jim who had entered the room behind the earl.

"By the blessed Virgin, how come you're here? Is Pierre here as well, is he all right?" he exclaimed, clearly delighted.

"His Grace sent us to search for you, Monsieur. He had a premonition that you might need his help."

"I did need his help, so why are you late and why hasn't he come himself?" Armand asked reproachfully, taking it for granted that Pierre should have known about his troubles.

"His Grace was indisposed. He had a sort of accident himself."

Armand nodded. "I had a feeling that something had gone wrong." Ignoring with nonchalance his own precarious situation, he continued, "Pierre always attracts trouble, I sometimes think he'll never grow up."

Jean was only half listening; he was already taking over. He opened the various bottles and flasks of medicine that were standing on the side table, sniffing at them

274

suspiciously. Automatically he started to fluff up the pillows, arranging them neatly and straightening the blankets.

"May I propose that I look after my lord Armand?" he asked the Earl of Wiltshire. "I know him so much better and I also know what kind of potion will make his headache disappear."

Armand grimaced. "You can't resist taking over, can you? But if you think that I'm going to take one sip of that evil tasting potion of yours, you're totally mistaken!"

"Your lordship may enjoy the benefit of a splitting headache for the next days to come then, it's entirely your preference, my lord," Jean answered very formally, in a glacial voice.

Armand sighed. "You win, but make it quick then, my headache is killing me."

The Earl of Wiltshire had followed this exchange with barely concealed delight. "I can see that you're in the best possible hands, Armand. I propose we leave you now, but the physician told me that you shouldn't leave your bed, it's far too early."

"Leave his bed?" Jean was horrified. "Over my dead body, Monsieur Armand."

"It's my lord, not Monsieur." Armand tried to impose his authority.

"That's correct, my lord, indeed," Jean replied, and then just to drive the point home, "May I suggest that your lordship behaves accordingly then?"

"Touché, Armand, I'd give up if I were you! I see that we're no longer needed and so will leave you in the capable hands of his Grace's valet. I shall ask my housekeeper to prepare accommodation for you and," he smirked, "our smuggler."

Having delivered his little speech, the earl left the room together with a grinning Jim.

***

Mortimer had sneaked back into his hiding place. The past days had taken their toll and he needed a rest before he'd be able to stage the final show-down. In the end he must have slept much longer than planned, as he awoke with a start, cursing, sure that he must have overslept. It was pitch dark already. He grabbed his pistols and felt his way to the exit in the darkness as he didn't dare light a candle for fear of being detected by the grooms on duty in the neighbouring stables.

Finally he reached the door. He cursed again, for as he was feeling across the rough wooden door with his hands to find the latch, a splinter went straight into his thumb. As soon as he felt the latch, he opened the door slowly to peep outside. All was quiet, a silvery moon bathed Wintershill Castle in its peaceful light. Mortimer's hand slid into his pocket where he felt the key he had stolen this afternoon – very negligent of the servants to keep all the keys on a board close to the servants' entrance, and very accommodating to have labelled them.

He held the door open as he had to get the splinter out of his painful thumb and prepare his pistols first. Luckily the rising moon provided him with enough light. After he had seen to his thumb, Mortimer set to the task of loading his pistols. The gunpowder appeared to be dry enough; at least that was one less thing to worry about. Soon his weapons would discharge their lethal load.

Armed and ready, Mortimer sneaked through the courtyard, making sure to stay hidden in the dark shadows cast by the estate buildings. All was quiet with the exception of the remote and comforting sounds of the horses and the busy noises coming from the kitchen compound. Finally he reached the servants' door; as expected, it was already locked. With a smirk Mortimer slid the correct key inside and felt it turn in the well-oiled lock. In no time the door opened, silently, as the hinges had been well maintained.

It's not always an asset to have well trained servants, he reflected sardonically as he closed the door behind him. Now the next challenge was waiting: he must climb the stairs undetected. If he was lucky, Elizabeth would be upstairs nursing Armand, worst case he'd need to wait for her until she came back from dinner. He had no idea how late it was, but the clattering sounds from the kitchen told him that the servants must still be doing the dishes.

Following the same way he had already taken this afternoon, he tiptoed his way up the servants' staircase. The stairs and the upper gallery were lit by lanterns, equipped with expensive beeswax candles that spread their sweet scent; no cheap tallow candles were used in Wintershill. The corridor was deserted, like the staircase, and Mortimer chose to hide in the same empty room that had provided him with shelter earlier. The room lay in total darkness and Mortimer had to feel his way to the armchair where he sat down to wait, keeping in his hands the loaded pistols, cool and reassuring, while his heart was beating fast. Mortimer felt like a lion ready to pounce on his prey. Sweet revenge was near.

Mortimer didn't have a clear plan of action yet, but he knew that the element of surprise would be critical. However he must first talk to Elizabeth, explain to her why it was his holy duty to execute the sentence of death, that the wickedness of her character had been established beyond any doubt. He would then raise his pistol and kill her, ignoring her pleas for mercy. Elizabeth had betrayed him, and only her death could grant him satisfaction and restore his honour. There could be no mercy.

Mortimer was unsure how to continue after that. Should he kill Armand de Saint Paul? Wasn't Armand guilty as well, hadn't Elizabeth been a virgin of the purest spirit before she had been seduced and corrupted by him? Armand certainly deserved death – but Mortimer would need to keep one shot for himself, as there was no way Mortimer was going to be arrested and be walked to the scaffold in order to be beheaded. This form of death would be his only privilege as a nobleman – not to be hanged from the gallows amidst the commoners. But maybe having to watch Elizabeth die would be punishment enough for Armand?

Suddenly he remembered his dagger. He could use the dagger to finish off Armand and then shoot himself. This would be the perfect solution. Now that Mortimer had a clear plan of action, he felt strangely calm and prepared. All he needed to do was to wait for the right moment and execute his plan.

His patience was soon to be rewarded. He heard the noise of approaching steps and briefly caught sight of a maid with a heavy tray in her hands heading for Armand's room. In her footsteps followed Elizabeth. As the candlelight struck her face, her short copper hair took on the colour of the candle flame, lighting up her face, forming a bright halo around her head. Dressed in an elegant evening gown, her beauty made Mortimer's hand shake and his heart beat like mad.

"She's wicked!" he had to remind himself. "I must not be blinded, it's beauty instilled by the devil."

The door of Armand's room opened and the small procession marched inside. Mortimer waited in his room, unsure what to do. His plan had not taken into account the presence of a servant. He was still pondering how to deal with this situation when the door opened again and the maid left the room.

This was just another proof of Elizabeth's shamelessness, that she was alone with Armand in his bedroom, Mortimer thought. With renewed resolve, he opened the door of his room, pistols ready in both hands. He listened, but all was quiet, there was no creaking of the stairs to announce the arrival of another servant – or worse, the earl.

There would be no more waiting. Mortimer lunged forward. Lifting the latch with his elbows he burst into Armand's bedroom, pistols pointing at the bed. In the candlelight he saw Elizabeth standing close to Armand, touching his hand in a scene of great intimacy. The candlelight played with the colour of Elizabeth's hair, caressing her skin. She looked lovely but flushed – most likely Armand had just been murmuring one of his obscene compliments.

Elizabeth turned around, startled by the noise of the sudden intrusion. As soon as she recognized Mortimer she wanted to cry out, but couldn't. His face and the weapons in his hands said it all. He had come to exact his revenge.

"Look at me, you harlot! Yes, it's Mortimer, the stupid, unsuspecting Mortimer you betrayed and cast off like a used glove – the moment you thought you had found better. But you forgot, my dearest Elizabeth, that we're betrothed. Man and wife in the eyes of God and together we'll go to hell or paradise, whatever the verdict of the final judgement should be."

The shot released by his pistol crashed through the room, echoing like the trumpets of Jericho in the small bedroom.

Revenge was sweet indeed.

The Dice Are Cast

"I wonder if Armand is all right." Pierre frowned.

"Consider it a miracle that you're even alive, have you thought about that?" Charles answered.

"I know, it was a close thing." Pierre smiled. It was impossible not to be taken in by his smile.

"Armand says that I have a bad habit of attracting trouble. I'm aware that I'm a nuisance, thanks again for coming like the famous white knight to rescue me."

"No need to thank me, you'd have done the same for me," Charles replied roughly, although secretly flattered by Pierre's compliment. "If only I knew who exactly is scheming against us."

"Halifax, that's obvious enough." Pierre looked at his cousin. "But Halifax must be in league with somebody in London. Probably Cromwell. As we discovered by now, my warrant was a fraudulent document, someone well connected had access to the seal and falsified the signatures. Yesterday a delegation of members of Parliament came to see us at Hertford House, offering their excuses. I had the impression that their consternation was genuine enough."

"Yes, it was. But all the same I think it's time we removed ourselves from the scene until we know who the winners and losers will be in this war, it's getting too hot. I have ordered the *Beatrice* to be ready in Dover, we'll set sail shortly and return to France."

"I won't leave London without Armand," Pierre answered. "I really hope that the two J's will find him."

"Jean and Jim? Be sure, if anybody can find Armand, they can. Jim is a clever man and Jean is like a terrier, he'll never give up."

"Yes, I know," Pierre sighed. "But I also know that Armand is still in danger. I simply can't help it, sometimes I think we're more like twin brothers than best friends. I simply know when something is wrong."

"Yes, it's amazing. I hope we'll know soon enough what happened to him. For the time being let's make sure that your estates are safe and well-run during our absence. But this means that we have to sign a sort of truce with the Puritans, as they're going to be running this island soon. Cheriton was a disaster, the King will have to retreat North," Charles said with a grimace.

"I know, I'm not the naïve Pierre anymore, Charles. I also saw it with my own eyes in Oxford. I understand now that the Stuarts are in grave peril." Pierre

279

shuddered. "It was disgusting, in truth, I saw nothing but rats around our King, feasting on his money but preparing to leave the sinking ship as soon as possible."

"You're absolutely right. And the fattest rats are Halifax and the Lord High Treasurer."

"Poisonous rats," Pierre added. "A very dangerous species." He sighed. "I need a brandy, Charles, I could swear that something is happening to Armand, right now, it's driving me mad. If only I could ride down to Hampshire myself!"

"Don't even think about it!" thundered Charles. "Armand is like a cat, he has nine lives. Don't forget it. I'll get you that brandy."

***

"The wine is delicious!" Antonio poured a generous new helping for the fortune teller and himself.

"Yes, I instructed Cook to procure us something special, no idea where she found this, but it's truly exceptional, I agree."

"I have an idea where. Her nephew works at the docks, he probably filched it from a consignment smuggled from France. It tastes like liquid honey, never in my life have I tasted a wine like this before."

Henri de Beauvoir, the mysterious fortune teller, was already feeling the effect of the heavy wine. His brain seemed to be floating, he felt like the careless young viscount he had once been, handsome, ruthless, desired by men and women alike. The world had been his oyster – until that bastard of a cousin had entered his life, and stolen his position, his castles, in fact had ruined his life.

But the Marquis de Beauvoir was no more. Antonio, his precious, beautiful Antonio had made sure that Pierre de Beauvoir, the usurper, would rot in a damp prison cell, dying slowly, soon to be extinguished like a candle that had no more fuel to burn. This was his ultimate revenge and it tasted as sweet as the wine.

"Pour me another glass!" he commanded and downed the next glass in one go.

"What will we do next, my lord?" Antonio asked.

"I will show you, once we're upstairs in my bedroom." Suddenly Henri started to giggle.

"Be ready for a special treat!" he laughed. A thin line of spittle dribbled from the corner of his mouth; although he was only in his twenties he suddenly looked like an old man by the light of the candle burning brightly in the empty skull.

Antonio looked at his master, abruptly sober. Since the fortune teller had helped him to escape the slavery of the London brothels, he had not only admired, but had worshipped his master. But today he saw his master drunk for the first time, and he saw a new face, different, disgusting. No longer was he the aloof and elegant man of the world – suddenly Antonio saw the true face, a man ravaged as much by his physical scars as by his years of hate, greed and desire. Henri de Beauvoir sat slumped in his chair, his wig askew, exposing the pulsating red scars on his head.

"Why are you staring like this at me?" Henri hissed, his eyes flashing, although his words were slightly slurred. "Something wrong?"

"No, master, I was thinking about Portugal, to be honest," Antonio quickly improvised. "I've never been away from London, I can't even imagine what's waiting for me."

"Portugal, I almost forgot, when does the next boat leave for Lisbon?" Henri asked.

"In four days, my lord."

"Then let's start packing. I loathe this country, I hate the food, the language, the cold weather. I'll buy a house in Lisbon, it's a wonderful city. The azure sea, the scent of flowers, it's amazing."

"I've never seen the sea, my lord, only the River Thames."

"It's beautiful beyond anything words can describe. You'll discover it soon enough. Now let's go upstairs, the celebration has to continue."

Henri stumbled out of his chair, clinging with difficulty to the table.

"Do you need help, my lord?"

The angry eyes flashed once more at Antonio. "I'm not a cripple, you idiot. I can cope."

"Let me tell Cook and the servants that they can leave, my lord. We'll have the evening to ourselves."

In truth Antonio had an urgent need to leave this room for a minute, to breathe – and to think. Suddenly he saw the gentle face of the Duke of Hertford in front of him – the duke who was dying right now. Had he committed the biggest mistake of his life?

"Yes, tell the servants to leave and then come to my bedroom. I may be a bit noisy tonight." The fortune teller smirked and limped out of the room.

"What have I done?" Antonio thought, and then, "What shall I do?"

***

281

Elizabeth didn't move. The world around her had come to a standstill. She must be seeing a phantom, a hallucination. Could this be Mortimer, her Mortimer, appearing in Wintershill Castle like the angel of revenge?

It had happened unbelievably fast, in a matter of seconds only. The door bursting open, Mortimer appearing in the room, pistols loaded, speaking to her. She didn't understand a single word however, as the shock numbed her mind. All she could grasp was that Mortimer had come to Wintershill Castle with the sole purpose of taking revenge.

Rochester – for once – hadn't lied.

Elizabeth was standing next to Armand's bed, paralysed and helpless. She gave a quick look to Armand, but he was no help either, sitting frozen in his bed, transfixed by the pistols pointing at both of them.

Elizabeth fixed her eyes on Mortimer and accepted the inevitable. *Make it quick*, she thought.

Suddenly a dark shadow pounced silently from the corner, toppling Mortimer. Taken completely by surprise, Mortimer fell forward but still managed to pull the trigger of one of the firearms. A deafening explosion sounded through the bedroom, followed by a short cry.

Swaying, Elizabeth uttered a short moan and pressed a hand against her breast. Then she sank down, right into Armand's arms. A red stain was spreading on her gown, glistening brightly in the candlelight.

Mortimer tried to scramble back to his feet but Jean got hold of a silver candelabra, swinging it as a Viking would swing his axe in battle. In one single blow he felled Mortimer who crumpled to the floor, blood trickling from a head wound across the floor.

"Bravo, superb, and just in time! But help me quickly, Elizabeth is wounded," Armand cried.

"It's nothing, I just did my duty, my lord."

Armand was holding Elizabeth in his arms. Her lips were moving, but Armand couldn't understand what she was trying to tell him.

"Help me Jean, we must stop the bleeding."

Armand spoke to Elizabeth, talking to her kindly as if he were addressing a frightened child. "Elizabeth, *chérie*, all will be fine, but don't try to speak, Mortimer can't harm you anymore."

"*Excusez-moi, Mademoiselle*," Jean murmured, as he tore Elizabeth's dress open in order to examine the evil-looking wound.

The Earl of Wiltshire would never forget the strange scene he encountered as soon as he hastened into Armand's bedroom. The whole castle was in turmoil since the sound of the shot had echoed through the corridor and the staircase. He found Elizabeth lying in Armand's arms, her bodice torn and covered in blood while Jean hovered about her, trying to find the best way to stop the flow of blood that was by now soaking the bed and Armand's nightgown alike.

Jean finally located the spot where the bullet had entered the upper arm and breathed a sigh of relief. The bullet had only penetrated Elizabeth's arm, causing severe bleeding, but he couldn't find any further injury.

"What do they usually do in order to stop the bleeding, Jean?" Armand cried. "There was a trick, but I forgot. I never had to treat any wounded soldiers and in my days in school in Reims, Pierre was the only one who paid attention and learned all the tricks."

"Use a belt," the Earl of Wiltshire intervened. "I've seen this in the field and it works."

"Yes, that's the best way," Jean nodded and before he could remove his belt, the earl had taken the initiative and handed him his own. Jean immediately set to work. In the meantime the earl ripped a cord from the bed curtains and was binding the unconscious Mortimer.

"Will he survive?" the Earl asked Jean.

"I'm afraid so, my lord. Maybe I should have hit him harder?"

"He used to be one of my best friends in Oxford," the earl replied, staring bewildered at the unconscious body lying at his feet. "I still can't understand what happened. He must have gone mad, I have no other explanation."

"Love," Armand commented knowingly. "It can drive men mad. But what I don't understand is why he turned against Lady Elizabeth instead of me. I always knew that he hated me and I was expecting to have a duel with him sooner or later. That's what a man of honour would have done, at least."

The earl raised his eyebrows ever so slightly but refrained from exploring why Sir Mortimer must have hated Armand so much. Instead he sat on the bed and disentangled Elizabeth gently from Armand's embrace, wrapping his arms firmly around her while he murmured endearments into her ear.

"Hmm, I can see I'm no longer needed here. A pity that I can't leave you my place in this bed though, as I'm somewhat incapacitated – and it wouldn't be *bon ton* anyhow," Armand joked.

The earl grinned back. "Do try to show good manners, Saint Paul, Lady Elizabeth will soon be the next Countess of Wiltshire."

"Congratulations, Wiltshire, the whole court will envy you. Better fill the moat around your castle and let me suggest some hungry crocodiles for your defences. You'll need them."

Their exchange was interrupted as they could hear Mortimer moaning. He opened his eyes with difficulty, moaning once again. He tried to touch his head, which must have hurt like hell, but of course he couldn't; the Earl of Wiltshire had tied him up securely like a parcel.

Hearing the stirrings of Mortimer, the Earl of Wiltshire left Elizabeth, albeit reluctantly, and confronted his former friend. "What the hell did you think you were doing?"

"Elizabeth," Mortimer croaked, "she's evil, Satan's harlot. Don't let yourself be blinded like I did, Richard. Listen to the advice of a friend."

"Some friend you are, invading my home. Hold your tongue, Mortimer, you're talking about the future Countess of Wiltshire. How dare you insult Lady Elizabeth and be her judge? Did you forget that you've been born and raised a gentleman?"

"I see that she's bewitched you like she bewitched me, Richard. One day you'll regret and realize that I speak the truth. Elizabeth is evil, she deserves to die, believe me."

"You're barking mad. You're the only one who deserves to die, Mortimer."

The earl looked at his former friend, disgusted, but as yet not sure what he should do. Delivering Mortimer into the hands of the local sheriff would trigger the sort of scandal that he must avoid at all costs, especially at a time when the Puritans were taking control. And – most importantly – he had to protect Elizabeth's reputation.

Jean sensed that the earl was struggling over what to do with his former friend. Cautiously he tugged at the earl's sleeve before he whispered, "Excuse me, my lord, but may I propose a possible solution?"

"You may, Jean. I have no idea what to do. I should have him sentenced to death. But he's been a good friend... and I have to protect Lady Elizabeth."

Jean nodded. "I understand, my lord. I therefore would like to suggest a less orthodox solution..."

He continued to explain his idea while the earl looked more and more sceptical.

"But that's against all the rules!" he exclaimed. "I'm bound by a code of honour."

"Isn't it against all rules to break into Wintershill Castle, try to murder a helpless lady and my lord Armand? Shouldn't it be your lordship's duty to protect them, especially Lady Elizabeth?"

The earl grimaced. "You're very persuasive, Jean. Go ahead, but I'd prefer you not to mention my name. Now remove Sir Mortimer, I can't stand his presence any more. Make sure that he is well guarded until he – disappears."

"I promise, my lord. Jim and I will take the best possible care of this maniac."

***

Having solved the most pressing issue, the earl insisted on carrying Elizabeth in his arms to her room, refusing the assistance offered by his shocked footmen. After the first panic and commotion had calmed down, hectic activity had started in Wintershill Castle. A groom had been sent to fetch the doctor and two maids were preparing Elizabeth's bedroom, making sure that a fire was burning brightly and that a hot brick had been placed between the linen sheets.

The earl dismissed the maids. He wanted to be alone with Elizabeth.

"Thank you," Elizabeth whispered.

"Does it hurt a lot?" the earl asked, his voice thick with concern.

"It doesn't matter. Where's Mortimer?"

"Armand's valets are taking care of him, don't worry, my love, you're safe."

"I'm not worried for myself, but I've caused enough trouble for you. Tomorrow I'll go back home, I made up my mind. There's no future for us, my lord, you have to understand this."

"Oh, I do understand perfectly," the Earl of Wiltshire replied cheerfully. "Your reputation is ruined forever, there can be no doubt. I should leave this room now as fast as possible."

"It's true, it's nothing to joke about, my lord."

"It's no joke," the earl replied, and taking care not to hurt her bandaged arm he kissed her gently.

"Will you marry me? That's all I care about."

"You're mad, Richard! I can't, I'll ruin you," she exclaimed.

"Will you consider marrying a man who's gone mad then?"

"We can't, Richard! The court will reject us, your mother will refuse to receive me, it's impossible. I'm an outcast, I told you what happened in Oxford."

The earl kissed her again, longer this time. "Let this be my concern, Elizabeth. I think I fell in love with you the first day I saw you. Now that fate has decided to reunite us, I won't let you go. Let me deal with the rumourmongers, nobody will dare to scorn Lady Wiltshire, don't worry. I ask you again: will you marry me?"

Elizabeth sighed. "You'll regret it, Richard, but if you insist, I think I have no option but to say yes..."

The earl kissed her again. "That's correct Elizabeth, there was no other option."

Journeys by Sea

To His Grace, the most honourable Duke of Hertford, Marquis de Beauvoir etc etc.

Pierre put down the letter he had just received by messenger from Wintershill Castle and smiled. "Sometimes I think that Jean is more enamoured by my titles than anybody else. It takes him almost five lines just to address me correctly."

"Well, that's how it should be," Charles said. "You're the head of the House of Hertford, a bit thoughtless from time to time, but you're our esteemed head all the same, and honour should be shown where it is due."

"Thanks for reminding me," Pierre grumbled. "I knew that I would – sooner or later – be scolded for my short sojourn in the Tower of London and I'm aware that it would be a complete waste of time to tell you that I didn't undertake this venture on purpose and didn't particularly cherish my days rotting away in a damp prison."

"Don't be ridiculous, Pierre, tell me what kind of news Jean has for us."

"For me, not us," Pierre muttered, feeling somewhat rebellious. But Charles had been so much part of their adventure, admittedly he had a right to know.

"Armand was found, unconscious, in a forest close to Winchester. The Earl of Wiltshire has been gracious enough to have him brought to his estate where he's staying and is being nursed right now, and most importantly, he's much better already and plans to return to London next week."

"That's excellent news. I knew that Jean would find him. Didn't I tell you that Armand is like a cat, he always falls on his feet." Charles looked smug.

"You did, no need to brag about it. I must confess that I am deeply relieved that Armand is in good shape and in good hands. What about François, when is he coming to London to join us? When can we all go back to France? Marie is waiting for me."

Charles rummaged in the depths of his pocket until he found a sheet of paper. "Here's a note I received this morning from François, I forgot to tell you."

Dear Charles, just a quick note to let you know that I'll escort HM to Bath. As soon as HM is safely installed, I propose that we all meet in Southampton and sail back home.

Your servant and friend,

FdT

Pierre frowned. "I must confess, my knowledge of English ports is limited. Why Southampton?"

"Its location is ideal, Pierre. Southampton is not far from Bath and – what's more interesting – only a few miles from Winchester. I suggest that we ride down and reunite with Armand before we meet François."

"That settles it. I'm so looking forward to going back to France."

"Aren't we all? It's time to leave London, there's too much trouble brewing for my taste! I'll miss the good air though when I'm back in France, nothing can beat London."

***

Henri de Beauvoir woke up, feeling sick. He opened his eyes with difficulty, trying to sort out where he was. Slowly his memory returned. He was on the boat that would bring him to a new and exciting life in Portugal. But he felt terrible. Not only was his stomach rebelling, his tongue was sticking to his palate, dried out, a strange object in his mouth. There was only one explanation: he must have drunk far too much wine yesterday evening after they had boarded the ship.

His head felt as if it was ready to explode any minute, he needed help, where was his servant?

"Antonio!" he croaked. Antonio would know what to do to soothe his headache, he'd know where to find the pomade that must be applied to alleviate the throbbing pain of his injured leg.

"Antonio!" he cried louder. *Where the hell was Antonio?*

"Antonio, *putain*, you lazy son of a bitch, come here immediately!" he cried.

Henri closed his eyes as a wave of pain reached his brain, blinding him. He desperately needed those powders he had brought from the Orient. Antonio knew how to use them and brew a potion, strong enough to send him sleep again, forgetting the pain, forgetting the world around him.

Finally the door opened and Henri opened his eyes, ready to scold his lazy servant. But it was the captain of the ship who appeared, not Antonio.

"You were calling, sir?"

"I was indeed, and it's my lord, not 'sir'. I'm calling for this lazy ass of a servant called Antonio."

"Keep on calling then, sir," the captain shrugged. "There ain't no Antonio no more."

"What do you mean?" Henri was flabbergasted. "I'll have him whipped as soon as I get hold of him."

288

The captain shrugged. "You've been sleeping the whole day in your cabin, we thought that you might be dead. Don't want a dead man on board, mind you, my sailors are a superstitious bunch."

Henri tried to think. He couldn't have drunk much, he remembered only drinking a tankard of the special wine that Antonio had taken from Cook and offered to him as a special surprise to celebrate the start of their journey.

"Where's my servant?"

"He left the ship before we set sail, sir."

"We must return, I'll kill him with my own hands!" Henri fumed. "He must have drugged me, that cockroach, that son of a bitch!"

"No way, we've already passed the Channel, we're on the open sea now. If you want to go back, you're welcome to swim." He paused, and then as an insult he added, "Sir."

"How dare you to speak to me like that!" Henri tried to get up but failed miserably. The swaying ship, his headache and the anger finally took their toll and he started to retch.

"Always the same, pretending to be a lord or something but all you can do is to throw up. Don't make a mess in my cabin, you braggart or I'll feed you to the fish. And I want my money now, otherwise you can help out downstairs on the deck."

Henri breathed hard, and finally managed to get up. Trying to find his way, barely able to see anything at all, he staggered to the chest where his gold was stored. With difficulty he opened the lid and grabbed the leather purse. He sighed with relief, it was still there, filled to the brim and heavy.

"How much?" Henri asked.

"Twenty louis d'or, that was the price I agreed with your precious servant."

"Are you mad?"

"Want to swim?" the captain asked and pointed behind him where Henri saw the shadow of two brawny sailors waiting at the cabin door.

Henri didn't reply. He opened the purse and froze with horror: the purse was full, but with worthless copper coins only.

The captain noticed his glance and moved forward. He took the purse. "Take him downstairs, lads, see if you can get some use out of him. His lordship…" he smirked, "is not capable of honouring his dues."

"I swear to God, I'll kill you, Antonio!" Henri whispered.

"Better pray to God that you survive the next weeks. My lads are known to be a bit rough sometimes, especially when they expect gold and receive copper instead."

As Henri was dragged out of the cabin the captain put his hand into his pocket. He could feel the cool and comforting touch of the louis d'or that Antonio had given him to make sure that his master would never return.

The captain smirked, wondering how much time it would take for Henri de Beauvoir to find out that they were not heading to Lisbon at all – but to Virginia instead.

***

The seagulls were crying as Mortimer woke up. Where was he?

Slowly he remembered: Wintershill Castle, Elizabeth lying on the bed next to Armand, bleeding. Then the two valets who had grabbed him, bundled him into a coach, his journey to Southampton, two – or had it been even three nights – in an inn until… his memory had a gap here, those bastards must have drugged him.

He felt the swaying of the ship, but he didn't breathe fresh air, it was the stale, mouldy air of the lower decks, the odour of unwashed bodies, the scent of the slimy mush they gave out as food on those ships accompanied by sour ale.

He swallowed deeply. He knew this kind of ship from when he had served briefly in the navy. Mortimer stirred and opened his eyes in shock.

"Our baby is waking up!" remarked a tattooed sailor and pointed at Mortimer. "Isn't he sweet with his red hair, a bit of fresh flesh will do us good." He laughed roughly and poked Mortimer.

"Don't scare our baby, see, he's frightened now," came another voice.

"Where am I?" croaked Mortimer, ignoring the insults. He knew better than to provoke the sailors.

"You're on your way to the colonies, baby. You signed up for service on this boat, you may have forgotten. It's the gin, the devil's invention."

"I never signed up!" Mortimer protested.

"That's what they all say. The captain's whip will make you remember, it can work miracles like that. He's not into jokes, better you remember this before he gets twitchy. Take it as a piece of advice from a friend."

Mortimer was dumbstruck. He had expected to be sentenced to death – better to be killed in a duel. But this was worse than anything he could have imagined, he was to be buried alive on a sailing boat heading to the colonies, if he even arrived there. He swallowed hard.

290

"Baby is going to start to cry," the brawny sailor commented, his voice oozing with contempt. "Have this, it'll help."

He emptied a bucket of water over Mortimer's head.

"See, so many tears. But that's just the beginning. Now move your sweet little arse. Plenty of duties are waiting for you, we don't like lazy sailors here. Better not behave like a weak little girl, it might put the wrong ideas into some people's heads. We tend to get a bit restless after weeks without a woman on board."

A Mission Accomplished

The elegant courtier was waiting in the antechamber of His Eminence, Cardinal Mazarin. François de Toucy was prepared to wait for several hours, as His Eminence was notorious for being late. His usual excuse was the Queen detaining him. François had some other ideas though as to what might be keeping the Cardinal busy in his private rooms.

But to his surprise it only took fifteen minutes and the Cardinal arrived, outpacing the monks that followed him like a flock of black crows.

"I want to be alone with M. le Comte," he declared, and the door closed behind them.

The Cardinal smiled. "Yes, you heard correctly. Her Majesty has been gracious enough to elevate you and has bestowed the title of Count of Clermont on you."

François bowed elegantly. "Your Eminence is known to be true to your word. I'm surprised though that it happened so fast, I might have failed."

His Eminence was concentrating all of his attention on finding the biggest candied cherry in the golden box that was always kept filled with delicacies on his desk, but he was smiling.

"But you didn't, of course. First of all, I knew the sort of person I was working with, and second, my agents kept me informed at all times. I know that Her Majesty was rather, ah, reluctant to leave Oxford. Her pregnancy is difficult, I've heard?"

"Yes, but now she's in excellent hands. I spoke with her physician and he's moderately optimistic," François replied. "It will be necessary to keep a ship ready though. If the forces of Parliament take Bath, Her Majesty will have to come back to France. "

"I know, and between you and me, it could happen faster than many people here might imagine. But in order to avoid any diplomatic incident, it will be a Dutch vessel that will be in charge. We don't want to upset the new government in London."

The Cardinal had chosen the biggest cherry and savoured it with obvious pleasure.

"Delicious!" he sighed. "But now let's raise a glass to the health of Her Majesty, Queen Henrietta Maria."

They drank in silence.

"How was your journey otherwise? I heard Beauvoir and Saint Paul accompanied you?"

"You know, Your Eminence, how those travels are. A bit tedious from time to time, but not very eventful…"

The Cardinal looked at him suspiciously. "You've always been a good liar, or should I say an excellent diplomat. I don't believe a word."

François laughed. "Trust me, Your Eminence, nothing special to report. It was a very ordinary journey – by our standards."

A Quick Note From the Author

This book is a piece of fiction and I hope that you enjoyed reading it as much as I enjoyed writing it. My story unfolds in the year 1644, against the historical background of the English Civil War, a war that changed Great Britain and the role of its monarchy profoundly. Maybe modern democracy wouldn't be the same if the forces of Parliament hadn't succeeded in imposing a system of government run by parliament rather than by the sovereign, even if parliament in the seventeenth century was still a far cry from today's ideas of a representative democracy.

I tried to keep the historical facts as accurate as possible but took the liberty of inventing a plot, therefore my principal characters are mostly fictional. Consequently, the story itself is pure fiction, especially Oliver Cromwell's involvement with a fortune teller, which is my own invention – it was tempting to imagine the esteemed head of the Puritan movement as being tormented by the devils of power and vanity. But has there and will there ever be an important leader in politics who isn't?

Although most historic locations are correct, I took the liberty of inventing Wintershill Castle, locating it close to the city of Winchester.

Some readers may recognize several characters from the 'French Orphan' series that I wrote three years ago. As usual I tried to keep my characters authentic to their time, even if their language has been modernized. It would be difficult to keep up the pace and suspense whilst having them speak the authentic language of England in the seventeenth century.

It's good to remember that the concept of political correctness didn't exist in the seventeenth century. Racism was a generally accepted fact of life, human rights were unheard of, and any kind of illness risked ending a man's short stay on this earth and despatching the poor sinner into the flames of purgatory. Therefore religion permeated all aspects of daily life and the promise of heavenly salvation was far more important than we can imagine it today.

However, in the end people are people. Love, greed, friendship, romance, pride and curiosity were driving forces centuries ago, just as they still are today!

Historical Characters

Charles, King of England, Scotland and Ireland

Henrietta Maria (Marie), Queen Consort of Charles, former Royal Princess of France, sister of King Louis XIII of France

Charles, heir to the English throne, Prince of Wales (later King Charles II)

Prince Rupert of the Rhine, Nephew of King Charles

Cardinal Jules Mazarin, Prime Minister of France

Queen Anne of France, sister-in-law of King Charles and Queen Henrietta Maria

The Cavaliers, men who supported King Charles, independent of their faith:

General Hopton

General Forth

Sir Henry Bard

The Parliamentarians, also known as Roundheads, and including the Puritans (a radical Protestant faction leaning towards the teachings of Calvin):

Oliver Cromwell, Member of Parliament

Lord Algernon Percy, Earl of Northumberland, Member of Parliament

Earl of Essex, general of the Parliamentary forces

Sir William Waller

Fictional Characters

François de Toucy, a French nobleman

Julia de Toucy, his Italian wife

Pierre, referred to either by his French title Marquis de Beauvoir, or his English title, Duke of Hertford

Marie de Beauvoir, his wife

Jean, his valet

Armand de Saint Paul, Earl of Worthing, youngest son of the Marquis de Saint Paul

Jim, a smuggler turned valet

Sir Charles Neuville, Pierre's cousin

Lady Elizabeth Huntville

Sir Mortimer Clifford

Countess of Portsmouth

Earl of Rochester

Marquess and Marchioness of Halifax

Richard, Earl of Wiltshire